TELEPATHIC MESSAGE FROM A DYING COMMANDO . . .

Please don't fail me . . .

Whatever I can do, I shall, my Islaen. The former Admiral steadied himself, battling to hold his control. He hesitated, but he had no right to pride now, or ever when the good of his unit and mission were at hazard. *It might be best if I turned command over to Karmikel. This is Commando work.*

No, she replied firmly and at once. *I wouldn't have made you my backup if I didn't believe you could do the job. When you bring the team back up to strength, choose another Commando to fill my slot, but you command.*

The Colonel, too, was fighting to retain her rein on herself. It was an incredible strain to maintain the contact she had initiated over this distance, and it was becoming increasingly difficult to keep her grief from pouring into her transmission. If she allowed that, she would break Sogan as well. A cold determination gripped the woman, an anger as frigid as the depths of interstellar space. *Contact Ram Sithe at once. Tell him everything. Whether we succeed or not, that fleet must be stopped. No. It must be annihilated, and those who sent it must be found and taken. I want them to suffer such a fate that would-be tyrants a thousand millennia from now will be held in check by the memory of it!*

Ace Books by P.M. Griffin

STAR COMMANDOS
STAR COMMANDOS: COLONY IN PERIL
STAR COMMANDOS: MISSION UNDERGROUND
STAR COMMANDOS: DEATH PLANET
STAR COMMANDOS: MIND SLAVER
STAR COMMANDOS: RETURN TO WAR

STAR COMMANDOS: FIRE PLANET
(coming in November)

STAR COMMANDOS

RETURN TO WAR

P.M. GRIFFIN

ACE BOOKS, NEW YORK

This book is an Ace original edition,
and has never been previously published.

RETURN TO WAR

An Ace Book / published by arrangement with
the author

PRINTING HISTORY
Ace edition / July 1990

ISBN: 0-441-78047-4

Ace Books are published by The Berkley Publishing Group,
200 Madison Avenue, New York, New York 10016.
The name "ACE" and the "A" logo
are trademarks belonging to Charter Communications, Inc.

PRINTED IN THE UNITED STATES OF AMERICA

10   9   8   7   6   5   4   3   2   1

To my friend,
Jane Elwood,
in honor of her own talent.

ONE

Varn Tarl Sogan ignored the invitation of his meticulously contoured flight chair and went directly to the observation panel. He stood before it, studying somewhat somberly the familiar scene outside.

It was still very early morning, and the light flooding Horus' vast spaceport was the cold, dim gray of predawn, but even so, the planeting field seemed to boil with activity. He nodded appreciatively. A planet hugger might have mistaken this for confusion only, but to him, there was the height of order, controlled and with purpose, in every movement. This was a fine fleet, one prepared to act to the full of its potential within an incredibly short time should the need to take action suddenly arise.

Sogan sighed then, and his head lowered. He had once commanded such a force, had led it against those very ships, those very soldiers, out there, until he had chosen to spare the world he had been ordered to destroy and so had earned for himself disgrace and perpetual exile.

So intense was the longing that gripped him that his hands whitened on the instrument panel in front of him. He wanted that armada, wanted to walk the bridge of its flagship instead of this minute needle-nose, had been trained for that. He had been bred for it . . .

Varn?

The former Admiral's shields flew up and snapped tight around his inner mind. *On the bridge, Colonel,* he replied with carefully schooled ease in that manner of speech he shared with both Commando-Colonel Islaen Connor and their Jadite comrade, the gurry Bandit.

He and the woman who was his commander and his consort had
discovered during their first days together that they could speak
directly thought-with-thought, a gift unique to them among all
humanity and one whose existence they took great care to conceal
save from the other members of their own small, tightly knit unit.
Normally, he cherished that strange, close bond, but it could
reveal too much, and he had no wish to burden Islaen with any
needless darkness.

His lips tightened. He had no wish for her to learn anything
about this. What right had he to whimper at all, much less before
the one who had given him life again in place of the shadow-
ridden existence in which he had been wallowing when they had
met on Visnu of Brahmin?

His head raised. He had declared to her that he would refuse
such a place if it were offered to him, that he would not allow
himself to be separated either from her or from the urgent, perilous
work they shared. He had not spoken those words lightly and did
not intend to be foresworn or seem foresworn now.

The man sighed. Neither that knowledge nor that determination
lifted the ache from his heart and mind, not with the close
proximity of those fine ships out there to fire his longing for all he
recognized as lost to him forever.

Varn Tarl Sogan had composed himself again by the time
Commando-Colonel Islaen Connor swung lightly from the core
ladder linking the various levels of the *Fairest Maid* and stepped
onto the bridge.

As always, his eyes brightened when he saw her.

Islaen Connor was a beautiful woman, almost prototype ideal,
although she lacked the softness favored in the inner systems. Her
body was slender and well formed, lithe and quick to respond to
her mind's commands. She moved with a spacer's grace and
carried herself with the air of one long accustomed both to
command and to danger.

Her features were delicately chiseled, nearly too much so. The
brown eyes were large and heavily fringed with lashes that were
the same rich auburn as her hair, which she wore tightly confined
in braids after the custom of most female spacers. It formed a
wonderful contrast to the pale, life-warm skin against which it
rested.

The stark black uniform of a Federation Commando did so as
well. Normally she preferred the more comfortable space garb
they both used when either at ease or on an active assignment, but

they had been summoned to Horus specifically for this meeting with Navy Admiral Ram Sithe, and the Colonel was too much a career soldier to present herself before her commanding officer without observing full military form.

Islaen, for her part, studied the man she had taken for her husband, or consort as he would have said.

Sogan was moderately tall, well built but wiry rather than heavily muscled. He was slim, too much so at the moment. He had not yet regained all the weight he had dropped following his wounding on Omrai of Umbar.

He had the olive complexion and fine, stern features of his race, features that could mean his death were they identified correctly in all too many settings throughout the Federation ultrasystem. The hatreds engendered in the great War so recently ended were both powerful and violent. It was with excellent reason that he held himself aloof, walled behind a mask of frigid reserve, from most of those in whose midst fate had cast him.

His hair and eyes were both a very dark brown, precisely the same shade, a trait only found in the highest ruling families of the Arcturian Empire.

She smiled, delighting herself in his pleasure at her arrival. *One would think you'd have the sense to sleep while you could*, she chided. *We may not have much time for such luxury once Ram Sithe gives us our flying orders.*

Whatever her words or the tone in which she transmitted them, she continued to study her husband pensively. The fact that his shields were closed over his inner mind was sign that some shadow was riding him, or had been when she had called to him. There was no forcing the smile he gave her in turn.

Varn hurried to meet her. His fingers brushed her cheek, then he scooped the tiny, brown-feathered creature accompanying her off her shoulder.

The gurry whistled in delight at his touch, and he could feel her purr as his fingers caressed her. "Good morning, small one," he said, using verbal speech as they both usually did when alone with her, although she could share her thoughts with them as readily as they did between each other. "Even the early hour does not seem to have diminished your cheerfulness."

Nooo! Breakfast was good!

He smiled again. He had never yet seen Bandit when she was not ready for a meal or pleased by having just eaten one.

She was the most unique member of their team and as much a part of it as any of its human members. If they still did not entirely fathom her nature, the fact did not trouble them. There was no doubting that she possessed the reasoning intelligence that was customarily considered to be the mark of humanity and its equivalents in the multiracial populace of the great Federation ultrasystem, and she had given ample proof of her courage and loyalty. It was only for the protection of her species and for their own protection that they chose not to reveal that information to the universe at large, even as they took care to conceal their own strange abilities.

She, too, had her gifts, apart from her telepathic talent. The gurry hen had bonded with Islaen on her homeworld, Jade of Kuan Yin. In so doing, she had revealed that she could link her thoughts with theirs, with the woman through that adoption and with him both because of his relationship with Islaen and because of his own power to interact with nonhuman species. They had discovered as well that, although she could not converse with other humans, she could understand their speech, and she could influence their feelings toward both herself and those in her company through the massive volume of goodwill she transmitted. Only the most debased of sentient creatures or those gripped by either furious madness or high, overpowering emotion were immune to that gentle charm.

No one suspected the power she exerted. Bandit was extraordinarily engaging in herself with an appearance appealing to most humans. She was very small, weighing not quite seven ounces, winged and feathered although a mammal. Her color was chiefly a uniform brown, but a thin line of black circled her head, crossing the merry black eyes in the manner of the masks once assumed by Terran robbers in prespace times. Her bill was a brilliant yellow and was flexible enough to give expression to her face. The legs and feet were also of that color and ended in toes supple enough to serve her as efficiently as any hand.

The man's fingers curved around the tiny, warm body so that they might both cradle and stroke her. She responded with such a storm of delighted purring that he laughed. "You sound like the *Maid* when she is getting ready to lift," he told her. "Well, small one, are you willing to work your usual magic for me today?"

Bandit will help Varn! she declared, indignant that he should even pose such a question.

"You have never yet failed to do so," he assured her soothingly as he gently set her on the back of his chair.

He sat on its arm. *It might be better if she went with you, Islaen.*

You both should come. Admiral Sithe summoned the unit, not just me.

No. Sogan caught himself. That sounded too emphatic, although the woman was well aware that he preferred to avoid his former opponent whenever possible. *We may need to lift quickly. I want to see to that valve while we have the chance.*

You take Bandit, then. Our mechanics look forward to seeing her. And Varn liked the security her gift provided, that and the willingness to work for them that it inspired, though in truth, she felt they were favorites enough now, in themselves and because of their reputation, that they would receive prime service even without the gurry's aid.

They look forward to overfeeding her, too.

It's up to you to see that they don't succeed.

The Commando straightened as if she were about to assume a heavy burden. *I suppose I'd best be going. As it is, I'll be late if I hit traffic.*

Sogan came to his feet. He had seen that look on her ever since they had been commanded to report to Horus.

Can you tell me nothing, Islaen? he asked quietly. *I have not asked before because our orders came in on scramble, but it is obvious that something is weighing on you.*

Sending that way was only a precaution, she said quickly. *I haven't told you anything for the simple reason that I don't know anything really, just the bare description of the problem we face.*

She turned abruptly from him. *Too many people who should have peace never seem to be granted the right to enjoy it.*

Jade!

No, the Colonel assured him. *Another world with which I've had dealings. —Why isn't it ever enough?* she whispered as despair suddenly welled up to overwhelm her. *All the fighting and the dying and the suffering, and in the end, one would-be conqueror is banished only to be replaced by another.*

The man was silent. Her unhappiness tore him, but what answer could he make her? Their work all too frequently brought them into that sort of situation.

We see that often enough, he agreed at last, *but, Islaen Connor, we have succeeded in thwarting it, too. Do not forget that. It is surely cause for satisfaction that worlds stand free today because of our efforts.*

Her head raised, and she smiled. *Aye, satisfaction indeed. —Thanks, Varn. I needed to hear that, even though I have no right to unload my cargo on you . . .*

Then I am no consort of yours. His dark eyes fell. _I am not always so good about sharing myself_ . . .

Her fingers brushed his cheek. _You're all I need, Varn Tarl Sogan_.

The Commando-Colonel's hand dropped back to her side, and she turned toward the hatch. _Take care of Jake and Bethe if they should planet before I get back. The_ Jovian Moon's _due this morning_.

Aye, Colonel, assuming I am back here myself.

Good enough. —Watch what that feathered glutton manages to cram down her throat. I don't want to have to start computing excess weight adjustments for her.

The man laughed at Bandit's protesting squawk. _I doubt we have much to worry about there, but I will do what I can_. He gave her an informal salute. _See to it that you bring us back a nice quiet assignment_.

Some hope you have, friend! I'll put credits down that we won't be bored, but apart from that, I'll make no promises at all.

Islaen activated the control rod of her flier. She gave one glance back at the beautiful, slender spire that was the _Fairest Maid_ and sighed. She felt so powerless sometimes.

Varn loved that needle-nose, and he did try to make himself content with her, but it was not hard to guess where his thoughts had been before she had come on the bridge this morning.

Space, the man was a war prince of the Arcturian Empire! That could not be stripped from him as his rank and place had been. He, and generations of his fathers before him, had been trained from infancy to rule star systems in times of peace and to lead his Empire's armadas in war. He had to want a command, a significant command, and no amount of acceptance of the knowledge that he would never again hold the like would in any way lessen his longing.

She had done all she could for him. Even Ram Sithe could do no more, not so much as raise the dark-eyed former Admiral's rank any further, much as Sogan had earned promotion. Sithe had taken an enormous risk as it was in granting his old enemy a Captain's place in the Navy, permanently assigning him to her unit.

Her eyes flashed with pride. His trust had been well repaid. Few people in the ultrasystem, few even among the military, had so much as seen a class one heroism citation. Since their chance meeting on Visnu of Brahmin, Varn Tarl Sogan had earned four of them and shared another with her.

Her shoulders squared as she came to a stop before the building housing her commander's office. She had best prepare herself for the interview ahead. There was no point to this agonizing anyway. What was lost was gone, and both she and the war prince had best face that reality and be grateful for the favors fate and the Spirit ruling space had granted them. The present and the future were theirs, and right now a mission loomed large before them.

Her eyes shadowed. It promised to be big, as most of her unit's assignments were, but she would be much more pleased if Anath of Algola did not figure so prominently in it.

TWO

SCARCELY TWO HOURS passed before Islaen Connor returned to the *Fairest Maid*.

She was pleased to see the *Jovian Moon* occupying the bay beside theirs. At least there would be no delay in briefing their comrades and getting under way.

Because the others lacked the ability to link thought, she gave a questioning signal on the communicator strapped to her left wrist. The Arcturian answered immediately, and she boarded the *Maid*, heading for the crew's cabin where they were awaiting her.

The chamber was small, as were all the *Fairest Maid*'s cabins, but it was more comfortable than the rest, being the one in which those voyaging aboard her spent their waking off-duty hours. Her team was gathered around the firmly secured table; Commando-Captain Jake Karmikel was leaning back against the padded wall, cradling a cup of jakek and watching the other two with obvious amusement while they fussed over a thoroughly gratified Bandit.

Like herself, he was a native of the planet Noreen and shared the fair skin characteristic of that world's citizens. He shared the red gene as well, but its influence was stronger in him, so that his hair was a rich dark flame color. His eyes were a bright blue.

He was a big man, taller and broader of shoulder than Varn, although he was not in any sense overmuscled in the manner of many of Terra's colonists.

Navy Sergeant Bethe Danlo formed a strong contrast to him in that respect. She was very small and slight in keeping with her stature. There was no mistaking the strength in the steady slate-gray eyes, however, or in her pleasant, basically Terran features.

The blond woman was space-bred and owned no specific planet as home, although she carried Terran citizenship since that was the world from which her clan had originally sprung. During the latter stage of the War, she had served with the Demolitions Unit, and it had been the experience she had gained there that had first brought her into contact with their team when she had been called in to aid them in their mission of Hades of Persephone.

Islaen frowned momentarily to see Sogan and the demolitions expert so near and at ease with each other. It had been Bethe rather than herself who had fought for him, rekindled his will for life, after that duel of minds with his renegade kinsman at the end of their last assignment. She who was his wife had done nothing, only waited for him to make his choice in accordance with his caste's custom, even if it was for death . . .

The unworthy emotion died as his greeting warmed her mind and spirit. Fortunately, she had instinctively raised her shields around her earlier thoughts and so had not shamed herself before him.

A chill touched her soul. She might have done far worse. It was half a miracle that a man who had suffered such awesome injury at the hands of his own race and had such ample cause to dread too-close contact with any Federation people was able to relax this completely with them. She could have destroyed that with her base and thoroughly groundless disapproval.

Sogan's welcome to her was quiet, reserved as the man himself. Jake's was not. They had been comrades a long time, ever since their first days in Basic training, and the friendship between them was strong and warm. No sooner had she passed through the narrow door than he was on his feet. In the next instant, she was enveloped in his enthusiastic bear hug.

Bethe watched them for a few moments. "Let her go, you space tramp!" she commanded at the end of that time. "You'll kill her. Besides, the Admiral might object to your mauling his consort."

"Not in the least," Varn responded, laughing himself as the Colonel disengaged herself and hastened to a more secure position beside him. "I cannot say I consider this an appropriate greeting for an officer to give his commander, however."

A flickering regret touched him. He could never meet her so exuberantly.

It was gone again even as it was born, and no sign of it had marred either his voice or expression.

Karmikel studied the newcomer critically. "You're looking

well," he observed. "Life on Thorne agrees with you, Colonel Connor."

"It'll agree with all of us once you two decide to report in like proper soldiers and settle in there. She is our official base now, you know."

He just grinned. "Navy personnel can go where they want on extended leave, which is precisely what we're supposed to be enjoying right now."

"It'll have to go in the bank along with all the rest of the time we're owed."

"Have a little pity, Islaen! We just found a lovely little planet with the best beaches . . ."

"In another minute, you'll have me in tears," she said archly. "Anyway, you don't belong on a beach. You'll just get yourself burned."

She thanked Varn for the jakek that he had fetched from the galley before giving her attention back to the redhead. "Be reasonable, Jake. You really wouldn't expect the old man to break tradition and actually let us finish a furlough before calling us back to active duty, now would you?"

They had been given enough time at least, praise the Spirit of Space, she thought. Even if Varn had not returned from that last one closer to death than to life and had Bethe not been carrying the aftereffects of her own injuries, they had all been thoroughly spent in body and in spirit. That was why Ram Sithe had called her in for a personal interview, to satisfy himself that they were indeed able to work again, instead of merely giving them their orders over the transceiver. He was not such a fool or so poor an officer as to sacrifice the best guerrilla team he had ever commanded on a mission that any other unit could have carried just about as well.

Karmikel threw up his hands in an exaggerated gesture of surrender. "All right, Colonel. I know when it's useless to argue. To what hole or paradise are we being sent this time? I'll put credits down that it's the former."

"Anath of Algola."

"Oh, space!"

Sogan and Bethe Danlo exchanged quick glances. The man's disgust was patent, and so, in more controlled form, was Islaen's.

"What is wrong with her?" the former Admiral asked quietly. After some of their past experiences, he dreaded the answer.

His consort sighed. "Nothing in herself. My old unit spent six months on penetration duty there before being sent to Thorne.

That's why Sithe wants us to take it now, because Jake and I are already familiar with her."

"Neither of you appears anxious to return there," he observed.

"No. Anath herself is a fine world, but we had a difficult time there. To put it charitably, her people were not as easy to work with as those of Thorne. In fact, we had to just about fight the whole damn campaign ourselves. —I've brought tapes for us to study en route, but I can give you a quick overview now.

"Anath is Algola's sole planet and possesses but one satellite herself. She's Terra-normal and basically an ocean world, of course. Land masses consist of two approximately equal-sized, large continents, both with varied topography showing all the major ecological categories in one place or another. There are also a great number of islands of every conceivable description. Wildlife is abundant everywhere, on land and in the waters."

"You mentioned people," Bethe interjected.

The Commando-Colonel nodded. "ExoTerran human, though we were unaware of their existence until we planeted. They inhabit only the middle southwestern portion of one continent and are very few for so large and fruitful a planet, less than a million individuals in all."

"A new race, in its stone age?" the Sergeant asked.

"No. They're barbarian stage, right enough, totally unmechanized, but they do have the use of steel. They marry late and have few children even then, and as is usual among peoples on that level, many of those die in infancy. As a result, their increase has been slow."

"Considering their total lack of ability to face invaders from the stars, their small population and primitive life-style worked to their advantage," Jake interjected. "They were scattered enough and knew their homeworld intimately enough that when the War came to Anath the bulk of them, even their rulers, were simply able to vanish and entirely avoid contact with their enemies, all save one unfortunate village."

Sogan gave him a hard, strange look. "That does not sound like my people. It was not our way to leave a populace, however small, unsubjected when we came in conquest."

"Your soldiers weren't there long enough, only about two years in all, and had too much else to occupy them to concern themselves with a relative handful of primitives who represented no threat and were of almost no use to them even as slaves. They were sent in to establish a support base for a planned major thrust against us, but between Anath herself and, later, our activities, they found nothing except trouble."

The former Admiral frowned. "I think I recall something of Anath now, though I had nothing to do with her myself. Our plans changed after her invasion, leaving her too far out of the way to warrant the continued effort and expense needed to hold her. We went after Thorne of Brandine instead and soon abandoned Anath."

The Commando-Captain grinned. "A crucial three months ahead of schedule thanks to our efforts."

His commander scowled at him. "Give Anath her due credit, Jake." She glanced at Varn. "It's the old story. Your commanders failed to study what they invaded. The fleet remained too long on the beach where it planeted. Even though your officers took warning from a severe storm that hit early in their stay to establish some impressive inland bases, they left their ships and the bulk of their troops where they were.

"The inevitable finally happened. Another storm, a tempest of awesome fury, struck the area, driving titanic waves before it. Only a handful of the starships, all of them severely damaged, were left after it had passed. As for those manning them, most of those sheltering on the surviving ships made it. Almost none of the others did.

"The inland garrisons were untouched and were large enough to hold a shortened perimeter, but they were withdrawn not long afterward."

Sogan did not respond at once. It was a too familiar tale to him. The Empire's homeworlds were all tame, lacking natural challenges, and Arcturian war leaders had never been compelled to concern themselves with such forces. As a result, they rarely took them into consideration when laying their plans against the very different Federation planets. Time and again, even near the end of the great conflict when stark experience should have taught its bitter lesson a thousand times over, they had ignored the possibility of encountering such perils on the new worlds to which they sent their fleets. It was the one consistent failing of his kind, and it had cost the Empire a brutal toll of valiant, well-trained soldiers and countless tons of the equipment supporting them. Even at the height of his career, he had not concealed the fact that he had considered that blindness to proven danger no less than criminal negligence, aye, and open treason against the Emperor's cause.

Varn? The gurry shifted uneasily and peered up into his face.

He checked his thoughts and caressed her. *It is all right, small one. This is battle talk. That is always disturbing.*

Yes!

The Arcturian stroked her again. Bandit disliked the kind of tension generated during such conferences, but she had never quit one for that reason, no more than she had ever held back from any phase of the work that was the lot and life of the people to whom she had attached herself. That was a great deal more than could be said of many a human.

There was nothing of humor either in Sogan's answering smile or in Islaen's. The Jadite mammal had risked herself and had sustained injury for their sake, and she was ready to endure that much again and more. It was enough to give both of them pause when they discussed a future campaign that needs must include her as well.

Varn forcibly concentrated on the discussion before them. "Jake is correct all the same about the importance of your part in our withdrawal from Anath. As I understand it, our fleet had strength enough left to hold on longer even without reinforcement or resupplying if all they had to face was a single potential threat from space. It was chiefly the constant guerrilla activity on-world, coupled with our growing need to strengthen our increasingly hard-pressed major fleets, that spurred our departure."

His dark eyes fell momentarily. That had been a coup for the Federation. Had that fleet remained a bare three months longer, Ram Sithe would not have been able to slip his ships past the planet to surprise . . .

"You organized the locals as you did those on Thorne, I suppose?" he asked abruptly.

Islaen Connor shook her head. "Thorne of Brandine had an active and very efficient Resistance before we ever planeted. —The Anathi did not, and they never did much more than scout for us and provide support and guards. Only a very few of them took part in any of the actual fighting."

Bethe Danlo's brows lifted. "You did a pretty impressive job, four of you against a whole fleet. What was wrong with those planet-hugging sons of Scythian apes, anyway? Raw cowards?"

"No way," Karmikel declared flatly. "They're courageous to the point of folly at times, but we couldn't arm them, and you can't send swords against pellet guns and blasters."

"Why in space didn't you outfit them properly?" the Sergeant demanded. "Even if you couldn't smuggle in enough weapons and ammo, you could always take them from the Arcturians. Commandos were famous for keeping Resistance forces supplied that way."

"Federation law. The surplanetary situation was such that giving our weapons to those people might too readily be tantamount to replacing one tyranny with another and totally disrupting their natural development as well."

"Rot!" Bethe tossed her head. "They were damn well disrupted before you space hounds ever showed up on the scene."

"I'm afraid we agreed with you," Jake admitted, "but Morris Martin made the mistake of reporting the situation as it stood, and he got a set of orders back as explicit on that score as a navputer's program. Maybe High Command wouldn't have been quite so adamant had Anath represented a key attack point for us, but no one saw her in that light, and we weren't given a micron's leeway. —Ah well. It worked out anyway."

The Noreenan woman saw and read Varn Tarl Sogan's contempt, quickly as he managed to veil it. She stiffened. "You disagree as well, Admiral?" she asked coolly.

"You were at war."

"Would you have had us violate the very principles millions of us were battling and dying to defend?"

"I am not of your Federation," he responded wearily. "A lot of your ways are and probably shall always remain incomprehensible to me. With us, military expedience has precedence over other considerations. To my mind, it should have ruled on Anath of Algola."

He scowled as his temper quickened under her continued challenge. "Commandos though you were, you would not have done as well as you did working alone had that storm not arisen to aid your cause. You could not have counted on its coming with such excellent timing—or did you enlist one of their witch doctors to summon it?"

The Commando-Colonel bit back the retort that sprang to her lips. "Sorry, Varn. I shouldn't have pushed you, especially since, as Jake said, we all agreed with your appraisal."

She shrugged. "It was a lot of weight to throw on us, all right, but in point of fact it was no more than we had anticipated from the start. Don't forget, we went in expecting to voyage solo. No one knew there was a surplanetary population until we came in and found them."

Her eyes seemed to look into the distance. "Our mission was merely to harass, tie down troops and matériel your people could have used to better effect elsewhere. That we so far exceeded that goal was a matter of great pride to us, however much we owed to chance for our success." She smiled. "We even managed to get the locals cooperating with one another as they had not done for centuries of their history. —Morris cherished that as an achievement greater than our military gains. He had been educated as a diplomat, you see, and that sort of work was his real love, not the waging of war."

Her eyes fell. The Anath assignment had been the last he had completed. Commando-Captain Morris Martin had been killed shortly after they had arrived on Thorne of Brandine, and she, then a Lieutenant, had assumed command in his place.

"They consist of the usual mix of small, ever-quarreling tribes, I suppose?" the blond woman asked after a moment.

Islaen shook her head. "No. The Anathi have a more complex society than that.

"Actually, they were once considerably more numerous and also more advanced, technically and socially. About eight hundred years ago, the bulk of the populace was organized in a theocracy dedicated to a goddess, Anath herself, whom they still honor, and were ruled by a hierarchy of priest-kings. Life under them was ascetic and increasingly more repressive, and at last, a backlash developed against it.

"Unfortunately, it took the form of another sect, one given to what Terrans would term demon worship, at least in its outer attributes."

The Noreenan man nodded. "They had it all—excesses of every sort, animal and human sacrifice, with and without torture—the full cargo, everything repugnant to the old order. But they got recruits. Very few may have been worshipers, but folks were apparently so sick of the chains loaded on their lives that many were willing to throw themselves in with any movement that might work a change. Others were swayed by fear as the power of the newcomers expanded."

"It came to rebellion?" Sogan asked. His voice was cold, haughty. As a prince of his own strongly governed race, he had little sympathy with rebels, and he could only despise those who would debase themselves in the manner Karmikel had described.

"Aye. —They were a proud folk who detested what was being done to them," the redheaded man explained.

"Pride gives the strength to endure until appropriate action can be taken, or merely to endure if no other course is possible. They were only treacherous, and they were stupid. I should not care to receive the brand of relief that vermin such as you have described were likely to dispense once they gained power."

Islaen silenced Jake with a shake of her head. The Arcturian's opinion was set and would not soften, whatever any of them might say. Besides, neither she nor Karmikel could conduct a very strong defense in this case. They were both just about of the same mind themselves.

"That was never put to the test," she told him. "They were utterly defeated in the end, and exterminated, every man and woman and every child of theirs old enough to have received the imprint of their ideas. However, they did succeed in part of their aim. The fighting had been long and hard and very costly; the theocracy did not survive it.

"The remaining populace hung on in their old places in the highlands for another two or three generations, but they could not rebuild their society, and in the end, they migrated to the gentler forest region to make a new start. Their King, now merely a temporal ruler, built his stronghold, a fortress called An Fainne, and those of his people not attached to his household settled in the surrounding woodlands."

"They became farmers?" Bethe asked.

"Most of them had been that. Some continued raising crops or practicing the crafts in which they were trained, but most turned to the forest itself for support."

"They reverted to hunting-gathering?" she exclaimed in surprise.

"To another sort of husbandry. Both the forest and the plains beyond are rich in a great variety of resources. The newcomers merely adapted themselves to managing and harvesting them as the inhabitants of the area were already doing.

"They did manage them, too, and continue to do so. Anathi have a wisdom rare in primitive peoples and recognized from the start the need to use their blessings carefully, the necessity of replenishing what they take and nurturing the whole. As a result, they haven't ended up raping their world, but rather have always worked with her."

"But not entirely with each other," Varn noted, forcing the discussion back to its original topic. "You did mention political differences. I presume that trouble has started between the newcomers and the people already established in the woodlands."

"Aye," his consort admitted regretfully. "That shadow seems to accompany intelligence wherever it arises. Anath of Algola was no more fortunate than any other planet in escaping its curse.

"Their argument is the product of greed and pride, as most such divisions are. It's doubly tragic in that the two factions should by every right be fast friends. During the uprising, the faithful were staunchly aided by the people of the forest, who shared their beliefs, although they did not give allegiance to the priest-kings. Despite that help and their traditional independence, when the loyalists' descendants settled in that part of the forest adjoining their allies' domain, their King tried to extend his authority over them. They resisted, naturally enough, and proved sufficiently woodcrafty and strong that they continue to resist to this day."

"Nasty," commented the demolitions expert dryly.

"It is that, and it could've been worse than that for us had we not managed our campaign well and avoided letting ourselves be trapped between the two groups. In truth, apart from the Warlord and a few of the others from An Fainne, we dealt nearly exclusively with the Foresters. They proved more accepting of us, and they were by far the better scouts for our kind of combat. —They should be, having waged a technically similar, if a lot less bloody, war themselves for a good seven hundred years."

"Warlord?"

She nodded. "That's one of their more politically sophisticated concepts. The Anathi had learned to their sorrow that a good administrator and ruler is not necessarily a good general. By the same token, they realized that a fine military leader does not always make an ideal head of state. On top of all that, they had too much experience with the disruption that the sudden loss of their King created in all branches of life to want to see future rulers rush off to battle.

"Their solution was to create the nonhereditary rank of Warlord. The man showing himself best suited in mind and warrior skills is named to the position. He can never rule whether he surrenders his title or not—that law is inviolable and is a major check against possibly metastasizing ambition—but he does have command in all military matters. He is also likely to command more of the people's affection and devotion than any King, particularly if he is of superior ability and happens to be serving in a time of exceptional trouble. That can lead to a lot of tension in a glory-oriented race like this one, although it is a situation that doesn't actually arise very often. Despite the constant ill feeling between palace and forest, Anathi prefer to live fairly peacefully, usually limiting themselves to relatively minor raiding on one another's stock. They all work and dwell too closely to the potential battlefronts, and they've had just enough experience with warfare to appreciate the consequences of all-out conflict."

"That is why they appear to have made no move against my people when they came?" the war prince asked contemptuously.

Islaen sighed to herself. If he was this hostile to the on-worlders now, what would she have to put up with when he learned the rest? "No. It is not. They stayed in hiding because they realized that swords and axes could not match the weapons you possessed. They are not to be blamed for not seeking purposeless racial suicide. When we came, they were more than willing to do their part, and a greater one than we would or were able to permit them to assume."

Sogan fell silent under the lash of her words, but Jake Karmikel grimaced. "Not that we didn't have to walk a narrow course with them between their own squabbling and that tension Islaen so casually mentioned. —You and Babaye didn't feel much of it, Colonel, so you can pass over it fairly lightly, but take my word for it, none of us males enjoyed our time with the Anathi."

"The King was jealous of you, too?" Bethe asked sympathetically.

"A Queen ruled An Fainne, fortunately a fine, sensible woman, no war leader in any sense but completely dedicated to her people's cause and well aware of the needs of that unprecedented situation. We had no problem at all with her.

"Her son, Prince Coronus, on the other hand, was a royal pain in the fins. He has good stuff in him, right enough, if he can ever manage to put clamps on that temper and stubborn streak of his, and there's no doubting that he's both a capable fighter as he understands warfare and brave, but he'd never have made Admiral in either ultrasystem. He managed to swallow the necessity of our presence and the role we played, but, space, how he resented us! He'd never been happy taking a poor second to Xenon, the Warlord, in most warrior exercises all his life—they were approximately of one age and had trained together—but custom at least made that acceptable. We were another matter with our exotic weaponry and our flamboyant successes in what he and everyone else saw to be Anath's war as much as our own.

"Islaen and Babaye Llyne fared fairly well since An Fainne's women did not fight, though those of the forest have long done so, and he didn't feel threatened by them. It was another matter entirely with Tomas Dyn and me.

"Morris, he hated outright, for his skill and courage and the glory they very quickly earned him, and at first because of the

woman who seemed to emphasize his position more strongly even
than the powerful weapons he carried."

He glanced at Sogan. "He didn't want Islaen for himself, but he
really didn't understand her place in the unit at the start, or
Babaye's. Once he did, that difficulty cleared up as if by sorcery."

The former Admiral nodded but made no comment. That
attitude was, apparently, frequently found in Federation men.
They based their self-image upon their supposed performance in
the reproductive act and so tended to subconsciously see an
association with a particularly attractive woman as indicative of
their own worth and place.

He smiled to himself then, banishing his rising feeling of
superiority. Arcturians were not any more reasonable in measur-
ing their manhood by their ability to maul one another in single,
weaponless combat.

Perhaps not, he thought, but their consorts and concubines at
least had an easier time of it. The men of the warrior caste
maintained harems, aye, but out of the necessity of preserving
both the ruling lines and general population levels, which would
not otherwise be possible for a people who had never been free of
war for so much as a single generation during all the millennia of
their long history. There was no seclusion and no overt or covert
slavery for their women. That was more than could be said of
similar arrangements where they had arisen in this supposedly
freedom-cherishing ultrasystem.

That line of thought passed from his mind even as it was born.
There were matters in this tale more difficult to understand than a
barbarian's weaknesses and of considerably greater concern.

"You chanced working with such a one, knowing how he felt?"
he asked incredulously. That seemed tantamount to introducing
the seeds of plague into an unimmunized community.

"To some extent," the Colonel replied. "We were more or less
compelled to use him when we had to to call out more of the
palace men than usual and, of course, we encountered him during
our visits to An Fainne. He was not one of the company Xenon
chose to aid him in the fight full-time."

She read his disapproval and the worry that fired it. "We had no
fear of betrayal," she assured him. "Whatever his feelings about
us or our other allies, Coronus was absolutely loyal to Anath.
While the forces of the Empire remained on-world, there was no
danger of treachery on his part."

"Especially with the good Colonel's talent for reading people's
supposedly private emotions," Jake drawled.

Islaen Connor could not receive actual thoughts save from Sogan and Bandit, but she was able to pick up emotion and other highly charged transmissions from human-level minds. In all the time since she had accustomed herself to the gift that had first awakened during her days in Basic training, she had never failed to identify a traitor or potential traitor.

Despite that assurance, Varn shook his head. "It is still a bad situation. —I do not like our becoming involved with it, Islaen."

"Neither do I," she admitted frankly, "but it would be as difficult for anyone else, and Admiral Sithe feels we'll be better able to deal with it with our previous experience to back us."

Her brown eyes fixed him sharply. He, too, had his talents. *Varn, have you any feeling against this?*

No, not as I had before some of the others. Logic just goes against involvement with Anath of Algola.

He was grateful that she had not raised that question verbally. The Commando-Colonel suspected that he might have some ability to sense particular danger in an upcoming mission. Some of their prior experiences did seem to bear that out, but it was theory only, and he was loathe to let the others know of it. He had no wish to broadcast that Varn Tarl Sogan went through a case of nerves before an assignment.

"Mind if I ask what may be a scramble-circulated question, Colonel?" the demolitions expert inquired.

"Fire away."

"If no one knew the Anathi existed until you ran into them, how did they pick up Basic or you their tongue to the extent that you were able to wage a war beside them?"

Islaen Connor smiled. "We all spoke Arcturian."

The other woman blinked in surprise and then smiled herself. "Of course!" She stopped. "But where did they learn that? You said they avoided the invaders."

"All except the one village Jake mentioned. That was located on the cliffs just above the beach where the fleet planeted, and most of its people were taken and enslaved, though their total lack of the most basic technical concepts limited them to general heavy labor. Some of the younger women were also reserved for possible use by their captors and were sterilized since they didn't possess the knowledge to prevent conception themselves.

"The Anathi were restive under their chains, and a number of them did manage to escape, most during the disruption caused by the first storm. Those who failed to make a break finally perished with a large part of the Arcturians in the great tempest at the end of the occupation.

"The fugitives were picked up by the Foresters and their wounded cared for by them, and they were eventually returned to their own people at An Fainne. Thus, they gave intelligence of the invaders and knowledge of their language to both native factions and aroused the deep anger and hatred of both.

"Slavery is unknown on Anath, and that in itself spurred fury, but the sterilization of those women horrified and revolted the entire populace. Anathi do not quicken often, and since children are relatively few, they are highly valued. It was all but inconceivable to them that any woman should be denied the right to bear."

Sogan listened without comment. He knew his people's ways and made no apology for them before their enemies, although he himself had kept atrocity to a minimum in his own command. Besides, he did not believe that any explanation he might offer would be well received by his comrades.

He, at least, could understand why the Anathi women had been used as they had. To his kind, with their intense pride of blood, it was a black disgrace for any man of the warrior caste to sire a child even upon a menial of their own race. To father a half-breed upon a barbarian alien would be unthinkable. It was essential to take whatever steps were necessary to prevent that since their commander had chosen to allow miscegenation with the on-worlders in order to lighten the burden of extended duty on the isolated planet. Had those locals not been too primitive to take care of the matter themselves, they doubtless would have been allowed to handle it in their own way.

Still, despite his comprehension of the invaders' probable motives, his lips tightened as the Colonel continued to speak, and his eyes fixed on the cup in his hands. Although some men in the lowest ranks of a few commands did deign to use for their pleasure patently unacceptable captive females, even near mutants, he had never tolerated the like from those serving beneath him. He had never been able to understand how any officer could. To his mind, to most of his caste, such unions amounted to little less, aye, and often worse, than the mating of human with animal.

Bandit stirred. *Varn?*

Quiet, small one, he said hastily lest Islaen pick up their exchange. *I was merely thinking.*

None of his comrades had challenged him, nor did he expect them to do so. They knew his record and were not likely to draw down the deeds of others on him even if friendship would have permitted that. Islaen only mentioned this now as background for their current mission.

Indeed, the woman was not thinking about her consort at all. She had been concerned about how Bethe Danlo would fare, but now she nodded in satisfaction. The demolitions expert had been given a crash course in the Arcturian tongue when she had been assigned to serve at the surrender ceremonies and had been practicing on all of them since she had joined the unit. She might not speak it as well as the rest of them, but there was no fear that she would not be able to communicate effectively should she find herself alone among the Anathi for any reason.

As for Bandit, she understood those tongues her two humans spoke.

Sogan drained his cup. His mind had already shifted to what might lay ahead of them, and he was only marginally aware that the jakek had gone cold and vaguely tasteless. He set the cup down.

"That is all history. What is drawing us there now?"

"Precisely the same thing as before. An invasion. —Although both palace and forest were unanimous in their decision that they wanted no further contact with the Federation, thereby insuring that their people would continue to develop naturally and not be overwhelmed by our technology and numbers, we did leave an interstellar transceiver with Xenon so that Anath would still retain the ability to summon aid in the event of some extraordinary threat.

"A transmission was received in Headquarters, in Arcturian and on scramble as the instrument had been set to send, using the Warlord's code sequence. He reported the planeting of a fleet and asked if its coming was by our order. If so, he wanted to know for what purpose. Xenon further stated that until he received our answer, his people would assume the worst and keep well away from the starships and those manning them.

"Sithe responded at once, stating that the Federation government had not authorized any such visitation. He directed that the Anathi should continue to avoid the newcomers, at least until we could investigate this violation of their neutrality."

"Space!" exploded Jake. "They deserve better than that. They worked hard enough for their peace during the War. It wasn't their fault that we wouldn't let them do more."

"My thought exactly, my friend."

"What was Xenon able to tell us about the invaders?"

"Precious little. Even if they dared approach the off-worlders, his people don't know any of our languages and wouldn't have been able to learn anything from them.

"The fleet consists of approximately the same number of ships as the previous one, but they're basically smaller, chiefly brigs and a slew of escorts along with three cruisers, one of them most probably a one hundred-class.

"They came down on the same beach the Arcturians used but didn't stay long before resettling inland on the plain. Part of their crews have remained with them; the rest have taken over a couple of the installations left behind by the Arcturians. They've done some work around the last, but Xenon couldn't say whether they were installing some sort of fortifications or alarm systems."

"Alarms, I'd say. They apparently know they have little to fear from a frontal attack." Karmikel's eyes took on the look of blue ice. "They seem to know something about Anath, both her weather and her populace."

"That's scarcely surprising. No one shifts a force of that size around the starlanes without meaning business. It's only reasonable to assume that those giving the orders would do a bit of research on their planeting site or sites. A quick look in the open planetary files would give all the information to which they seem to be responding."

"Well, they have power and obviously purpose and some store of brains. What else do we know about them?"

"Almost nothing. They hunt for pleasure, which doesn't endear them to the Anathi, as you can well imagine, and they use pellet guns almost exclusively for that purpose. Many of them also sport blasters, but pellets seem to be their weapon of choice. They're fully mechanized, naturally.

"As to who they are or whom they represent, we have no idea. Our informants simply don't know enough about us to come to any conclusions. They are definitely military, not pirates. That much is apparent from both their behavior and their uniforms."

"Uniforms?" he asked hopefully.

"No help. Khaki and basic spacer style from Xenon's description."

"Oh, wonderful!" he snapped in disgust. "Do you know how many planets outfit their forces like that?"

"No. There are too many of them."

Every Federation planet maintained some sort of official armed force, either exclusively on-world or equipped for service in space, though most rarely ventured beyond their home star

systems. The only stipulations the Senate made was that they must
in no manner resemble either the Navy or the Stellar Patrol and
that they should neither violate interstellar law nor infringe upon
the security or peace of any other people.

She spread her hands. "It's part of our business to find out just
who they are and what in space they want with Anath of Algola."

"And the other part?" her fellow Noreenan inquired with
deceptive mildness; he knew full well what her answer would be
before he ever voiced his question.

"To kick their fins off-world again."

"Rather a stellar order for four humans and one gurry," Bethe
observed. "I realize it was often necessary to tackle odds like that
during the War, and even now when we happen to walk into
something unexpectedly, but don't you think we might have just a
bit more help on this one? A small fleet of our own, for example,
might prove real handy."

Islaen laughed softly. "We have one, in a sense anyway, but a
full-scale assault is likely to leave Anath, or the affected part of
her, in a pretty bad mess. That just happens to be the region where
her entire human population is located. That's why it was decided
to try guerrillas to see if we can't just learn what we need to know
and maybe neutralize them without resorting to a major assault. If
we call the Navy in after studying the situation, or if we should fail
to report reasonably on schedule, then they'll strike. —That's
about all I can say for now. We'll have to see precisely what's
going on before we can decide what to do or how far we'll actually
have to go."

Varn Tarl Sogan's frown deepened as she spoke. As usual, they
would be carrying a lot of responsibility, more than enough to put
concern on the officer who must lead the expedition, but he
thought he sensed another worry on her, something that went
beyond—or beside—the conditions she was describing. A touch
to Bandit's mind confirmed that the hen was receiving the same
input.

"You might as well tell us the rest, Colonel," he said softly.

She looked at him sharply, then sighed. "Aye, though it's
nothing actually definite." The Commando scowled. "Xenon
closed his transmission with the injunction to take great care when
planeting and to meet with him in Vanya's cot before making our
arrival known to An Fainne."

Jake's eyes narrowed. "By the Spirit of Space, what's happened
there now?"

She shrugged. "There was no explanation in his transmission, but if it's their own games that they're playing and it's gotten to the point that either we and/or Anath have something to fear as a result, then our efforts may be doomed before we start. The Anathi were at least united behind us when we fought the Empire."

Her voice changed, subtly, but her comrades would not have cared to have the promise it now held turned against them.

"We still have no choice but to go in, but we do have a few gifts on our side of which our surplanetary hosts are totally unaware. If they think to betray us, to use us or our weapons against each other in their private squabbles, then their fate'll fall smack down on their own heads by their own doing. We can and shall rightly wipe our faces and hands of the lot of them."

Since only the *Fairest Maid* would risk the entry onto the occupied planet, Bethe and Jake returned to the *Jovian Moon* to collect the gear and personal items they would need.

Varn rose as well. *I had best get the navputer programmed.*

Hold up a minute, will you.

He turned again, frowning slightly. There was a strange note in her tone, and he knew she had some business with him that she had not wanted to share with their comrades. *Do you intend to ream me for expressing my opinion of your Anathi as I did?*

No! she snapped. *Did I ream Jake or Bethe? That was a war council. Your opinions were wanted.*

The former Admiral returned to the table. He sat on its edge. *Something is bothering you, Islaen. I take it that it concerns me.*

Aye, she admitted, then hesitated before going on. *Anath's people arose independently, but had they been Terra's seed originally, they'd be classed as mutants.* She felt him stiffen, although there was no outward alteration in him. *The variation from prototype isn't extensive compared with some of the changes we've seen, but it's there, and it's apparent.*

Her eyes caught and held his. *We'll have to deal with them to some extent, Varn.*

Are you questioning my ability to do so? he demanded frigidly.

The woman sighed. *Personally, no, but as an officer, I have no choice. —I know how you respond to mutants. I've felt your reaction too often when we've encountered them.*

Then you know, too, that I function as I must. Our maintenance crews on Horus, aye, and the team transferred to Thorne for our benefit are a well-mixed lot. I have had no trouble with any of them.

In short-term interaction, no. This may not be. She studied him a moment. His anger was plain to read, but she went on. *We're facing a delicate political situation and maybe a full-scale war. I don't need any problems with my own unit.*

Varn Tarl Sogan shot to his feet in fury, but that died almost in the next moment. He raised shields to cover the shame that replaced it. The Commando-Colonel was all too right to question him. He had gone to Hades against all sound advice and reason and had shown such little control there that he had nearly sabotaged their entire mission. Could he expect anything but doubt from her now, in the face of his distaste and disgust for those altered races his kind considered not merely not human, but an abomination against creation itself?

He compelled himself to meet her eyes again. "I am an officer of the Federation Navy, Islaen Connor," he said in tight verbal speech. "I shall not forget that again. I lay my word and my very soul on that."

THREE

VARN TARL SOGAN'S hands moved over the *Maid*'s controls, minutely adjusting her angle of approach. He was bringing her in straight out of Algola's face. It was a maneuver they had used with good effect before and one that should serve them equally well here. The sun-star's brilliance could be counted upon to shield them from any chance observation from the surface of the pearl-white planet now filling a full fifth of the near-space viewer.

It was merely a precaution in this case. If they were detected, it would either be by nonoptical sensors or through fortune's curse by some other ship chancing to pass through this particular portion of space during this same brief span of time. Nothing could actually be seen of space through the cloud cover that gave Anath her exquisite, vaguely mysterious beauty.

No one could do much about luck apart from hoping it would at least remain neutral if it could not be good. There was no point even in dwelling upon the possibility of betrayal from that quarter apart from keeping a careful watch out for other spacecraft, which would almost certainly belong to the invaders, and Sogan tried to banish that possibility from his mind entirely.

He could not dismiss the danger of running afoul of mechanical devices, sensors of one sort or another, so easily. That was a concrete threat, one they had to fear until they were on-world and under cover. Any party capable of putting a fleet of the size Xenon had described into space would also be able to equip it with every nonclassified security device available. The only question was how much protection had been deemed necessary on an isolated, unvisited planet like Anath of Algola and to what extent that equipment would be monitored when no alarms were anticipated.

Or perhaps the invaders did expect trouble, he corrected himself. Commando wavelengths were of necessity very tight, but if the Warlord's transmission had been detected, even if it had not been deciphered, they could find a fully alert enemy prepared for just such a response on the Federation's part. If so, their death might well already be poised and waiting to receive them.

His palms were sweating. He unconsciously rubbed them against his knee to dry them.

This was the third time he had made such an approach, brought a small craft into the space of a planet held by a larger, hostile force. It was an experience that did not seem to become easier with repetition.

The war prince surreptitiously glanced at his copilot. Islaen was no stranger to such planetings. She had made several throughout her service career, a number of them in the face of highly trained Arcturian commands, before joining with him. She was taking care to broadcast no alarm, but he was gratified to see from the stiffness of her posture and the way in which her eyes flickered between the observation panels and the instruments that she regarded their present challenge no more lightly than he did.

Varn quickly brought his attention back to the work before him. He stared at the ever-nearing planet somberly. Their time of greatest peril would begin when they broke through those clouds. He would have to bring the *Maid* down very quickly—but without allowing her hull to heat up at all—and get her into the clearing Islaen Connor had selected as her bay. If he failed and she did heat, she would appear like a comet or titanic meteor, certainly betraying their arrival to the on-worlders and most probably to the invaders as well.

That was assuming they would be able to planet at all. The Arcturian's heart went cold at the thought of their target. He had nursed the *Fairest Maid* into some tight places before, but to take her almost literally through the branches of a tree, where any significant tip could overbalance her and send her crashing to her doom, that was the stuff of a spacer's nightmare.

As if that were not enough, he would have to maneuver her through those last crucial moments using absolute minimum power. The little needle-nose was no fire tail of the old days, but she could still do a lot of damage to the greenery around her if she were to come down on full jets. That would create a fine beacon for either an air search or for any of the forest-wise surplanetary dwellers happening to wander into the area.

His grip tightened on the controls. He was good—few in either ultrasystem were better on the bridge of a starship—but he was not at all sure that he was the equal of meeting and mastering the multiple challenges looming before him.

You'll do fine.

Is my nervousness so apparent? he demanded curtly without looking at his companion.

Not really, Islaen replied smoothly. *I'm on edge, and I'm not carrying any responsibility for us at the moment.*

He gripped himself. *Sorry. And thanks for the confidence. Rest assured that I shall do my best to bear it out.*

Well, you do have some stake in the outcome, she teased gently.

Varn won't crash, the gurry told him serenely from her specially outfitted place on the Colonel's chair. She radiated no fear whatsoever.

Sogan smiled, soothed despite his appreciation of the difficulties just ahead by the magnitude of her certainty.

"Thank you as well, small one. Do not worry. A little humility is beneficial in moments like this. If not carried too far, it helps sharpen one's mind and responses."

A great swirling mass filled the viewer. Varn moistened his lips with his tongue and opened the ship's intercom.

"Jake, Bethe, strap down if you have not already. Next stop is Anath's surface."

Or the realms of their various gods.

The Federation ship plunged into the mist that was the pearl planet's outer face.

The former Admiral's eyes lowered to the instrument panel. He would have to depend on their guidance for as long as the starship remained within this blindfold. Even the most basic, trusted senses could become confused when confronted by that vast, fleecy sameness outside.

He wondered about the world rapidly rising up to meet them. Despite the assurances contained in the tapes he had studied and the two Commandos' testimony, the thought nagged in his mind that a cloud atmosphere like this was often the visible signal of an air mixture inimical to life as humanity knew it. Even more frequently, it heralded a runaway greenhouse effect rampaging beneath, with surface temperatures high enough to soften and maybe melt many of the common metals.

To a certain extent, that phenomenon was in force on Anath of Algola, but it worked rather to her good than her ill. The masking layer was too thin to trap heat that completely, and it did not totally envelop the planet; there were clear skies over one pole, alternating with Anath's yearly revolution around her sun-star, that allowed still more of the excess to escape back into space. What remained of it was beneficial. Without that pent-up warmth, the rich variety of living things she supported could never have come into being on a planet set so far from the cherishing rays of her sun.

Tension rose in him as the seconds passed. Would they never break through?

Suppose Islaen and he had miscalculated? Only a minute veering from course, and they could wind up over one of their foes' strongholds. A graver error might put them above the other continent or far out to sea, forcing them to keep to the air far too long . . .

Varn's eyes lifted to the observation panel. No change. Surely this stuff should have begun to thin out by now!

He drew a deep breath to steady himself. The clouds were less dense. Barely perceptibly at first, then more rapidly and obviously, they dissipated until, moments later, the *Fairest Maid* broke free into the clear air of Anath's perpetually shrouded surface.

Below, for mile upon countless mile, stretched a vast forest, a wonderful, tufted carpet of green broken here and there by patches of vivid color where some tree or stand of trees was in flower and by spots of brighter emerald marking grass and shrubs, natural clearings in the ocean of growth.

None of them was large enough to accommodate even so small a vessel as the *Maid*. The former Admiral slowed as rapidly as he dared. They must not remain airborne any longer than a few more seconds, but where in all space was he to put his ship? There was no sign of the oddly configured clearing the Commando-Colonel had recommended.

He glanced at his instruments. No, it would not be visible yet. Soon now, assuming he had not mishandled the approach.

What if they found it only to discover it was too small? Perhaps they should have insisted on being dropped from some Navy battlecraft near Algola's space and made their way in with the flier, which was unique in its ability to serve as both a surplanetary and, for short hops, as a space vessel. They had rejected that option, which would have greatly increased their chances of exposing themselves—no innocent traffic passed near this place—but he wondered now at the wisdom of that caution.

There!

Sogan saw it as well, a break in the trees, larger than the others he had noted but still looking impossibly narrow.

He kept a tight hold on himself. They should be able to make it, barely, with care and a measure of luck, if the Empire's harsh gods and Anath's did not work against him.

He went into the final descent pattern immediately. His sensitive fingers cradled the controls, in spirit cradled the *Maid* herself, as he guided her down so delicately that he seemed not to interfere with her movements at all.

Leaf-crowned branches surrounded them on every side. A few brushed the starship's smooth skin, but their touch was soft, as if welcoming. She struck none of the strong, inner limbs that might have disturbed her delicate balance.

At last, all motion ceased. Varn automatically cut the engines, but even after he had done so and with the instruments confirming that the *Fairest Maid* was resting squarely and safely on the planet's surface, he did not for a moment quite believe that he had succeeded.

He released the breath he had been unconsciously holding and then turned to receive Islaen's smile and voiceless congratulations.

Sogan activated the intercom once more. "Time to get to work, you two," he told his comrades. "We are on-world."

FOUR

THE WAR PRINCE'S attention fixed on his companion. He could feel the energy streaming out from her as her mind swept the surrounding treelands for any indication that they might be under observation.

Is there a welcoming committee? he asked at last, quietly so as not to startle her.

Nothing human, at least not yet. The rest is your department.— Let's go, Varn. We seem to be all right for the moment, but company could still be on its way.

Even as she spoke, she released her safety nets and helped free the gurry from hers. Sogan moved as quickly to unfasten his own webbing and scooped up his carefully readied pack almost in the same instant that his consort reached for hers.

They scrambled, nearly dropped, down the core ladder until they reached the main hatch where Bethe and Karmikel were waiting with the flier. It was in position to exit, its engine already running.

"Is it safe to open up, Colonel?" the Captain asked.

"As safe as it's going to be."

"Get under cover," the Arcturian told them. "I will secure the *Maid*. We just might be wanting transport off this rock."

As soon as Islaen slipped behind the controls of the machine, he opened the lock, then bent to the task of guarding his starship as best he might, not so much as pausing to watch his comrades' departure.

Islaen Connor kept the flier at full speed until they reached the shelter of the trees. She stopped there and turned, holding the vehicle on hover so that it would leave no mark on the ground to betray them. All three had their blasters at ready to give Sogan cover should he require it in his exposed position.

Her eyes ran once up the length of the graceful ship, and she allowed Varn to feel her admiration for the precision with which he had placed her. There was no room whatsoever for error in this tight bay.

He was so good with a ship, she thought, or with many ships. It was criminal that such a great part of his talent had to lie idle, never again to be used.

Perhaps. There was one possible out for him. She did not like to consider it herself, but it was viable despite the heavy price it carried. The military was Varn's life, and it was hers.

No matter. She was not about to keep the proposal from him because of that. It was his future and his decision. She had failed him utterly after that mess on Omrai by merely standing aside and allowing him to choose by himself whether he would live or die by his own hand, instead of fighting for him with all the force at her command. She would not now deny him the chance to secure a measure of real fulfillment in this life in exile. If any man had earned that right, Varn Tarl Sogan certainly had.

Whatever her determination, all that must be postponed until their work on Anath of Algola was done. If they did not keep their minds on the work in front of them, they might not live long enough to be able to take up any other.

She studied the starship critically and was satisfied by what she saw. The *Maid* looked strange in her dull-finished coat mottled over with camouflage patterns, but that unattractive dress was eminently more suitable for screening her while she sat unattended in Anath's wild forest than her usual clean silver skin would have been. Their maintenance crew on Horus had done well, particularly in the face of the little time in which they had been given to work. She smiled briefly. But then, those servicing Commando equipment should be pretty used to doing things on short notice.

The former Admiral was still inside the *Maid*, but she knew his routine for safeguarding her on-world well enough to follow his progress almost without the need to make mind touch.

At first, the number and nature of the multiple defenses he had installed and habitually set whenever he left the ship had seemed little short of mild paranoia to her, but she had not been in his company long before she, too, had come to see them as no more than the wise precautions of a man for whom the universe was often a very hostile place.

Jake Karmikel's attention was not fixed on the starship herself

but on her makeshift berth. His lips formed a soundless whistle
when he saw how closely the wide-spreading crowns of the
surrounding trees pressed in on her. "I don't count myself any
novice on a bridge, but by the Spirit of Space, I would not care to
try a planeting like that!"

"I don't even care to remember that we were part of it," the
Sergeant muttered in agreement.

Sogan left the *Fairest Maid* at last. He darted across the narrow
space separating her from the trees, unerringly guided to the flier
by his contact with Islaen Connor.

He sprang through the door she opened for him. Varn cast a last
look at his ship. He wished mightily that he could have raised an
energy picket around her, but the intense light that emitted
prohibited its use. The *Maid*'s titanone skin and the guards he had
set would have to suffice.

He made himself turn away and face the maze of tree trunks
stretching seemingly into infinity all around them. "Where now,
Colonel?" he asked. "One of your old camps, or do we break new
ground?"

"The latter, Admiral. As long as we have any doubts at all
about our former allies, I wouldn't feel too comfortable settling
down in known territory. Jake and I think we've figured out a
good spot for us."

"The rest of us are in your hands."

The Arcturian fixed his eyes on the windshield and stared
through it rather bleakly. He had done well with that planeting, but
that probably would be the last time he would excel at anything
until they were spaceborne and back in his element once more.
Already, Islaen was seeking Karmikel's opinion rather than
his . . .

He gripped himself sharply. That kind of fouled thinking had
very nearly wrought disaster on Hades of Persephone. He was not
about to give it rein again.

He cautiously tested the tightness of his shields and, to his
relief, found them sound. At least he had not betrayed his burst of
jealousy to his consort.

"You are not picking up anything?" he asked more to distract
her from any tension she might sense in him than to confirm what
he already knew from her relatively relaxed attitude.

"Nothing.—What about the wildlife? How are Anath's nonhuman citizens taking us?"

Just as she could detect the transmissions of fellow humans and their equivalents, Varn Tarl Sogan had the ability to receive the patterns of animalkind possessing any perceptible sentience.

Sogan opened his receptors to the full and sent his mind out in search of other living things.

Physically, there was little sign of Anath's creatures, no sight of them and no sound near the flier, although birds did call and odd chitterings could be heard high above and at some distance from them. That in itself was no cause for concern. The presence of strange people and their even more alien machine was enough to render most wild things shy and silent. It was not mere unease sparked by their passage that he sought to detect but sharp, concrete fear or a more widespread disturbance that would signal the presence of others of their race, though Islaen's senses should already be giving them warning of any other travelers—or spies—in the area.

"There is a large population around us," he informed his comrades at last. Varn had expected that, but it amazed him all the same, as it always did, to discover such numbers in a place that seemed almost devoid of life to eye and ear. "Most of the variety seems to be above, though. Down here, I can feel only a few distinct types. One species overwhelmingly predominates, just about exclusively in most places."

"Junners probably," Jake suggested. "Curious, harmless little mammals?"

"That is the impression their transmissions give." It was also what he expected to find here. There was little other life on the floor of Anath's deep forests; the bulk of their denizens dwelled high above in the richly leafed canopy.

"You probably picked up the other touches as we passed various streams or springs. These woods're well watered, and every wet place is a regular miniature ecosystem."

"Well and good," cut in Bethe, "but what's their mood, Admiral? Anything to worry us?"

"I do not believe so. They are strange to me," he added frankly, "and I could be missing a great deal because I simply do not know what clues to seek, but they appear to be quite content. We are giving the nearer ones a start, but chiefly they seem to be more concerned with feeding than with our presence or anything else."

"That's about right for this time of day," Islaen agreed. She smiled as her husband suddenly joined his mind with hers so that she, too, could experience the contacts he was receiving. She loved to share consciousness with the supposedly lesser creatures of the universe and envied Varn his ability to do so at will. Her talent allowed her to touch only the stronger transmissions of people, and so many of those were dark, filled with hate and the will to death.

They maintained the contact only a short while, then regretfully separated again to return to their own individual watching.

Sogan eased off his probing and settled back, keeping his receptors open so that he could remain in contact with Anath's wildlife without exhausting himself in a constant, active search. This method of scanning worked well and he had learned to utilize it. The concentration needed to maintain a continuous search was impossible to hold, and intermittent attempts were all but purposeless. Peril could appear and strike in a moment.

Since he occupied the passenger seat for once, with no responsibility for guiding the machine, he permitted himself the luxury of allowing his mind to wander where it would.

Their surroundings were fair in a shadowed, solemn sense. The trees around them were old without weakness, dizzyingly tall with the trunks straight and bare to their crowns, where they exploded into mighty umbrellas of green.

Such green! Islaen called it super chlorophyll. That was no scientific pronouncement, just a commentary on the intense color universal to Anath's vegetation and to its remarkable richness and success on a world whose sky was perpetually clouded, a world that, save at her poles, never beheld the face of her sun.

Even for their height, these trunks were broad and sturdy-looking, but there was good room between them, enough to have allowed a choking jungle of undergrowth to rise up in another place. On Anath of Algola, the ground was bare save for a thick mat of moss, which softened and shrouded the whole surface. The light was dim, and although there was movement in the air, it was gentle, tamed by the great baffle through which it had to pass. Humidity was high, for the area was well supplied with surface water, and rain came both frequently and heavily, but the temperature was just cool enough that it did not become a burden.

His eyes traced the length of one of the great trunks to the place where it blossomed in a sudden exuberance of branches.

Reason seemed to call these trees the product of a miracle. How else could they exist, and in such great profusion, under that eternally gray sky?

That was a ridiculous notion, of course. Anath's offspring had developed to meet the challenges she presented, and her growing things were well adapted to utilize diffused rather than the direct sunlight they were fated never to receive. Leaves were generally of two basic types—very broad, miniature solar traps or else delicately feathered masses with multiple slender needles to expose an enormous total surface area to capture the vital rays they required. Their well-nigh incandescent hue seemed to proclaim the intensity of the sensitivity and activity of the cells comprising them.

What a pity that glorious green could not be mated to a firmament of equally vivid blue, he thought, a sky such as Thorne of Brandine possessed. He tried to imagine what it must be never to see the like of that, never to behold the stars in an ebony sky, never to wonder at the phases of a moon. It was poverty in truth not to know that such glory even existed.

He wondered how their blindness to all but their own realm would affect the Anathi's growth as a people. Memory of visitors from the stars would gradually fade, maybe into vague legend, maybe entirely, with the passage of time. How was curiosity, which was the privilege and goad of humanity, to develop fully with no far distant mysteries to draw it? Would this race be forever confined, unaware that they were confined, within the narrow bounds of one planet's lower atmosphere?

Islaen Connor sensed the pensive mood on him, and her mind brushed his quizzically.

He opened himself to her. *It is nothing, my Islaen. I was only collecting stardust.—I would not trade our Thorne for Anath of Algola, however worthy she might be.* The image of the sealed sky he had glimpsed from the clearing returned to him. *Even the smallest ship has observation panels.*

I know, she agreed slowly, concealing her surprise, *I could never quite accustom myself to her when we were here before.*

She managed to keep her eyes away from him. She had known Varn loved Thorne of Brandine, but she had not realized he felt the sense of personal association with her that he had just revealed. The Noreenan sighed to herself. The war prince only rarely allowed her any glimpse of that part of him, not wanting her to read the longing and consciousness of loss that rode him all-too frequently. She could not force herself or her help on him, not in this. His kind considered it rank weakness to admit to a pain or difficulty that could not be altered. He could not so forget himself as to permit her to share it. She could only accept the confidences he chose to give and react very carefully to them.

The woman took care that her thoughts did not pass her shields. *I wish that we'd been given a bit more time there,* she said a bit sadly, *at least to the conclusion of our furlough, but I suppose we were lucky to get as much as we did.*

His smile reached his dark eyes. *Perhaps we should be glad to be needed,* he suggested.

The gurry hen had been listening quietly to the pair from her perch on the seat back between them. Now she gave a sharp whistle. *Let's go back to Thorne. Everyone's nice there.*

Everyone's nice to you everywhere, Islaen told her unsympathetically. *Don't worry, love. We'll probably get more leave after this assignment, just like we did after the others. That's usually the way it works.*

Normally because at least one of us has been smashed up and has to recuperate, the Arcturian pointed out.

Nooo!

Varn, don't tease her!

I was just being realistic.

Nooo!—Let's leave now!

Varn!

Very well, Colonel Connor, he laughed, *I surrender.* He stroked the gurry with the tip of his finger. *Power down, little Bandit. We shall try to take better care of ourselves on this one, but you know that we cannot lift until our work here is done.*

Yes, she replied with a resignation that would have been comical had she not been so serious. *Bandit will guard Islaen and Varn,* she added with equal gravity.

Bethe Danlo leaned over the back of the seat. "What's going on up there? Bandit's all worked up about something."

"Just a discussion about the possibility of our incurring casualties again," the Noreenan woman answered.

"You were tormenting her, you mean! A fine pair of heroes you two are, upsetting her like that!"

"Your maternal instincts are showing, Sergeant," Jake told her lazily. "Unnecessarily, I may add. Our Jadite friend manages us all very well with no need of assistance."

"That little bundle of feathers saved my life, remember? I'm usually surprisingly grateful for such services. She also saved yours."

"A fact that I'm not likely to forget, and if our two commanders continue pestering her, they're going to find themselves walking in pretty short order."

"All right," Islaen laughed. "You don't have to mutiny. We'll treat her with proper consideration and respect from here on in."

* * *

The off-worlders' good humor held over the next hour, and the time was not long in going before the Commando-Colonel brought the flier to a stop. "Here's home for a while."

Sogan and Bethe looked about them. The place was not really a clearing, although more than the usual quota of light did reach the forest floor. Many of the trees seemed younger than their fellows. At least they were perceptibly shorter and more slender of trunk, and their crowns were proportionally smaller and less dense.

The explanation for that and for the abnormal brightness of the site was readily apparent. One of the forest giants had fallen here long years in the past, so long ago that only its skeleton, part of its skeleton, remained. All the soft inner wood had vanished, and even most of the iron-hard bark that gave the tree its surplanetary name was gone save for one relatively long section. This part of the shell was so situated as to receive good shelter and had survived virtually intact since it had not endured the same weathering pressures.

What remained was a huge, almost perfectly circular cavern, dank inside and perpetually shadowed at its center, although both ends were open to the light.

"Memory did serve us right," Islaen Connor said with satisfaction. "There should be plenty of room in there for the flier with enough left over to provide us with living quarters."

The former Admiral kept his face and open thoughts bland, but Bethe eyed the hollow tree dubiously. "There won't be a whole lot of space in there," she ventured cautiously. Or comfort, but that was hardly a matter for discussion.

Jake Karmikel chuckled. "The luxuries the space-bred expect!—Sergeant, as a campsite, this place is a half step from paradise itself. Just think, we might as easily be sitting on some mud hill in the center of a swamp, and battling a generous variety of insects and slimy types for the privilege of staying there."

She shuddered. Anath, she knew, hosted only a few insect species, and most of those were totally innocuous. That was a matter of no small consequence to soldiers compelled to dwell in close association with the land. Even the leeches and stinging flies of Terra's jungles could be a torment well nigh beyond endurance; the monsters of Tabor were meat for nightmare. A chill went through her. Her three comrades had met and fought a nightmare direr still in the ravagers of Visnu.

The spacer hastily turned her attention to the campsite itself. Even with her less-than-practiced eye, she could see that the

Commandos' choice was sound. The place was well concealed, and there seemed to be many possible routes of escape from it. A small stream danced its way across its farther end, they supposedly would be able to supplement their rations from the surrounding treelands without undue effort, and they even had shelter from Anath's sometimes questionable weather. Guard duty should prove no problem, either, between Islaen's gift and Varn's. They might indeed have found themselves in far worse straits.

The Commando-Colonel did not leave her companions to idle observation for long. She brought their vehicle into the shelter and concealment of the dead tree and then set her team to cleaning their quarters and constructing doors for either end, placing them well in so as not to draw the attention of anyone chancing to pass through the area, unlikely as such a visit might be.

All four turned to that last work with a will. The barriers would help keep back the damp and night chill, and they would permit them to use lights without broadcasting their presence throughout all the region during the planet's dark nights.

They would also keep out unwanted visitors. More lived in this wilderness who might or might not be friendly to them than others of their own kind.

Major predators should not be a problem this far into the forest, although they existed in plenty on the plains where the great herds of huon and bands of equii roamed. Here, forage was sparse, and the little moss-eating junners formed the bulk of the ground-dwelling animal populace. Few among the richer fauna congregating near the streams and other watering places were very much larger. The creatures hunting them were sized accordingly.

Reptiles were common, however, and a large number of those were serpents. Although not big, many were strongly venomous, particularly among the rare arboreal visitors. Apart from these, the canopy supported at least one large feline species that could prove a serious threat if an individual should ever venture down to this realm.

The job was soon finished, and Islaen surveyed the results with satisfaction. They would be as comfortable and as secure here as was possible in a camp like this.

She glanced at her timer and then at her companions. "We've had a busy time of it, but it's early yet in Anath's day. Would you be up to taking on another task?—You particularly, Varn? You had to carry all the strain of bringing us down."

"I am fine. What do you have in mind?"

When the other two nodded as well, she went on. "I'd like to get some feeling of the invaders' penetration and behavior before contacting the Anathi. Since they're hunters, the wildlife could tell us much. Bethe and I will check out the woods around here, but I want you and Jake to take the flier to the edge of the treelands and see if you can pick up anything of their impact on the prairie."

She saw the Noreenan frown and quickly cut off the protest he was about to make. "Between the visible signs and the impressions Varn receives, you should be able to discover a good bit in a few hours. In any event, I want you back here before dark. We'll do better to accustom ourselves to Anath's night again before attempting to function in it."

"Aye, Colonel," Karmikel answered with a reasonable semblance of good grace, although he knew full well that she had silenced him.

The gurry flew to her shoulder. *Bandit can help?*

"Aye, love. You'll stay with me and tell me what you can learn from the forest creatures, just like Varn will do for Jake."

Yes.

"We'll leave right away," the Commando-Captain told her.

"Good, and good hunting."

Sogan did not turn at once to follow him.

I am no reader of tracks, Islaen . . .

She whirled about. *Don't give me trouble, Varn! If you're tired, say so, and I'll reschedule this for tomorrow, but you have a talent for reading animals, and by all the Federation's gods, you can be damn sure that I'm going to make use of it when our work calls for it.*

She stopped herself. The Arcturian's anger rose at her words, but his hurt was stronger and kept him silent. *I'm sorry, Varn. Something else riled me, and I was taking it out on you.* She was not about to tell him that it was Jake's doubts concerning Sogan's ability to fulfill his part that had irritated her. Varn apparently had enough of his own at the moment without her reinforcing them.

No matter, he replied stiffly. *What I can do, I shall.*

Varn, if I didn't think you'd be of good use, I wouldn't send you. There's plenty you could be doing here.

He smiled, mollified. It was not Islaen's concern that he did not want to fall on his face, particularly in front of Jake Karmikel. He would just have to make certain that he would not. *If I do not bring you some information, it shall not be for want of trying.*

FIVE

THE FLIER HEADED west at top planetary speed. They had a lot of distance to cover before reaching the prairie, and the Noreenan intended to make their search a thorough one. For that, they would need time, and their commander had not relented in her order that they be back again before full dark had fallen.

There was little talk between the two men. Jake kept the controls. His knowledge of the country made it more reasonable for him to do the driving than to turn the machine over to his companion, who would then have to wait for his instructions. Besides, Sogan was better left free to pursue his own peculiar brand of hunting.

Karmikel had quickly gotten over his initial feeling that the war prince would be little more than company. He found himself listening ever more closely to Sogan's reports, correlating the impressions he described with his own knowledge of Anath's wildlife, and he realized Islaen had done very well in pairing them for this.

He was ashamed for having wronged the other man as he had. The Arcturian might usually channel such contacts directly into Islaen's mind, but he had heard him verbalize them like this often enough before to appreciate the value of his gift. Then, too, though Varn Tarl Sogan might not equal either Commando— probably never would equal them—in the physical reading of a wilderness, neither was he any longer a total novice. They all owed him their confidence, and he was both glad and relieved that the Colonel had prevented him from making a royal ass of himself, not to mention insulting his comrade, by venting his unfounded objection before they had started out.

Sogan himself remained uncertain as to how well he would succeed, but an assignment had been laid on him. The intelligence he brought back would help determine the course his unit would follow on Anath of Algola and, perhaps, the ultimate outcome of their mission. He would not permit himself to fail.

Jake's eyes constantly swept the world around him. He did not expect to make any discoveries, startling or mundane, as long as they remained within the forest proper, but he had long since learned to make no such assumptions or to significantly relax his guard while in alien and possibly hostile territory.

At last, almost without warning, the land beneath them dropped as if some incomprehensibly huge giant had cracked and flattened the planet's surface. The march of the trees halted abruptly at the edge of the precipice marking the end of the higher ground, while a great swampland replaced it at the lower level.

Sogan straightened a little. This place reminded him far too much of the way Visnu's swamps met the plateau where the Amonite settlers had tried to establish their colony.

He said nothing. The situation was not the same on Anath of Algola. Danger did dwell in that wet country, aye, unknown danger for the most part as far as the off-worlders were concerned, but it was not of a nature to threaten a world's life. The presence of both humanity and animalkind in great variety gave vital testimony to that.

If the Commando was aware of his companion's reaction, he gave no sign of it. The marsh was of no concern to them at the moment apart from the fact that it indicated their journey would soon end, and as long as they were not forced down into it, it represented no difficulty or danger at all.

The flier had no more trouble crossing the treacherous, half-liquid soil than it had above the firm floor of the forest, and they soon left the area behind. That would not have been the case were they much farther south or about 1,500 miles to the north. Here, the great fault running the entire length of the continent that had created the swamp narrowed to a mere strip; elsewhere, a person on foot would be days passing through it.

Trees once more claimed precedence, but not to the same extent, and the countryside assumed more the nature of a wood. The trees were smaller and less fine. They were significantly more widely spaced as well, and underbrush was fairly heavy, in some spots nearly impassable for a surface vehicle.

Both men were on the alert now. These woods were all but

created for ambush. It was not likely the mysterious invaders had penetrated so far or that they ventured here frequently if the lack of concern their flier aroused in the creatures around them was any indication. It sparked curiosity and natural wariness only, not the fear a known hunter's tool would elicit.

The Anathi, human and animal, were another matter. They had not yet determined that the on-worlders were still their allies, and occasional parties from An Fainne were not rare to this region. Possible betrayal aside, the prairie was close enough at this point that big grasslands predators would almost certainly venture here now and then, and those were never to be taken lightly even by blaster-armed soldiers from the stars.

Again the terrain altered radically, although the change came more slowly this time. The trees began thinning out, diminishing from a solid forest into ever more widely spaced thickets and then to single individuals standing alone. Finally even these vanished.

What remained was a vast plain of chest-tall, swaying grass that stretched far past the distant horizon to the foot of the massive mountain chain that formed the boundary between the continental interior and the coast.

The Noreenan brought his machine to a stop. "We should separate," he suggested.

"Aye. Keep the flier. You will do best to check whatever signs there are over as broad an area as possible. My power will enable me to range fairly far afield without too much physical travel. Just take care that you are not spotted out there in the open."

"I've had some practice avoiding that.—Watch out yourself. Stick reasonably close to the trees, and if you run into any wolfcats or a thorik, forget dignity and get up into one. Fast. Then call for help."

The war prince touched the communicator on his wrist. "Do not fear on that account, my friend. I have no intention of winding up in some predator's stomach."

Karmikel kept the flier low to the ground, moving slowly and stopping regularly to examine in closer detail the grass and the soil supporting it.

It was pleasant work. The air was heavy for the time of year, and Algola seemed exceptionally hot, a welcome change from the usual biting chill of the prairie. The breeze was mild. It wafted lazily across the plain, carrying with it the sweet scent of freshly broken grass and the stronger smell of equii.

A small herd of the tall, spotted mammals had been feeding in this place very recently. The ground showed their spoor and the inevitable trackings of the area's junner population. Birds flitted overhead or chirped from nests hidden in the tall grass. Of a certainty, nothing had been near to disturb the peace of the perfectly balanced natural community, not recently at any rate, or in this particular spot. There were indications in plenty that this was not the case everywhere on the great plain.

The Noreenan drew farther from the woods, so that the outermost trees receded into tiny, scarcely visible smudges on the horizon.

He stopped suddenly. A sour, distinctly unpleasant smell was heavy in the air. It was very strong, not a subtle scent that only one familiar with Anath could have detected. Varn Tarl Sogan or Bethe Danlo would have picked it up as readily, though they lacked the experience to identify it. Thorik.

He frowned. Flier or not, the prospect of meeting with the most feared of Anath's hunters while he was out here alone was not one he cared to contemplate.

Jake searched the area and was not long in locating the fouled circle of broken grass that had formed the predator's nest.

Tracks were scarce in the vicinity of the temporary lair itself—few creatures were foolhardy enough to venture too close to anything bearing the scent of thorik—but they existed in plenty elsewhere for those with the eyes to see them. He could be sure now if he had not been before. Everything he saw bespoke a mass exodus; large numbers of animals were in motion, and it was not difficult to guess that they were fleeing the pellet guns of the machine-riding invaders.

The prairie junner population did not seem greatly affected. The wily, wary little creatures did not venture too near to large concentrations of humans, and it took a good, experienced eye to spot one in its own habitat. Besides, they were small and inoffensive, not likely to attract much interest from sport hunters seeking trophy prey.

The lesser predators that fed upon them seemed to be present in a somewhat heavier than normal concentration, but they, too, were small and likely to escape serious notice, and the signs he found were scant enough that he might be misreading them.

More definite were the tracks of equii and of both species of huon, the heavy, multihorned animals that were the most numerous large denizens of the plain. They had crowded into this area in great numbers, to the extent that they were stressing the ability of even the fertile, rapidly regenerating prairie to support them. In some spots, the tall grass had been grazed completely down, and wide trails had been flattened out that had not yet sprung back, marking the passage of big herds.

Many animals of various sorts were visible on every side, more than he had ever thought to see in a single section of Anath's plain, and he was wary whenever he left the flier even when none of them were particularly near him. All appeared nervous, and most started when his vehicle drew near them. The forced migration had left them jittery to start with, and it looked as if they had had some very bad experiences with machinery from the stars. The slightest thing could set them running, and if he were caught by such a stampede before he could get back to his flier and bring it up beyond their reach . . .

Even without that threat, the man had reason in plenty to keep every sense strained and alert. Other spoor were present in the tall grass besides those of the grazers. He could be thankful that none of the creatures leaving them were currently in evidence, but he knew too well that they were not far distant. Where the herds went, wolfcats inevitably followed.

Another of Anath's major predators, wolfcats hunted in prides that were as noted for their adaptability to suddenly arising or uncommon circumstances as they were for their courage and unexampled ferocity. Large and fleet enough to bring down an equi buck, brave enough to do battle with the banks of razor-sharp horns and flaying hooves of the biggest huon bull, these animals were even more respected than the thoriks, although individually they were less powerful and lacked the latter's formidable array of weapons. He had no wish whatsoever to find himself facing a pride or even a lone male, a misfortune that could too readily result in the sudden and permanent termination of his role in this mission.

Varn Tarl Sogan, too, had learned a great deal, much of it highly disturbing. The animals whose signs he discovered were all supposedly creatures of the prairie, but many of them appeared to be pushing into the woods and remaining there. This had always occurred, he knew, but once in a while, as the act of individual animals. The present invasion was on a larger scale. It had to be, he thought bitterly, for someone as inexperienced as he was to be so strongly aware of it. The poor beasts must be experiencing heavy pressure indeed to be so altering their usual habits.

The transmissions he was picking up from them confirmed their unrest, and not for the first time in his life, he wished he could enter into their minds and read their active thoughts as he did with Islaen Connor and Bandit.

At least, he did have experience with the denizens of other worlds to back him now as he tried to decipher and make sense out of the flood of raw emotion bombarding him from every side. It also helped that the greater part of this was similar in nature and so was reasonably easy to classify. There was a vague uneasiness whose probable cause he could not identify and a strong, nearly universal mingling of anger and fear in those he believed to be the larger beasts, a wordless rage that made him shudder at the thought of meeting with any predator carrying such feeling against humankind. Unlike the grazers, Anath's hunters were not slow to attack, according to the Commandos' reports.

Algola had long since left her zenith and was now well on her descent. Sogan had come fairly far out on the open prairie in his eagerness to supplement the mental contacts he was receiving with physical clues to help him piece together the situation on Anath. He turned back toward the trees now and raised his communicator to his lips to let his comrade know where to pick him up.

Before he could speak, the instrument came to life.

"Sogan, get under cover! A water storm!"

Even as he received Jake's warning, a sound like the distant roar of a waterfall filled the air behind him.

He glanced over his shoulder. A gray wall extending along the whole of the horizon was bearing down on him with the speed of a fast transport.

Varn fled. He had heard of these storms from his comrades, enough to realize full well what his chances of survival would be if he had to face what was approaching unshielded. They struck anytime of the year, always suddenly as this one had, roaring over the prairie and dropping a seeming ocean of water with such ferocity that its very force and weight could quickly beat the life out of any creature whose body had not evolved over the eons to meet its challenge. Even the weaker of those well provided by nature to endure the deluge could perish in a bad one.—Scant wonder the creatures of the plain had been uneasy earlier!

They had a chance at least, he thought. A man possessed no defense against it at all.

The trees were his only hope, not a single specimen open on all sides to the elements but a grove large enough to shield those sheltering within it with the united strength of many stout trunks and firmly interlaced branches.

Only one such place was anywhere close to him, and even that was a terrifyingly distant goal in a race with this mindless, utterly ruthless foe.

The Arcturian ran for his life, ran as he never had before. He had nearly gained the grove when a mighty blow threw him to the ground. Once, on Thorne, he had taken the edge of a blaster bolt. It had not felt very different from the hammering of countless gallons of water torn from the heavens with a force that seemed almost sentient in its violence and power.

Varn strove to rise. To remain down was to die, to be broken and beaten to death as if with sledges.

With a desperate surge of strength, he regained his feet and staggered across the remaining yards to the beckoning haven of the trees.

Their promise was not false. The force of the water was less with the thick branches breaking and absorbing much of its fury, but it still fell in a hard, seemingly solid sheet, and many tree limbs, some as large as small trees, came crashing down with it to testify to the pummeling his living shields were enduring.

It was safest closest to the trunks, he decided, although no spot could be termed really secure. Sogan chose a large one with a pronounced lean so that he was screened somewhat from the downpour. He crouched as closely as he could get to it, facing inward and burying his face in his arms as the rain poured over his back.

A small creature that he assumed was a junner peered out at him from its well-dammed burrow among the roots.

As Islaen had indicated in describing the species, the Anathi animal was quite appealing. Small, only about four pounds in weight and not a foot long, it presented a low, round profile and was predominantly a brownish gray color, somewhat lighter on its underparts, a logical hue for a gentle, ground-dwelling creature. Only the face and forepaws were different. They were a bright yellow-tan that provided an excellent backdrop for the brilliant amber eyes, huge eyes filling almost all its upper head, a common feature in Anath's offspring.

The junner seemed particularly small and helpless in the face of the fierce storm raging around them, but it was not in the slightest degree perturbed by the fury of the elements. It was perfectly warm and dry and chirruped sympathetically before diving back into its nest.

The man laughed despite his discomfort. Large size was not

always an advantage, it seemed. He could imagine few creatures more miserable and bedraggled than himself at this moment.

The violence of the storm increased steadily for well over an hour. Twice during that time, the continuous roar of the water was punctuated by the more solid crash of a tree as it fell, broken by the relentless force of the tempest beating against some long-hidden weakness. Both times, Sogan glanced uneasily at the trunk sheltering him. The angle it formed with the ground was sharp, and the constant weight of the water pressing on it could conceivably topple it if the root system was not both very deep and widely spread.

He did not move. The junner would warn him of danger by sudden flight. The fall of trees during these savage storms would not be all that rare an occurrence, but he did not think that the little animals would often be trapped by them.

At last, the fury of the rain slackened.

For the first time, Varn studied the area surrounding his place of refuge. He was not the only creature to have come here. A large huon cow stood nearby, a half-grown youngster pressed against her, vainly trying to keep dry, and when he opened his mind, he received a myriad of responses. Nearly every tree must be shielding some animal or animals of the savanna or wood.

He left the place as soon as the tempest lessened enough to permit him to do so. Karmikel would be waiting for him, impatiently probably. The flier would have afforded him protection enough whether he had been able to reach the trees or not.

A cold wind followed the rain. His saturated clothing clung to him like an icy skin, and the war prince was soon shivering violently.

"Sogan?"

The Noreenan's voice sounded sharp, worried, and Varn Tarl Sogan quickly activated his communicator. "I am sound out," he replied hastily. He should have reassured the other well before now. "Can you get a fix on me?" It was an effort to keep his teeth from chattering audibly, but he willed himself to speak as normally as possible. Jake would come for him as quickly as he could; making a display of his discomfort would not hurry him any.

"Easily. Just activate the homer.—It'd save a bit of time if you start walking north to meet me."

"Very well." If nothing else, the exercise would help to keep his circulation going.

* * *

It was not a pleasant journey. The wind did not ease off, and its bite seemed only to increase as his exposure to it lengthened. His progress was slow as well. The ground was muddy and slippery, and the tall, drenched grass between the stands of trees was proving difficult to penetrate and cross.

He spotted the flier in the end and stopped, waiting for it to come to him.

Jake Karmikel made a heroic effort not to laugh when he saw the other, but Varn knew the picture he presented and smiled himself. When he had seen the water storm's approach, the Noreenan had run for the vehicle and hastily closed and sealed the canopy. He had remained as warm and dry as the sympathetic little junner back in the grove.

"No remarks," Sogan growled. "Just push the heat up another notch."

"Sure thing, Admiral."

The war prince took the passenger's place once more. His nerves were tight with the worry he could no longer hold in check under the demands of his own danger. They had survived the storm with no more than an inconvenient wetting, but what of their three comrades? There was no harm in trying to contact Islaen now, with the tempest past, and his mind went out from him, seeking her across the distance.

Karmikel saw him tense and then, moments later, relax. "Islaen's all right?" he asked quietly.

"Aye." His eyes fell momentarily, as if he had been caught gratifying a weakness. "I knew that she must be with the trees to break the rain's force, but I feel better for confirming it."

"So do I, friend. Accidents are always possible.—Bethe? And Bandit?"

"They were together and weathered it in the camp. They suffered even less than you did."

The Arcturian leaned back in his seat, trying to force warmth into his body. His uniform held the wet and cold, and even the heater set at high could not drive the chill out of him.

Jake watched him for a few minutes. "You'd better get out of at least that tunic, or you'll be a good candidate for Quandon Fever." He reached back to the supply case beneath the rear seat and pulled out a spider silk blanket and a flask. "Here, wrap this around you."

Sogan was glad enough to shuck off the wet garment. The Commando handed him the blanket, steeling himself to show no reaction to the glimpse he got of the other man's back. Varn Tarl

Sogan had come late to renewer treatment, and although the scars
he now bore were but shadows of those that had marred him, he
would always carry the mark of the Arcturian executioners.

"That is better," the war prince said gratefully. "Thanks."

Karmikel held out the flask as well. "I know an officer of the
Empire doesn't usually indulge, but consider this a medicinal
draught."

"What is it?" he asked dubiously.

"Opaline, high quality and well aged." He scowled at the
other's grimace. "This happens to be one of civilization's more
pleasant concoctions, Admiral. I'll thank you to show more
appreciation for it."

Varn smiled. "That appreciation is an acquired taste that I do
not desire to develop, Captain. Its flavor is precisely like that
which a strong poison should have." He gave a contented sigh.
"Besides, I do not need it. I am beginning to warm up now."

"Arcturians!" Jake grumbled in disgust.

"We are not totally incorruptible," Sogan assured him lazily.

His eyes closed, and he let the warmth take him for a while. He
was tired, and he felt as though a couple of Malkites had gone to
work on him with boots and fists. It was good just to sit back and
let another take on the work and what worry there was for a while.

SIX

THE ARCTURIAN DID not want to let himself drift into sleep entirely, but as they approached the camp he dozed for a few moments despite himself and came alert again only when Islaen's questioning welcome sounded in his mind.

We will be there in another few minutes, he told her, then stretched and reluctantly reached behind him for his tunic. Even with the worst of the water dripped out of it, he did not look forward to putting it on again.

"I wouldn't do that if I were you," Jake advised. "Neither of us may be in Bandit's class when it comes to arousing sympathy, but as it is our two comrades're likely to be fussing around us like a couple of brooding fowl."

Sogan hastily returned the garment to its former place. It was bad enough to be coming back looking like something washed up out of a flood without courting an extra dose of attention to remind him of the fact. "For that warning, I thank you, my friend."

"I rather figured you might."

They reached camp less than five minutes later. The effects of the water storm, though less dramatic, were apparent here as well. The ground shone with moisture it was not yet capable of absorbing, and with every breeze droplets from the surrounding trees sprayed the world beneath like a miniature rainfall.

None of that was of much concern to the two men. They would bring the flier in immediately and were not likely to be forced to venture outside again for some time.

Bethe Danlo appeared as if by magic at the entrance, a dazed

expression on her face that was half mock, half real. She raised
her hand in greeting and then waved them inside.

It was dry within. The iron-strong wood and the doors the
off-worlders had constructed that morning had held the water
back, and their miniature stove ably kept both damp and chill at
bay.

While the newcomers ate, they reported all they had learned and
deduced. Well before their meal was finished, all four humans
were heartily glad of the stout barriers capping each end of their
temporary home. It was highly unlikely that any creature of the
prairie would cross the swamps, or penetrate this deeply into the
forest if they did do so, but with wolfcats and their prey migrating
into the woods from their usual feeding grounds and at least one
thorik near the edge of the trees, none of them would have felt
secure sleeping open to Anath's night.

Bethe peered through the door. "It's almost dark, Islaen. If we
need water or anything, I'd better go for it now."

"We do, but hold up a minute. I'll . . . ."

"Don't trouble yourself, Colonel," Jake told her quickly. "I'll
play bodyguard."

That was a necessity. Visitors from the canopy were not
uncommon in the aftermath of a heavy rain, and the coming of
evening always brought out a number of the natural ground
dwellers, several of the more poisonous reptiles among them.
They had learned the last time they were on-world that it was best
to work in pairs, even if venturing only a few feet from one's door,
once Algola had seriously begun her descent.

It took only moments to cross the short space to the stream. The
demolitions expert paused there after filling the canteens and
glanced up at the snatches of sky visible through the spreading
branches. There was good time yet, but not a superabundance of
it.

Anath's night was very black, lacking as she did the light of
moon or stars to scatter a small part of the shadows released with
the sun-star's setting. Some afterglow or natural phosphorescence
did diffuse through the eternal clouds, but it was not nearly
sufficient to effectively stimulate the off-worlders' eyes, sensitive
as they had become to low-level illumination. Even the bulk of the
planet's own offspring were primarily diurnal, although the huge
eyes that were the mark of nearly all of them did provide a certain
amount of guidance when they were forced to move after their sun
had dropped below the horizon. None of the bigger predators and

precious few of the smaller ones ever hunted once the day was completely flown.

Suddenly, Bethe chuckled softly.

Karmikel looked at her in surprise. "What's so funny?"

"I was just thinking that I've never seen Varn look so unlike a war prince."

The man grinned. "You should've seen him when he met up with the flier."

"You didn't comment too gleefully on his appearance, I hope?"

"Didn't have to." His brows lifted. "No similar concern for my feelings?"

"You didn't come back looking like so much wreckage," she pointed out. "I imagine your feelings were every bit as comfortable as your person." Her voice tightened. "I was a damn sight more than concerned before the Admiral contacted Islaen."

"Praise the Spirit of Space for that gift of theirs," he agreed quietly, moved by the emotion on her. "We were worried as well, even though we knew you should be all right, but we couldn't have justified broadcasting over the transceiver to find out how you were doing, and the communicators probably wouldn't have reached so far. We went well south after crossing the swamp."

Suddenly he faced her squarely. "Look, Bethe, you claim you love me. I want to marry now, as soon as we get back. No more delays . . ."

"Forget it."

"Give me a time, then—or do you mean forget it literally?"

"No, I do not!" she snapped. "What in space's wrong with you? All I'm asking you to do is wait a bit."

"I waited for Islaen, too. Then Varn Tarl Sogan rose from the dead, and Jake Karmikel ceased to exist!"

"I love you. Islaen Connor did not. She was considering marrying you so she could remain on real active service, even if she had to officially leave the Navy to do it, instead of being forced to spend the bulk of the rest of her career behind a desk. Both of you'd accepted that."

"How . . ." he began in fury.

"Women talk, Jake. She's bitterly ashamed that she ever considered doing that to you, and she's as eager as I am to see you happy."

"Oh, you're eager all right," the Noreenan said sarcastically, "and maybe just as eager to work on someone else's happiness."

Bethe Danlo straightened. "You bastard! Do you imagine you'll be slapping a chain on me by marrying me?" Even in the half light, he could see the rage on her. "Think again, you son of a Scythian ape! If that's your plan, aye, and your opinion of me, space'll be white a hell of a long time before I'll be tying myself to you! Now get out of my way, or you'll be wishing you were facing a few Arcturian invasion troopers instead of me!"

"Bethe, wait!—Listen. Please. I don't think that. It's just that I . . . don't want to lose you."

"Well, you won't lose me, not to anyone. Not even to Varn," she added a bit more sharply.

The Noreenan cringed. "You don't have to draw that down. I know I was off the charts there."

"Friend, you were so far off that you weren't even in this galaxy."

Bethe gripped her temper. There was no point in arguing. She did not want to argue. In truth, the man did deserve an answer from her. This indecision was unfair to him, to both of them, yet . . .

"What's driving you, Jake?" she asked wearily. "I'd understand it if you were a boy, but you're not."

He sighed. "Bethe, if we were a pair of farmers back on Noreen, I wouldn't mind waiting, years if you wanted, but space, woman, how long do we have? If it hadn't been for Bandit, you'd have died on Omrai, and one minute miscalculation would've finished me as well. One or both of us could easily wind up in a similar situation here or on our next mission or on the next, and maybe we won't be quite so lucky."

His hands balled. "I want some of what they have. I can buy gratification in just about any port in the ultrasystem, but the rest, that closeness and sharing . . ." He shook his head. "That can only come with you, Bethe Danlo."

"Don't you think I want the same thing?" The woman turned away. "I can't do it, Jake, not yet. The fault's entirely mine. There isn't anyone else, and I do believe you love and want me the way you say you do. I want you, too, but until I resolve this—if I can—I just can't say I'll marry you!"

To his dismay, he realized she was crying. Bethe? The strong-willed spacer who had held her own in a war-torn galaxy from the time she was a girl? It threw him into confusion to see her like this, and for a moment, he was at a total loss as to how to respond.

Feeling took over then, and he folded her in his arms. She made no resistance, and he pressed her closer to him.

"Gently, lass," he murmured softly. "I can wait." His eyes closed. "Just take your time. I'm not forcing anything on you."

She drew away from him, her hold over herself in place once more. She was grateful for the comfort he had so freely given her, and she was proud of this man, proud of his silence, of the sensitivity that held him quiet despite the questions that must be burning the heart out of him.

He had a right to know, but in her shame, she could not face that. No one was going to learn of her weakness, much less Commando-Captain Jake Karmikel. "Back off, Jake, just for a little while. I won't keep you suspended like this forever."

Varn Tarl Sogan allowed himself the luxury of awakening slowly. He lay still a moment, enjoying the warmth of his sleeping bag and testing muscles that turned out to be not quite as stiff as he had anticipated.

He reached out in mind for Islaen's familiar pattern only to find himself alone. Even the gurry was not near.

He sat up. The shelter was empty save for himself. Bethe passed by the entrance, which had been opened to admit the daylight and conserve their raditorches, so he knew one at least of his comrades was in the camp, but he heard no voices or other sounds.

His probing sharpened and lengthened. *Islaen?*

Awake at last? The answer came swiftly and with a natural humor that proclaimed all was well. *Jake and I are collecting some berries I spotted yesterday. They'll go far toward improving the palatability of supper tonight.*

That will be easy for them.—Why did you not call me?

I figured you'd be sore after that hammering you took yesterday and wanted to let you sleep off as much of it as possible.

Soft fingers seemed suddenly to move within him as the Commando-Colonel switched from communication to searching his body for injury, an aspect of her talent that had proven extremely useful in the past.

Her concern in the face of so minor an incident embarrassed him. *I am sound out, Islaen,* he told her irritably.

She only laughed. *Aye, and your vanity's intact, I see.* Her mood changed. *Get up now. We'll be coming in soon, and then I want to see about contacting the Anathi.*

I will be ready, Colonel Connor, he told her as he withdrew from the contact.

Sogan dressed and ate dutifully, although he could work up no enthusiasm for the rations that would be their mainstay for the duration of their assignment. A hot mug of jakek would have been good, but he did not delay to make it.

He stowed his gear and then stepped outside into what proved to be a bright, fresh day.

Bethe Danlo saw him and gave him a bright smile. "Morning, Admiral. How . . . —Oh, look!" she finished in a whisper. "Over there. That has to be a junner."

He followed the direction of her gaze. One of the small forest dwellers was indeed sitting by the stream in full view of them. Literally sitting. It had risen up on its haunches to better watch them, its mind radiating fear but also a lively curiosity. "So it is."

The man joined his mind with their visitor's, reassuring and calming but also stressing the need to behave with its usual caution around members of their species who were not of their particular party.

"Kneel down and hold out your hand," he told the blond spacer softly. "Move very slowly so as not to startle him. I will try to bring him to you."

Bethe obeyed. She stretched out her hand and willed herself to hold it steady. Wonder filled her. Would the war prince really be able to soothe the shy little thing to the point that it would actually approach her?

The junner eyed her, then encouraged by Sogan's reassurance, it began to hesitantly inch toward her. It took several minutes, but at last it came near enough to sniff her fingers and even to accept a caress from them.

The man sent his mind out in search. Islaen Connor would love to see this. *Colonel?*

We're almost home, Varn.

Come carefully. We have a visitor.

As he spoke, he linked his sight receptors with hers and was rewarded by her gasp of delight.

A few minutes later, the auburn-haired woman emerged from the trees to the right of their shelter. She carefully sat on the still-damp ground and froze. In the next moment, Jake, who had come up just after her, followed suit.

Karmikel smiled to see the spacer play with the Anathi creature, and he watched human and animal closely, with real interest, for several seconds. This was a rare opportunity to observe one of the normally elusive junners, and he wanted to make good use of it.

He scowled when his attention drifted to Sogan for a moment. That dark-eyed demon was an arrogant bastard, he thought. There was something basically wrong with a sense of dignity that would not permit a man to get down on his knees with the rest of his companions and join in their enjoyment of a situation like this. Living with him day to day must not be any prize charter for their commander, whatever the mental link and the love binding them.

The junner gave one final sniff of Bethe's hand, then shook its head and bounded away.

Islaen sighed in regret and came to her feet. She joined her husband while their companions went inside to examine and store the results of the morning's foraging expedition.

Her eyes were glowing when they met his. *Varn, that was wonderful. We were never able to come anywhere near that close to them the last time, and you may believe that we did try.*

I believe it. They are winning little beasts.

Not like Bandit! The gurry knew enough of the unit's discipline to hold her peace and her temper while confronting an alien creature, however innocuous it might appear, but now that they were alone again, she gave vent to her annoyance.

"Of course not, small one," the Arcturian agreed. "There is no one like you anywhere. You should know by now that you do not have to be jealous."

Varn's jealous of Jake.

Bandit! Isalaen snapped angrily, in thought rather than voice to avoid any possibility of attracting their companions' attention.

The gurry squawked in surprise at her tone, but the woman did not relent. *Get out of here. I'll deal with you later.*

Without waiting to see where the hen went, she faced Sogan.

He was scarlet with shame, and she could feel the mortification and stark fury warring for supremacy within him.

Power down, she told him calmly. *No one expects an Arcturian officer to enjoy playing second to a former farm boy in anything. You've admitted to it yourself, and there's no real harm in it. If there were, we would've been forced to tackle it long ago.*

Bandit has "tackled it" quite effectively! Varn Tarl Sogan snarled.

He turned on his heel and strode away, sealing himself off from her both physically and mentally.

The Colonel's mouth was set in a furious line.

Bandit, I can feel you nearby. Come here.

The gurry, who had been huddled on top of the felled tree, flitted down until she had reached Islaen's eye level. She clung to the rough bark, making no attempt to approach the human or to perch on her shoulder. *Yes, Islaen?*

Whatever moved you to make a scramble-circuited remark like that? she demanded coldly.

Varn is jealous! Bandit protested.

So what? It wasn't your business to announce the fact.—You've been with us some time now, long enough to know that people don't like to have their weaknesses broadcast to all and sundry, especially not Varn Tarl Sogan.

Varn is mad?

Varn is furious, and believe me, you're none too popular with me at the moment, either. I can anticipate sufficient trouble on this mission even in my own team without your handing me any more. It's bad enough that Jake and Bethe can't seem to work out a charter and keep going at each other, and now you have to set Varn off as well.

Bandit will try to fix . . .

Bandit will stay out of sight and give us both a chance to cool down. She straightened. *Fortunately, we have to get down to business shortly, and Varn won't allow his temper to interfere with that again. Just see to it that you're on hand when we're ready to go and that you don't pull any more blunders.*

SEVEN

As soon as the flier was checked out for fitness, the Federation party left their camp. It was imperative that they meet with Anath's leaders and learn what they could about the interstellar force that had invaded her.

The former Admiral took his place beside his consort. He said nothing to anyone, and his mind was sealed so tightly that no shadow of thought or feeling escaped his shields, but he was determined not to compromise their work on Anath of Algola as he very nearly had done on Hades.

Bandit meekly settled on the seat back in her usual spot, but she hunched there, her feathers fluffed out in misery. The minds of both humans were shut and glacier cold with respect to her.

The Arcturian felt her presence and the unhappiness she was broadcasting, although he would not look at her. There was no avoiding that much contact since it was his responsibility to scan the wildlife they passed for any warning or other information their transmissions might afford.

He fought pity but could not eradicate it. This was the first time the gurry had ever experienced real anger directed at herself, and it was coming from both of her humans, those beings to whom she was attached above all others. Rejection by them was the ultimate loss, and she had brought her ruin on herself . . .

His heart seemed to stop. Even as he had done.

He looked at Bandit and felt sick with self-loathing. She was but a wretched shadow of the merry little creature who usually started on an expedition full of importance and the determination to help and guard them. He had done this with his unrelenting fury, because she had revealed the truth about him.

Tentatively, Varn reached up and poked her in the breast with his finger as he sometimes did when he played with her.

The little hen brightened. *Varn's not angry?*

No, small one, not anymore. I just wish you had not been quite so truthful, especially in front of Islaen.

Bandit's sorry—Varn doesn't hate Bandit now?

I love you, small one, he replied smoothly and without delay, although the admission did not come easily to him. He was comfortable expressing that only to Islaen Connor.

Bandit responded with an ear-shattering whistle and flung herself rapturously against him. She clung to his chest, her wings outspread as if she were trying to embrace him, her needle-sharp claws driving through his tunic and the skin beneath.

"Bandit! Damn it, ease off! Do you want me to be as badly scarred fore as I am aft?"

Sorry, Varn! she said contritely but with no sense of fear. There had been no annoyance on him at all.

Islaen Connor doubled over the controls in laughter, to the point that she was forced to stop the flier.

"Good!" she said when she could talk again. "Now you know what it's like. I'm usually the one she winds up impaling, to your undying amusement!"

Bandit whistled again. *Islaen likes Bandit, too?*

Aye, love. We all make mistakes.

"What in space is going on up there?" Jake demanded testily. He and the Sergeant had been growing increasingly more upset by the little hen's obvious distress, and the sudden transformation in her only heightened their confusion. Mind talk was fine enough in its place, he thought, but it also could leave a lot to be desired by those who were not privy to it. At times, and this was decidedly one of them, it was both exceptionally annoying and outright rude.

"You don't want to know," his commander told him. "Just trust me that everything's all right now."

Her mood sobered in the next moment. "Hang on, comrades. We should be acquiring an audience very shortly."

"Aye. We'll be crossing into Forester territory in a few minutes," Karmikel agreed. "You're not picking up anyone yet, Colonel?"

"No. —I'm going to open the canopy so there won't be any mistakes in identifying Jake and me. If you get cold, Bandit, go under Varn's tunic or mine."

She did not speak after that but concentrated on her driving and on the hunt she was conducting with her mind.

Fifteen minutes passed, then suddenly she stiffened.

"Watchers?" Bethe Danlo asked tightly.

"Aye."

As she spoke she linked her receptors with Varn's so that he, at least, would be able to share the information she was receiving. The others would have to rely on her description.

There were two sentries. The had not really anticipated visitors, or off-world visitors, for their initial response was surprise. Anger followed fast upon it, but then came recognition and with it both relief and real pleasure.

"We're wanted here, at any rate," she said after concluding her report, "whatever reception we'll get at An Fainne."

"By these two," her husband corrected. "A Yeoman's feelings need not necessarily reflect his Admiral's."

The Commando-Colonel did not remove her eyes from the way ahead of them. "We're all aware of that fact. We'll be finding out whether they do match or not soon enough. Word of our arrival will have reached the Chieftainess long before we get to her cot."

Word of the off-worlders' coming passed from sentry to sentry, and in every case, their arrival was greeted with the same pleasure and renewal of hope, with the trust that all would now be well.

Islaen's old unit had made a powerful impression, Varn Tarl Sogan thought, to have inspired this kind of confidence years after their previous visit.

That should hardly surprise him. On Thorne of Brandine he had a lot more experience than he had wanted with those same Federation Commandos, or with four of them. Their original leader had been killed shortly after beginning what had proved to be their longest and final War-time assignment.

Because of that old familiarity with guerrilla capabilities, the war prince took care to hold his inner thoughts to himself. It was taking the full grip of his will to keep him sitting quietly and seemingly at ease. This journey was too much like a return to the past, to the time when he had traveled thus in a flier or transport, knowing unseen eyes were on him, perhaps aiming the blaster or pellet gun or explosive charge that would finish him. The fact that there was no hostility on the present watchers was no comfort whatsoever, and the old sensations rose up from within him with ever-increasing force to chill and tighten every nerve.

He felt no shame in the fact that fear of such foes died so

slowly, not as long as he was able to conceal his nervousness from
the others. It only surprised him that it should be this strong. He
could not recall feeling its fangs so sharply even during the height
of the Resistance's campaign on Thorne. Probably the very fact
that it was war then, that and the blunting effect of familiarity,
even with horror, had helped him accept it all in some strange
manner and to shunt it away from the foreground of his awareness.
Without that adaptation, it would have been difficult for him to
function effectively, or maybe to have functioned at all.

A strong pride filled him. No personal attack had actually been
launched against him, but death had been constantly around him.
All too many of those serving under him, officers and Yeomen
alike, had perished in Resistance ambushes. The same dread
gnawing him had to have been the lot of all, yet no soldier of the
Empire, not one to his knowledge, had visibly hesitated to assume
his duty. His had been a fine command, one worthy of better than
the cold reception accorded the defeated fleets by their people,
worthy of a commander who brought them honor. His head
lowered momentarily. If only fate had not thrown that accursed
choice on him . . .

The Arcturian's thoughts returned abruptly to the present. The
contacts Islaen was receiving increased suddenly in number. It
was not the thoughts of a couple of ever-changing sentinels now,
but those of a good-sized company that were coming to her, and
although the welcome remained strong in their transmissions,
wariness was there as well. These people might be barbarians, but
they were no fools. They realized all-too well that people and
circumstances alter with time and that the strangers now invading
Anath of Algola might easily not be the enemies of those who had
aided them in the past.

He knew their journey must be nearing its end and was not
surprised when the Noreenan brought the flier to a stop at the edge
of a small clearing, keeping it far enough beneath the trees that it
could not be spotted from the air.

A squat, square building stood in the center of the open place.
Its steeply pitched roof was thatched with the ubiquitous moss and
reached to the ground, completely covering the walls save for the
breaks made by the two tiny windows and the door. There was no
sign of a chimney.

"How do they cook or heat the place?" Bethe asked in surprise.
The absence of smoke in so primitive a dwelling struck her as
totally wrong, and anything grossly amiss could also be deadly.

Jake chuckled softly. "Well asked, Sergeant! You'll make a

Commando yet. —It's not a house. The Foresters don't take people not of their race to their living places, especially not to their leader's. This meeting cot is the only structure of theirs that we've ever seen."

"Trusting, aren't they?"

"We're being careful enough as well," Islaen pointed out, "and we can pick up their emotions if not their actual thoughts. —There's Vanya." She frowned. A man was with the Forester Chieftainess. "Xenon! What in space is he doing here? They could never have gotten word to An Fainne in this time, much less brought him back here."

"Maybe you missed an observer or two around the camp," Karmikel ventured. He was frowning as darkly as she.

"No, I did not."

"Perhaps we were spotted yesterday," Varn suggested. "Or maybe I was. I do not have the skill either to detect or to hide myself from master woodsmen, as you claim these people are."

"You're not all that bad," Jake told him sharply. "Besides, even if we missed Anathi scouts ourselves, Anath's animals wouldn't, not all of them, and you were monitoring those good and tight."

"We'll find out soon enough," the Commando-Colonel told her comrades. "Stay here. I'll call when I want you." She smiled at them. "It's for their peace of mind, not ours. We at least know they aren't plotting any treachery."

Varn Tarl Sogan was not much comforted by that assurance as he watched the woman step out into the open place. If anything were to happen, she was now a clear target.

To distract himself from a worry he could not mend, he fixed his attention on the couple waiting to greet them and forced himself to study them closely.

In dress, neither was impressive.

The female wore a long skirt of some coarse material, a dull brown save for two brightly woven, broad panels set into the garment to the front of each hip. Her blouse was several shades lighter and was simply made with wide, wrist-length sleeves and a plain, round neck, completely devoid of decoration.

Her companion's clothing seemed to be made of slightly finer material, linen, perhaps, rather than rough wool. His loose trousers were dark green, and the shirt, what little they could see of it, was a bright white. Over it, he wore some sort of leather doublet studded with round, hard disks, which Sogan decided after a moment were probably made of iron wood. Islaen had mentioned the trees were used for fashioning shields and personal armor.

Both had short, broad scabbards slung from their belts, and Xenon carried a dagger as well. The Forester bore a second weapon, too, a slender axe that had patently never been fashioned to hew wood. For all the Arcturian's experience with the slaying power of the mighty interstellar battleships in which he had spent the greater part of his adult life, that primitive thing seemed more to symbolize war than blaster or laser or pletzar.

A tall bow leaned against the wall of the building, although no arrows were in sight.

In person, the surplanetary leaders were very alike. Whatever their differences now, it was obvious their peoples had risen from the same stock and had remained part of that line for well nigh the whole of their developmental history.

Neither was tall. The Warlord was about Islaen Connor's height, and Vanya barely equaled the diminutive Bethe's. Their bodies were stocky and well formed, the Chieftainess' showing a womanliness he had not expected to see here. It was a softness he associated more with the easier life of long-established, flourishing colonies or the inner systems themselves.

The hair of both Anathi was straight and a true black. Vanya's was shoulder length, only slightly longer than her companion's. Their skin was a distinctive pale green unlike that of any other people he had yet encountered. The eyes were green as well, the vivid emerald of Anath's plants, and they were huge in keeping with those of the rest of their homeworld's life, comprising a full third of their faces. Their lips were very full, their features cleanly cut albeit flat, their expressions, what could be deciphered of them, were intelligent and, despite their present tension, pleasant.

Mutants all right, he thought in a disgust he could not quite quell, or they would be had they been Terran stock. They were not terribly far off prototype, but there was no mistaking the adaptations their homeworld had forced on them. That was even more obvious in person than in the images he had studied while en route to Anath. The invasion commander here had shown more open-mindedness than he himself would have done in admitting the possibility of intercourse with Anathi women, but then, he would not have encouraged that even with captured females of a standard race. He had always insisted on the same control from his subordinates as he did from himself. His fleet had never been the worse for that strict code of conduct, and even in the lesser ranks, individual honor had of a certainty remained on a higher level than was common in an occupying force.

The former Admiral frowned as he continued to study the pair. He could feel himself shrink from them, over and above his normal response to mutants. Why? He had not experienced any such reaction when faced with their pictures. Objectively there was nothing repulsive about them, nothing grotesque except for those grossly enlarged eyes, which seemed much more like masks than parts of a human head, but the sight of them made his skin crawl. Insects, with their great, multifaceted sight organs, might have such faces . . . ·

His throat closed, and he nearly gagged. Ravagers! They reminded him of the vast, ravenous horde that had so nearly been his death on Visnu of Brahmin. Spirit of Space! He could feel their mandibles tearing into his flesh . . .

Varn Tarl Sogan gripped himself. That was entirely his problem. Those two people had nothing to do with it. According to Islaen Connor, they were worthy allies, and he was sworn by his oath both to the Federation and to the Commando-Colonel herself to work with them. Whatever the personal difficulty involved, he was resolved that no sign of revulsion and certainly no irrational horror would escape him to interfere with that.

Islaen Connor hastened toward her former allies. She searched their faces eagerly and found that they seemed older, both of them, beyond the flow of time since their last meeting, even for citizens of a planet not benefiting from Federation medicine's defeat of senescence. The strain of the War, and perhaps other trials as well of which she as yet knew nothing, had taken its toll.

She extended her hands to them, crossing the right above the left to clasp first Vanya's, as head of this state, and then Xenon's. "It's good to see you again, my friends," she said softly and with real feeling.

"And we rejoice to see you," responded the Anathi woman. "May Anath's blessings shower down upon you and yours."

Vanya glanced toward the trees from which the off-worlder had emerged. "Are our other old comrades with you?"

"Jake is. Babaye and Tomas retired from warrior duty after the defeat of our foes, as was their right." Her eyes lowered momentarily. "Morris fell within the year after leaving Anath."

"For that, I am sorry," Vanya replied gravely. "He was as good a man as he was a war leader."

"He was a man who loved Anath," Islaen said, then she

straightened and turned slightly, beckoning to the rest of her party. "I would have you meet my other comrades."

She nodded to each as he appeared. "Jake, you know. Navy Captain Varnt Sogan is second to me . . ."

A double wave of shock and hate seared into her mind, and the Noreenan cursed herself for her stupidity.

These people were familiar only with their own race, and to their eyes, the similarities characterizing the offspring of another planet were far more apparent than the differences marking individuals of any such population. Varn's origin was as plain to them as if he were again wearing the scarlet uniform of an Arcturian Admiral.

She spread her arms wide as the on-worlders dropped into a crouch to make smaller targets of themselves. If their followers loosed a flight of arrows from out of the woods . . .

The Anathi had not lost their control with the passage of time, praise the Spirit ruling space. Death might be poised at the ready, but they held off loosing it.

Islaen faced the pair slowly, schooling her expression to show the correct mixture of surprise and anger. It required no art at all to summon the image of fear. "Hold up, will you! That man's not only my second-in-command but my chosen as well. I'll thank you not to kill him."

At that instant, Bandit rose as if by magic out of the flier. She whistled loudly enough to draw the attention of the three people in the clearing and flew directly to the war prince. She settled familiarly on his shoulder and rubbed her face against his cheek.

"Bandit, be still!" he commanded sharply in Basic; he might be expected to speak Arcturian fluently if he traveled in this company, but it would be well to give the impression that it was not his native tongue. *Praise all the Federation's gods for you, small one*, he told the gurry even as he cautiously raised his hand, as if to restrain and fondle her. He could feel the power of her particular gift flowing out from her and wondered that so tiny a creature could generate and sustain a transmission of this volume.

The Anathi woman laughed. "No Red One would bother himself with such a creature! —I have never seen a bird like that."

"Come, Bandit!" the Commando-Colonel called. "She's not a bird, actually, but a mammal."

"Where did you find her?" Xenon inquired curiously as he studied the newcomer.

"She comes from a world called Jade. The people there usually guard them pretty jealously, but she attached herself to us, and since Varnt and I had given good service to the colony, we were allowed to bring her away with us."

Islaen stressed very slightly the half alias the semiconscious former Admiral had accidentally given himself when questioned by his rescuers after having been pulled out of space near Dorita. His executioners, as a final ignominy, had cast his supposedly lifeless body into a near-derelict lifecraft and set her adrift in space. The old ship had crossed the better part of the galaxy and had very nearly passed out of it into the vast emptiness beyond . . .

The gurry landed on her outstretched palm. *Bandit is helping? You've saved us again, love, at least from some pretty fast explaining. Just keep it up if you can.*

No trouble! Bandit likes doing this!

She held up the hen for the on-worlders' inspection and was rewarded by the further softening and brightening of their expressions.

The Noreenan quickly completed the introduction of her party and then nodded questioningly at the cottage. "We have some matters to discuss, I think."

"Yes," the black-haired woman agreed. "It is best that we begin at once since you have come so far to hear our tale."

Islaen Connor allowed her comrades to precede her. Bandit might have charmed their hosts and thereby disposed them to look favorably on all the Federation unit, but their faculties of judgment and observation had not been suspended. She did not miss the way the pair spoke quietly and briefly together in their own tongue or the fact that only Vanya went inside with the others.

The Warlord of An Fainne held back. She waited with him since it was apparent that he wished to speak privately with her.

She faced him directly. "Aye, Xenon? What's troubling you?"

"This second sword of yours," he answered bluntly.

The Noreenan straightened. "He's what I told you, a Captain in the Federation Navy and second to me in my company."

"And you are his chooser?"

"I am."

"He is much honored, then."

"I'm honored. Varnt Sogan is the finest and most valiant man I've ever encountered, and he has stood for life, Xenon of Anath, at heavy cost to himself."

There was no point in pretending ignorance of what was bothering him. "Will he have trouble here?" she asked somberly.

"We've had our fill of that among our own people, much to their discredit."

The Anathi was silent a moment. "Hopefully not, but he will do well not to wander alone until the word that he is one of your party has spread. Even then, he should take care. Many a Forester bled or perished through the efforts of men very like him."

"What about those of the palace?"

He scowled and then sighed. "We might as well wait to discuss An Fainne until we join the others."

EIGHT

XENON NODDED ONCE to the Chieftainess when they entered the surprisingly brightly lit single room of the meeting cot.

Sogan had been watching for the pair and caught the gesture. His eyes met Islaen's. It was not difficult to guess what the subject of their conference had been. *Problems?*

Everything should be all right. We'll just have to watch ourselves.

I shall have to watch myself, you mean, he said bitterly. *I seem to be more complication than help to you at times.*

Put it on freeze, Varn. I don't have time right now to worry about nonsense.

There was no slap or force in that rebuke, and he accepted it with a mental smile. *You usually tell me that guerrillas must worry about everything, Colonel.*

Commando-Colonel Islaen Connor took the remaining seat, a high-backed wooden stool of excellent workmanship, at the table filling most of the room. Preliminary speeches were unnecessary, and she turned immediately to the Warlord.

"Your report was good enough to draw the admiration of my commander, Xenon, but we need more if we're to accomplish anything, or even to begin. What else can you tell us?"

"Not a great deal," the man responded grimly. "We do not often get very close to the invaders, and we cannot understand their language when we do." He grimaced. "We are not about to sacrifice another village in order to acquire the knowledge of it."

"Hardly," Jake agreed. "You were lucky your people didn't resettle the cliff above the beach. —What makes these strangers so difficult to approach?"

"Their defenses. They have set some sort of killing field around their strong places and strange warning devices outside those, different systems from those used by the Red Ones. A lot of animals fell victim to them at first, but our creatures are not stupid, and most of our wildlife now avoid them. We humans learned from them, and have not repeated their initial mistakes."

"We could probably dismantle them, temporarily at least, using the knowledge you gave us," Vanya added, "but we've held off making any attempt until we have some real purpose for doing so. We do not want these strangers to know what we can do until it is too late for them to counter us with something else."

"A wise decision. That ignorance on their part may serve us all well."

"You say they have strong places," Sogan prompted. The Anathi's grasp of Arcturian was excellent, although they spoke it with a resonant accent that set his nerves on edge. Communication would be no problem, even as his comrades had said.

Xenon nodded. "Yes, damnably strong. They took over and further fortified works left by the Red Ones. The Arcturians," he added for the benefit of the two strangers. His lips tightened momentarily. "I would we had pulled them down years ago."

"They're using the whole chain?" Islaen asked sharply.

"No. They do not have nearly enough manpower for that. They have about the same number of ships as the Red Ones did, but most of these are much smaller. I think I mentioned that."

"You did. —Go on, Xenon. Which buildings have they appropriated?"

He spread out a roughly drawn but clear chart that had been lying folded on the table before them.

"They are using only two, those closest to the place to which they brought the fleet. They moved their ships off the beach almost immediately, as you know."

She nodded. "So your report said."

He ran his finger along a line representing a long spur of high, rugged mountains extending perpendicularly like the frozen tributary of some rocky river from the coastal range to the blunt finger of stone that was its end far out on the prairie.

"They settled here, on the left side of the tip. It was a sound choice, providing both good shelter from seaborne storms and ready access to the largest of our old enemies' structures.

"Here, well to the south of them, is the Red Ones' communications center. They have taken that and appear to be using it as some sort of command area. The arsenal here on the right has retained its original function to judge by the kind of matériel we saw them bring to it."

"They'd be damn glad to have that," the Colonel agreed. "It's comfortably far but near enough to be useful, and no one'd chance leaving too much volatile stuff lying around a starfleet on a planet with Anath's history of very successful guerrilla activity, not if he could help it."

He frowned. "How would these strangers know about the War we fought here?"

"The Federation keeps general records on every planet we contact. It would be easy to learn that Anath suffered invasion during the War and fought back to good purpose with Commando aid.

"Details of the battle are another matter. That's classified information. Researchers would be forced to fall back on supposition, and they'd be likely to assume that we armed and trained you as was done in most such cases. These newcomers may well believe that your people are quite capable of doing them very severe damage should you choose to strike. That's plenty good reason for setting a virtual fort about themselves as they have done."

"There's a lot of land between the outposts and the fleet," Karmikel observed. "Are they putting it to any use, or is it just there as far as they're concerned?"

"They hunted until the big animals left," Vanya replied with open distaste. "There were some bad massacres before that, and with no use of the meat. Since then, we have seen them fill little packages with dirt, grass, seeds, and the like. They take different kinds of rocks and soil from the mountains away with them as well."

Jake frowned darkly. "So they're testing. That means they're looking for minerals to rape or work, or land to settle."

"Our land," the Chieftainess claimed proudly.

"Aye," Islaen answered her, "and you can put credits down that they have one plan or another for eliminating you as a serious factor in any contest for control of it. They're probably only waiting to be certain Anath does test out before putting it into operation." She gripped her temper, which was threatening to get away from her. "At least, that's what it looks like at the moment. I doubt it, but we could be reading them all wrong."

"You have read the thorik's spawn right," Vanya stated.

"Maybe. Maybe not. Motive can show surprising variety, and

it's too easy to fit facts into preconceived theories. —What about the invaders themselves? What do they look like?"

"To us, strange," Xenon replied readily, "but they probably would not seem so to you. Nearly all of them are snow skins like yourselves. Most or all of them are men, tall by our standards, between . . . Varnt's height and Jake's, and all carry themselves and behave in a manner that recalls the Red Ones to my mind."

"Career soldiers?"

He nodded. "Apparently. They are well schooled to that life at least, more"—he hesitated, seeking the right word—"organized than we are, although all of us are warrior-trained."

"I think I know what you mean."

"Their hair is mostly some shade of brown, but there are a lot of straw heads among them. Eyes are usually some light color and are small, like yours."

"A typical northern Terran gene mix," Bethe Danlo said with disgust.

"They are all of one people," the Forester told them with certainty. "Despite the differences Xenon describes, they are as alike as babes of one birth."

"I'd expect that," Islaen told her. "Private, uniformed armies usually originate on one planet."

"There are no flame heads among them, or so few that we have not noted them," the Anathi woman added suddenly as her eyes fell on Karmikel.

"The gene, the seed, for that isn't present in every colony populace. Jake and I just happen to come from a world where it's very prevalent."

"You can't tell us anything more about their uniforms?" the Commando-Captain asked them.

Both shook their heads.

"They seem similar to what you wore before," the Anathi man replied.

"Shirts rather than tunics like these?"

"Yes."

"Stripes, any notable markings at all?"

"Nothing," Xenon told them. "Their dress is plain. They do wear small red patches on each shoulder, but they show only a little writing, or what we think is writing, and no pictures. —We have not been able to reproduce that," he added, anticipating the off-worlders' next question. "We have not gotten close enough for a long enough time to get a sufficiently good look at them." His hands balled into fists. "I just wish we had more information for you. You will not find it easy to work with so little."

She shrugged. "It's part of our business to ferret that out. What you have told us is more useful than you might imagine. Our people have computers, tools, that can take such details and draw a great deal from them. As for the rest, that's up to us, for the present at least."

"Whatever help we can give is yours," the Warlord assured her. "Every man and woman in the forest is ready to serve under you as we did against the Red Ones."

She studied him a moment, her eyes narrowing. "The forest, Xenon? What about the palace? What are Magdela's feelings about all this?"

His head lowered, and he sighed. "The Queen is dead these three years. Coronus is King in An Fainne now."

"Son of a Scythian ape!" muttered Jake Karmikel. He caught himself. "Sorry, Xenon, but he wasn't a very comfortable ally, and I doubt he'll have had any change of heart with respect to us."

"He has not," the other replied honestly. "If anything, his resentment has deepened. Your company's exploits have gone to our songsmiths, whereas his deeds remain unmentioned. —Coronus is a good ruler in the judging and leading of his people, the work rightly his, but he has a blindness with respect to war. It is not the province of an Anathi King, yet he longs to excel in its ways."

"He never will," the Commando-Captain declared flatly.

"A fact well known to him and to everyone else. All the same, the desire is there and a shame for what he sees as Anath's nearly passive role during the Red Ones' invasion. He has declared more than once that he does not intend to see it repeated."

"Surely, he can't be thinking of attacking these people!" Bethe exclaimed, her horror sharp in her voice.

"No, or at least not openly. He is no madman." Once more, his eyes wavered. "This is my thought only, and I would not repeat it before any others, but I fear at times that he is dreaming of performing some deed of his own that would win him renown. The invaders provide a target for that."

"Then he is considering suicide," Islaen Connor said, "or murder if he is thinking to draw any others in with him."

"That he will not do," the man assured her. "He is too much aware of his responsibility to his followers for that, even if any of us should consent to accompany him."

"Couldn't you stop him from making the attempt if he tried?"

asked the demolitions expert. "I thought the Warlord commanded in such a situation."

"I do," he replied wearily, "and I should do so if it were forced on me, but that would open a breach between us that no power of human or of Anath herself could ever heal, and it might well rend the kingdom, later if not during this current crisis. Coronus is respected but not well liked, and many believe, correctly, that he tries to overstep a ruler's rights on occasion." He was silent a moment. "I do not want to shame the man who is my liege and my friend despite all, and I do not want to be the springboard of rebellion."

The Colonel's breath caught. "It could come to that?"

He nodded. "Possibly, though we are an honorable people." His green eyes fixed on an invisible distance. "The Warlord must never rule. Once that happened, the time would inevitably come when war would be made to gain the crown, either in revolution or as a means of winning notoriety and favor."

"That would be a tragedy stretching beyond your single lives."

"Xenon is too good a friend to the King to permit that, little though his loyalty is appreciated."

"What do you mean?" the Noreenan woman asked sharply. She did not like the note she heard grating in Vanya's voice as she had said that last.

"Xenon has all but lost Coronus' regard because he chooses to work for right rather than war," she answered with a harsh bitterness.

"Peace, Chieftainess," the Anathi man interjected hastily. "This is our . . ."

"No peace!" she snapped, "not when there is none of it in Coronus' heart." She faced the off-worlders, her eyes flashing. "An Fainne's King has decided that a good way of gaining the fame he craves is by subduing and bringing to check the 'forest rebels,' as he terms us. For more than two years now, he has been pushing to have his folk march against us in force."

"What!"

Both Commandos looked from one to the other of the surplanetary leaders in fury and dismay.

"He has a short memory, doesn't he?" Karmikel demanded sarcastically. "You so-called rebels worked pretty hard for all Anath, harder than he did or the bulk of his own people."

"It is just talk and will remain that," the Warlord assured them tightly. "It takes my command to form and move an army, even if one could be raised in so base a cause. Most of us are not so inclined to forget our allies or what they did. We would sooner welcome them as the friends they have proven themselves to be even than continue as we have been throughout the ages since the breach first opened between us."

"This King of yours should first learn to command himself before he thinks to rule others," Varn Tarl Sogan interrupted coldly, "but that is Anath's concern. It is not our business or worry if you cannot resolve it. We came here to take care of a fleet that has planeted without your leave and in violation of your neutrality agreement with the Federation government. You have offered us the Foresters' help, presumably with the consent of their Chieftainess, but you have said nothing about An Fainne. Does that mean Coronus is opposed to our work here?"

The other eyed him speculatively. "He does not know I sent for you. He wants no outside help, and he knows we're in no position to do battle with these starmen ourselves, so he is resolved to avoid them altogether, to wait and see what they do." He sighed. "Maybe he is right. They have not tried to seek us out or shown themselves to be actually hostile as yet."

There was no humor in Sogan's answering laugh. "As yet? It will be a light year too late to act once they are on you with lasers."

"That is why I summoned you," the other answered quietly.

Sogan relented somewhat in his mental condemnation of this race. He might not feel comfortable with the large-eyed man, but he did respect him almost despite himself, and there was a chilling familiarity in the situation before Xenon of Anath.

"So you concealed the fact that you contacted the Navy?" he asked more gently. "Because you wished to avoid setting his temper off or because you were in violation of his command?"

Xenon's head raised. "I fulfilled my duty. The Warlord, not the King, decides in matters of security."

The former Admiral's gaze wavered for an instant so brief as almost not to have been. "Such duty can prove costly at times," he said softly, as if to himself.

Islaen Connor had been watching the two men, her frown deepening as their exchange continued. She had felt her husband's growing annoyance and contempt as well as his strangely intense revulsion, and her look was not friendly when she bent it on him, but his last comment and the partial alteration in him that had accompanied it caused her to fix her attention on Xenon in real alarm. "Comrade, you haven't been exiled from An Fainne?"

"No," he answered, more surprised by the sudden softening in

the Red One's attitude than by Sogan's quick appreciation of his
danger; Islaen's ready and personal concern once she became
aware of his situation was quite predictable. "I have not betrayed
myself. I was in the forest today merely by coincidence. I have
been working with Vanya's people since the invaders landed and
meet with her regularly."

"You don't suggest that we contact Coronus?"

He shook his head. "At this time, no. The very idea of
accepting off-world help for Anath's problems is repugnant to
him. You have questions only and a few guesses, no answers to
make him listen to you, and he might try to banish you, though I
suppose the invaders' presence does give you some sort of right to
operate here as well. If needs be, I could and will order that you
be given support in spite of his will, but as I have said, I would
prefer not to oppose him so openly. If you could bring us some
facts, some proof that these strangers intend us, or Anath herself,
real harm and maybe score a successful stroke against them to
illustrate that you can sting them despite their numbers and
weapons, even as your old company stung the Red Ones, then he
would be forced to give you a hearing and probably would have to
grant you his help and our people's as well."

The Colonel was silent for some minutes. "That seems to be our
only practical course," she said at the end of that time. "Very
well, Xenon. We'll work on our own for a while and draw on the
forest for any help we may need—if that's agreeable to you,
Vanya?"

"You need not even ask. You know how to contact us. We will
be ready to act when and if you do."

"Xenon? How can I reach you?"

"Through Vanya, though I cannot guarantee an immediate
response."

"Fair enough."

Islaen came to her feet. "Let's go, comrades. We'd best find out
what kind of war we have to wage, or if it'll be necessary to fight
at all."

NINE

The Commando-Colonel fell into step with Sogan as they headed for the flier.

What in all hell was the matter with you in there? she demanded. *Why did you start on him like that?*

If you mean about King Coronus, I was right, was I not? —Your Xenon is fit to rule. The other one appears not to be, and he could be a threat to us.

That was a suggestion, and she reacted to it as she would to the sight of an assassin poised to strike. *We don't meddle in politics, especially not in the politics of a neutral planet!*

He shrugged, stung by her rebuke. The affairs of these barbarians meant nothing to him. *If the choice were mine, I would lift now and leave the Anathi to solve both their petty surplanetary quarrels and the question of the fleet.*

I doubt it, his wife said, refusing to be provoked. Openly provoked. What ailed the man? The Anathi were mutants, but, damn it, he should long since have cast off this nonsense. He had been in the Federation long enough now for that.

The pair took their places in their vehicle. Sogan's hands closed on the controls. *It is a rhetorical question anyway, is it not?* he asked, continuing their conversation. *We are required to investigate the fleet, and some involvement with the locals will be all but inevitable.*

Right on all counts, Admiral, she replied, relieved that he seemed to be relaxing into his normal manner again.

The intensity of his response to the two on-worlders still puzzled and troubled her. He had not shown any powerful dislike of their appearance during the voyage to Anath, nor had she

expected that he would. They were different, aye, but they were
not an unattractive people.

What are mutants, Islaen?

The woman started, then relaxed. Bandit had penetrated her
closed thoughts, those unreadable between herself and the war
prince, to question her. Varn did not know the gurry could
communicate at that level, and so they would be able to talk
without his becoming aware of what they were saying.

*In this case, mutants are humans whose race was originally like
the Terrans you've seen but which changed significantly in one
sense or another so that now they look quite different in at least
one feature and usually in many.*

That's not wrong!

*No, of course not, and it let us colonize a lot of planets that
would've been hard to settle if their people hadn't adapted.*

Why does Varn . . .

*Quite, love!—He knows he's not right, but his people dislike
mutants, anyone who's very different from themselves, to the point
that those who were here would eventually have killed all the
Anathi had they been given the time, or others of their kind would
have come to do it. Their Admiral really didn't have much use for
wholesale slaughter when he could avoid it.*

Varn wouldn't do that! Bandit exclaimed indignantly.

*No, but he can't help the way he feels, either. His people
trained that into him.*

The Anathi make him think of ravagers, she remarked.

Space! No wonder he had felt like being sick when he had gone
into the cot. Those monsters had very nearly eaten his legs to the
bone, and he would have lost both of them had it not been for the
rapid renewer treatment he had received. *Bandit,* she said carefully, *do not raise this subject with Varn, and if you have any love
at all for peace, don't let him realize that either of us knows what
was riding him in there.*

Jake settled quietly into his place. His thoughts were somber,
and he felt considerable relief as they began to put real distance
between themselves and the Foresters' meeting cot.

That could have turned into a very nasty situation had it not
been for Bandit. Sogan could give the impression of being a
proper bastard at times, but he did not merit the reaction his
appearance could provoke or the prospect of a future of assaults
and near assaults such as those he had already endured since he
had been dumped into the Federation. The Noreenan gave a sharp

shake of his head. He would lock himself behind a wall, too, he supposed, if he risked sudden and unpleasant death every time he showed himself among strangers. It was enough to make one hate his own rather than the Arcturians whose atrocities had fired this hostility to all their kind.

Well, he thought, bringing his mind back to their immediate situation, they should have no more trouble of that sort here, at least not from Xenon or the forest people, and they apparently need not worry about their reception at An Fainne for a while. In the meantime, they had a mission to occupy them. "What now, Colonel?" he inquired, breaking the silence that had held them all.

"History repeats itself, Jake. The commander must study the fleet proper while her valiant comrades spy out the rest of the installations . . ."

"Your circuits are completely fried if you think we'll let you go off alone . . ."

"It's no more than Morris Martin did before, Bethe, and we were playing with Arcturians then."

"No insult meant to the Admiral, but how do we know these sons aren't even worse?"

"We don't. That's one of the things we have to find out. —Study the arsenal first. Learn everything you can about it. What'll hurt them the most to lose, and we'll strike it as soon as I get back, or you'll go for it if I'm taken out. If possible, reconnoiter the command center or whatever it is now as well."

"Aye, Colonel."

"Thanks, Jake. —See if you can spot any major changes the new tenants have made. We'll want as few surprises as possible when we go in."

"Will do."

Varn? she asked as the war prince continued to remain silent. *No objections?*

It must be done, and you are our commander.

He kept his eyes carefully fixed on the windshield. Only Jake Karmikel would have been good enough to accompany her, and the Commando-Captain's skills would be needed to fulfill their own assignment. They would be essential to the mission itself if Islaen did not return.

He fought to keep his outer mind and his appearance steady. Once again, he had failed Islaen Connor, this time through his slowness in acquiring the abilities he was striving to master.

His eyes closed momentarily. If she needed him, and he was not there for her . . .

The gurry stirred beside him. *Bandit will help Islaen!*

"No, love, I think you'll be more useful here." She slipped into closed thought. *Stay with Varn, little Bandit. He'll need you, especially if he's forced to deal with the on-worlders. Don't let him get into any trouble.* She sighed then, remembering his reaction to the Anathi. *Don't let him start trouble.*

The Commando flier skimmed through forest, swamp, and wood as rapidly as the obstacle-laden terrain could be negotiated.

Islaen paused briefly once they reached the outer edge of the trees, until Algola had completed her drop below the horizon, then she started out again on the long journey across the darkening prairie.

She flew by instruments. The black of Anath's night was almost palpable, and she dared not chance lights, not even while far from the invaders' strongholds.

The Noreenan had always disliked night travel on this starless, moonless planet, but now, at least, she did have Varn's gift to keep her in some sort of contact with the invisible world around them. He linked his mind with hers as he probed the rapidly passing countryside, giving her full access to the transmissions he was able to pick up.

All of them were normal, praise the Spirit of Space, with no sense of the alarm that the presence of alien hunters would have induced in them. They could ride easy as long as that held true.

She kept the vehicle at maximum planetary speed. Varn would have to be back under cover again before day broke, and nights were short this time of year.

She glanced at her companion. He had said very little to her since she had laid this assignment on herself and almost nothing since they had set out from camp, and although he had given her access to his mental receptors, his thoughts themselves had remained closed to her. He might be too much a soldier to protest an action he acknowledged as necessary, but it was easy enough to guess that he heartily disliked her setting out on it alone.

Sogan felt her gaze but did not react visibly to it. Islaen was acting as circumstances demanded of her, and there was no point in burdening her with his dislike of the course she had deemed necessary to take. Even Bandit, who he was certain must be aware of his objections, seemed to recognize that and was for once keeping quiet.

Still, they could not go on with no word passing between them. He did not want them to part like that. It was self-defeating anyway. His consort was no fool. She would realize he was not in favor of her going merely by reason of his silence, and she might come to imagine that he lacked confidence in her ability to carry out her part. He did not want them to separate in doubt, when it was possible that they were not fated to meet again . . .

I am opposed to this, you know, he told her suddenly.

She sighed. *It's necessary, and it's no more than Morris did before me.*

I know, but I do not have to enjoy abandoning you to the night.

That's a somewhat dramatic way of putting it.

She felt his short-lived smile.

Life has been dramatic since my meeting with you, Colonel Connor. He grew serious once more. *I do accept the need for your doing this, Islaen, but why was your former commander also compelled to work alone? Every one of you was capable of handling any phase of the reconnaissance. He should have been able to have help with him.*

So that was it, the woman thought. She should have known that mixture of damaged pride and supposed inadequacy would be tearing at him, and she could not even ream him for it this time. It was not vanity-fired jealousy of Jake's abilities that was driving him now, but a rending frustration. He knew as well as she that, however careful she might be, there was danger in this undertaking, danger multiplied many times over by her lack of backup. He was afraid for her and wanted to help her a lot more directly than circumstances and his own capabilities permitted.

The same reason I have to go alone, she answered carefully, as if she were unaware of what lay behind his question. *Time. Morris had a much greater distance to go, all the way to the coast, and your people were holding the whole chain of outposts. Like me, he wanted to start our war as soon as he got back, and he wanted us to have all the necessary information on hand before we made our first strike. We were all well aware that access to any Arcturian position would be far more difficult to gain once we made our move and announced our presence on Anath.*

This is different all the same, he told her somberly.

How so, basically?

I was not in love with your Captain Martin.

The woman just laughed, and Varn Tarl Sogan settled back, satisfied. He had given her this much, at least. Maybe later, before they parted, he would speak more directly of what lay in his heart, but for now it was best that she be able to go on with as light a spirit as possible.

* * *

The Colonel began to feel uneasy when her instruments indicated they were passing over the gentle knolls that were the outriders of their target spur. The mysterious fleet was not terribly distant, not for machines such as the invaders might be expected to possess. *Perhaps you should drop me here,* she suggested. *I can . . .*

No! he replied curtly. *I will take you as far as the highlands themselves as we originally planned.*

There was no arguing with him, and she just let it go. It would not be that much longer anyway before they reached their goal, not long enough to make an issue over her tightening nerves.

Half an hour later, Islaen Connor brought the flier down, hastily adjusting its angle of descent to accommodate a slope steeper than she had anticipated meeting.

The war prince felt numb now that the moment of parting had come. Abandoning her to the night, he had said in a forced half jest, and now those words echoed in his heart like the formula of a barbarian's curse. Whatever the reason, he was leaving his consort on this bleak mountainside, nearer to the unknown and probably hostile strangers than to her own small company.

The Commando's hands left the controls. *You're in charge until I get back,* she said as she tightened the fastenings on her pack.

I know. Militarily and diplomatically. —Do not worry. I shall do whatever must be done.

I have no doubt of that, Islaen replied quietly. She sighed then. It was time for her to go. *Take care of my unit, Admiral.*

That I shall, Colonel. He made himself smile. *Our friends will probably be right glad to have you back after several days under Arcturian command.*

They'll survive, she said dryly. *I'll see you here, or on the prairie if I finish up early.*

He nodded although she could barely see the gesture in the dim light cast by the instrument panel.

His arms came around her, and Varn Tarl Sogan's lips found hers. In that embrace, he gave her all he was carrying within him of passion and love, of his need for her and his tenderness. Only his fear, he kept to himself, that and the aching loneliness he knew their separation would bring him. *Take care, my Islaen. Return to me soon. If you were to fall, all the universe would go down with you.*

I'll be back, the Spirit of Space and Anath herself willing. Just listen for me, in mind and on the communicator.

You may depend upon that, Islaen Connor, he said and then

turned from her while his resolution to do so remained firm. He did not watch, or try to watch, since the dark would have defeated the attempt, when he felt her slip from the vehicle to disappear into Anath's night.

TEN

THE COMMANDO-COLONEL dropped lightly to the ground. They had chosen their site carefully. The place was well sheltered with good cover, both rock and vegetation, and it was far enough from their enemies to make it highly unlikely that her arrival would draw any notice.

She did not take the chance. With a pencil-thin beam from her shielded raditorch to guide her, she cut sharply to the right, diving beneath the hardy shrubs covering the slope into a shallow channel probably carved by water running off during Anath's sometimes fierce storms. This she followed until she had gone a good three hundred yards.

Only then did she stop and look around. All was deathly quiet. The flier was already gone, and she was completely alone. Even Varn's mind was closed to her. Barring stark emergency, they would not try to contact each other until she was ready to come home, a discipline they had imposed upon themselves early in their association together to avoid the danger of distraction at a time when full concentration was required to combat some immediate threat.

She would have to wait out the remainder of the night where she was, without so much as the glow of the raditorch to comfort her. Tomorrow, she would begin her ascent of the spur, a climb that she estimated would take her into part of the following day; the distance involved might be short in terms of straight miles, but once she hit the mountains themselves, the going would be rough. It was not likely she would be able to both scale them and descend their opposite face with sufficient daylight remaining to allow her to gather meaningful information. No movement at all would be possible at night, not on those high, steep slopes.

She had allowed three days in all to complete her mission, two for travel, one for spying itself and for the slow, cautious maneuvering required for her approach to the fleet and her retreat from it. On the night following the third day, she would signal Varn Tarl Sogan to pick her up in this place, unless she finished so quickly that she deemed it best to start out on her own across the plain, a decision of which she would inform her comrades by mind, or by communicator if she could not reach Varn for some reason. One more day would be allowed to her beyond that, but if she did not then contact her unit to explain the delay, she would be assumed lost.

That was what Sogan hated most, she knew, the fact that they might have to abandon her, not even knowing her fate. The idea did not appeal very much to her either . . .

The woman yawned. There was no profit in that line of thought and less in ignoring good time given her for rest. Space only knew where or how she would have to pass the following couple of nights.

A Commando could sleep just about anywhere, and her present surroundings were palatial compared with some of those in which she had found herself in the past. Wrapping the spider silk blanket from her pack around her, she curled up and gave herself over to sleep, trusting in Anath's black night and her sharply honed warrior's senses to guard her from danger.

Islaen awoke with the first graying of dawn. She ate sparingly of the rations that would have to last her for the next three days and then set her pack to order.

She slipped it onto her back, wriggling her shoulders to settle it more comfortably, and started out.

The Noreenan did not move quite as rapidly as the terrain should have permitted. It was very dark as yet, and there was always the possibility of sliding on a loose stone, maybe sustaining an injury that she could ill afford even if she did not actually wind up in some crevasse or at the bottom of a slope.

The danger of a fall increased the farther she climbed, and in the end, she stopped again to wait until the morning was more advanced. A slight delay was preferable to courting avoidable disaster.

* * *

When Algola did rise for a fact, she revealed a world of startling beauty. Islaen stood among the high hills, low mountains whose slopes were gentle enough for her to negotiate without heavy effort. They marked the merging ground of the lowlands—the forests and prairie—with the true barrier range, of which this spur was a part.

Before her flowed the blue-gray panorama of the mountains. They were sharp and young with clouds encircling their heads like cornets of giant kings. The greatest peaks rose 30,000 to 40,000 feet into the rarefied air, far above their lesser comrades, and towering over all soared the Knife, chief of all the heights in this part of Anath.

The view behind was no less magnificent. The prairie was an ocean of shimmering green stretching eastward for endless miles. Green and something else. The silver grain currently heavy on the tall grass gave an otherworldly sheen to the whole scene that was both eerie and very lovely.

The immensity of the plain was broken only by the myriad of streams and deep pools watering it and by large herds of huon moving slowly over its farther reaches as whim and the run of the grazing decreed. In the far distance, barely visible on the horizon, was the faint line of darker green that signaled the beginning of the treelands.

The hills normally teemed with life. The soil here was rich and the supply of water plentiful. Lush grass sprouted in sensuous abandon, and masses of flowers begemmed the slopes. Almost every form of animal life found in this part of Anath of Algola abided here, and within half an hour, she had heard the song of almost every day bird she knew from the forest and many much less familiar besides. Junners and their highland cousins, the golden mistreks, scurried through every field in enormous numbers.

Still, despite that apparent abundance, it was obvious that something was direly amiss. Too many other creatures who should have been present were not visible or else showed themselves in drastically reduced numbers. She saw no sign at all of either the small highland huon or of equii save for a few old tracks, and even igline were both scarce and skittish in the extreme.

Her expression hardened. These slopes had been hunted, not as brutally as the prairie and, probably, the face overlooking the fleet, but heavily enough to have driven off or terrified the larger wildlife.

Large? The thought of killing harmless and beautiful igline, the biggest of which did not reach her waist, merely for the joy of it sickened her and filled her with fury. Bad as the Arcturians were, they had not sunk to that. But then, few of them slew for pleasure. Their reasons had been many and often wretchedly poor, but that had not been one of them.

She forced her mind back to the present. Reason said that the predator population would have followed the grazers, but this mixed country welcomed wolfcats and thoriks and even warbirds from the heights. All of them hunted by full light as well as during the transition hours, and she had no wish to meet with any of them that might have lingered behind.

The morning was still young when Islaen left the gentle hill-mountains behind and entered the true highlands.

It was as though she had come upon yet another world, one of breathtaking grandeur. The soft beauties so often found in the other sections of Anath were missing here among the towering rocks. The cliffs were frequently naked, their features sharply defined, almost like the ranges of a weatherless satellite. There were no trees as the lowlands knew them. Shrubs existed in some places, twisted, stunted things that eked an impoverished life from the thin soil. It was difficult to believe, looking at them, that some of these dwarfs might have been fighting the violent winter gales for more than two centuries, but if the example of other worlds held true on Anath of Algola, they might well be that old or more ancient still.

These high places were the most barren on this part of the planet, but even they were not utterly desolate. Pockets existed that were shielded enough from the force of the wind to permit the formation of tiny but exquisite meadows. The soil trapped there was quite fertile, and streams flowed through most of them. At this time of year, they were a mass of lush vegetation.

The Commando chose to take her first break at the edge of one such field. The ever-present bite of the wind was less sharp there, and by virtue of its sheltered nature, it offered her protection from unfriendly eyes, Anathi or off-worlder.

Others besides herself found safety here as well. A herd of igline was nearby, on the nearly invisible ledges of the cliff towering above her. They were not easy to see, and it was only by chance that she had spotted their slender, slate-blue bodies against the rock. It was a small herd, four does with fawns at their sides and a buck who kept constant watch on the sky, either for

warbirds, which instinct proclaimed would be out, on the hunt for
the still-tiny fawns, or for the crueler fliers of the newcomers. The
animals were uneasy but not urgently so, and Islaen nodded,
satisfied. It was probably safe to assume that there was no danger
in the immediate vicinity.

The Colonel started out once more. She was climbing for a fact
now and knew that the demands of her journey would increase
with each foot of altitude she gained.

She encountered the little meadows ever less frequently, but
those that remained seemed all the fairer by reason of their rarity.
She would often pause for a few moments beside one of them to
watch the jewel larks flit from flower to flower in search of nectar,
their only source of nourishment. In the process, the down-
covered legs of the minute birds were dusted with pollen, which
they carried away with them to the next blossom, thereby giving
life even as they received it.

As she stopped for the third such break, she froze. A faint, sour
scent clung to the air, and a brief search of the meadow's rim
revealed the abandoned nest of a thorik. It was an unpleasant
discovery. The scarcity of its natural prey meant that the big
hunter was likely to be hungry and eager for any source of meat
if it was still in the area. She would have to move with greater care
and even closer attention to her surroundings from here on.

Hour followed hour. Her encounters with Anath's wildlife
dropped drastically in number once the altitude increased to the
point that the last of the sheltered meadows was left behind. Few
creatures besides transient predators and igline had inhabited these
peaks by choice even before the invaders had violated the region.

The Colonel made good use of the igline trails. The agile cliff
dwellers were capable of leaping from ledge to ledge when the
need arose, but they preferred to travel more secure paths offering
easy footing for their young and good cover to shield them from
the savage mountain gales and from the eyes of hunting warbirds
that, when hungry enough, did not hesitate to attack and carry off
a buck. The Federation's engineers could not have chosen or
created a better route for her.

Her greatest worry as yet was of meeting with that thorik whose
nest she had found or one of his kin on the sometimes narrow
trails. Igline had little to fear from the big killers since their
remarkable speed and maneuverability would quickly carry them
out of danger, but Islaen Connor had no desire whatsoever to try
such an escape, though chance it she would rather than attempt to

face down one of the hunters. Thoriks preyed upon the huon herds
of the prairie, the largest species of all the creatures on Anath, and
could break the back of a prime bull with one blow. Further armed
with razor claws and the speed of a fast Terran racing steed, they
were one creature wisely avoided by the best human fighters on
Anath in all but the most urgent circumstances.

The time at last came when she was forced to take up a
mountaineer's rope and pick and travel without protection from
any scouting patrols the invaders might choose to fly over this
section of the highlands.

That afternoon was bad. The mountains themselves made travel
unpleasant. In the rarefied air, the exertion of climbing tired her
quickly, and she felt hot despite the gnawing of the seemingly
eternal wind.

In one way, though, she was blessed. Although the work she
did kept her sweating and no tree or shadow shielded her from the
sky, the heavy cloud cover held Algola's burning rays firmly at
bay. She did not forgo the silicates designed to protect skin from
rays stronger than nature had intended it to bear, but she had no
real fear of a burn.

She smiled. Varn loved her pallor. He would often place his
hand or arm beside hers to emphasize the contrast between her
whiteness and his own olive complexion, and when they were
alone together . . . It was worth guarding herself, if only to
watch and enjoy his pleasure in her.

The evening shadows lengthened. She greeted them gladly,
although she realized too well that they would bring her still more
discomfort. They also heralded the rest she would be compelled to
take. However poor her bed would be, she welcomed the thought
of any prolonged break.

The Commando still kept on, ever watching for a place to pass
the night. The search for a real campsite proved fruitless, as she
had anticipated it would, and in the end she was forced to remain
where she was, on a narrow ledge that gave no scope for comfort
and made no allowance at all for carelessness or thoughtless
movement.

The night ahead would be as unpleasant as the day before it had
been. The temperature was already dropping, and her sweat-
soaked clothing would freeze if it became low enough, as it well
might. Once again, she wrapped herself in her blanket. If she
could not be comfortable, at least she would not perish or suffer
actual cold damage.

Islaen wedged herself between two rocks so that she should not fall during her sleep and ate a cold meal from her rations. She sighed when she had finished. It was necessary to use her supplies sparingly, but she was ravenous after the exertion of the day and could have eaten twice what she would allow herself.

Full darkness fell with Algola's setting, and she composed herself to take what rest she might.

The silence of Anath's night was very pronounced among the high peaks. The usual chorus of night birds and the occasional late movements of the animals were absent, and the only sounds to break the utter stillness were the howling moan of the wind and the constant singing of moving water. That chorus eventually lulled her, and she slept at last, lightly, with her senses still alert to receive the faintest warning of danger.

Morning came, too soon for Islaen's weary body. She ate quickly and prepared to leave her uncomfortable campsite, checking carefully to be sure that no sign of her stopping remained to betray her. She did so out of habit and the dictates of her long acquaintance with danger. She had known that this bare rock would show no mark even had she acted in such a manner as to abuse it.

She did not make good time. The trails were steep and less well defined than had previously been the case, and her skill as a climber frequently came into play, although she tried to avoid the major faces of these raring towers.

Two hours passed slowly. The woman's body screamed for rest. The climb became even more strenuous, and in the thin air, even mild effort was exhausting. Despite her excellent progress of the previous day, she had soon fallen behind the schedule she had set for herself.

Great though her weariness was and despite her growing concern over the time she was losing, Islaen Connor was not blind to the wonder around her. The majestic aspect of the mountains had replaced the barren, dead rock, and while her body was strained to the limits of its strength, her senses drank deeply of the grandeur that met her gaze at every turn.

She crested the final peak, and all sense of exhaustion left her. The path she had chosen for herself ended abruptly, or rather, it dropped, straight down onto the plain lapping at the mountain's base.

The scene that met her eyes was impressive, aye, and beautiful, too, in its own way, but her heart chilled as she beheld it. There, just beyond a long, comparatively low ridge formed of the debris that had broken and fallen from the great cliff with the battering of time and storm, lay the invading fleet.

ELEVEN

THE COMMANDO-COLONEL studied the starships closely for several minutes before shaking her head in disgust. They looked tiny at this distance, like the ultraminiature models so popular with Horus' children. The people manning them and the smaller equipment were not visible at all.

Her distance lenses helped. They still could not provide the detail she needed, but they showed the battlecraft well enough to allow her to classify them—brigs and escort fighters mostly plus three cruisers, even as they had deduced from Xenon's report.

Those manning them could now be seen as well. They were still insectlike, but their movements showed the order and control of a well-managed and trained military force. The Warlord had been right about that. They were dealing with a professional navy, not a mongrel association of pirates such as they had encountered above Astarte or on Mirelle of Eri.

There was nothing more she could learn from her present position, but she had known that would be the case and felt no sense of disappointment or frustration. Slowly and with infinite care, Islaen Connor began working her way down the mountain, clinging to every shred of cover. Her danger now was not of discovery by Anath's deadly predators but of betraying herself to potentially more brutal killers of her own kind.

There was a ledge, almost a tiny plateau, about three quarters of the way down. It should offer both good shelter and an excellent observation spot if she could reach it undetected. Even if sentries were posted there, a development she did not anticipate, she should be able to discern a great deal merely by watching them.

She had done as much with Arcturians many a time during the War.

Her descent was painfully slow and nerve-wracking, but at last the Colonel found herself crouched at the foot of the cliff base where the ledge joined it. She sent out her mind but detected no human consciousness near at hand. There was no visible sign of danger in any direction, and she cautiously started to creep forward.

Suddenly she froze. A strong, deeply vile ordor was heavy in the air. The smell of old death.

She searched the area until she located the corpse. Though she was accustomed to slaughter in its more unpleasant forms, her stomach knotted painfully at the sight. The body had been horribly mutilated and so fouled that it would be a very hungry scavenger who would have touched it. A familiar, sour smell was also heavy in the fatal air.

Islaen frowned. The body had not been eaten. The thorik had not killed for hunger. One quick stroke of its razor claws would have served for that. This man had taken many wounds while he still lived, and he had survived a long time after the attack had begun. Other lacerations had been inflicted after death. Hate killings were rare in Anath, but it was obvious that this hunter had slain from blood lust rather than out of need.

Her face hardened as she examined the corpse. Nothing remained of his face, and there was little recognizable in the rags of his uniform, but she could just make out the bloodstained insignia on the shattered right shoulder.

Britynons. So. The worst she had imagined in terms of motive and potential consequences for Anath of Algola might well not be out of line with reality if those sons of Scythian apes were behind this invasion. There was little she would put beyond them including the genocide for which the Empire had been so justly condemned. Of a surety, they had worked the murder of almost all that had been natural on their own four planets.

She eyed the body coldly. She could not even pity the man very deeply, not with that pellet gun lying where it had fallen when the thorik had struck. He had doubtless come to this ledge, probably had been flown up to it, to kill, to begin a hunt. The only game left anywhere nearby were igline. If he had met the Grim Commandant himself instead of slaughtering gentle creatures from afar, well to her mind justice had only been served.

Islaen stopped herself. She blamed Varn Tarl Sogan for retaining his people's ages-old aversion to races differing greatly from his own, but she was showing herself to be no better. It had been a vast span of generations since Brityne had made her ill-fated attempt against Noreen, yet she was reacting to this discovery with a hatred scarcely less implacable than that held against Arcturians by their erstwhile victims, and it was a hate directed, not against what they had done or might do but against what they were. She would have to manage herself better than that if her observations and judgment were to be of value to her comrades.

The Commando bent and examined the body, but there was little to be learned from it. There were no papers of significance in the pockets; the belt pouches, those that remained intact, contained nothing more than the standard gear required for a short-term trek in the wild. The pack was just about a total loss. It had been light to begin with, she believed, and the thorik had thoroughly ravaged it. Whatever foodstuffs it had contained were gone, devoured most likely. The rest of the equipment was scattered, and all of it that could be destroyed was shredded or in pieces. Again, there was no sign of any documents that the off-worlder might have been carrying.

That was hardly surprising. The dead soldier was only a Yeoman and would not have been entrusted with any great military secrets even if she was wrong about his being engaged in a simple pleasure jaunt. She held to that theory. Hunting would be about the only way in which to spend a short-term pass on a planet as primitive as Anath of Algola for a people who found or could imagine no satisfaction in a wilderness environment.

Islaen came to her feet, glad to leave the gruesome remains behind and turn her attention elsewhere.

The ledge was typical of the many such formations scattered throughout the highlands, although it was exceptionally large both in length and breadth. A litter of boulders and broken stone covered its surface, all but the largest hidden by thick stands of sturdy mountain brush. On the right side rose the mountain to which it was fixed, a smooth gray wall broken only in one place, by a dark, low-mouthed cave. On the left, it fell away abruptly in an almost perpendicular drop ending on the floor of the plain far below.

The woman glanced around a little uncomfortably. The cover was good. Maybe too good. That thorik might still be near.

She relaxed again in the next moment. No, the hunter was gone. Its smell was still clinging to the place, but only because it had laired here, probably in that cave, for some time. It was old now and fading.

She frowned. It would have been very fresh—and strong—when that Britynon's comrades had dropped him on the ledge. The sour, sharp odor of thorik was distinctive and should have been an ample warning even to inner-system men. She could not believe that this had been the invaders' first encounter with the animals, that the victim had been unfamiliar with the long-lingering stench or ignorant of what it portended. Had the fool thought to match the big hunter with his pellet gun at close range? Alone?

Her puzzlement and contempt both cleared even as they were born. Of course! She remembered now. Britynons had no sense of smell. It was jokingly said throughout the outer systems, and particularly on her own Noreen, that this was why they could endure the discharge of their own factories, which kept most off-worlders who had no urgent need to be there as far as possible from their planets' surfaces. The poor bastard! she thought. He really had not realized he was in any danger until his death was upon him.

Islaen completed her inspection of the place, giving particular attention to the cave. That proved to be higher inside by several feet than its entrance indicated and considerably deeper than she had imagined it would be, though a sweep of her raditorch did reveal the rough stone of its back wall. It had indeed served the thorik as a nest for several days at least, but was definitely abandoned at this point.

She moved away from the black opening and crept over to the edge, making sure she kept low and well under cover so that there would be no chance of the invaders' spotting her either from below or from the air.

She studied the fleet intently. It was located fairly far out on the plain, farther than it had appeared from above. The Britynon commander had wisely decided to keep his battlecraft well away from the rubble ridge to avoid the possibility of having his ships involved in any new falls. It was more than many an Arcturian officer would have done in similar circumstances.

That leader would be a Commandant, she decided. There might be a lot of individual ships down there, but they were nearly all small, too small to merit the attention of an officer of higher rank, whatever their number.

The starships were an impressive sight despite their lack of bulk. They were grouped in a technically perfect invasion formation with the more maneuverable and readily activated fighters clustered protectively around the brigs and the three big cruisers. The largest of the last, definitely a one hundred-class, held the center place as befitted the flagship. Her two fifty-class sisters stood to the right and left of her. All the ships were needle-noses.

The bright line of a powerful energy picket formed a semicircular shield stretching from the base of the cliff wall on either side out onto the prairie before the encampment, effectively screening it from any frontal attack the invaders could expect even a Commando-armed surplanetary army to mount. With the mountain itself forming a seemingly equally strong rear guard, it was readily understandable why the inner-system newcomers had felt secure enough to quarter themselves outside their cramped starships.

Islaen Connor smiled coldly. It was obvious that they knew very little about what guerrillas, Federation or on-world, could accomplish.

She forcibly returned her attention to the camp. It was rather too early to start savoring any victory just yet.

Small figures of people and surplanetary vehicles moved among the ships themselves and throughout the orderly quan hut city that had been erected to the far right of them to house the troops and crewmen.

Islaen sighed. She knew now that the fleet was large, military in character, and prepared for trouble, and the fact that the Britynons had brought those quan huts with them proved that they planned an extended stay. That was not enough. She had to find out more—their purpose in coming to Anath of Algola and, more urgent still, the means by which they intended to accomplish that purpose—and she was going to have to get a light year nearer before she could hope to ferret out those answers.

The Commando-Colonel thought deeply. As she saw it, she had two choices before her. She could work her way down and penetrate the alien camp, or she could stay where she was and wait for some of the Britynons to come to her. In either case, she faced a serious risk of discovery.

That last was unavoidable. It had to be accepted and everything possible done to minimize it, but the information, she had to have.

In the end she decided to remain on the ledge. The soldier had been dead about three days. That was the customary length of a short-term pass. Even if she were wrong in assuming that he had probably arranged to have his comrades pick him up here and save him the strenuous climb down to the camp, someone was likely to come seeking him if he overstayed himself. Men, particularly

inner-system men, did not voluntarily vanish, permanently or
temporarily, on a planet offering neither refuge nor any temptation
whatsoever to draw them away.

If no one came within a reasonable period of time or if she did
not learn what she needed to know, she still had the option of
making the descent herself and trying her luck in their encampment. That would mean another day here, but no matter. They had
allowed for that much additional time in their planning.

She would have no problem understanding what she overheard
at least. If this were a mixed party, all would speak Basic. If it
were homogeneous as she believed would prove the case, well,
Britynons used a bastard tongue compounded out of modern and
ancient Basic and the old language of their first-ship forebears,
which had itself been a major root of Basic. She would be able to
comprehend more than enough for her needs.

Islaen worked swiftly to erase all sign of her presence on the
ledge and establish a secure blind for herself. Potential sites were
legion, but few met the twin requirements of good vantage and
acceptable security. Had she been less experienced, less sharply
honed by years of guerrilla warfare, she might well have fallen
into the trap of neglecting that last, of underestimating her
enemies. No Britynon had ever served with the Commandos, and
to her knowledge, none of them had joined the Stellar Patrol
Rangers, but she could not allow herself to forget that there were
other ways for individuals to acquire wilderness skills. Off-
worlders possessing them could be hired as well, and hired
readily. It was not sufficient to assume she would be safe in any
hide-hole merely because it was potentially too small for a thorik's
use.

She found what she wanted after a brief, intense search. A huge
stone slab, thin but a good ten feet in length, had at some point
flaked off from the cliff and come to rest on a flat-topped boulder,
creating a crawlway just high enough and broad enough for her to
look back over her shoulder—and fire over her shoulder—while
lying within it. The shelter it provided encouraged the tough
highland brush, screening both ends well but not to the extent of
obstructing her view. Its situation was good, nearer to the mouth
of the cave than she liked, but directly overlooking the corpse.

She hesitated before claiming it. She could be trapped in there
if fortune betrayed her, but further searching revealed nothing
better, and the Commando finally crawled inside, carefully
pushing aside the vegetation so that it would spring back naturally
after her.

She settled herself as comfortably as she could on the pebble-strewn ground. Islaen gagged as a sudden, sharp gust of wind drove the stench of the body directly into her face. She held her breath until its force was spent and then composed herself for her vigil. Hopefully it would not last too long.

TWELVE

TIME CREPT BY. Her mind ranged out again and again, each time to be met by the same dull murmur, the mental babble of a large number of individuals going about their lives. No trace of excitement or other strong emotion on which she might have fixed was troubling any of the invading horde.

She kept her receptors open. Visitors could arrive at any time, and men at ease with themselves and their situation would not be broadcasting very strongly. She wanted some brief warning before any of the Britynons came near the ledge.

Three hours passed, interminable hours, then she stiffened. Some of the transmissions filtering into her mind were sharper, nearer. Seconds later, her straining ears caught the whirr of a flier.

The woman concentrated on those inside the machine. There were three, none of them radiating very strongly, although she thought she detected a trace of annoyance on them. They must have been expecting some sort of signal from the dead man, she decided, and were probably put out because they had not received it. Enough time had not yet gone by for real worry to have set in.

The flier crested the lip of the ledge. As it did so, the sendings of its occupants altered abruptly and violently. Shock, fear, anger, the wrenching need for vengeance, all screamed into her mind.

Islaen had experienced the like before and had anticipated and braced herself to receive the onslaught. Even so, it was a moment before she could force her thoughts to center on her own situation. Once she did, her eyes went nervously to the stone above her head. Would her cover hold against the air and ground searches to come?

The invaders swept over the big ledge several times at low altitude before at last setting down beside their slain comrade.

One, a Sergeant, knelt beside the man. He examined him much as the Commando had done previously, then came to his feet again, cursing bitterly. He spat out a word that she did not recognize but supposed to be their term for thorik to judge by the context and the emotion on all three as he voiced it.

Contempt filled her. Three men, well armed and with a flier on hand for quick escape, and they cringed in fear at the mention of an animal!

She quelled that in the next moment. None of her team were any more enthusiastic over the prospect of meeting with one of the creatures. Thoriks were formidable opponents, and there was grim proof of their prowess in front of them.

"With all the planets on the rim, the Prime must've shorted his circuits to pick a bleeding hole like this!" one of the Yeomen exclaimed in a rage that was more than half grief.

"Easy on the drive, mate," the Sergeant said, his hand closing momentarily over the younger man's arm. "None of that talk below," he warned none too roughly.

"More than one of us is thinking it," the second Yeoman muttered sourly.

"Everyone's free to think what he likes. —Anath won't be so bad once the worst of the wildlife has been cleared off. There's good land here for cattle and crops, and there'll be more once we've harvested those trees. Our people weren't microwits in picking her." He paused. "If she tests out, I'm going to grab some of this land and get out of the navy at the end of this hitch."

"Go on!" the other said. "You're shipping us a comet's tail!"

"No, and I'd advise you to do the same thing. Cogs like us'll never get beyond Sergeant, and there's even less for us as civilians. I sure as space don't want to wind up pushing buttons or turning screws like my da did. We could change that on Anath if we get in at the start. She wouldn't be half built up in our lifetime, or our kids'. We'd earn big for our work, and there'd be a chance of making grade and maybe even breaking into the ton."

The others were silent a few seconds. They were young men, open to reasonable hope, and the suggestion that their class might be improved, an impossibility on their homeworld, held an intense appeal for them.

"Why're we wasting all this time?" the first man demanded. "Even if no ores are found on land, the ocean's rich . . ."

"The spot checks aren't done," his Sergeant explained, as if to an overeager child. "The whole planet has to be worth taking, not just this one section of her. We're not going to get another chance to make a grab like this without the Senate getting wise and clamping down on us again. We'd be decades in recouping our war losses then."

"And there is the little matter of the locals."

He just laughed. "No point in worrying about them until Anath checks out. Once she does, we'll locate their stronghold—they have only the one supposedly, in the forest someplace—and drop a few missiles on it before we bring our settlers in. We shouldn't have any trouble with them after that."

"We haven't had any trouble with them period."

"Whatever role they played in the War, it seems they've had a bellyful of fighting," the other Yeoman agreed. "If they did fight. I'm beginning to think the Commandos did it all."

"Routed an Arcturian invasion fleet?" His comrade laughed. "I doubt it. —They may be legendary, mate, but sure as space is black, they're human. No, I'd say our neighbors've stayed quiet simply because they realize they can't face our weapons. They're probably hoping we'll lift again and not come back."

"My credits go with yours," the Sergeant agreed. "So do the Commandant's and the Prime's apparently. They'd be too few to bother with otherwise. We could just absorb them if there wasn't too good a chance that they might try their guerrilla tricks once the fleet lifts. We can't risk exposing our colonists to attack by savages." He sighed. "Cogs like us don't make those decisions anyway. We just get our orders and carry them out. —Come on, let's put poor Stoke in the flier and then give this place a proper going over. Bring the blaster, Briggs. We could need it if that thing's still lurking around, even with three of us here."

Islaen had no difficulty in holding her temper in check although her fingers were white on the grip of her blaster. A Commando who could not control herself did not survive long, and those serving with her did not survive. Her hate and her anger were of a different nature, cold, hard, and sharp with determination. What those Britynons intended was as bad as anything laid against the Arcturians, worse since they were a Federation people, the seed of Terra herself. They must, would, be thwarted, and she hoped to the depths of her soul that it would be at such cost to them that even their greed would shrivel under the blast of it.

She lay very still. That just might happen, but she would see none of it if she were discovered now.

The Britynons had begun their search of the big ledge, and they were making a thorough job of it. The muscles of her stomach tightened in familiar fear. Would they find her lair? Would she be able to fight her way out if they did? There was a chance—she would not have chosen this place if there were not—but she would have to move fast, particularly if the three were together when they found her. Worse, the invaders would then be alerted to the presence of blaster-armed opponents on Anath of Algola and would prepare themselves accordingly. She could only hope the gods of this place favored her . . .

The cave quite naturally claimed much of the soldiers' attention, bringing them far too close to her. Twice while they scoured it and its environs, she could have reached out and grasped one of them by the ankle. The woman held her weapon at ready, set to slay. She tried to quiet her very breath, fought herself to keep perfectly still despite the discomfort of the cramped position she was forced to maintain in order to watch her enemies' movements. The rattle of a single pebble could be enough to betray her.

The men passed her by. They were not careless and studied the broken ground as closely as their knowledge permitted, but their lack of wilderness skills blinded them, that and the fact that they did not even consider the possibility of a human spy being here with them. The Arcturians had been similarly hindered, she recalled, and she blessed Anath's wildness; neither group would have been at such a disadvantage in an urban setting.

At last it was over. The invaders returned to their flier with heavy spirits but satisfied that no enemy remained on the ledge. They did not so much as look back as they rose from it.

The Commando waited a long time after they had gone, until the excitement and anger generated by the flier's grim burden ebbed again and the mental murmur rising from the camp returned to an approximation of its former amorphous hum. She preferred not to have too many eyes fixed on the ledge when she made her move.

That must come soon. This place was likely to receive other visitors, and it would not be well to presume too long on fortune's good graces.

Her journey home was not going to be a pleasant one, at least not the first part of it, she thought grimly as she studied the route she would have to follow. The ascent was a difficult one in itself, more so than the climb down had been. Cover or its absence would have to be the determining factors this time, and it was obvious even from here that the heaviest growth and most broken ground did not follow the gentlest slopes.

That was irrelevant. Apart from a brace of cliffs that would require mountaineering skill and equipment to scale, she would have to resign herself to tackling everything else. The excitement might be spent down below, but many heads would still be turning toward the scene of the tragedy through what remained of the day, and anything seen moving on the mountainside, human or animal, was likely to become a target for the firepower of the entire invading force.

THIRTEEN

ISLAEN'S HAND SCRAPED along a sharp fang of stone, but she retained her grip and her balance and did not slide back over any hard-won ground. She rested a moment, catching her breath, then continued her climb. There could be no thought of taking a real break yet, not while she was on the same side of the mountain as that accursed fleet. Besides, there was some need for speed on her. The day was well on already, and she must not only be over the crest but well down the opposite face before night fell. She was considerably to the west of her original path, and there might well not be so much as an igline trail on which she could wait out the hours of darkness on the upper slopes.

On and on she pressed for what seemed an interminable time until at last she found herself on a gently rounded hump of real grass with only the gray sky above her. The crest was almost incredibly narrow—she could have straddled it—and she squirmed across it in the next moment.

The woman gasped as she looked around her and then down along the way she must go. It was as if she were standing upright overlooking the whole world. The grade here, and as far below as she could discern, was as close to 90 degrees as she had ever encountered on a planet's surface without being fully equipped with mountain gear.

Fortunately, that would not be needed here. The mountainside was steep only, not a true cliff save in a few readily avoidable places. Basic skill and care would master it. Height in itself was no problem for her, and she felt only awe and a practical appreciation for the difficulties of her proposed route when she studied her position more closely.

The scene, near and far, was magnificent. Behind her, the Knife and its companion peaks soared into the heavens. Before lay the great plain and the distant treelands.

Much of the slope below was hidden by its incline and by the thick, blurring mantle of vegetation, which was amazingly rich and varied even at this altitude.

Its presence was not so surprising, she thought after a moment's consideration. The ground was dry where she was, but there seemed to be a great deal of wet below, and not very far below either. That was the unusual part. Springs did not often break surface at this height.

Several apparently did so here, and their combined discharge was significant enough to maintain the respectable little river racing some four hundred yards beneath her.

This, too, was somewhat unusual, for it flowed more westward than directly down. She supposed it had cut itself a channel in a natural fault and was following that.

Islaen lay back and closed her eyes. Space but she was tired! Two strenuous days and the uncomfortable night between them were taking their toll, and she would like nothing better at this point than to dig into her evening's rations and settle down right where she was until morning. Had conditions been otherwise, it was late enough that she might well have done precisely that, but instead she forced herself to start off again. This springy high-altitude vegetation made a wonderful mattress, but it was not tall enough to screen her should an unfriendly flier pass overhead, an eventuality well within the realm of possibility.

Her mouth tightened. It was not human enemies that she feared most greatly. Her receptors were open, and her talent would give her at least some warning if any of her own kind came near. She possessed no such defense against animals. Thoriks hunted by sight. Their vision was excellent, and they could move both quickly and quietly. One of them could be upon her before she had any more idea of its presence than that poor Britynon soldier had known.

With that thought and the memory of the Yeoman's torn body to spur her, she did not have to struggle quite so hard to keep moving. It was far preferable to be bone tired than dead. Besides, she did not have all that much farther to go before she should be able to find a reasonably secure nest for the night.

The Colonel had to go slowly. There were many small ledges and steps, some of them miniature cliffs, that had to be negotiated carefully, and most were difficult to see in the rapidly waning light until she was all but upon them. At last the way grew so treacherous that she determined to halt at the next likely spot.

Five minutes more did not pass before she came upon a site better suited to her purpose than she had hoped to encounter. It was a small, level patch of ground nestled against the base of a perpendicular step about four feet in height. There was good shelter from the sharp wind on three sides and good cover from unfriendly eyes. She would be cramped, right enough, but if she wedged herself in well, she should be able to pass the night in peace without having to tie herself in place to avoid sliding halfway down the mountainside as soon as she drifted off to sleep.

Islaen dropped down to her campsite, landing lightly in a half crouch. She straightened immediately, glad of the chance to stand erect for a moment, but as she did, her foot suddenly turned under her. There was a sickening, perceptible crack—she felt rather than heard it—and the simultaneous surge of searing agony that tore through her whole being, driving awareness out before it.

The Noreenan was conscious only of pain when her mind again returned to her. An instinctive effort to sit up was met by such a wave of dizziness and protest from her battered body that she fell back with a half-smothered cry. She lay still until peace once more returned to her system but did not try to move again.

That was not necessary, not for the moment. She had gained one glimpse of her surroundings, brief but sufficient to tell her where she was.

What had happened was evident, or easy enough to reconstruct to be considered evident. Poor technique or even carelessness had not struck her down. It was luck pure and simple, foul, rotten, bad luck. A fall like that could have taken place anywhere—on the bridge of the *Fairest Maid,* on Noreen, on the paved streets of Horus—with the same result.

She groaned. Not quite. Someone would have quickly picked her up in any of those locations and carted her off to a renewer to repair the damage she had done to herself. She could expect no such rescue on Anath of Algola.

Her eyes closed. She needed help. She was hurt. She did not as yet know how badly, but her injuries, some of them at least, were significant. What she felt, from several independent centers, was pain, not merely the outrage of banged and scraped flesh.

It was small wonder, she supposed. As near as she could reason out the sequence of events following the initial accident, she had

rolled after her fall, tumbling ever more rapidly until she had
slammed into the stone tooth now at her back. Her blood still
glistened wet and red on it where a sharp knob had opened her
scalp.

That cut must be more of a rip than a deep wound, she thought.
If she had taken a real crack, she would have been out longer; the
degree of light still remaining told her she could not have been
unconscious for more than a few minutes.

The Commando knew she should be thankful. Had she not been
stopped, she would have gone into the river. Only a short space of
land lay between her and the bank. That stream might be no major
body of water by any real standards, but it was more than deep
enough to drown an unconscious or stunned person. She would be
properly grateful, she thought, if she did not fear so strongly that
she had just been delivered from a relatively fast death into a much
slower and very unpleasant one.

What was she to do now? The cover was good enough, if not
precisely here then near enough to her, that she need not turn her
blaster on herself save at the very end to spare herself further
torture and the unlikely but still-present danger of capture once she
lost the ability to seek that final escape. But she was not ready to
lie back and wait for death. Besides, she had succeeded in her
mission and had information she needed to get to her comrades.
She could not give over yet.

She was not hurting quite so badly now. Perhaps . . .

There was one easy way to find out. Islaen Connor not only had
the power to send her mind out in search of thought and emotion,
she could also direct it inward, into a human body to examine it
for injury and also for sign of many illnesses. It could only
diagnose, not heal physical damage, and she might accomplish
nothing more than to confirm her imminent death for her trouble,
but it would still be better to know precisely where she stood.

It was a slightly more difficult process to use her talent on
herself than on someone else, but after a few moments, she felt an
eerie sensation begin within her, as if gentle fingers were probing
every cell. She wanted to squirm under the strangeness of it but
held still, although there was no one here to witness her reaction.

Soon, her mind withdrew into its normal seat again. Islaen took
a long, shuddering breath and turned her face toward the river.
That was all. She would learn nothing more by this means.

Things might have been much worse. Her back was not broken
as she had more than half feared. It was not even sprained, just
pulled a little, and a short rest would put it reasonably to rights

again. The same was true of her shoulder; it would not be pleasant using it for a while, but exercising it would cause no further damage. Even the cut on her head was more messy than significant. There was no inner trauma apart from a very slight concussion.

She had not been so fortunate with her other injuries. One rib was broken outright, and two others had hairline fractures. Her right leg had snapped, half snapped, in the upper thigh. Part of the bone was still intact and so the whole remained together, but any real pressure could complete the break.

Relatively minor injuries, all of them, the woman thought bitterly, or they should have been. A few minutes under a renewer would clear the lot. Unfortunately for her, the nearest one might as well be halfway across the galaxy instead of back at base camp. She would have had about the same chance of reaching it.

Islaen sat up, wincing at the pain the effort cost her. That would have told her in itself, without knowing how badly she was hurt, that she would not be seeing her comrades again. She could not make it to the pickup site on this leg. She would not have been able to do so had the way been smooth and straight instead of a strenuous trek across a lot of very tough country. By the same token, she was far too near to their enemies to so much as consider permitting the flier to come for her. No such approach could be risked until they were ready to start raiding the fleet itself if they chose to attempt that, certainly not for so poor a cause as her rescue. She had always accepted the risks inherent in her work and could now only bear her fate.

It was hard all the same, and neither courage nor duty required that she not grieve. She did not want to die merely because she recognized that she must. She did not want to lose Varn's love.—Spirit of Space! She had known it for such a short time, and now she would never again link her mind with her husband's or feel his strong, astonishingly gentle arms around her.

Poor Varn. The blow would be heavier for him even than it was for her. About the only anguish he would be spared was the foreknowledge. He would at least not have to choose to stay where he was and go on with his work while allowing her to perish alone.

Tears started into her eyes. She was wrong. He would have to suffer that as well. Her duty did not allow her to spare him. It was her responsibility to transmit the intelligence she had gained to her unit.

The Commando-Colonel raised her communicator but let her wrist fall back again in the next moment. No, not yet anyway, even if it could reach so far. Use that, and they would get a fix on her whether she disabled the homer or not. They were simply too good, all of them.

It would have to be mind touch. They had intended to use that anyway, albeit from a slightly nearer range. Normally she would not have been concerned about trying it from here, but she was not sure she would be able to reach so far with her strength impaired as it was. Varn's experience on Jade had shown them that transmitting over a great distance was incredibly draining, and she already felt spent and ill.

There was no choice but to make the trial. She was on Anath's surface at least. Varn Tarl Sogan had contacted Jade's goldbeasts from space, using Bandit as a link and catalyst. She should be able to draw on the gurry for help as well if the distance was too great for her to reach her consort unaided. At any rate, she had to put it to the test and do it now. She was not going to get any stronger.

FOURTEEN

VARN TARL SOGAN leaned against the ironwood trunk and gazed into the rapidly darkening, painfully blank patch of sky above them.

He detested it! The gods of his Empire only knew how much. Space was cold and deadly, implacably cruel to the careless and the ignorant, but it was beautiful as well, majestic, a worthy ally and foe alike to those who understood and respected it. That was his element, and he longed to be voyaging out there once more. Anath of Algola felt too much like a vast prison.

A soft smile gentled his features for a moment. He would not mind being on Thorne. Memory of her vast, vibrant sky flashed into his mind. There was nothing smothering about that world.

His head lowered. Her people were fine, too, brave and fair to look upon. He had always liked them, even when it had been a sort of heresy to do so. It was easy to sympathize, to empathize, with them.

The Anathi were different. Their planet had put heavier demands on her offspring, and they had altered in response to the challenges she presented. It was to his shame, but he knew he would have been hard-pressed to deal as justly and humanely with them as he had with the Thornens. Even now, with all his experience with Federation peoples, he had been heartily glad the Warlord or the Forester Chieftainess had not clasped hands with him as they had with their old allies. He shrank inwardly and in body from the very thought of coming into physical contact with any of them.

Mutations. There had been so many in so many races. He had not realized, gut level, how diversified intelligent life actually was

111

until he had been cast into the Federation ultrasystem and
compelled to make his way here. There were several nonhuman
species who shared full membership in the Senate, but humanity,
prototypical or altered, formed the bulk of the galaxy's populace.

Why? And how? Terra was responsible for a lot of it, of course.
Her prolific and varied offspring had established themselves on
planet after planet in their spread across space, but they had been
met on many a world by people very like themselves, humans who
had arisen independently in their own places under their own
sun-stars. His race was part of that group.

How was that unity, that repetition of design, possible?
Granted, the basic form was good, a logical evolutionary choice
and style, but how in space and beyond could the vastly greater
majority, Terran and exoTerran alike, have developed so closely
as to make possible a single standard of appearance and type? Had
all those various and varied races indeed come into being
independently, as both Arcturian and Federation scientists believed, or were they actually the seed of some other people, now
long vanished from even the earliest shadow-memory? Were they
all really no more than offshoots, perhaps mutations, of another
line and time, equal brethren in the misfortune of genetic
corruption? Terra's experiences throughout the stars were strong
proof of how quickly changes could occur and become
established . . .

That thought depressed him unutterably, and he pushed it from
his mind. It would profit him nothing to squander his energy
pondering such questions. He had enough concrete concerns to
occupy him.

Bandit's head pushed free of the breast of his jacket where she
had taken refuge from the evening chill. He petted her, comforting
her as best he could. The gurry missed Islaen as well. She loved
him and spent a lot of time with him, especially since he usually
had the greater need of the shielding her talent provided, but it was
the Colonel with whom she was bonded, and she did not like at all
that they were separated now.

The man sighed. Neither did he. He had grown accustomed to
the unique intimacy they shared. Even when they were not
actually speaking or consciously in nonverbal contact, even when
they locked each other out in some dark mood, yet still they were
together. Islaen's absence had left an emptiness inside him, a
longing rivaling the gnawing hunger of a black hole . . .

The hen picked up on his mood. *Bandit should be with Islaen!
Not needed in camp!*

"No, small one," he replied softly, "but you might be needed very much if we have to deal with these Anathi."

Islaen is Bandit's human!

"She is my consort, too. —We should both be glad that she is so able, little Bandit. This waiting would be even more unendurable than it is if she were not." He veiled his thoughts as he spoke. Now was not the time to dwell openly on the fact that misfortune could strike anyone down, no matter how able he or she might be.

Suddenly the small mammal started.

Varn, Islaen calls!

"What?" His heart gave an ugly leap. Why had he not heard her? Had they miscalculated the effects of distance that badly?

He strove to reach the Colonel and felt her call as well. It was faint, but with the weakness of the sender, he believed; not because of the miles between them. He could detect pain and, he thought, misery as well. By the Empire's cruel gods, what had gone wrong? "Try to link us, small one! I cannot hear her."

The gurry's power swept out, joined with his. There was an instant of seeking and intense striving, then he was in Islaen Connor's mind.

The woman received him with a surge of relief. *Varn! Praise the Spirit of Space! I knew Bandit would be able to do it.—I have the information I came to get.* She recounted all she had learned and concluded with a brief, almost offhand description of her own situation.

Where are you? he demanded. *Can you give us the coordinates or describe the place? You could open your sight receptors* . . .

No! I'm too close to the fleet.

We will not abandon you, Colonel.

You will do as the situation before us demands, she told him coldly. *You have work to do, Admiral. Get on with it.*

The Commando softened suddenly. She could not leave him like this. He must at least know their assignment was important to her, that he would be working for her as well as for Anath of Algola. *Varn, I didn't fight for Anath just out of duty, because I was ordered to do it. I care about this planet and her people. I care a great deal. Don't fail her. Please don't fail me* . . .

Whatever I can do, I shall, my Islaen. The former Admiral steadied himself, battling to hold his control. He hesitated, but he had no right to pride now, or ever when the good of his unit and mission were at hazard. *It might be best if I turned command over to Karmikel. This is Commando work.*

No, she replied firmly and at once. *I wouldn't have made you*

*my backup if I didn't believe you could do the job, nor would
Admiral Sithe have seconded my choice. Draw on Jake's experience, aye, and when you bring the team back up to strength,
choose another Commando to fill my slot, but you command.*

The Colonel, too, was fighting to retain her rein on herself. It
was an incredible strain to maintain the contact she had initiated
over this distance, and it was becoming increasingly more difficult
to keep her grief from pouring into her transmission. If she
allowed that, she would break Sogan as well.

Her eyes flickered to the river rolling beside her. She stiffened.
*Varn, go on with the reconnaissance, but keep your communica-
tors open. This stream here's quite a respectable little waterway,
and it's going in the right direction—away from those blasted
Britynons. If it's half as deep as it looks and stays that way, it'll
be able to support my weight, keep it off my leg. If I can get far
enough, I'll call for a pickup.*

We will be ready.

A cold determination gripped the woman, an anger as frigid as
the depths of interstellar space. *Contact Ram Sithe at once. Tell
him everything. Whether we succeed or not, that fleet must be
stopped. No. It must be annihilated, and those who sent it must be
found and taken, including and especially the Prime of Brityne. I
want them to suffer such a fate that would-be tyrants a thousand
millennia from now will be held in check by the memory of it!*

We will do our parts, he replied, surprised by her vehemence
and bitterness, *but most of that will be beyond us.* He could
promise nothing he would not be able to fulfill, not now.

I know, his consort answered, checking her hatred once more.
*You can begin the work and trust the Navy to finish it. Too many
died to stop invasion and murder from beyond. I very much doubt
it'll be tolerated from within.*

Her love for him waxed high, sweeping all else before it. In
another moment, she would have to sever contact with him,
perhaps—probably—never to link with his vital mind again or
experience the love and care he felt for her. *The Spirit of Space go
with you, Varn Tarl Sogan. I've left you with the worst of it. I'm
sorry.* With that, she parted from him.

Sogan buried his face in his hands, but sharp claws tore at their
backs and forced him to look up again.

Bandit whistled shrilly. *Islaen needs us!*

We cannot help her.

Find her, Varn!

I cannot!—Can you trace her, Bandit?

Nooo.

Nor can I. She intended that, so we would not be tempted to chance a rescue before it was safe. Once again, fear and pain as deep as the void threatened to overcome him, but he mastered it. *Come, small one. Islaen is right. We do have work to do, and . . .* His eyes closed. *And we cannot betray her trust. It might be the last she will every lay on any of us.*

Jake Karmikel glanced up as a blast of cold air from the entrance struck him. "Close that door, will you . . ." He stopped and came to his feet. The Arcturian looked as if the Grim Commandant had just manifested himself in visible form and laid hand on him. "What's happened, Sogan?"

Varn tersely related what Islaen Connor had told him.

The redhead's fist slammed into the side of the flier. "The witch! The bloody little witch! If she'd used the communicator, we could've traced her!"

"That is patently the reason why she did not."

Jake gripped himself. "Sorry, Admiral. —You and Bandit can't . . ."

"No."

Bethe Danlo's fingers brushed Sogan's arm. "We'd best call headquarters. The sooner Ram Sithe gets this news, the sooner he can act on it. The rest'll have to wait until morning."

He nodded and went to the interstellar transceiver.

The transmission was a long one, for there were questions, close, sharp questions, to be answered after he had finished his report. By the time he had dealt with the last of them, he had told everything either Islaen or the rest of them had discovered, everything except the means by which she had communicated her news, that and the aching emptiness in his heart . . .

He sat where he was for a moment, his head lowered in a deadly weariness, then he raised it again. "Who are these Britynons?" he asked. "You two reacted strongly when we discovered their race, even without any knowledge of their intentions, and I have never felt hatred like that in Islaen before. She meant what she said about the fate she willed on them."

"I don't doubt it," Karmikel told him. "Noreen has an old grudge against them. Actually, most colony planets don't care for them much."

"Neither do spacers," the demolitions expert added, "or Navy and ex-Navy people either at the moment. Those sons're living proof that a lot of the things rim folk claim about inner-system types isn't just so much space tripe."

The Noreenan chuckled. "All of which tells him nothing.

"Brityne was settled very early in Terra's colonization of the stars, and as a result her people definitely are of the belief that everything refined and civilized rests with them and that we ruffians on the rim should properly look on them with awe and deference.

"Normally, folk just laugh at that debris and label inner-system denizens machine-ridden fops in turn, but Brityne developed in ways unpleasant or downright repugnant to most of the rest of us.

"First off, they brought with them the love of political manipulation and the empire-building characteristics of the subrace from which they sprung. Granted, they were ingenious about it. Instead of settling just one world, they spread from the outset to all four planets in Empress' system. The Federation was a lot smaller then, and they reasoned that once their ten generations were up and they gained full member status instead of a dependent colony's half vote, they'd be a pretty strong block."

He grinned. "They forgot that the rest of Terra's offspring were also politically astute. The Senate recognized damn well what they were doing and declared their effort to be one colony, Brityne I through IV, not four separate developments.

"To their credit, the Britynons didn't pull out. They held on to their toeholds and went ahead on all fronts."

The former Admiral frowned. "That would seem rather to their honor than otherwise. It is no small task even now to settle and develop a new world. They worked with four, presumably across a climate spectrum ranging from ultratropical to superarctic, and they did it with primitive technology and communications."

"No one's slighting their accomplishments," Bethe answered, "but the length to which they carried that 'development' is another matter. I'm space-bred and have no real feeling for any particular world, but even I'm disgusted by what happened to those planets. They just took out every bit of native life. All of it. I don't believe so much as a microbe or species of natural Britynon algae is left. A lot of planets suffered badly during the early days of colonization, but the fate of Empress' system is regarded as one of the worst disasters and is cited as a, as the classic example of total criminal exploitation."

The Commando nodded. "Then, too, like many other old-time settlers, Britynons let their population climb to maximum levels. They've never exceeded that, but they've never bothered dropping it, either."

Sogan had been long enough with his companions at this point to realize how they would respond to abuse of that nature, particularly on this scale, but the intensity of his consort's enmity still puzzled him.

"What has any of this to do with Noreen or any other colony for that matter? You all apparently profited from their example and have made very sure you didn't repeat their mistakes."

"The desire for an empire dies slowly, my friend, especially when it's coupled with economic factors and greed. Our Brityon comrades were occupied for a long time with their own concerns, and in the end, they had created and were in complete command of a thoroughly mechanized, high-tech society that gave them a good, secure living, chiefly through interstellar trading, monetary exchange, and heavy industrialization.

"They found that paying a fair price for raw materials, once they had depleted all their own resources, and in open-market competition for the sale of their finished products did bite into the profits they would have preferred to be enjoying, and they started looking around for a solution.

"They weren't long in coming up with one. The most obvious, they discounted almost at once. Developing a new planet was, as it still is, a costly, time-consuming, very long-term business— even if the by then well-established Settlement Board was likely to turn over another victim for the ravaging. However, there were more attractive possibilities. Noreen and a number of other colonies were well past the first-ship stage by that time and comfortably on their way. Brityons bought land on our world. They didn't farm it like the rest of us. They started to build despite our avowed intention of remaining a low-impact, low-population society with no urban centers whatsoever. The plan, of course, was to build up their numbers real fast, literally overwhelm and absorb us, and use Noreen to their ends, all the while pretending she was still under our control, she and several other worlds slated to follow her."

Blue fire rippled through his eyes. "They grossly underestimated those with whom they were dealing. Our ancestors had suffered enormously on prespace Terra, and at the hands of the Brityons' forebears. We had retained our age-old mistrust of them, and none of us, including our leaders, liked their sudden rejection of what had become nearly inviolable custom—that a new planet be settled entirely or almost entirely by people of one race or subrace or from a specific place of origin. We did not like the way they were conducting themselves on Noreen, and we weren't fools enough to allow matters to develop to their conclusion before having a good look at what was actually going on.

"Our investigation turned out to be what amounted to a full-scale guerrilla mission, far and away the best in Federation annals prior to the War and on par with most Commando missions since in all but wholesale destruction. There was nothing of that nature involved. Our agents got the evidence we wanted, and Noreen's leaders presented it—and not just to the Senate.

"My subrace is a very old one with a very long history of wandering and colonizations of new and wild places, migrations very frequently instituted because we were forced in large numbers from our original homeplace. People of our blood had settled a large proportion of the planets comprising the Federation both as full members and dependent colonies, and all but one of the worlds chosen to follow Noreen's takeover belonged to one group or another of them. Our leaders knew full well what they were doing when they lay our case before the people of the ultrasystem as well as before its ruling body. The outrage was instantaneous and bitter and utterly erased any hope Brityne might have nurtured of a lenient sentence, much less of escaping with a stiff censuring and a warning."

"There was never any possibility of that anyway," Bethe interjected. "We had a strong Senate at that time, praise the Spirit ruling space, and those sitting on it recognized the magnitude of the threat posed in that case. If this serpent were not killed fast, crushed utterly, everything Terra's seed and those others allying themselves with us were trying to build was doomed. The Federation would tear itself apart within decades or in a few centuries at the most. You can believe they struck hard, and they did so economically, with all the long-term effects of such a move, rather than merely physically.

"The sentence was hard, and there would be no lifting of it. Ever.

"Because Britynons had so abused the worlds already in their care, they were denied access to any others. They would never be permitted to claim a colony in their own name, and no Britynon would be allowed to live outside Empress' system or to own or control property or a business off their own worlds.

"These were the severest sanctions our government had ever placed on any people, and because of that severity and the fact that it has been enforced to the letter and in spirit, no similar measures have ever had to be used against any other, though the old gods know, we've never lacked for trouble from individual thieves and tyrants."

"Harsh treatment of its erring citizens by an ultrasystem supposed to be dedicated to its individual members," Sogan observed rather sarcastically.

Jake started to frown, but he checked his temper. "Don't misunderstand us," he said. "Brityne was by no means doomed. She was and remains a powerful, very rich system, but her people have to work for that wealth and pay as well as take in the accumulating of it."

Varn made no reply to either of them. This was a facet of his comrades he had not encountered or suspected before. Bethe had a spacer's temper and the implacable sense of justice of a people all too often compelled to make and maintain their own, but what he saw in the Noreenan astounded him. Karmikel's kind had carried this sense of outrage through the generations, without allowing it either to wither or to warp into something less. He shook his head. What was even more astonishing was that it made no difference. Islaen Connor and Jake Karmikel would have gone to Brityne with all that aflame inside them and would readily have given their lives to prevent a threat similar to that shadowing Anath of Algola from falling there.

His eyes closed. Perhaps that was the answer to an older question of his own—how they could have received a man with his history into their company . . .

Noo! Varn's part of us! The gurry looked up at him from the door of the flier where she had perched, her little face anxious and troubled that he should doubt his place with them. *Islaen loves Varn! You belong here!*

I know, Bandit, he said wearily. That was a reminder he had not needed at the moment. "That explains your dislike of these invaders," he said hurriedly to the two humans, "but what has the military against them? Bethe mentioned the Navy has no liking for them either."

"Their lack of interest in fighting Arcturians," the Sergeant told him. "Throughout the whole course of the War, Brityne sent up barely sufficient recruits to stave off conscription, and ninety percent of those were criminals." She caught the dark-eyed man's look of dismay. "Oh, aye. You don't think the ton'd risk their cultivated hides, do you? Those guilty of minor offenses were sentenced to the Navy. Those suspected of deeds that would have made them ineligible were given the choice of prosecution or enlistment. Since Brityne's penal code is particularly harsh, most took the latter. You can imagine the kind of soldiers they made, though to be just, a good number did excel when the time of proving came. Some even found the life congenial, to the point that they fought to remain with the Navy after the War's end."

"Why not?" Jake asked. "At least they had a chance to advance in the service."

"What do you mean?" Sogan ʼasked. "What is this ton you mentioned? Some caste?"

"Aye, to answer your last question, Admiral," the woman said. "Their society's completely frozen. The ton are the descendants of the first shippers to any of the four planets and hold all significant political power, all high rank in their navy, and own and manage all major industry and large-scale commercial ventures. The grade consists of those born of the second-wave settlers. They hold the lesser political and civil posts, military rank to about Captain, and own small businesses and the system's few farms. The vast majority of people are cogs. They man the factories, do whatever heavy or menial work's to be done, and serve as general laser bait. There's no grinding poverty, and the government provides for their physical welfare, but no one moves except, rarely, down. Conviction of a crime strips all rank, as would the improbable event of a misalliance. Mate below your station there, and you irrevocably drop to your partner's level."

The war prince nodded slowly. "That explains a great deal.—I was wondering why men would risk settling a planet they would never be allowed to keep. Losing their work would not matter as much, would it, if they gained status by it?" He looked into some distance invisible to his companions. "There would also be the hope against hope that they would not be discovered, that they would be able to remain, to do more than rape and flee. The desire for something better, for one's offspring if not for oneself, seems to be inherent in Terra's seed. I do not suppose one subrace is very different from the others in that respect."

"No different at all," Bethe Danlo replied softly.

Varn Tarl Sogan straightened. "We must also assume that they possess something of your ultrasystem's stubbornness and the fighting skills to hold what they have claimed. From Islaen's description of their encampment, they appear to have the discipline that usually accompanies that will and ability."

"You can count on that, friend," Karmikel agreed. "What now?"

"You two get some rest. I will take the first watch. Tomorrow we step up our examination of their installations. The sooner we strike at them the better."

"Aye, Admiral." Jake hesitated, then went on. "Sogan, Islaen Connor's flown on one tube before. She's always made it back, and you can put credits down that she's not going to jump into that river with the intention of drowning. Don't count her out yet."

"I am aware of that." Light rekindled briefly in his eyes. "Adjust your communicators for fine reception. And take a look at our maps. We know the general region where she must be. There cannot be that many streams of such depth flowing through there, particularly in the direction she describes. It would help when we do get her signal to have some idea of where we are going."

The redhead grinned. "You're turning into a fine Commando, Admiral. I'd planned on doing both before knocking out tonight."

Bethe waited until they were alone before moving close to her companion. "Thanks, Jake," she said quietly. "I'm glad you answered him like you did instead of reaming him for that crack about the Federation."

"I'd take a lot more than that from him at the moment."

"I know, but you're hit hard, too." Her voice tightened. "If Islaen goes down, we'll need him more than ever."

"Aye."

She shivered. "I've seen people look like that, Jake, just before . . ."

"Varn Tarl Sogan won't snap, and he won't put a blaster to his head, not while he has this mission or our safety to consider." He glanced at the door and was silent a moment. "After that, I don't know."

Karmikel fixed his eyes on the demolitions expert. "If that's his choice, you'll have to let him go with it. Don't try to intervene this time."

"I won't."

The spacer turned away from him. "This is what I'm afraid of," she whispered. "For us."

Bethe's head lowered in shame, but having begun, she went on. "I remember what it was like when Norm was killed. I was a girl then. I'm a woman now. I've lived with loneliness and know too well what that kind of loss means, far too well to want to risk suffering like Varn is now." She bit her lip. "I'm even more terrified of being the cause of inflicting that pain on someone else, especially on you. I love you too much to do that to you."

Karmikel came to her side but for the moment did not touch her. "Why didn't you tell me this instead of letting me think I was doing something wrong or lacking something?"

"I knew I was playing the coward, and-I was ashamed to have you know that." Her eyes lifted to his. "I knew you, too. Once you learned what was holding me, you'd have insisted on the marriage, however right you realized I was. —I wanted to protect you, Jake."

The man took her in his arms. "It wouldn't be like that, Bethe, not the way it is with Varn and Islaen. It couldn't be. We're not the same as them. That mind link of theirs has to make them different, their situation different. So does their history. We aren't bound the same way, and severing wouldn't hit us the same blow, however deeply we love each other. It's sad in one sense, but it is a protection, too."

She rested her head against him. "I hope you're not wrong, Jake Karmikel, because I don't want to delay any longer. You're right. We may have a lot of time or a little, and I don't want to squander any more of what's been allotted to us." She paused to steady herself. "There's a priest of your belief on Horus? I know that's important to a Noreenan . . ."

"The same one who married Islaen and Varn."

His hold changed a little, significantly, but she shook her head and gently drew away from him. "Not now. Not with him outside like this and Islaen missing. I . . ."

"No," he agreed, making himself relax. "We've waited long enough to do it right. There shouldn't be any clouds over what we want to share between us."

FIFTEEN

ISLAEN CONNOR SAT for several long moments after she had severed contact with her husband. She had betrayed him, she thought dully, as surely as had his own people. However unwillingly, she was abandoning him in a universe that had shown him almost unremitting cruelty . . .

Her head raised. No. Not yet. She was not prepared to lie down and die. The plan she had announced to Varn was not merely a contrivance to make their parting seem a fraction more bearable. It was a sound one, a possibility at least. There was a chance—not good, perhaps, but she intended to grasp and to play it while any spark of life or will remained in her.

Before she began, Islaen made herself eat. She took a full portion, more than double her allotted ration. By this time tomorrow, she would either be dead or home free. There was not likely to be much or any opportunity to take food later, and she would have need of all the strength it could give her. She would need all the heat it could generate within her as well. Anath of Algola was not a hot planet, and mountain streams were rarely noted for their warmth. The water in which she meant to immerse herself was frigid, enough so in itself to eventually numb and kill even one whole in body, and her injuries would drastically reduce her resistance to its effects.

It was fully dark by the time the Commando-Colonel finished replacing her gear. She worked without light as she had trained herself to do, mentally checking off each of the few items she had removed for her meal as she slipped it back into its place and carefully running her hands over the ground around her in case she had inadvertently dropped or overlooked something.

The little river was so near that she did not even consider coming to her feet to approach it. She doubted she could have managed it anyway. The crawl hurt abominably, but it lasted only a few seconds.

Once she reached the bank, she rested a few seconds, then played a thin beam from her raditorch down along the route she would follow. She did not like using the light, but the chance of its being spotted was a far less danger than what she would risk by dropping down that inner bank without any knowledge of what it was like or what might actually lie below. A moment later, she switched it off again and braced herself. She had learned as much as she was going to know until she actually entered the water.

Islaen wriggled over the edge and cautiously let herself down into the river. The shock of the water brought a gasp from her. It was freezing, more than she could bear, she thought for an instant. She steadied after that. It was this or resign herself to death on the bank, a death that would come all the more quickly now with her wet clothing to draw and amplify the cold.

She started moving. She had been right both about the stream's uncommon depth and the support it provided. The water was breast deep here, and she could walk, albeit not without discomfort. Should she encounter somewhat shallower or much deeper sections, she could swim or float across. The current was more than strong enough to carry her along with only a minimum of effort on her part, and unless the volume of water all but gave out, she should be able to keep going. Her worst danger at the moment, apart from the cold, was that of falling and being held under by the force of the flow. That she would have to take great care to avoid.

The Commando had not gone more than a hundred feet before the river took a distinctly downward turn. She felt heartened by the change, evidence as it was that she was at least heading in the correct direction.

It was well that something cheered her. This was not a pleasant journey, and she was ever conscious of the scope it gave for disaster of one sort or another. Its difficulties kept the perils inherent in it all too sharply before her for her to forget or ignore any of them.

The dark was almost complete. Her pupils had expanded to their full capacity to no avail. They were not sensitive enough to utilize the ghostly shimmer her mind told her existed in Anath's night. She had to be content with the flow of the water against her body and an occasional touch to the bank to guide her.

Her pace was of necessity dreadfully slow, but at least she was moving. Despite all its numbing cold, Islaen was grateful for the river. Any advance at all would have been impossible on dry land. She would have been forced to quit before she had gone a quarter of a mile, or else she would be either dead or very close to it. Several times, she felt the sickening jolt of the ground going from under her in a sudden drop, but the water supported her, and she swam across the holes unharmed.

She stayed with the river for seemingly endless miles. Her body screamed for rest, and she longed to lie down, even for a short while, but the most she could allow herself was to lean against the muddy bank for a few minutes, permitting it to take as much of her weight as possible.

Even those breaks were rare. Islaen learned very quickly that it was best to keep to the center of the stream, away from the projecting mass of roots, branches, and rocks of every size studding most of the land bordering on the waterway. It was impossible to avoid them in the dark if she ventured anywhere near either shore. It was impossible to avoid them entirely. The stream was too narrow. Once again, the water shielded her somewhat, but she took many a slash and blow as the night wore on.

Her pace grew slower and still slower. Her senses were numbed by cold and exhaustion, and even when some change in the river bottom signaled a drop, she was unable to perceive it. She fell more frequently and found it more difficult to fight her way back to the surface. The force of the current increased along with the grade, which steepened as the altitude dropped, to the point that it threatened to sweep her, almost did take her on several occasions.

At last she felt she could go no farther, not without some little rest. Islaen battled her way cross current to the bank and caught hold of a sturdy root to which she could cling to hold herself in place. Even with that help, she had to struggle to remain where she was. The river was urging her to move on with such insistence that it was nearly easier to keep walking than try to fight it.

That said a great deal. The break in her leg had worsened despite her effort to use the limb gently. All her injuries were worse, and she was in almost constant pain . . .

She heard it then, a dull roar in the distance. Tears of dismay sprang to her eyes. Not now! Not after all this suffering and all this labor.

She angrily gripped herself and tried to make her numbed brain function. The Colonel fumbled for her raditorch and switched it on. She used broad beam this time and was just able to see what her body could no longer feel. There was a change in the current, a backlash, a drag that slowed its forward thrust somewhat. She frowned. That should not be the case if a waterfall lay ahead as she had believed.

Curiosity piqued her, that and the fact that she knew there was no escape. The riverbanks were steep in this place, slick and high, and her strength was almost completely gone, sapped by cold, pain, and exhaustion. Even if her injured leg would have supported the climb, she was not capable of making it. Whatever her fate was to be, it lay in the water.

The roar and drag became increasingly more pronounced as she inched her way forward. Her senses were alive again, fired by this new stimulus, and she did not miss the slightest of changes in her surroundings. She realized now what was happening, what she had overlooked in her weariness. The river was either about to plunge underground or into a tunnel it had bored for itself through the low cliff up ahead that her beam had revealed looming up at the far end of its range. Which of the two was actually responsible for the phenomena she was witnessing made little real difference to her. What mattered now was that soon there would be water only in the path she must follow, a grim, closed path of stone with little or no space at all for the air upon which her life depended.

Her eyes shut. Varn had conceived a strong dislike for caves, for underground ways in general, during his time with her unit. Though he strove to conceal his reluctance to deal with them and succeeded fairly well, she knew he felt an almost superstitious repugnance for regions of perpetual night, as if deep within himself he believed they gaped for him and his with sentient maleficence. It seemed he was not far wrong, she thought numbly. Danger appeared to loom for them when they entered such settings, and now it was all too likely that she would soon meet her end in that drowned hole ahead.

The Commando stopped once more. It was no longer difficult to remain still with the backlash partially neutralizing the heavy current.

Probable death lay only a few feet ahead, but she was without choice. She had to go on. She knew that. There could be no returning now, and she did have a chance, a slim one, of making it through. That bottleneck might be very narrow, a mere hourglass of stone. Similar formations were not unknown on other planets. At least, some hope did exist for her if she went ahead, none whatsoever if she tried to retreat.

Islaen Connor approached the cliff until she felt she would be thrown off her feet if she went any farther. She breathed deeply for several seconds, working her lungs until they were filled to their full capacity with air.

She could do no more. The Colonel involuntarily glanced back in the direction she had come, then took a final breath, deeper than all the rest, and plunged into the water.

The boiling current gripped and tossed her like a twig on a wave. She allowed herself to travel with it, expending as little energy as possible.

The seconds flew. They seemed like years. A burning knife twisted in her chest. Very shortly, her breathing reflex would react against even her strong will, drawing water into her lungs . . .

A blast of cold air shocked her back into full consciousness. Islaen looked around. She saw grass and brush and the sky overhead.

She was lying half on an arm of the bank, half on the partly submerged rock that had snagged her. She had wit enough to drag herself fully onto the shore but lacked the resolution to crawl farther under the shadow of the thick stand of bush above, although she was dimly aware that she was readily visible from the air.

All of a sudden, a weird, terrible cry rang out from on high, shocking the life back into both her mind and body. She knew the call and glanced upward, expecting to see winged death plummeting down upon her.

It did not strike. The warbird was there, a raven black male the size of a Commando's flier and half that again, but he was only circling, although he could not but be aware of the potential victim lying helplessly beside the river.

Why? What was holding him back? Those birds were known for their swift, merciless attack, yet this one merely soared over the same area, ignoring the woman below.

Again the cry. It was answered this time. An instant later a dark speck appeared on the horizon and grew in size until it was almost upon the winged hunter. Another warbird, this one significantly smaller in size and of a dark charcoal color. A female.

The male circled her. Occasionally he made a feint approach, but she drew back each time, as if threatening to flee.

He pulled out of the slow circle abruptly and shot upward with

such speed that he was soon gone from sight. The warbird dropped
with the terrifying whistle that could freeze the hearts of Anath's
bravest warriors.

The speed of this drive was beyond even the tremendous
velocity normally achieved by the species. Instinctively, Islaen
cringed and clutched at the ground beneath her. The great bird
could never brake that descent in time!

He did halt, stopping almost from full speed on a level with the
female. He faced her for perhaps half a second, then dropped a
little lower in his flight.

She hesitated no longer but settled herself on his back. His
burden cost him no altitude since her wings were still supporting
the most of her weight. They flew a very short distance, no more
than twenty feet, in this position, then the female rose from him
and returned to his side. After that, the pair flew rapidly to the
southwest, disappearing from sight as quickly as they had appeared.

The woman drew a deep breath and released it again. The
courtship flight of the mighty birds was a rare occurrence. They
were not numerous and mated for life, and this might well be the
first time it had been witnessed since the great War had begun.
Possibly it was the first time anyone of her species had seen it
since Xenon's people had quit the highlands for the forest.

The strength the incident had sparked in her was fading rapidly,
but the Commando-Colonel utilized what remained of it to drag
herself under better cover.

She tried to take stock of her position. She did not know where
she was. The nature of the countryside and vegetation told her that
she had not yet reached the prairie, although it could not be very
far away. The hills that she could see were low, rolling rises,
gentle outriders of the peaks she had left behind.

That did not help her much. She still could not place herself to
be able to direct her comrades to her, and without them,
everything else had been for nothing. She could not go farther.
She was ill now on top of her injuries and was so weak that she
would not be able to defend herself against the poorest attack.

Islaen activated her communicator. She did not try to contact
the others, knowing too well that she was beyond the instrument's
range, but she set the homer to full power. That had been given a
greater reach.

Marshaling all her remaining strength and will, she cast her
mind out, seeking her husband and the gurry hen.

There!

Varn, come . . .

The tenuous contact broke. She had not the power left within her to maintain it or to try to establish it again. The woman lay back, her eyes closing. She did not even know if Sogan had detected her attempt, so light and brief had their linking been.

Her hold on consciousness drifted quickly after that. She was aware only of the overpowering, long-delayed effects of complete exhaustion and a sensation of intense cold so overwhelming that her body no longer felt even the pain that had ravaged her since that accursed fall.

SIXTEEN

JAKE LOOKED SHARPLY at the war prince. Sogan seemed to be asleep, but he was restless and moaned softly even as he watched.

Karmikel went over to him. His face, what could be seen of it in the sleeping bag, gave Jake a start. It was stark white, strained as if after battle, and it was slick with sweat. Space! Had he been wrong about the former Admiral's not breaking?

"Sogan!" he called softly. "Wake up, man! Are you all right?"

The dark eyes opened. They were focused and quite clear although very tired. "Karmikel?"

He sat up and pressed his fingers to his temples. "I was trying to reach Islaen."

"No luck?"

He shook his head. "None, even with Bandit's help. She probably has her mind sealed against us."

Or she was dead, but the Commando did not have to say that. Sogan was all too well aware of the possibility already.

Varn sighed and stroked the gurry, who had fluttered from his shoulder to his hand. "Poor little thing. This business is very hard on her."

"It's hard on all of us, comrade," he said, wondering at the Arcturian's compassion. No one could be suffering more deeply than Sogan himself.

The war prince's head lowered. He did not look at the other. "If anything happens to both of us, you and Bethe will take Bandit?"

"That's already been arranged." He made himself speak irritably, as if he considered the question unnecessary and was annoyed by it as a result, but his eyes, too, fell. Varn had already made his

130

decision, then. What he had gained among his former enemies was not enough to hold him without Islaen Connor.

Bethe stirred at that moment, sparing him the need of saying more. "What's going on?" she demanded in a sleepy voice.

"Nothing. The Admiral's been trying to contact Islaen, but she's not having any of it."

"She won't, not until she's ready."

The spacer got up and began rolling her sleeping bag even as the others were doing. "What now?"

"Review our battle plans, I suppose," Sogan replied. "We have about all we are going to get on those installations."

They had done well, he thought. Islaen would rightly be pleased with the results of their efforts. If she returned to learn of them . . .

He was somewhat surprised by all they had accomplished and more so by the part he himself had played both in the accumulation of detail and in the plans they had already formulated for the downfall of the two outposts. He had always been capable of unconventional thought, to the sorrow of both Federation fleet officers and the Resistance on Thorne, and he had learned a great deal during his time with this unit, but Varn had fully expected to take a strictly supporting role now, with most of the weight falling on Jake Karmikel. It was both pleasing and very satisfying to discover that he had been wrong. The Commando-Captain had of a certainty made the heaviest contribution, but his own input had been anything but minimal. It had far outweighed Bethe Danlo's.

Sogan banished his sense of accomplishment. He had no time to squander on personal trivialities at the moment. They would soon be ready to act. In point of fact, they could make a move now, but he preferred to have all the data they could get on the fleet first and then go after the three strongholds in quick succession, assuming they decided to include the last in their efforts. For his part, if circumstances permitted, he would much prefer to leave that for the Navy's attention.

The decision was theirs. Admiral Sithe had ordered them to prevent the Britynons from initiating any of their planned measures against the surplanetary populace, or to minimize its effects if an assault could not be entirely blocked. It was up to them to choose the methods by which they would accomplish that.

The Arcturian's eyes darkened until they were almost black. Another burden lay on them, a heavy one. The Britynons here were doomed. Those who did not die in battle would face Federation justice for some of the darkest crimes a sentient being

was capable of committing. None of them, not the lowliest
Yeoman cog, was likely to get off.

That was not enough. Sithe, like Islaen Connor, wanted the
system's government as well, her Prime and every other official
and private individual involved in the outrage. For that, they had
to have better evidence than the single conversation the Colonel
had overheard, which had named only the Prime and might not be
sufficient to convict even him. The old communications center
appeared to be serving as a field headquarters and could well hold
what they needed, enough at least to permit civilian or military
prosecution. Simple, total annihilation would not serve there. The
place would have to be examined first.

Sogan flexed his shoulders to take out of them some of the
stiffness left after his bad night and sighed. Dampness bothered
his back even under the best of conditions.

No matter. It was a minor discomfort, and the activity of the
day to come would soon loosen him up.

They would be beginning soon. Breakfast was over, and Algola
was well up behind Anath's cloud veil.

A tremor passed through him that he was powerless to check. It
brought a corresponding whimper from Bandit. His head lowered. No word, nothing, despite their repeated efforts to make
contact. Everything within him rebelled against accepting the
inevitable, but if Islaen Connor had made it, she would
surely . . .

Varn, come . . .

His heart leaped. The call was gone almost in the moment he
had heard it, but death had not broken the connection. Of that he
was certain, although a strong attempt on his and the gurry's part
failed to reach the Noreenan again. She was probably in a bad
way, but he knew now that she was not dead. Not yet.

The war prince recalled himself to the others. They knew
something had happened and were watching him closely, hardly
daring to move. "Open the homers! Islaen's just contacted us."

After several attempts, he gave up trying to quiet Bandit's
excited whistles and went ahead with a description of the brief
communication.

Jake did not so much as shrug when the instruments failed to
pick up any transmission their commander might be sending out.
He grabbed his pack and raced for the flier.

"Come on, you two! We've made a pretty good guess as to the
river she took, and even if we are wrong, we're bound to come
within communicator range at some point." He stopped as he was

about to pull the rear door open. "Sogan, will you be able to drive while you're searching?" He knew the Arcturian's gift had some peculiar side effects at times.

"Aye. Bandit will be doing most of the active probing. Bethe can ride with me, just in case." Varn, too, appreciated the double-edged nature of his talent and preferred to have someone close at hand to grab the controls if he should abruptly be drawn into some other awareness or sensory perspective.

"Good enough." The redhead's eyes danced for a moment. "Do try to bear in mind, Admiral, that the straightest course isn't necessarily directly through any trees."

"I shall do my best to navigate to your satisfaction, Captain Karmikel," he replied dryly as he slid in behind the controls.

Varn Tarl Sogan kept the vehicle at as close to space speed as he could without threatening to destroy them all in Anath's atmosphere. There was no doubt in his mind that Islaen's case was urgent, and he feared above all else that she would die now, after having called for help, that she would die knowing he had failed her.

The journey was long. They cut diagonally across the forest, well south of the areas they had previously explored. The marshlands rushed out to meet them far sooner than they did to the north. They were a lot broader as well, a deadly morass a man on foot would have required many long days to cross, if they could be passed at all in this place.

The morning was gone before they at last left the wetlands behind and entered healthier country once more. Still the flier never slowed save when the Arcturian surrendered the controls to Bethe Danlo for a while and when he took them back again several hours later.

By that time, they had a strong fix on the Commando-Colonel's communicator and were making directly for it, traveling back along its signal. Excitement and determination were powerful within all four, driving them to use greater and still greater speed, but the humans watched both the sky and the instruments carefully. They were far out on the prairie, and they were not fools enough to count on their enemies being so lax from Anath's lack of opposition that they would not send out occasional patrols. They had to be ready to dive into the tall grass at the first sign of trouble and scatter from their machine on the chance that it might be spotted before the vegetation could cover it over. In the event of a directly overhead pass, nothing on the plain would screen it from the Britynons.

They crossed the course of a small, deep river and flew up along it, traveling against its flow. The water was crystal clear and grew ever more turbulent the farther they followed it.

Varn's hands were wet on the controls, although the schooling of caste and rank held firm otherwise and he gave no more obvious sign of the fear eating him. There had been nothing from Islaen in all the time since he had heard that short-lived call, and he felt sick with the dread that the signal they were tracing would lead them only to a corpse.

Islaen lives.

The gurry hen sounded so serene that he shot her a quick look. *Have you reached her?* he demanded.

Nooo.—We'd know, Varn. Gurries always know.—Hurry, Varn! She might die!

I can go no faster, small one.

He tried to steady himself. It was something, everything, to know that Islaen Connor still lived.

They had to reach her in time! He could not even imagine this emptiness inside him enduring for the length of time it would take to finish their mission and win the right to seek release. She must not die alone, not now, when they were so close. That vibrant, valiant soul must not be permitted to vanish from the universe.

The Federation party came upon a strange place that would have been a delight had any of them been in a frame of mind to appreciate it. The stream they were following had bored through a low cliff, a final elbow of the highlands, and sprang again into the open air like a great fountain to continue its lively course.

Islaen's signal was powerful now. She was somewhere in the area, probably within sight if they only knew where to look. The communicators could tell them nothing more. They were too near the source of the transmission.

Once again, a sense of desperation started to grip them. They could fail yet. It was almost dark . . .

There! A big, unclean-looking animal was lying on the bank, watching a section of thick underbrush with great impatience. It seemed undecided about whether to go in, although it obviously desired to do so. Even as they watched, it began to slink forward.

Get out of that, carrion eater! Sogan shouted at it in mind, at the same time sending a stream of blaster fire sizzling before its muzzle.

The scavenger fled, and he leaped from the still-moving vessel, leaving the Sergeant at the controls.

He peered into the underbrush, and his eyes closed. Islaen.

Varn quickly uncovered the still form of his consort.

Bethe brought the flier close. "Dead?"

"No, only very ill." Sogan raised the unconscious woman gently. Her face was very drawn and thin and still bore the signs of pain and exhaustion. "Give me the renewer, Jake. We can take care of the worst of this. The rest will have to wait until we get her back to camp."

The Commando-Captain had already prepared the instrument and handed it to him. He stood by, silently watching while the dark-haired man played the ray over her body.

After several minutes, Varn returned it to him. The Arcturian did not come to his feet immediately or try to raise Islaen. His mind went out to hers. With her beside him like this, he had no difficulty in reaching her. She had still not roused to the point that real communication was possible between them, and he lacked his wife's ability to diagnose the extent of injury, but mind and spirit were both there and stronger than he had expected to find them. His hands balled to keep them from trembling in his relief. With luck and the Spirit of Space willing, she would make it.

Islaen Connor was still a very sick woman. He lifted her and with Karmikel's help settled her on the back seat, taking the place beside her.

The Noreenan man, who had done none of the driving thus far, claimed the controls. "How is she?" he asked as the flier rose off the ground, breaking the silence that had been holding all of them.

"The physical injuries are gone, but there is a high fever. It is probably the result of all she has gone through, but I am giving her the full range of shots just in case of infection. There is nothing more to be done after that except wait for her to sleep it out."

All the next day and most of the following passed before the Colonel's temperature started to drop. Once it did, her recovery was rapid.

She felt a scratching at her throat and looked up to find bright black eyes peering into hers and a yellow bill pressed against her nose. "Bandit! What are you doing, love?"

The gurry responded with a whistle that caused the human to wince. *Islaen's awake! Varn, come!*

Sogan had not been far off to judge by the speed of his response. Islaen smiled up at him, then struggled to sit. Instantly his arm was around her. He raised her gently and slipped a rolled sleeping bag behind her so that she might rest against it.

Easy on the drive, Colonel, he told her severely. *I am not certifying you for active duty for a while yet.*

You just want to keep the command, she responded archly. Islaen studied him. He looked tired but not spent. He had shown some good sense during her crisis, then, probably because there was a mission involved as well as her life. She would not trust him to take care of himself otherwise. *What's been happening?*

The former Admiral gave her a full report both of their work and of their efforts to find her.

Well done on all counts, she said appreciatively after he had finished. *It looks like I owe you all for this one.*

He smiled. *It just goes against our grain to lose things, especially personnel, and we all know how hard it is to eliminate a Commando . . .*

The gurry stopped purring under Islaen's stroking and looked up at him. *Varn was afraid the whole time!*

Sogan glared at her. "Bandit, so help me, if I were not so happy right now, I would wring that little neck of yours."

She gave a surprised squawk. *But, Varn, you were . . .*

The woman laughed. "Never mind, love. He's not denying it. Now go keep Bethe and Jake company.—*I guess they're outside?* she asked her consort.

Getting water.

Good. Varn, open the door for her, please.

The Arcturian let the gurry out, then quickly closed the entrance again, before his patient could take any chill.

He shook his head ruefully. *There is no changing her,* he grumbled.

Islaen's soft laugh sounded in his mind. *I'm afraid not. Just be thankful you're not a serial murderer or something of that ilk. She'd blab that on you, too.*

Her great eyes shadowed, and she was silent for several seconds. *I was scared as well,* she said at last, slowly, as if she were groping for the words. *It wasn't so much the prospect of dying itself that got to me, but the thought that I was losing you, and betraying you on top of it all.*

What?

I'd have left you to face everything alone again.

Hardly by choice.—My Islaen . . .

Her head lowered, and he could not read her face. *I know I'm not being very reasonable, but that emptiness where you should have been . . .* She shuddered despite herself. *I would be gone at least, but you would've had to go on enduring it.*

In answer, he opened himself to her, allowed all his love to pour into her. He took her into his arms, pressing her against him. *It did not come to that, praise the Spirit ruling space. We will do best to be thankful for the time we have been given and not dwell on what might have happened had your plan gone wrong.*

SEVENTEEN

Islaen Connor rested for another day but then grew impatient with inactivity. Her strength was fully restored, and her comrades had completed their reconnaissance of the invaders' strongholds. The time had come to begin to take action against them.

She hoisted her pack to her shoulder and left the shelter, a happy Bandit flying out before her.

It was early morning, and the others were busy about the affairs of the camp. She waved in response to their greetings and made a face at Jake, whose brows raised at the sight of her burden. "The vacation's over, friends," she told them. "It's time we got down to some real work."

"What do you think we have been doing, Colonel Connor, and shorthanded, too, while you were napping the hours away?" Karmikel demanded archly.

He smiled then, shyly, and drew his arm through Bethe's. "Before we start, I guess you three should know that Sergeant Danlo will be taking over half control of my *Jovian Moon* once we get back to Horus. She'll also acquire full control of the *Moon*'s master at the same time."

"Jake! You're getting married? At last?"

"With full ceremony," he admitted.

"And you had to wait until I was out of the way before making up your minds?" the Colonel demanded accusingly.

"Well, we did have to talk about something while waiting for you to report in. I can assure you that your consort here wasn't very lively company.—At least we did wait for you to get back on your feet before making any announcements, didn't we?"

"That you did," she agreed, laughing.

Islaen kissed Bethe, then threw her arms around the redhead in a bear hug approximating his usual manner of greeting.

The former Admiral, always a spectator during these displays of his comrades' exuberance, offered his congratulations more quietly, but he, too, was smiling broadly. "I was beginning to wonder at the length of time it was taking you two to make up your minds. It was beginning to seem like indecision must be part of the basic Federation character, with a few exceptions of course," he added, glancing at Islaen Connor. There had been nothing slow about her response to him.

"Not at all. We just believe in studying a situation from all angles before leaping into it."

The Commando-Colonel raised her hands in mock surrender. "Jake, please! In another moment, you'll have us believing you.—Come on! This, we have to celebrate properly. We've got time enough for that before setting out."

So saying, she started off at a fast pace, leaving her comrades to follow after her in complete puzzlement, even Jake, although he quickly divined her intention from the direction in which she was walking.

Their commander finally came to a stop in another clearing, or more rightly in a hint of a break in the trees several hundred yards from the base.

Tiny as the place was, its beauty alone would have made it well worth more than a single visit. Cascading down each of the surrounding trees and spilling out into the open patch was a creamy curtain that appeared solid at first glance but quickly resolved into a number of heavily flowered vines that draped their host trees from their uttermost crowns to the ground.

The blossoms themselves were trumpet-shaped and huge, each extending more than eighteen inches from a base as large and round as a small bowl. They proved not to be all of one shade upon closer examination but rather ranged in color from brilliant white to dull yellow. Some were still in bud, and a few had brown petals withering back over clusters of swelling orange fruit.

Islaen drew her knife and severed a white one from the nearest vine. With a deft hand, she pared away the petals so that nothing remained but the cuplike base. This was filled with a pale golden liquid.

She drank from it, smiling in delight at the sweet, light flavor of the nectar. Islaen could readily have emptied the whole cup but confined herself to that one mouthful. She handed it first to her husband, and he in turn passed it on to the others, who made certain to leave a good swallow behind for the enraptured gurry.

"This makes an excellent food if supplies should run short," she explained after they had all finished drinking, "but if you want to use it, take care to choose only the young, white flowers." She repeated the husking process on one of the yellow blossoms. It, too, was filled with liquid, this time of a darker color.

She raised it in salute to the engaged pair, sipped from it, then passed it to Varn as she had the first. "Careful," she warned as she did so. "Take only a little."

He tasted it and found the flavor still sweet but tempered by a refreshing tartness. "This is excellent," he told her appreciatively, but looked at her in surprise almost in the same moment as he felt his head begin to swim. Arcturians rarely drank, but they were not unduly sensitive to the drug that a mere sip should produce any effect whatsoever on him. "What is this?" he demanded.

"The Anathi call it power nectar. Like many of Anath's plants, these vines are pollinated by small animals, so the reservoirs that draw them are large. Once the seeds have been quickened, the remaining nectar ferments rapidly, protecting the slowly ripening fruit since it very soon incapacitates any creature still willing to taste it. Actually humans're just about the only ones who bother with it, and even they've learned to go easy. A gobletful produces heavy intoxication, and it wouldn't take much more than that to kill someone."

"That I well believe."

Jake took the cup from him and gave it to the spacer. "As you mentioned, though, Admiral, it does taste good.—If we ever want to corrupt you, at least we have a possible . . ."

"Not a chance, Commando! I am forewarned now."

Islaen eyed the two men. "Lay off, Jake Karmikel, or I'll have to recount the tale of your first power-nectar encounter."

"That's a pleasant memory. Part of it anyway." He glanced at Bethe. "Well, what's the verdict, Sergeant?"

She sipped the dark liquid gingerly, then whistled. "This is wonderful! Jake, if you and I ever regain our sanity and get out of the Navy, we could make our fortune exporting this stuff. Hedon'd buy every drop of it we could bring in."

"I've thought precisely the same thing myself. Makes one want to get Anath's neutrality rescinded, doesn't it?"

He sighed and drank his own portion. With a great show of regret, he poured out the remainder. "This affronts my delicate sensibilities, but I don't think we'd be smart to mix any more power nectar with the work before us. It's effect is as long-lasting as it's potent."

Bandit gave a screech of protest. *My turn!*

The Noreenan woman only shook her head. "That's not for you, love. Even a few drops would be too much. The young nectar's much nicer anyway, and we let you have plenty of that."

Islaen likes this! the gurry wailed.

"Only as much as I took. See, it's the same with all of us, and we're a lot bigger than you."

She retrieved her pack. "All right. Let's have a go at those Britynons and find out what kind of scouts you four make in my absence."

The day was clear and beautiful. A slight chill refreshed the air, keeping it light and crisp, pleasant for travel and for the heavy, fast activity they expected to encounter at the end of this journey. Under other circumstances, the off-worlders would have enjoyed the flight, but the fact that they were engaged in an active raid gripped and held them all. The tension that always preceded battle was high in them, and their minds were fixed chiefly on what lay ahead and the part each would have to play, that and with watching the world around them for sign of potential trouble.

Islaen Connor sighed inwardly. If this were Thorne of Brandine, she would be going into battle with a powerful, superbly skilled Resistance force behind her. Here they must work without help.

No matter, she thought, or it must not be allowed to matter. Commandos had fought alone often enough before and conquered. Her team was the equal of any other in the Federation's service, now or during the War, and what had been accomplished in the past, they could do as well.

There was no doubting the havoc they could wreak on the invaders' outposts if fortune were at all with them. They should be able to take them both out and in so doing hold the main body in a constant state of turmoil, keeping them off balance and forcing them to concentrate on guarding their camp rather than working further damage against Anath of Algola or her creatures until the Navy could arrive with the force necessary to sweep the whole rotten crew away.

Their first attack would have to be impressive, and the arsenal should give them good scope for making it so. It should also supply them with means in plenty for creating the chaos they

hoped to loose here, enabling them to conserve their own
equipment almost indefinitely.

Luck did seem to be smiling on them, at least with respect to
timing. The Arcturians had been considerate in the placement of
their installations, and the Federation guerrillas did not have to
worry about distance, which frequently presented a major problem
on penetration missions. By keeping the flier at high speed, they
should reach target just prior to predawn. That would allow them
to make the raid and be well away again before true morning.
They would still have a large stretch of open country to cross, aye,
but the Colonel was not unduly worried. She anticipated no
trouble once they got away from the immediate environs of the
attack. Anath had shown no resistance to the Britynons thus far.
They would be at ease, lulled by the quiet, and if her comrades did
their work well, neither the fleet itself nor the other outpost would
so much as learn of the assault until it was well over.

Time passed, seeming both to fly and to crawl. The guerrillas
had left the shelter of the trees for the open prairie. All were
acutely conscious of their increased and ever-increasing vulnera-
bility, and their eyes flickered constantly from the instruments to
the sky and to the surrounding countryside.

Islaen's receptors were wide open as she both scanned their
surroundings herself and linked with Varn in his own searching.
She heard and shared his quick laugh at a junner's startled
annoyance when their vehicle's strong air jets ruffled the grass
where it was feeding, but then she frowned as his mood darkened,
or rather deepened, again almost immediately. She realized
suddenly that although he had joined his talent freely with hers
since they had set out, the Arcturian had remained very much
inside his own closed thoughts. He had the controls since he knew
the way as well as she, but the demands of driving were hardly
sufficient to account for his preoccupation.

Is something wrong, Varn? she asked. *You've sensed trouble
for us before.*

No, he answered hastily, bringing himself back out of his own
thoughts. *I do not always anticipate danger,* he added defensively.
*We cannot depend on a gift we do not even know for certain that
I possess.*

*Maybe not, friend, but you've been right often enough that we
can take warning to watch ourselves when you feel particularly
uneasy about a project.*

He kept his eyes fixed on the way ahead of them. *This is*

nothing like that. He hesitated, and the woman read his embar-
rassment. *Back on Thorne, I used to wonder what it must feel like
to be a Resistance fighter waiting to attack one of our installations. Since joining up with you, I've gotten some part of an
answer.*

All this doesn't bother you, Varn? she asked quietly. *These
people aren't soldiers of the Empire, even if your kind did build
the structures they're using.*

No, of course not, but still it is strange. He gave her a rueful
smile. *I used to believe I was not an imaginative man.*

She laughed at that. *Admiral, no member of Thorne's Resistance would've shared that delusion.*

The Noreenan sat back, relieved that there was no real trouble
on him. Her hands absently cupped over Bandit, who was
snuggled on her lap out of reach of the wind whipping through the
open flier. *You're very quiet yourself, love. I hope nothing's
bothering you?*

Nooo.—Islaen?

Aye, love?

Bandit wants to help!

Both humans looked at her in surprise.

How do you mean, Bandit? the Colonel asked. *You help us all
the time, really help.*

Bandit's always safe! Friends might get hurt! She whimpered.
Bandit wants to stay with you!

*You can't fight, love. You're not strong enough. Besides, you
don't want to hurt people, not even very bad ones. It's not in you.*

Islaen and Varn need Bandit!

Aye, small one, we do, the former Admiral told her, *but you
must help us in ways befitting your abilities. We all work like that,
and our team is strong because of it. No one of us is equally good
at everything.* His dark eyes rested on her. *Directly or indirectly,
you have saved the life of each of us at some time or another. How
much more could any of us expect from you?*

But . . .

Bandit, the Colonel told her severely, *apart from the fact that
we love and want to protect you, we need the services you provide.
We're not about to risk losing them. You understand that, don't
you, that you're too valuable to us to be cast away?*

Yes.—You'll come back to Bandit?

We'll do our best, love. You can count on that.

EIGHTEEN

THE NIGHT WAS still black when the Federation unit at last neared its target. Sogan carefully lowered the flier into the tall grass and settled down to wait. There would be no approaching that installation until they had light enough to work.

Tension was high in him. The prairie growth provided a good screen, but it was by no means perfect, and their enemies were very near.

His eyes closed to shut out all extraneous stimuli as he tightened his link with Islaen and with Bandit. All three of them were scanning the dark world beyond their vehicle, piecing together the details they could discover about the invaders and their defenses.

To their relief, they found that the information the team had gathered and the conclusions they had drawn from it were apparently sound. The Colonel detected the dozen individuals they anticipated finding here—a Lieutenant, Sergeant, and ten Yeomen. Peace rested on the camp, and boredom was the primary emotion riding those still awake. As expected, the better part of the company was asleep. That would probably include both leaders and half the enlisted men. The remainder, those on watch, were performing their duties with little care and no interest, much less any sense of urgency.

They would soon pay dearly for their laxity, the war prince thought none too sympathetically. Varn Tarl Sogan of the Arcturian Empire expected a higher quality of performance than this from soldiers on active service, particularly in hostile territory. The fact that they had encountered no trouble thus far should only have made them more alert. But then, Britynons had never been

on the receiving end of Commando attentions or the activities of
a capable and dedicated Resistance.

Besides, the invaders were not really depending on their own
senses for their safety. They were making the mistake his own
people initially had and were putting their trust in the elaborate
system of alarms and death traps surrounding their outpost.

It was an obstacle to be respected, too, he conceded, well
placed and varied enough to treble its efficiency, one his unit was
going to have to penetrate undetected before even beginning their
attack. Good as they were, that was not going to be an easy task.

They would have to have light to accomplish it. He glanced
nervously at the unremitting blackness above them. Predawn
would be enough—they did not want too much brilliance for their
kind of work—and that could not be far off. So reason said. Every
slow-crawling moment seemed an eternity to his straining nerves,
and he knew it was the same with each one of his companions.

At last a faint shimmer appeared on the horizon. It was so
nearly imperceptible that the off-worlders at first could not be
certain they were not imagining it, but the glow steadily strength-
ened, and finally Islaen Connor pointed in the direction of their
target.

We might as well get at it, she said in mind, but she spoke no
audible word, nor did any of the others. Sound carried too readily
and too far in a stillness such as prevailed here, and anything out
of the ordinary could alert their enemies, however lacking in
wilderness skills the sons of Brityne might be. Strange human
voices most assuredly would do so.

Varn Tarl Sogan snaked his way through the tall grass. He tried
to ignore the cold wetness of the heavy dew and concentrated on
the task laid on him. His was the responsibility of detecting the
trapped area and warning the others when they reached it.

His mind and Islaen's were linked, and he felt the outpouring of
power from her as she swept the outpost and its environs, but
he was seeking more strongly still, reaching for every contact he
could find with Anath's wildlife. There was a vast multitude
surrounding them, but most of the creatures comprising it were
low on the evolutionary scale. Their transmissions were difficult
in the extreme to read, more mere indications of existence than
anything else. A great many were barely discernible at all. There
were no large animals, of course, not this close to the murderous
invaders. The most consistent readable patterns he received were
those of the ubiquitous junners. Those lively, wary little beasts

seemed to be everywhere and go everywhere, even close to their world's deadly foes.

Close, but not too close. To a point, the junners were all around, conducting their lives as they always did, as if nothing whatsoever were amiss. Beyond that point, nothing. They had long since learned to avoid the circle of traps and alarms the Britynons had laid to ensnare larger and more powerfully motivated prey.

The change was abrupt. All around him, there was life. Ahead lay a void, or a near void, where only insects and a few small reptiles seemed to exist. Even the patterns of birds were missing.

As soon as his mind encountered that emptiness, he froze. *Islaen!*

The woman stopped as well. She listened a moment with him, then her nail hit her communicator, tapping out a warning in the team's terse combat code. The killing field was before them.

The off-worlders divided, the two Commandos separating from the others. Islaen moved to the right, Jake to the left to neutralize the alarms and traps on this part of the perimeter.

Bethe stirred beside Varn. His hand closed over hers for a moment. It was steady, offering comfort and reassurance, although he fully shared her nervousness and fear. There were so many devices out there, working on every conceivable principle— light, sound, body heat and temperature variance, movement, even a few ancient trip wires. Every one of them had to be located and deactivated. A single mistake could slay the guerrilla making it and alert their foes to the survivors' presence.

Bandit grasped his shoulder tightly. She would not accompany them farther, but she did have her part to play. She took wing at his command, following after Jake Karmikel to monitor his progress, even as the Arcturian was doing with his consort.

Sogan forced himself to lie still, to continue breathing normally. This was bad, the waiting, not knowing whether disaster would strike or whether their comrades would succeed.

At least this part of it would not last long. Islaen was working quickly, carefully, almost matter-of-factly, severing wires, jamming sensors with the highly classified device she played over each new discovery after first altering its transmissions to suit the particular trap she was attempting to nullify.

The sensitive work was finished at last. Both Commandos signaled that the way was open, and Varn and Bethe Danlo began inching their way across the cleared space.

The light had bettered perceptibly while they had waited, and the gray outlines of the installation were clearly visible. It was typical of countless such depots that had been hastily erected during the long course of the War, so familiar in form that the former Admiral felt a chill grip him. It was as if the past had somehow returned and he was once again in the nightmare position of assaulting soldiers of his own Empire, as he had been forced to do on Omrai.

He checked himself sharply. There were no Arcturians in and around those buildings, just a pack of Federation brigands, would-be murderers whose very presence was a desecration of those who had designed and constructed the place.

Sogan studied the complex closely, intently, as if he were seeing it for the first time. There was a difference, an urgency, to his observations now, with the time of attack on them.

The central building, the major and by far the largest one, was strongly constructed of titanone to shield its volatile contents from the shocks of nearby battle and to guard the rest of the installation from any accident or sabotage from within, unthinkable as that last should be.

Some distance apart were clustered the smaller buildings housing the garrison. These, too, were well built, for by the time they had been raised here on Anath of Algola, the Empire's Navy had resigned itself to the fact that its surplanetary structures might and probably would have to be defended, and all installations were designed accordingly. Besides, though the members of the elite Arcturian warrior caste were expected to sacrifice themselves readily, their lives were not squandered needlessly. This was an arsenal, dangerous in itself because of its contents, and all possible protection had been provided for those manning it.

It was an arsenal still, valuable as such to those utilizing it, and so it was guarded, though not nearly so well or so strongly as it would have been by its original builders. Three sentries paced near the central structure. Two others were patrolling the remainder of the camp, ready to surprise any intruder. Supposedly ready. It was obvious from their deportment that none of them had any particular interest in his duty.

The guerrillas remained concealed a long time, watching carefully until they were certain they had indeed located all the guards.

At last the Commando-Colonel gave the signal to begin. She and Jake Karmikel moved in first. Each slipped up on one of the unsuspecting outer sentries. Their knives struck so fast and surely

that both Britynons were dead before they realized they had been
attacked, much less that they were injured.

Sogan and the Sergeant sped across the open area like a pair of
shadows. Their targets were the two barracks, their purpose, not
to slay but to neutralize.

Varn worked rapidly to lay the silwire he had removed from his
pack before starting his run, activating each tiny, powerful coil as
it fed out between his fingers. Thirty seconds, fifty, and the circle
was complete. He stood back, smiling coldly. When those
Yeomen snoring away inside awoke, they would find themselves
enclosed in a ring of deadly energy. They probably did have the
firepower to blast through the picket, but it would take time to do
it. Even if they should somehow rouse now, the Federation unit
would still be able to finish its work and make good its escape.

The war prince shuddered suddenly and felt glad of the strength
of his Navy's structures. Those inside would have sufficient
protection when the arsenal went up. It was one thing to kill
soldiers in battle or to fell a lax sentry and quite another to crisp
men while they slept or were helplessly imprisoned in close
quarters. That was atrocity, sometimes unavoidable, perhaps, but
he had never been compelled to resort to the like during the War,
and he gave thanks to the Federation's many gods that he was
spared the need of doing so now, even as a by-product of his
actions.

He looked around. Bethe Danlo had finished sealing off the
officers' quarters in the same manner. He tapped his communicator in signal and raced for the depot itself, keeping low and to the
shadows in case the Commandos had not yet taken out the rest of
the sentries.

The demolitions expert joined him at the door. Varn studied the
seals. He nodded curtly. They were simple locks, of a kind
familiar to any Federation spacer. The Arcturian invasion commander must have ordered the originals removed or destroyed so
as not to leave them for his enemies' study. That was to their good
now. They should be able to pry these open without having to
delay to set explosives.

He tried once and then again. They would have no more time to
waste on it after that, but his second trial worked, and the lock slid
back.

Scarcely had the pair activated their torches and flashed the
beams around the high-piled supplies stored within than they
heard the soft, nearly soundless sigh of the flier. Jake set it down

and sprang to the floor beside it. The Colonel had remained outside to keep watch at the door.

Working in total silence, all three loaded the machine. When it would hold no more, the men leaped inside. They paused at the entrance to pick up their commander, then sped to their rendezvous point in the tall grass beyond the trapped area.

Bethe stayed behind in the depot. She looked around her. Tons of supplies remained, and she sighed regretfully. It was a pity they could not carry everything off. Her team would have been well supplied for the duration of their active careers, much less for this single mission. She shrugged. Since that was not possible, she could at least see to it that the Britynons got no good from any of this.

Dealing with such matériel was an old and familiar task for her. There were a dozen different kinds of explosives stored within a few feet of one another, and it was the work of seconds to run a slow fuse from the door to the center of the most volatile of the munitions. She activated it, then raced for the high grass, heedless now of the soldiers quartered in the barracks. Her comrades would wait no longer than five minutes after the explosion. Reinforcements could reach this place very quickly from the fleet, and they dared not risk capture after this night's work. It would be difficult in the extreme to make her way back through this type of country once full day came and Britynon patrols were scouring the countryside for those who had dared to attack them.

The Sergeant had not quite crossed into the disarmed killing zone when the shock of a massive blast lifted her off her feet and flung her down. She lay still, momentarily stunned. Flames shot skyward, tearing hundreds of feet into the air, and huge balls of fire and flaming material were tossed out in every direction from the fiercely burning arsenal. One fell within ten feet of her.

Bethe struggled to her feet and again began to run. The others must be feeling very nervous just now waiting in that flier loaded with its highly explosive cargo.

She reached the machine and leaped through the door Karmikel held open for her without breaking stride. Jake slammed it shut even as the Commando vehicle shot forward and raced for the safety of the forest.

The sky was red behind them for a long while, but in the end it was the glow of still-smoldering embers that provided the color. The fire itself had been extinguished relatively quickly, far more quickly than any of them had imagined would be possible considering its violence and the casualties they had inflicted on the garrison and the fact that the survivors had been forced to first break free of their prisons before they could begin battling it. The Britynons had proven their efficiency in rising as they had to this completely unanticipated emergency.

The Arcturian kept their speed high while they were on the plain, flying partly by instrument—chiefly as a guard against pursuit now—mostly by sight. Twice, they had to drop into the grass as patrols passed near, but the enemy fliers were too far south, and they were able to continue their retreat without trouble or the fear that they might have been sighted.

The prairie was alive with activity, which covered any motion of their own that might otherwise have been noted. Everywhere, herds of huon and other creatures could be seen still fleeing in the aftermath of the explosions and fire. He sighed at the sight of them and more so at their terrified transmissions. The animals of Anath, if not her ruler, would be glad when the invaders were gone.

NINETEEN

NONE OF THE Federation company really relaxed until long after they were within the forest, not until they had actually reached that part of it familiar to them. They knew they were home free then, although their work was not yet completely finished.

Islaen, who had taken the controls from Varn over an hour before to give him some break after his long drive, brought the flier to a halt and let her fellow Noreenan out. "Sorry for the long walk, Jake, but I want to cache our loot before calling it a day. Give the camp a good once over for us."

"Aye, Colonel." He sighed, thinking of the hike ahead of him. "Sometimes it doesn't pay to be the team's second Commando."

"Poor thing," Bethe said unsympathetically. "At least you won't have to lug all this blasted stuff around again. Just have a nice supper ready for us when we get back. I'm famished right now."

He grinned and gave her a smart salute. "The tastiest rations in our store," he promised.

He started walking as soon as the flier left him, keeping well to the deeper patches of shade although he anticipated no problems.

The Captain frowned when he realized he was hugging cover far more tightly than need and a guerrilla's instinct demanded. He was nervous, not cautious. It took him several minutes to figure out what was troubling him, and when he did, he was not pleased with himself. For years, since their days in Basic training, he had depended on Islaen Connor's unique gift for warning of potential enemies. He had grown dependent upon that alarm, and later upon Sogan's similar skill, and now felt naked and somewhat helpless without their backup. That was a weakness he was going to have to battle in himself. Commandos worked as a team, right enough, but each one had to be able to function fully independently as well, or no one was likely to survive long term.

He reached their base without mishap and paused at its border to examine it before venturing into the opening.

The Noreenan froze. It took no woodsman to see that the place had been disturbed. The ground cover had been much broken and trampled, especially along the bank of the stream and by the entrance of their shelter. There was no mistaking the rank, sour reek permeating the area.

He could see no sign of a nest, and he doubted the thorik had denned here, not unless it had been able to break into the hollow trunk and had slept there.

The smell was too strong for that, he thought. A stink like this would never remain after only a single night's occupancy. The beast had probably scented them and its fury and eagerness to hunt them down had caused its marker glands to release, not once but several times.

Humans were not the creatures' natural food, and Jake remembered at once the hate-killing victim Islaen Connor had discovered. Had their visitor been the same animal, or had the invaders' depredations been so bad that a number of the big animals had been driven to the same madness?

He drew his blaster and inched forward. After assuring himself the thorik was gone, he began to examine the damage it had wrought.

After a short while, Karmikel rose to his feet again. It was not as bad as it looked at first glance. With a little work on their part, a lot of it on the more heavily trampled and torn places, they should be able to eliminate the signs of disturbance. That was a relief. This was a good campsite, and he had not looked forward to abandoning it at this point.

He had left the shelter itself for last. If the thorik had gotten through the doors, there would be a galactic mess inside. They would not be crippled by the destruction, praise the Spirit of Space, thanks to Islaen's caution. On her orders, they had split their supplies into three separate lots and had cached the bulk of them elsewhere. They would face a massive cleanup, though, and that was not a pleasant thought in the wake of all their recent activities.

To his relief, both entrances were unbreached. They had been tried but had held firm, and the thorik had probably abandoned its efforts after two or three blows. Its sense of smell should have been more than strong enough at that range to tell it there was nothing alive within to justify further efforts. The doors would have to be kept firmly shut from here on in, unfortunately, limiting the amount of light and air within the shelter, but that could not be helped. It was better by far to sleep securely.

That was for later. He would be only a few minutes inside, and it was not worth the trouble of lighting his raditorch for that length of time. The long chamber had patently not been disturbed and would need but a quick once over before he started repairing the damage outside.

Jake holstered his weapon and began walking the length of the trunk, nodding in satisfaction as he went. Aye, everything was in its place, precisely as the team had left it.

Suddenly the light from the opening dimmed. Karmikel whirled about to find a remarkable and terrifying creature blocking the entrance. It was large, at least a foot taller than the Noreenan and broader of shoulder, biped, and proportioned like a man. Its limbs were muscular and clean of fat. The body was covered with a short coat of dun-colored fur except for the tail, which was naked of hair and resembled that of a giant reptile. It was heavily scaled. The face was a gargoyle's.

The beast was undoubtedly formidable. The great fangs it bared and the six-inch claws tipping its hands were sufficient to fell either its natural prey or any human unfortunate enough to encounter it when it was angry or hungry.

Jake's blaster seemed literally to appear in his hand, but fast as he drew it, he could not match the thorik's speed of response. One immense hand slammed down on the back of his, breaking his grip on the weapon before he could raise it to fire and sending it clattering across the wooden floor.

Jake sprang back, just avoiding the animal's follow-up blow aimed at his belly.

His right hand was numb. Maybe it was broken, maybe not, but it was useless for the moment. With the left, he slowly drew his knife. The thorik had started to move in but immediately slowed its advance and approached more cautiously. The man, too, became more wary. All Anath's major hunters possessed a considerable degree of intelligence, and it was obvious that this one knew enough not to charge a knife-armed man without care. That was hardly surprising in view of the fact that it had not only recognized the danger of a blaster, but had anticipated his draw and had effectively countered it. At this stage, he hardly dared allow himself the vanity of assuming that had come about by mere chance.

The thorik need not worry, he thought bitterly, not in these close quarters. His stupidity had seen to that. His dagger would be of little enough use to him. All the advantage in this confrontation lay with the animal. It used its claws as much as a man would a knife or a short sword, and its longer reach permitted it to strike at him while holding him at a distance. He was the faster on his feet, but he had no room in which to maneuver, and it was only a matter of time before those claws savaged him. A few good strokes from them—or probably only one—and he would be out of the battle.

Jakc lcaped into the air. That damn tail! A swipe from it such as he had barely avoided would break both legs!

The thorik expected the jump. Its arm lashed out, catching the man squarely and slamming him against the wall.

Karmikel lay still, stunned, blood running from his nose and mouth. His mind fought desperately to dispel the unconsciousness threatening to engulf him, to bring his body into action again before his foe moved in for the kill. By some miracle, his dagger was still in his hand, and he did not have to grope for it.

His attacker gave him little time in which to recover. It caught him up, pinning his knife hand to his side, and held him in what amounted to a wrestler's hold.

It used all its great strength to bend him backward. The pain became almost unbearable. The Noreenan struggled to free himself but could not. In a few more seconds, his power to resist would be gone.

His right hand was still free. He did not know what if any use it would be, but he forced it to move, to come into contact with the other. His fingers closed over the hilt of the knife.

The thorik was bending all its concentration on what it was doing and seemed scarcely aware of its victim's increasingly more feeble struggle.

The dagger was free! Without pausing even to strengthen his hold on it, he drove it deep into the creature's side. The thorik screamed in agony and fought to tear him away. It succeeded, but as it doubled over from the resulting pain, Jake struck again. The dagger went home, sheathing itself in the hunter's heart.

The thorik screamed a final time. It was mortally hurt, but with its last strength, it strove to slay its killer. It fell forward, its powerful jaws closing on the Commando's throat . . .

* * *

Islaen's eyes closed. Her very bones seemed to radiate weariness, and she longed for nothing more at the moment than to be back at base and snuggled up in her sleeping bag.

She roused herself after a couple of minutes and looked from one to the other of her comrades. Both were tired even as she was, but there was a satisfaction on them that required no special gift to read. They had accomplished everything they had set out to do and had done it with well-nigh theoretical perfection. They had cause to be pleased with themselves. "I guess you two can count yourselves genuine Commandos after this one," she told them.

"I wouldn't mind that," Bethe Danlo replied in a sleepy voice. "You get paid on a heck of a better scale than the rest of us mere mortals." She leaned back comfortably. "You'd be more interested in the glory of the transfer, I suppose, Admiral?"

"I do not know," their driver replied in keeping with the women's mood. "Mine is not entirely an impractical race, and I do have to keep our feathered comrade in chocolate somehow."

Yes! Bandit's answer came quickly and eagerly although the humans had believed her to be in a deep sleep. The whistle that accompanied it told Bethe her answer, although the Sergeant was deaf to her mind talk.

Varn scowled. "This is all your fault, you know, Colonel Connor. Synthetic sweets abound throughout the ultrasystem, and you had to introduce her to all the genuine articles."

The Noreenan sniffed. "Synthetics! I wouldn't eat them myself, much less pawn them off on a gurry!"

"That, Colonel, is why she is spoiled." He would have given the little hen a playful poke with his finger had they been alone, but with the demolitions expert watching, he felt constrained to confine himself to a verbal exchange.

Bandit's not spoiled! Bandit would eat them if she had to! Islaen laughed and translated that into oral speech for Bethe, who reached over the seat to stroke her.

"Aye, pet," the spacer assured her. "We all know you're very willing and very self-sacrificing when needs be, but no one's going to force you to do that. —Right, Islaen?"

"Right! Nothing but the best for our little friend. —Why don't you fly on ahead to the camp, love, and see if you can't get a treat out of Jake? He hasn't any more resistance to your wiles than Varn does."

Good! Bandit will go!

Islaen and Bethe both laughed, at her and at Sogan's glare.

"Never mind, Varn," the Colonel said in the end, taking pity on him. "We must all be a bit groggy for want of sleep. We'll rectify that as soon as we reach base."

Several minutes passed in silence. Suddenly the two in the front seat straightened as a terrified call rang in their minds.

Islaen! Varn! Jake and a big animal! Dead! Hurt! Hurry!

"A thorik!" Disjointed as they were, the visual images accompanying the jumbled, panic-stricken transmission were clear enough to tell her that much. "Move, Varn! On all burners. The son's got Jake!"

The flier tore into the clearing. Even as it jerked to a halt, they caught the animal's smell.

"Cover me," Islaen Connor commanded as she sprang to the ground. Bandit reported that both contestants were still out and that the thorik would not move again under its own power, but none of them was about to risk that she might be wrong in her fear and excitement.

The Commando pushed into the shelter, lighting her raditorch as she did. Her companions followed after her, blasters drawn and set to slay.

Two bodies were there as Bandit had reported, one lying atop the other. The thorik's teeth gripped Karmikel's throat, frozen even as they had closed.

"Varn, help me!" If Jake still lived, it was imperative to remove the crushing weight of the carcass from him before it stopped his chest from expanding altogether.

It took some time to pry the stiffening, tightly clamped jaws loose from his throat, then, working together, they rolled the thorik aside. Jake was covered with blood, but they could not immediately determine whether it was his own or his attacker's.

Bethe knelt beside him. She looked up at Sogan, her eyes huge with dread, but her fingers were steady as they pressed the redhead's neck in the same moment, seeking a pulse in the carotid artery.

"Islaen?" Sogan asked. He, too, was afraid. The Commando-Captain had been a good friend to him and a good friend to Islaen Connor. He did not want to see him die.

"He's alive." Her mind confirmed that even before Bethe detected the faint but steady pulse.

The blond woman moved aside to give her full room for her examination. Sogan's hand closed on Bethe's shoulder, but he did not speak either to her or to his wife.

What would Islaen find? Their renewer could take care of broken bones, damage to muscle and skin, to nerves or blood vessels, even to a great extent to the head, but it could not repair the organs of the chest or abdomen. With no access to regrowth equipment, they could offer little more than support and prayer if Jake Karmikel had sustained serious injury to any of them.

When Islaen raised her head and faced them, she was smiling. "He'll be all right. He's taken a hell of a beating, and he'd be sore as the galaxy's wide if it weren't for the renewer, but there's no sign of what I'd feared to find, praise Anath and the Spirit of Space." Her mouth hardened momentarily. "If Bandit hadn't gotten us here when she did, it might've been different. I don't know how much longer he could've continued drawing air against that weight."

She started playing the renewer over him, sweeping the healing ray slowly up and down the length of his body. "He'll probably sleep through until morning. He was pretty spent as it was."

So were they all, the Arcturian thought, but that was not going to help any of them for a while. He examined the slain creature grimly and rather gingerly. To have fought that monster with only a knife . . .

"I don't suppose we can afford to just dump this or burn it?"

Islaen looked up. "Hardly. It'll have to be buried."

"I will get the flier," he said with a sigh. "There is no point in our lugging it farther than we must."

By the time he returned with the vehicle, the Colonel had laid aside the healing ray and taken her place at the thorik's feet to help him lift the big corpse. "I'll go with you. Bethe had best remain here with Jake. Bandit, you stay as well. If he starts to go sour, call us back fast."

TWENTY

KARMIKEL GROANED AS he opened his eyes. "Who dropped that mountain on me?"

"No one dropped anything on you, you big ape," Bethe told him sharply as she knelt beside him, "but that'd be nothing compared with what'll happen to you if you ever give me a scare like this again."

He just grinned. "Now isn't that something to look forward to all my married life?"

The others joined them, and he sat up. "What time is it anyway?"

"Late afternoon. The next day," the Colonel told him. "How do you feel?"

He tested himself. "Fine. I can thank the renewer for that, I suppose?"

"Aye, and some old-fashioned good luck. You had a near miss, my friend. —Take it easy for tonight. If you feel up to it, you can come with us in the morning. Otherwise you can stay behind and look after the base."

"I'll go with you," the redhead told her flatly. "I'm not sick. What do you have in mind? The command center?"

She shook her head. "Not yet. An Fainne. We shouldn't put off paying our call on the King any longer."

Jake nodded, but he was quiet for a few moments. "Islaen," he said at the end of that time, "I've been thinking. We don't need Coronus' help. We've already got the Foresters, and we aren't even planning to draw much on them. Why bother with An Fainne at all?"

"I don't intend to use the palace for help. This is strictly a courtesy visit, though I may not choose to stress that fact, at least at first."

"Why go at all, then? I can almost guarantee that it won't be a pleasant visit."

"Because I'm the Federation's representative here as well as a military commander. Coronus is ruler over the major part of Anath's populace, and as such he has a right to a report about this invasion as long as we haven't reason to fear for our safety or our mission by talking with him. I don't believe that we do."

"No," he agreed slowly. "We may get a cool reception, but I can't see any of our old comrades betraying us, Coronus of An Fainne included."

"I'd pick up any hint of treachery in good time anyway." Her face tightened. "Courtesy aside, those people are in real if not immediate danger. They have to be warned, and directly. We can't depend that information passed to Xenon through Vanya's people will be sufficient to secure their safety."

"Will Coronus listen? Or act?"

"That's another matter."

"What can he do?" the Sergeant asked. "He can't fight them."

"No, or save An Fainne either if those Britynon sons decide to blast it, but he can guard his followers."

"How?" She frowned. "Why didn't the Arcturians find the palace anyway? They were long enough on-world, and from what you've told us, it's a reasonably significant structure."

"Of course they found it, but they believed it to be a long-abandoned ruin and simply didn't bother with it, apart from checking it out periodically to make sure no guerrillas had moved in. They could've leveled it, I suppose, but to give them their due, they let it be."

"Was it abandoned in actuality?" Sogan inquired curiously.

"Oh, aye. When the Queen heard of the invasion and learned of the newcomers' weapons and that they had the power of flight, she realized it couldn't be hidden and ordered her people to take to the woods. Apart from those attached to An Fainne itself, the populace is so scattered and lives in such low concentrations that concealment was easy for them.

"It wasn't so remarkable that Magdela took correct stock of the situation and left a building complex behind to save her people and government, but the steps she took to preserve the place sure as space were. She had all the furnishings, the wood paneling, everything of that nature removed and then had her folk so treat An Fainne as to make it appear like a remarkably well-preserved ruin centuries old, and not a dwelling or government center either, but a temple. The Anathi drew on their legends and what was remembered of the old priest-king days to design it since they use no churches or images now."

She shook her head in an amazement that had not faded with the years. "How a woman who had never before encountered any people but her own and the nearly identical Foresters could have come up with a ruse like that, I'll never know, but it was the perfect touch. It was precisely what your people expected of such primitives. They accepted the idea completely. Since Arcturians never took any interest in exoarchopology or natural phenomena, they didn't have the expertise to detect any flaws in the execution, and believe me, there weren't many to find." Islaen smiled. "When Morris saw that piece of handiwork, he lost all worry about our allies. Primitive or not, he knew we were dealing with pros."

"The present King appears not to be of the same quality."

She sighed. "No. —Magdela might have been created specifically to meet Anath's great need. At times she seemed more someone out of mythology than a real woman, so well did she meet the crisis of the invasion, and her line before her had been nearly equally good. Her father was a strong, wise ruler, and his father and that King's mother. Those four were responsible during their long reigns for forging the scattered remnants of their people into a strong, vital race once more.

"Poor Coronus simply isn't made of the same stuff. He can be a fine ruler, just and thoughtful, but he doesn't have his forebears' strength or their charisma. It's hard to follow greatness, especially several generations of greatness. —We might be wronging him, too. Coronus was young when Jake and I knew him, and the boy and the man are often totally different people."

"Maybe," Bethe Danlo said somewhat abruptly; spacer youth had to mature fast in their demanding environment, and her kind regarded the prolonged adolescence enjoyed by so many on-worlders with contempt. "Suppose he refuses to listen to us, for whatever reason?"

Islaen shrugged. "We'll have done our part. Xenon has the authority to force an evacuation, and even if he chooses not to use it, I can't see too many being willing to sit down and wait for doom to land on their heads, much less expose their families to the same fate, to fit some pique of the King's. These Anathi're nothing if not levelheaded."

"Suppose he simply orders them to stay?"

"An Fainne's King rules by the consent of his people, and there are all too many others of his blood well able to replace him should he ever overstep his bounds."

Sogan's brows raised. "Sounds like ideal seeding ground for palace revolution," he remarked.

"Not really. The King's office carries a lot of responsibility and work, with, as I've said, only moderate authority to compensate. The ruler does live in comfort by Anathi standards, but there's no want on Anath and nothing of what the inner-systems would call wealth, no enormous disparity in life-style between the highly and lower born. Add to that the fact that the love and adulation of the populace goes to the Warlord, and you can see why the crown is regarded as much as a heavy duty as a privilege."

The war prince only shook his head. She smiled, understanding the doubts he was taking care to screen. "I know," she said. "With a larger population or in a more complex society, or with a race bound by another ethic, it probably wouldn't work. Maybe in another few centuries it no longer will work, but here and now on Anath of Algola, it does."

Sogan remained within his own thoughts a great deal for the remainder of that day and while they checked out and loaded their vehicle the following morning.

He again took the passenger seat since Islaen's familiarity with the route made it reasonable for her to handle the controls. He kept his own council until they were well under way, but then he at last broached the subject that had been troubling him.

Islaen?

Aye?

The woman knew something had been bothering him, but she had long since learned to let Sogan make his own approach when he seemed hesitant about discussing any matter. Press him too strongly or prematurely, and he was likely to retreat into himself entirely.

You made yourself speak for Coronus last night, he said after a moment, *but you do not like him. Neither does Jake. Why?* Varn saw her frown and half decided to drop the question, but he was concerned and continued. *My reasons for reacting unfavorably to some people might not strike you as logical or even tolerable, but I have never known that to be the case with either of you. Did he give you that much trouble?—Islaen, we are risking our lives on this hole of a planet, fighting alone because of a surplanetary situation that this King is at least responsible for exacerbating. I know you say you believe you can trust him, but . . .*

Power down, Varn. If I were worried about treachery or anything more serious than some unpleasantness from him, I wouldn't be trying to conceal the fact. We wouldn't be going at all. Don't you have any faith in me?

She scowled, not at him but at the situation in general. *No, I don't care for Coronus of An Fainne. It's impossible to like everyone. Personalities do clash, and that's what happened here. In spades. The situation was just such that any friction was going to be bad. We managed well enough—we all knew we had no choice about that—but it wasn't always easy.*

The Noreenan was quiet for several minutes while she gave her attention to guiding their flier through an exceptionally closely set stand of trees. When they were clear of it again, she took up her tale once more.

We told you already that Coronus was a difficult person with his presumptions and temper. Even his hotheaded brand of courage could be more trouble than benefit if it wasn't carefully monitored. Only his youth excused him at all . . .

His youth! Varn snapped impatiently. *Was he a child, then? I assume you fought beside others as young both here and on Thorne.*

Many, she admitted. *His cousin Herald's a year his junior and was twice the soldier.* Her eyes narrowed. *You're opposing him pretty strongly yourself. You have from the start. What have you got against him, Varn?*

Personally, nothing, he replied slowly. *It is chiefly what I picked up from the Warlord during our interview with him.* The Arcturian paused, collecting his thoughts and trying to separate them from his dislike of Anath's race as a whole. *That one is a sound man, Islaen, steady, thoughtful. I may not agree with his patience in this matter, but it is clear that he is a good officer and a conscientious leader. He truly grieves for what is happening and fears where it all might lead. I, for one, do not trust the source of that difficulty.*

You admit that and yet you would have had to compel yourself by force of will to take his hands had Xenon offered them to you, Islaen thought wearily. *I don't like the sound of any of that either,* she agreed. *It's proof that Coronus hasn't lost his other major flaw. His jealousy of Xenon has if anything worsened.* Her eyes darkened. *He used to be violently jealous of Morris and was only a little better with Jake and Tomas.*

So you have mentioned. —What about you and Babaye?

Oh, we were mere women and no threat, though I must admit the Anathi got over that rot a lot quicker than some supposedly advanced groups we've dealt with. I suppose the Queen's strength and An Fainne's history of female rulers helped establish us, that and the active role the Forester women were playing. She shrugged. *Whatever about that, neither of us ran into real hostility from him, not the way our men did.*

Her consort smiled. *Naturally not. You were strangers, and not just outsiders like the forest women but total aliens. You would not be expected to behave properly.*

Islaen Connor stared at him for a moment, then broke into soundless laughter. *I wouldn't have put it quite like that, but you're precisely right. Female service personnel, and to a lesser extent spacers, run into that more often than you'd think on planets with relatively isolated societies. It's annoying as all the Federation's hells, but it does let us get on with our work without undue interference, and so we don't usually gripe about it.*

The Federation soldiers went first to Vanya to inform her of what they had learned regarding the invaders and also to be certain Xenon was not in the forest that day. They would want the Warlord in An Fainne when they had their meeting with its King.

Before leaving, they arranged to have a watch kept on the sky for any sign of enemy aircraft sweeping over the treelands. That would be a signal that the Britynons were seeking the Anathi stronghold, either in the wake of the Commandos' work or because their own tests were completed. Destruction would follow fast upon its discovery, and the on-worlders would want as much advance warning as possible to escape its worst consequences.

That done, they set out in earnest for the palace. Their journey was a long one, for it lay well to the south, but at last they came to the chief seat of Xenon's people.

The two newcomers to Anath stared at it in awe. They had expected to see a cot like Vanya's meeting place, larger in size, perhaps surrounded by a palisade of logs, but nothing more. The structure before them was something else entirely, a major fortification and a stupendous feat of engineering for so primitive a people.

It was a vast fortress of solid rock surrounded by four distinct barriers so that, if one circle fell, the defenders could drop back to the next, stronger wall. The gates piercing them were massive, and they were not set in a line. Each was placed a quarter around the circle from the one before it. Attackers could not break through them one after the other in a single surging charge but would have to form up and attack each succeeding entrance anew, always under the fire of the defenders. In the center were low buildings, fortresses in themselves, the palace of the King and the living quarters of his chief supporters. As long as food and water held out within, it would be next to impossible to take the place by any form of warfare known on a technologically undeveloped world like Anath of Algola.

"Incredible," whispered Bethe Danlo.

"Aye," her fiancé agreed, "that it is. An Fainne was built soon after Xenon's people left the highlands. They still had most of their old knowledge and capabilities then. They've lost a lot of ground since and may well lose more before they start to climb back again." He shook his head in regret. "Already there are some who see this as the handiwork of ancestral superfolk rather than of men like themselves."

"A real pity."

"Truly," Varn interjected, "and even this will be lost to them if we cannot stop these Britynons in time. —Do we just fly up, announce ourselves, and request an audience with their King?"

"Almost precisely," the Commando-Colonel replied. "In keeping with Anathi custom, we'll go directly to Xenon's own palace," she added, pointing to what appeared to be the finest of the smaller buildings. "That'll be a clear declaration both of the gravity of our visit and its nature. Coronus will then either send for us or come to us, but he will have to include Xenon in our discussion. Even in the unlikely event that he refuses to see us at all, we would still be able to formally meet with the Warlord."

"Which would probably be to everyone's advantage," muttered Karmikel.

"All right, Jake," she warned.

Her fingers touched Bandit's back. *Stay close, love. We'll be needing you in there.*

Bandit will help!

Thanks, love, she said gloomily. *I have a feeling that you'll have your work cut out for you on this one.*

The off-worlders were admitted readily, and the two Commandos received warm greetings from the guards and from those who gathered within the complex to meet them when news of their arrival spread. No one delayed them long, however, or showed any surprise when they made for the Warlord's dwelling instead of for the palace itself.

Xenon did not welcome them himself, but a liegeman threw open the door for them and asked them inside, promising to bring word of their coming to his lord and to the King.

The four looked about them curiously, for even Islaen and Jake had never seen An Fainne as it was meant to be. The exterior of the building was forbidding, as must be the case with all places constructed with defense as the primary consideration. The room in which they found themselves was of a different nature. It was light and airy, looking out on a large pleasure garden. The furnishings were basically of the Spartan nature to be expected in a society relatively poor in large-scale possessions, but what there was showed a surprising touch of luxury, the belongings of a soldier and a prince.

They were not given long to study their surroundings. The door opened, and two men came in. One, the foremost, was typical of his race, well muscled with a pleasant face only slightly marred by the signs of pride and temper stamped on it, which the two familiar with his kind were well able to read. He wore a long cape of green velvet. That plus his bearing and the richly worked silver skullcap covering his black hair proclaimed him to be Coronus, King of An Fainne.

His companion was of more singular appearance, notable even to the off-worlders. He was taller than most of his people but comparatively slight of build with finely wrought, almost feminine features. If prettiness in a man was admired on Anath, Bethe thought as she studied him, he was probably counted very handsome. Despite his delicately elegant appearance, though, he was patently not some court fop. His eyes were brave and intelligent, and the grace of his movements did not speak of a life of constant ease. His unconscious habit of keeping his hand within inches of his weapon of a certainty did not.

He smiled with genuine warmth when he saw his old comrades, but he remained silent. Custom demanded that he allow the King to speak first.

Coronus bade the Federation soldiers welcome but did not extend his hands in the personal greeting the Warlord and Forester Chieftainess had offered. He was King now and would do nothing that might reduce the dignity of his position before these off-world warriors.

Islaen Connor's chin lifted. So. If it was a game of images that he wanted, she was well trained and prepared to play it.

She held herself straight, as the Anathi themselves did before those legitimately bearing authority, but she did not give him the salute he had so often seen the members of her old unit accord the Queen, his mother. Her own greeting was as ritualized as his, as befitted the representative of one sovereign people to another, respectful certainly, but with no trace of subservience or sense of lesser before greater rank.

He scowled, but his eyes flickered to her companions in that moment and widened in shock. "What have you brought on us, woman?" he demanded furiously.

This was different from his previous posturing. Coronus' anger was real and in a sense well founded, and real, too, was his instinctive surge of fear at the sight of the war prince. The Noreenan glanced at Varn with an inner sigh, wondering for the thousandth time if he would ever truly be free of this and knowing full well that he would not.

Sogan himself was not helping matters, she thought. He was responding to the Anathi's petty arrogance with his own stronger pride and the old bearing of his line. He looked every inch the Arcturian officer and ruler he had once been. Anyone who had suffered under his Empire could not but react as Coronus was doing, aye, and with violence as well once surprise crystallized into action.

Her expression hardened visibly. "Navy Captain Sogan is second to me in our unit," she informed both Anathi coldly. "He is a much-decorated officer, and his valor has won him not only the citizenship of two planets but the love of their people as well. He is not to be faulted for his appearance, nor is it of any importance to our current mission. The fact that he has come in my company should in itself be testimony enough of his worth for you."

Islaen, do not beg . . .

This would be my answer if you were a Federation-born man.

The second Anathi took a quick step forward, extending his hands in Anath's traditional gesture of welcome. "Your pardon for my staring, Captain Sogan. We of Anath do not see many people of other races, and your resemblance to the Red Ones is striking."

Varn's hands clasped his seemingly without hesitation, although he had to brace himself to meet their touch. The ridiculous sensation that he was in the presence of gigantic ravagers was gone, praise whatever gods ruled this place, but the man was still a mutant. Something deep inside him felt defiled by that contact with him, short-lived though it was. "No matter," he said calmly, "I have encountered similar trouble elsewhere."

Islaen breathed an inner sigh of relief. *Well done, Varn.*

He flung his answer back into her mind. *Did you think I would blow the mission and maybe our lives for the sake of my pride?*

It was a situation that could very easily have been mishandled, she responded calmly.

It still is, he replied, forcing himself to be mollified. *It could too readily turn sour on us.*

Coronus had recovered himself and now stepped forward as well, acknowledging the off-worlder's position as his guest. He might want no part of this man, whom he still saw as one of their old enemies, and an officer of theirs to judge by his bearing, but that made no difference. A visitor to his stronghold was entitled to courtesy, whatever his purpose in coming, aye, or his race. He had very nearly failed badly in that charge. "You have Anath's welcome, Captain, as do your comrades."

"She is a brave world," Sogan responded evenly. "We are privileged to be here to serve her."

Islaen introduced Bethe and mentioned Jake's new rank, then the King presented the Lord Herald, his cousin, to the two strangers.

Bandit had been watching the proceedings from the place she had quietly chosen for herself above the door. She judged that the time had come for her to enter into the meeting. Whistling shrilly to draw the humans' attention, she fluttered down to the tall back of a chair placed near where the two Anathi were standing.

Bandit doesn't like this King! she grumbled as her toes closed over the intricately carved wood.

Do the best you can, Islaen told her. *Try not to make any of us look silly. He sets too great a store by the form of dignity, and we can't afford at this stage to lose status in his eyes.*

Bandit will try.

The gurry made a bobbing motion in the ruler's direction that he could not but take for a completely accidental bow. Coronus laughed, softly, with gentle humor rather than vanity, and like nearly every human not utterly debased who came into contact with one of the small mammals, he put out his hand to her in delight. She responded to the caress with such a storm of purring that she seemed to be in danger of falling off her perch.

"A mascot?" he asked. "What sort of beast is it?"

"Bandit's a gurry, a native of a planet called Jade of Kuan Yin. She attached herself to us there."

The hen flew to Herald and pretended to examine him, then went to Islaen, first pausing to receive a seemingly casual pat from her dark-eyed companion.

The Colonel mentally voiced both her thanks and her admiration. Bandit's entrance had been perfectly timed and masterfully handled, and the level of hostility in the room had dropped enormously.

"An attractive addition to your party," the King said. He paused only momentarily. "Some are missing whom I would have thought to find with you. What has become of our other comrades?" In truth, he was relieved to find two of the men with whom he had clashed in the past apparently gone from the guerrilla unit, but both simple courtesy and curiosity compelled him to inquire about them.

"Tomas and Babaye have left the Navy and are pursuing their lives as civilians. Morris didn't survive the War. He was slain within the year after leaving Anath."

"A brave and strong man," he said after a brief silence. "I am sorry for your loss."

Coronus' mind returned to the present. "That War is over and the Red Ones are gone, my friends. Why have you come to Anath again?"

"It's a rather long story," the Commando-Colonel replied cautiously. "We'll do best to wait until Xenon's here and spare all of us the repetition of it." Coronus knew as well as she that the Warlord must be present at such a discussion, and from past experience, she was not about to put much trust in this man's military judgment or expertise.

"I am King!"

Islaen feigned surprise. "Would you have us violate An Fainne's custom, its very law, Crowned One?"

The Anathi caught himself. "No. Certainly not, and you are unquestionably right that there would be no point in going over it all again. The Warlord will be here shortly. He was just detained outside. —Herald, will you see if he is not coming now?"

"Aye, Crowned One," the other man said and went quickly from the room, though not so speedily as to betray his eagerness to have the war leader present. Were it not for the Noreenan woman's talent, there would have been no indication whatsoever that he had not been pleased with the composition of the gathering.

I would put a month's credits down that Xenon was detained all right, Varn Tarl Sogan muttered darkly as he watched the Anathi lord disappear through the door.

Mine'd match yours, his wife agreed. *Coronus appears to take a lot on himself these days.*

A great sight too much!

Herald soon returned, this time accompanied by An Fainne's Warlord.

As he had done at their first meeting, Xenon clasped the hands of his former comrades. He started convincingly when he turned to the Arcturian, but there was laughter in his eyes when they touched momentarily with Sogan's. To Islaen's surprise, Varn's returned it, although she felt him cringe as their hands met.

Once the formalities of welcome were ended, Islaen Connor carefully detailed what she had learned about the new invaders and their intentions and described her party's successful raid on the arsenal. She concluded with her suggestion that An Fainne be evacuated at once and that it be stripped so that the loss of the buildings would not leave Anath's people bereft of all their major treasures. Finally she asked that watch be kept on the sky, even as the Foresters were doing farther north, though she was careful to make no other mention of the extent or nature of her dealings with them.

Coronus' anger had grown sharply as she continued to speak, to the point that Bandit's power could no longer check it. Now he glared openly at her. "So once more you would have Anath's warriors crouch like junners in their holes while others fight their battles for them—this time against your own people?"

"Not *my* people!" the woman answered sharply. "They're one of the many other races comprising my ultrasystem and will be punished for the wrong they've attempted here. As for the rest, you know full well that you're not capable of facing the Britynons' weapons."

"Then, damn you, woman, arm us and train us to use those arms!"

She sighed. "I can't. By Queen Magdela's own decision . . ."

"My mother is dead. I rule now."

"The choice—the wise choice—she made still stands. Even if she had willed otherwise, my own government would've insisted upon leaving your world untouched. —Think, man! Our goods and our numbers would destroy what you are, prevent you and yours from ever attaining what Anath intends for you to become. That must not happen."

His mouth twisted. "Neither must this! Not a second time."

His eyes narrowed, altering his face unpleasantly. "You claim these newcomers are criminals and intend us great ill, but we have only your word for that. They have not shown any sign of hostility against us, little though we might admire their actions here. They might prove better friends to us than you now are." His lips curled into a sneer. "At least they do not travel in company with former enemies of ours and, supposedly, of yours. —Or is this second sword of yours but a renegade, a traitor to his own kind?"

A deadly silence fell on the room.

Searing fury poured from the war prince, although as yet he was outwardly frozen behind a wall of superiority and almost palpable contempt.

He's not worth . . . Islaen began in alarm. If Sogan let loose either with his blaster or his hands, they would face a war with An Fainne. That she did not want, and they could ill afford it with the invading navy still to be countered.

I would not soil myself with this misbegotten filth!

The gurry listened to them unhappily, knowing that for once her gift had failed her humans. *Bandit can't help!* she wailed. *King won't listen!*

I know, little Bandit, the Noreenan told her. *It's not your fault. I'll have to handle this one.* If she could. She, too, was furious. That was appropriate and need not be concealed entirely, but she dared not lose control of herself or, to any greater degree, of the situation.

The Colonel's head raised. Her eyes flashed dangerously although her voice was icily still. "Very well, Coronus of An Fainne. You have made it clear that you remain the scant man you always were. Now understand this. These renegades are going to be brought to justice. They have to be, or countless other worlds would face the threat of the same peril that presently shadows Anath. That is the Federation's concern, and you have no say in it at all, whether you choose to believe the reality of the need or not."

The King eyed her coldly. "I do not believe it. It is my thought that you are the enemy, that you have come to work these strangers ill and Anath ill. I want you back where you came from. If you do not go at once . . ."

The woman silenced him with an impatient gesture of her hand. "Don't even think it! —You bloody, pride-besotted fool! You'll never be a ruler in fact until you learn to stop meddling to your great discredit where you have no right of decision!"

She pointedly turned away from him entirely.

"Xenon, this King of yours has given us no choice but to work alone. Do what you want about an evacuation of An Fainne, but I'm telling you now that those renegades must be eliminated even as I've said. My party will try to confine the battle as much as is feasible to our own forces and to theirs, but if Coronus gives us trouble, my Navy will come in, to the great sorrow of all this part of Anath."

Once more she looked at the Anathi ruler, contemptuously. "Don't misjudge the strength of our purpose or my government's in this, Coronus. What has to be done will be. We can't afford to act otherwise, not to spare one ill-advised people and their unfortunate planet."

The man's eyes locked with hers but soon fell. He knew the guerrilla leader well enough from past experience to recognize that she meant precisely what she said. It was no threat or blackmail demand, just a statement of irrevocable fact. Try to thwart these guerrillas, and he would bring disaster and maybe annihilation upon his people.

"Very well," he snarled. "Fight your war on my victimized world, and may ill strike every one of you as a result. As you have said, you will fight it alone. The men of Anath will stand no sky watch for you or give you any other aid, and there will be no convenient evacuation while you threaten to shatter the proof of my race's greatness . . ."

Here he stopped himself. "No. I am responsible to my people. That suggestion I will discuss with my Warlord and my councilors and will abide by their judgment, but the rest that I have said will hold."

"See that you cause us no difficulty. The rest is Anath's business and of no concern to us. Your Warlord will have to act as he deems best and hope that you can escape unscathed from whatever is to come."

With that, she turned on her heel and, signaling her companions to follow, swept out of the room.

TWENTY-ONE

JAKE KARMIKEL LEANED over the seat of the flier. "Say the word, Islaen. My fingers'd fit very nicely around that chunky throat of his."

"Never mind, Jake. We didn't expect a rapturous greeting from him."

"You actually worked with that cur?" Bethe demanded incredulously. "You should've collected a couple of citations for that, whatever you did with the Arcturians! —You tore him a new set of fins for a fact, Islaen, but you should've gone on and mined his nuggets proper. You could've had them, too. He broke a lot of what you've told us are Anathi laws and customs in there."

"It's Xenon's business, and maybe Herald's, to take care of that." She pressed her fingers to her forehead to combat the headache she felt forming and which she knew would be throbbing fiercely before she had a chance to swallow tablets from their first-aid kit to counter it. "It's all to our benefit. We don't have to concern ourselves with An Fainne now. We'll function more smoothly without having to consult with them or worry about including any of them, with the possible exception of Xenon, in our plans. If we do need help, which I doubt we shall, we can get it in plenty from the forest."

A smile brightened her weary face as she gently ran her fingers down the gurry's back. "Things would probably have turned out even worse if it hadn't been for our little friend."

Bandit tried to do more! the Jadite mammal said unhappily.

"You did everything that was possible by getting rid of the irrational hostility. Coronus' anger is real and, if rather badly

172

twisted, is still based on some solid substance. He and his fellow
Anathi have every reason to be furious over this second invasion
of their world from the stars. It's also perfectly natural that he
should want to actively defend her."

"King Coronus is a menial boor," Varn Tarl Sogan snapped.

"A boor, aye, at least with us, but his claim to royalty's sound
enough." Her eyes closed. The Arcturian was still fuming. She
was not about to check him, but she felt too spent to put up with
any more anger at this stage.

She could not ignore him, either. He had kept his temper when
the natural response of any member of the Arcturian warrior caste
to such an insult would have been to burn the offender down
where he stood.

I appreciated your holding on in there, she told him. *Killing
Coronus or slamming him through a wall would've meant a lot of
bloodshed besides.*

*I know. You have friends you value here. That on top of our
mission kept me from finishing him.*

He scowled. *He was right in a sense. I am a renegade . . .*

Don't ever let me hear rot like that again! she snapped. *You
know a hell of a lot better. —By all the old gods,* she muttered,
*there are times, and this is one of them, when I wish I'd stayed on
Noreen, married one of our neighbor's sons, and spent my life
raising fine angora steers.*

That idea might have been possible once, but it was now so
ludicrous that Sogan laughed, completely casting off the weight
that had suddenly settled on him. *Think of all the excitement you
would have missed.*

*I'd have missed a lot of aggravation I could well do without,
too.*

*That would have come anyway. It is part of being alive. Only
the source would have been different.* His mood sobered. *I am
sorry to have been the cause of it this time. That brand of self-pity
is detestable.*

It was unworthy of you.

They fell silent for a few seconds. The man flexed his shoulders
to work some of the stiffness out of them. *Space, but I am tired!
I feel as if I had spent a day and a night in battle.*

That makes us a pair. She yawned and said aloud, "No one's
trailing us. Drive on for another hour, and we'll hunt up a
campsite. Once we've all had a good sleep, I want to hit the
Britynons again.

* * *

It was well into the night by the time the Federation party found
a suitable place and set up their camp. They ate a hurried meal,
and those not on watch bedded down.

Islaen Connor believed all her companions were asleep, although she did not bother scanning them, and so she was surprised
when the war prince joined her near the end of her tour on guard.
His mind touched hers briefly in greeting, but he said nothing to
her. She felt the power streaming out from him as he searched the
night around them and held her peace as well.

Varn's eyes closed. He was physically tired, but his senses were
alert to the signals of this vibrant world. Anath was silent tonight
or nearly so. There were few insects to hum and chirp, and the
forest animals normally browsed or hunted by day or twilight.
Only the night birds were active in number. Their songs trilled
from a myriad of invisible perches, hauntingly beautiful as the call
of no day dweller could be. The swish of the branches in the mild
breeze and the quick rush of running water formed a fair backdrop
for their chorus.

His company could relax, for the time at least. All was well.
The life normal to the great forest was flowing smoothly around
them. There were hunters abroad, aye, along with the more
peaceful foragers, but that was part of nature's cycle. Nothing
abnormal, nothing human apart from themselves, was ranging this
night, not anywhere close to this place.

He looked at Islaen. *All is quiet,* he assured her.

*Aye. I'm not picking up anything beyond our patterns either.
—No stray thoriks?*

None, Colonel. He tried to study her, but the dark was too thick
to allow him a proper view of her face. *How is the headache?*

*Completely gone now. I should've known I wouldn't be able to
hide that from you.*

You should not have tried, he chided with good humor. He did
not announce minor weaknesses of his either.

Sogan's fingers brushed the back of her hand. He was uncertain
whether he should go on, but he knew the scene in An Fainne had
upset her, apart from its political implications. More, even before
the break had occurred, he had sensed her prepare to receive and
conceal a blow, and he wanted to offer her comfort and support.
He, too, understood loss, and he knew the burden of trying to bear
its pain alone.

*Coronus did not like Captain Martin, but he did not rejoice in
the news of his death.*

No. No, he did not, she replied slowly. *I was ready for that, but . . .* She just shrugged. *I had enough trouble holding my temper as it was.*

There is little else I can say in his favor, but he did appreciate your former commander's worth as an ally, even as a man. He scowled. *An Fainne's King is a poor excuse for a ruler. Xenon compares with him as a diamond to coal.*

Herald's a good man as well, she added quickly.

So I saw. He handled himself well in covering for both of them. —I am a nasty shock for these locals.

The shadow of a smile flickered on the woman's lips. Varn Tarl Sogan could look at himself with amusement for all his self-consciousness. *Most Anathi are worthy of a great deal of respect.* Her eyes fixed on his hard, fine face. *They're a reasonably comely people as well, Varn. Even your own officers stationed here believed the women might be of interest, at least to the lower ranks, to the point that they took measures to prevent the possibility of any disgrace coming of it.*

I should not have allowed that had I commanded this occupation! He stopped himself. *I could not condone it anywhere now.*

Now or before, Islaen Connor replied quietly. *You always came down damn hard on atrocity, even on Thorne of Brandine, and her populace was in no way objectionable to you.*

The Arcturian's head lowered. *I will always be a disappointment to you in this. I do not wish to respond as I do to so many of your ultrasystem's peoples, but it is impossible to discard everything that was drilled into me since the time I was conceived. Whatever my reason says, in my eyes and heart, your mutants and near mutants are not-acceptable.*

Don't, Varn, she said quickly. *It's not necessary. You've never betrayed yourself or us. Your control's just about perfect. I just wish you didn't have to draw on it so often.*

Islaen moved closer to him. His arm slipped around her shoulder. Its weight felt good there, and she sighed in contentment. *That's what I miss most on these missions. There's so little chance to be really alone with you.*

He held her closer, but when he made her no answer, either light or tender, she looked up at him. *What's the matter, Varn?*

Nothing really. I have been thinking about your previous stay here. It appears to have been very much Captain Martin's mission.

Aye, more than any other. Anath of Algola had his heart, the way Thorne later took mine, and that was reflected in his fighting, in everything he did here.

Her thoughts softened marvelously as she said that, and the man's lips brushed her hair. *You loved him, my Islaen?*

Aye, she replied, surprised. *A great deal.* She paused. *You don't grudge him that? Or me?*

No. I never have. It is only that Morris Martin is such a definite presence on this planet, and I have been wondering about him. About him and about you. His fingers traced the line of her cheek and the sensitive, exquisitely formed lips. *You loved each other, and yet you never became lovers?*

The woman stiffened. *You know very well that we didn't! When we married, I came to you a . . .*

I know, her husband assured her hastily, *but I have never understood why. Everything seemed to compel you to it with your future, the time left to you, so uncertain.*

Sogan fell silent then, and once more his fingers brushed her face. He had never dared raise this subject with her before and regretted having done so now. By what right did he question her? He could not yet easily talk about those the War had taken from him, those his own choice had destroyed. Did he imagine Islaen Connor felt her losses any less intensely? *Forgive me, my Islaen. I should never have reopened this wound, most especially not here.*

She shook her head slowly. *No. I cherish my memories of Morris. It'd be a sad testament to him if I couldn't recall or speak about him.*

All the same, despite her brave words, his consort drew away from him, and her shields raised over her inner mind. Varn cringed behind his own shields. It was his fault for having drawn barbs through her, but he could not now simply withdraw and leave her alone with the thoughts he had raised. *That should become easier with time. He was a fine man from all I have heard, one whose memory should rightly be honored. I am sorry I was never privileged to know him.*

You would've liked him, she said, *maybe more than any of the rest of us. You two were very alike.* The Commando's eyes closed. *We wasted so much time,* she whispered. *It wasn't until we were sent to Thorne that we decided to marry—a necessity for the success of any such relationship with a Noreenan partner—but by then, it was too late. Morris fell before we could make the arrangements.* She shuddered openly. *I'm glad Jake and Bethe aren't making the same mistake.*

Praise the Spirit of Space that we did not, he said, *that we recognized our minds and acted according to their dictates. We have taken everything that has been granted us.*

A hand cold as the depths of space seemed to close over Islaen's heart. *I couldn't bear to lose you, Varn, and we've come so close to that so often . . .*

Islaen . . . Sogan did not attempt to embrace her, not physically. She was fighting to regain her control, and a touch, even a movement from him, now would shatter her. His mind gently reached out to hers, asking her to open herself to him.

The woman accepted the comfort he offered, but only for a moment, then she was herself once more, strong, able, the battle leader of the Federation's most elite troubleshooters.

She smiled at him with lips and mind. *You are the finest thing that's ever happened to me, Varn Tarl Sogan,* she told him, *but now you'd best look to yourself for a while. Your watch'll come around all too soon and not long after that the morning. We'll need you fresh when we pay our next call on those glorious sons of Brityne.*

The guerrillas left their temporary camp with the first light and made for their base at the greatest possible speed. The fruitless interview was behind them, and the work they had come to Anath of Algola to perform had been delayed too long already because of it.

Although it was late in the day when they reached the camp, they did not remain there longer than was necessary to give their vehicle a thorough overhaul and load the additional supplies and munitions they would need to make their upcoming raid a success. Food and sleep they would take in turn on the move.

Nothing would be allowed to interfere with their war now. Commandos operating against a physically and numerically superior force had to keep their foes off balance, strike and strike again until all sense of security was shattered and the invaders lived in perpetual uncertainty, never knowing when the next blow would fall, never knowing who was against them or how many or how strongly armed. It had worked time and time again in the War, and it would work now. For Anath's sake, they had to make certain that it did work until the Navy arrived to finish off the threat for good.

All of them were silent as they started out. They appreciated full well that this attack was very different from their previous one, and the four humans felt daunted by the difficulties ahead of them. Only the gurry was at ease with respect to its outcome. Her confidence in her companions was such that she felt no concern about their ultimate success, although she quailed to think of the danger each one faced.

They had reason in plenty to be, if not cowed, at least humble, Islaen Connor thought grimly. The raid was important, and it was spectacular. The mere taking of that installation would be an astounding accomplishment, even without the evidence she hoped to secure there. It was heavily guarded and well armed, and the Britynons were as sure of it as they were of their own fleet, the more especially since it had been obvious from its condition when they found it that the Resistance had succeeded in inflicting almost no damage on it during the War. Its destruction would go far in crushing their morale.

If it could be destroyed. That was anything but a certainty. Indeed, to a conventional military mind, the building complex would have seemed well-nigh impregnable to any form of warfare likely to be conducted on Anath of Algola, by Commandos or by surplanetary soldiers. It was constructed entirely of huge stone blocks brought from the cliffs along the coast, reinforced and sheathed with top-grade solar steel. The windows were covered with shutters of the same metal, slotted to fit the muzzles of the defenders' pellet guns and blasters. These loopholes were so positioned that the whole of the surrounding area could be covered.

That was extensive. The complex was set on an artificial hill overlooking the countryside for miles in every direction, which was among the flattest stretches of land on all the prairie.

To further reduce the possibility of surprise attack, all possible cover had been removed from an area one hundred yards in diameter around the buildings, and every form of alarm at all effective on a Terra-normal planet had been employed to guard them. Nothing and no one should be able to approach it without the knowledge and will of those inside.

Perhaps that would prove the case despite all their experience. It might well turn out that they were fated to waste their strength and their lives attempting to accomplish the impossible. Commando teams had died trying to do that since their founding in the deadly days of the great War.

TWENTY-TWO

ALGOLA WAS NEWLY high the following morning when the Federation party reached the place where they would be forced to leave the cover of the treelands for the open plain. Islaen hesitated. It was contrary to her instincts and to all her deeply ingrained training to expose her unit to such a degree, but she only squared her shoulders and moved out onto the prairie. Their target was much farther than the arsenal had been and if they were to reach it before full nightfall, they would have to begin now.

She grew ever more cautious and more nervous as the day progressed. All of them did. They kept careful watch on their instruments and scanned the western sky every few seconds visually and with mind. The chance that an enemy patrol would venture so far inland was slim even with the knowledge that guerrillas were at last active on Anath of Algola, but they had too much experience with the quirks of fortune to ignore it.

The flier skimmed the top of the tall grass in nearly utter silence. The wake created by its air streams vanished almost as they formed so that their passage was all but unmarked. It was as efficient and safe a method of transportation as could be devised for the use of those in their profession, but all of them were heartily uncomfortable and would remain uncomfortable until they had completed their work and could disappear again into the protection of Anath's dark night. They appreciated too well that there was no way to conceal the nature of their vehicle should it be sighted. That black misfortune would call down an extensive hunt for them from the command center and from the fleet, one they would have great trouble avoiding while there was any light at all to guide it. None of them had any illusions about the outcome of a battle between the flier and a large, well-armed surplanetary wolf pack such as the invaders could doubtless put into the air in very short order.

Varn Tarl Sogan's thoughts ran along very similar lines to those of his consort although he was equally careful to conceal them behind tightly sealed shields. He knew the difficulties they faced, perhaps better in a sense than did any of his Federation-trained comrades. He had commanded buildings similarly defended, three of them, on Thorne of Brandine. They had been the only ones outside of his own headquarters that his enemies had either refrained from attacking entirely or had managed to damage only lightly. The Thornen Resistance had been a large, powerful organization, an army in truth. What could the four of them expect to accomplish where those others had failed?

To make matters worse, they were not even free to destroy and run. They had to penetrate the installation and search it for the evidence their ultrasystem's justice needed to tie the rulers of the Britynon planets to this atrocity and pull them down. What the invaders would be doing while they conducted that examination, he did not like to think.

There might be no purpose to it at all. Islaen was convinced they would find files in the center sensitive and explicit enough to give them what they wanted. He was not so sure and had pressed his argument strongly against banking on any such possibility. Of a certainty, he would never have kept material of that nature anywhere but on his own flagship, under his own charge, nor would any of the officers with whom he had served throughout the War.

Perhaps the Colonel was right, he thought wearily. Britynons were not soldiers of the Arcturian warrior caste, and this was not the time of active, formal war with all its threat of espionage. It was a supposedly secret invasion, and the command center, not the fleet, was very probably intended to become the core of on-world activities once colonists began arriving. In fact, it might even be the safest place to hold potentially incriminating material. An attack from space would focus on the starships, giving those stationed away from it time to destroy whatever their government would not wish Federation authorities to see . . .

He sighed in his mind. Time would tell which of them was right and whether they would live long enough to resolve the question at all.

* * *

Twilight was well advanced into near dark when the two buildings they sought at last appeared on the screen of their surplanetary viewer. Sogan, who had the controls, dropped the flier into the grass and, grabbing his pack, sprang from it.

His companions moved as quickly. None of them wanted to be anywhere near the machine if their enemies had detected its approach.

It took time, a seeming eternity, to work their way to the cleared area, but there was no help for that. They had to move carefully, so carefully that no motion, no violent agitation of the prairie grass, would alert Britynon guards or casual observers to their arrival. Even with the night almost fully on them, they dared not take any risk or leave any danger caution might avert to chance.

There was a long wait before the Commandos signaled that the alarms and the more active defense devices surrounding the outpost had been nullified. The invaders apparently respected the potential prowess of Federation-trained guerrillas and had tried to provide against their efforts, but they had made the mistake of using the same kinds of circuits, the same standard devices, for practically all of their safeguards. Specialists of Islaen's and Jake's caliber had little difficulty in ridding the field of its protection, although they had to exercise great care in doing it.

The few sentries were relaxed despite the fate of their comrades at the arsenal, depending on their alarms to warn them of danger. The Noreenan woman smiled coldly. Therein lay the peril of entrusting the task of vigilant humans entirely to manufactured tools.

The off-worlders moved with the utmost care, watching for any live devices the Commandos might have missed.

Karmikel and Connor stole upon the sentries, each in turn, and none but one knew death was upon him until it had come. The last turned, warned by some sixth sense, to see Jake as he leaped upon him. The Captain's fingers closed over his throat, preventing any outcry as his knife bit home.

His fall was Sogan's signal. He crept to the door of the single, large barracks, and as he had done on the previous assault, he set an energy picket around the building and attached a magnetic wedge so that those inside could not attack the Federation force en masse. He then ran for the entrance of the center itself.

Islaen and Bethe Danlo were already crouched there, examining it. The door was of heavy metal and could be opened only by a tiny, three-pronged key programmed with its specific code and held, no doubt, by the officer in charge.

His consort had already noted all that. From a pocket next to her skin, she took a piece of soft, flesh-colored material. This she kneaded in her hands for a few seconds. When she was satisfied with its consistency, she broke it into five roughly equal pieces that she molded to the door at key tension points. From a pouch on her belt, she took the hair-thin detonator fuses that would bring the compound to life.

Before she could attach them, their luck broke. The last man felled by Jake had not died immediately. His dazed mind rallied at last, enough to realize what was happening. Because there was nothing else he could do, he screamed. The cry, which ended in a horrible gurgle, rent the erstwhile still night with the force of a siren.

Those inside the barracks threw themselves at the door. When they found they were unable to move it, they turned to defend their installation from within. Flares created an artificial day, and a steady stream of pellets laced with sizzling blaster bolts poured from the loopholes. The picket could not stop energy or the tiny metal missiles as it did human-sized bodies.

It was a strange battle, more stalemate than fight. The invaders were secure enough, for the moment at least, in their stronghold but could not break out to overwhelm their grossly outnumbered attackers. The Federation soldiers by the door were shielded from their fire but could not maneuver into a position either to shoot back or to finish setting the charges without exposing themselves and being quickly cut down.

Jake Karmikel, the only one whose duties did not require him to enter the command center, was still free to act, and this he did with the cold efficiency of his profession. He watched the barracks until he got a sighting from the muzzle fire of a blaster or pellet gun, then loosed a narrow, deadly bolt directly at the spot. An occasional shower of impotent sparks told of a miss, but the Noreenan's aim was excellent, and the end was generally assured for the unfortunate soldier behind the slot.

The situation was not good. As with most guerrilla conflicts, the fight could not be allowed to go on too long, or help would assuredly arrive to relieve the beleaguered garrison, summoned either directly by transceiver or by the sight of the constantly renewed flares. Their brilliance would be seen and would call to the fleet in the otherwise unrelieved blackness of Anath's night.

Karmikel lay his blaster aside and quickly removed four bulky

cylinders from his pack. Each consisted of two parts, crown and
base, that could be rotated and fixed at a variety of settings.
Seemingly without thought, he adjusted and activated them and
almost casually sent them rolling over the dark ground toward the
building. One by one, each reached its target, settling softly, with
controlled force, against the wall so that it stopped without even
the faintest of clicks. Moments later, all four detonated as if they
were a single device, covering the whole wall with a curtain of
raging flame, blocking every window, every firing port.

The Commando nodded, satisfied. That would hold them for a
while. The defenders could not send a stream of chemicals
through the narrow slots, not enough to douse those fires.

Now Islaen moved swiftly. She set and activated the fuses and
flattened, signaling her companions to do the same.

For a breath's space, all remained still, then the door shattered
with a loud blast. The concussion that accompanied it was strong
but was less than might have been expected. The explosive had
been designed to waste as little energy as possible.

With the way opened before them, the three leaped into the
building, firing rapidly.

Varn held the point. A large crew was on duty inside, and they
were fully alerted to the attack by the battle raging outside,
although their orders held them to their own post to meet any
assault that might be launched against it. His task was to keep
them away from his comrades. Speed was essential now. Jake's
fires would keep going only so long, and that wedge he had put
under the barracks door would not hold forever. Once that went,
the defenders would be able to blast through the energy picket in
fairly short order.

The fighting was hard, bitter, but it could have been much
worse. The speed with which the guerrillas advanced took the
inner guards and staff by surprise and carried them before it,
making it easier to drop them.

Within minutes, they had gained the central chamber, that
which had once housed the Arcturian's heavy communications
apparatus. Now it was a vast information processing and storage
center.

A new dilemma faced them. None of them had anticipated
finding an operation of this magnitude at so early a stage in the
takeover. Given time or many hands, they could have searched the
material stored here and destroyed both the files they did not want
and the equipment for managing the data crowding the room.
They had neither. They could blast most of it with the remainder

of their explosives, but they could not read all this, not a fraction of it, and to miss what they needed most . . .

The Commando-Colonel refused to let herself accept defeat. There had to be order in the management of so much data. Figure out the Britynon's storage system, and she should have what she wanted.

Her brows drew together. It should be simple, something intended for their own use . . .

She studied the room. Shelves of tape cartridges and disks occupied two walls, so very many of them standing like soldiers in an army on parade behind the transparent panels guarding them from dust and accidental damage. Carefully, she scanned each line, making herself take her time despite the battle raging between her comrades and the Britynons in the hall outside.

At last she spotted what she sought, a section of locked shelves. All the rest were patently freely accessible to all comers. She hastened over to examine its contents and found that the materials did not follow the clear labeling characteristic of most of the media here. These were arranged and marked by some sort of numerical coding.

Islaen dove for the floor as sparks rose from the huge surplan-etary computing console near her. Many of the guards had escaped their charge and were now firing into the room.

Varn, can you cover me? I think I've found what I want, but I'll need time to get it out.

Take all you want, Colonel. Just pick the right stuff. I do not want to go to this trouble for a listing of the Commandant's gambling debts.

Sogan dropped into a position that was sheltered yet open enough to draw the Britynon's fire.

It was an eerie fight. They had cut the lights on their way into the room, and only the dials of the machines and the dim emergency system were operating inside. The glow was sufficient for their work, but the guards in the brightly lighted hall outside were at a disadvantage—perfect targets if they showed themselves at the door but unable to really see the Federation troops. There was remarkably little sound despite the heavy firing. The hiss of the almost-silent guns and the sharp ping of ricocheting pellets were the only regularly repeated noises, punctuated by the discharging of the less numerous blasters and the furious crackling of the energy they spat.

The Colonel fumbled in a back belt pouch and withdrew a ring of curiously bent, inflexible wires. She examined these critically, selected one, and began picking at the tiny but powerful locking device holding the shelf sealed. The gross violence of an explosion would not work here; that would only serve to erase or hopelessly scramble the data inside.

The woman smiled wryly. Hers was a strange profession. It did not fit her at all for a factory or office position, but she would make an excellent cat burglar should she ever demobilize out of the Navy, that or slip readily into any one of a half-dozen other equally shady occupations.

She worked cautiously, watching for booby traps and destruct devices that might eliminate the evidence she sought even as she reached for it.

She did not expect to find anything of that sort and did not. Once again, the invaders had not expected that anyone would make a try for this material and had failed to defend against that eventuality.

It did not happen quickly enough to suit her nerves, but at least the lock turned silently, freeing the case door. Islaen Connor began sweeping its contents into the empty pack she had brought to hold them. Hopefully, she thought, she was bringing off the correct material. There was no time to run any of it through a tape reader. Thus far the defenders had contented themselves with simple antipersonnel weapons, probably because they hoped to preserve their data, but sooner or later stronger force would be brought to bear against her party.

Varn was holding the door alone now, she saw as she began wriggling her way toward him. Bethe Danlo had stopped fighting to attend to her own assignment, that for which she had been trained since her enlistment before the War's end.

Islaen crawled over to her, freeing the remainder of her explosives as she moved.

"How much longer?" she whispered as she reached the other.

"A few more minutes. Five. Maybe less."

The Noreenan sighed in her heart. An eternity, but they would have to win it for her.

A sudden sputtering sound caused both to glance in the direction of the contested door. The charge in Sogan's blaster was spent!

Almost without thinking, the demolitions expert tossed him hers, but then she forgot about her companions entirely. She made herself forget them. The task before her was delicate and important, and she was as well aware as the others that almost no time remained in which to complete it.

Everything within this room had to be destroyed. Utterly. Not enough must be permitted to remain intact to allow the invaders to guess that anything had been removed from here. If that became known prematurely, the consequences could be dire, for themselves and for Anath. The invaders would act then, fast, to prevent them from transmitting their knowledge off-world. Whatever plan they had devised for dealing with active resistance on the part of the Anathi would be put into motion long before the Navy could get here. She had no doubts that its effects would be far reaching and would probably sweep up her team along with the planet's citizens.

It might not come to that. The Britynons had believed they would be dealing only with primitives, however well armed. It was possible that they would not be prepared to counter Federation Commandos. . . .

That meant nothing, she thought savagely. The potential for disaster was here, and it rested on her to counter that, to set her charges so well that no evidence would remain to call it forth.

She could accomplish it. Although the bulk of her work during the War had been the disarming of unexploded missiles and traps, she had both training and experience in this aspect of her art. She knew what to do and knew she should be able to do it, provided she was not cut down before her job was done.

While Islaen attached her putty and incendiaries to the wall shelves and the larger consoles, she worked to coordinate the blast to come, to orchestrate what would actually be a chain reaction of several different explosion centers. That would assure success even if some of the material should be found and rendered harmless in time despite her care in concealing her handiwork. As an added precaution, she planted a few other charges, equally deadly, which she did not camouflage as well so that searchers would lose precious microseconds disarming and dismantling them.

At last, she signaled that she was done. Her comrades charged through the door, firing as they ran. The guards fell back from them. They cleared the long hall and raced for the door. Outside, the fighting had resumed.

They leaped the shards of the door without pause, Bethe following a pace behind the others.

She just passed through the entrance when something struck her shoulder a violent blow that flung her to the ground. In the next instant she was torn by a numbing shock.

A pellet. She was done . . .

Varn Tarl Sogan sensed rather than saw her go down. He whirled about, dropped the sniper who had felled her, and doubled back for her.

The spacer was still conscious. She tried to wave him away. "There's no time for heroics, you scramble-circuited fool!"

He only laughed as he swung her to her feet. "Up, Sergeant! Those sons in there can only try to kill me. Jake would do it for sure if I left you behind."

There was all too good a chance that the Britynons might succeed. The guards had reached the entrance and were firing at them from behind the cover of the broken door. The two guerrillas were in the open, exposed both to their fire and to that of those trapped inside the barracks if the cover Karmikel was providing should slacken.

One pellet whistled by Varn's cheek. A second cut the sleeve of his jacket, then the Britynons were forced to drop back by a withering stream of blaster fire from out of the darkness: Islaen!

With that aid, they were able to race out of their enemies' range, Sogan supporting, actually carrying, the Sergeant.

The strangely muted sounds of the battle were all around them, then they were gone, drowned in a roar that seemed to rise out of the heart of the Empire's deepest hell.

The Arcturian did not pause. The flier was still a long way off, and their foes would soon break free, if they had not already done so, at least those inside the barracks. He doubted many, if anyone, could have survived the blast in the command center itself.

Bethe was reeling badly. He swept her up into his arms. She was a small woman and slight even for her height. With the danger pressing on them to drive him, he was scarcely aware of her weight at all.

Jake Karmikel appeared out of the darkness, his blaster in hand, ready to give them cover should they require it. "Hurry!" he hissed. "Islaen's bringing the flier in."

Minutes later, the machine came to a stop in front of them. Sogan maneuvered Bethe into the rear seat and slid in beside her even as the redhead vaulted into the vacant place up front. With her comrades aboard and once more secure, Islaen wasted no time in reversing and beating the fastest retreat she could force out of the machine's responsive drive.

The demolitions expert hovered on unconsciousness. Pellets were efficient antipersonnel weapons. The electric charge they carried was both surprisingly strong and fairly long-lived, and one

of them did an excellent job of immobilizing anyone in whose
flesh it managed to lodge.

She roused when she felt the war prince's knife slice through
her jacket and the tunic beneath. "Easy on my wardrobe,
Admiral," she told him weakly but steadily.

"Our generous Navy will be delighted to reimburse you." Jake
leaned over the back of his seat. "How bad?"

"Not very," he answered after a moment's examination. "It is
in the muscle just below the bone. The renewer will take care of
it once we dig the pellet out."

He studied her as closely as the half light would permit without
shining the raditorch directly into her face. The spacer was tough
like all her breed and made no complaint, but he could see the
lines of pain and the strain of trying to master it. "I could take it
out now," he suggested doubtfully.

"No thanks, Admiral. No insult meant to your steady hand or
our commander's driving, but I think I'd rather wait until we're
back on solid ground. The charge's nearly spent now anyway."

So was she, Varn thought wearily, but he let it rest. He did not
like the idea of performing even such basic surgery in a speeding
vehicle either.

Bandit had been watching the proceedings closely and now
hopped onto Bethe's sound shoulder. She licked the woman's
cheek with quick, rasping strokes of her pink tongue.

Poor Bethe! Bandit couldn't help, and she got hurt!

What could you have done? the Arcturian asked irritably.

Let her alone, Islaen Connor told him. *You've got a pretty
strong talent yourself for shouldering unearned guilt. —He's
right, though, love. None of us could've done anything to stop it,
or she wouldn't have been wounded.*

The blond woman was unaware of their discussion, but the
gurry's attention and her obvious distress held her completely.
"She really does care, doesn't she?" she asked softly, although she
was well aware of the little mammal's affection and intelligence.

"Aye," Sogan replied. "She is bonded to Islaen, but she has
adopted the whole unit. She wants nothing to happen to any of us
and will do all in her power to help and protect us, as she
has proven to our benefit often enough."

"That you have, little friend," she said, gently rubbing her face
against the Jadite creature's soft feathers.

The off-worlders fell quiet after that. Varn's eyes closed, and he
opened his receptors to Anath's life.

It was hard to read the prairie dwellers accurately with the terror of the attack still driving them, but from what he could sense, he did not believe the hunt for them was up as yet. Even if it was, and he doubted the invaders would mount a real search until there was at least some light to augment their scanners, it had not spread out nearly this far.

He turned his head so that he might see Bethe. She looked to be asleep, and he hoped that she was. A pellet was a burden to bear for all its minute size.

It was a pity Jake was not back here with her instead of him, he thought, but there had been no time to arrange their seating when they had started out, and he very much doubted that Islaen would stop at all before they reached base, however much she might sympathize with the Noreenan man's desire to be with the spacer.

One good had come of Bethe's wounding, at least for Varn Tarl Sogan, though it was nothing he would have been proud to own—Karmikel's reaction. The fear and anguish he had shown was not the response of a soldier to a comrade's danger and suffering but that of a man for the woman he loved. Varn had felt relieved to see that. He knew full well that the Commando-Captain had loved Islaen Connor long and well and that it had not been any decrease or alteration of feeling that had caused him to step back but only a yielding to the inevitable. Given that old, close relationship and Jake's still significant superiority in on-world work, he had good reason to be glad that Karmikel had at last turned for a fact to another.

No. He was wronging himself. That did in truth constitute a great part of his reaction to his comrade's revelation, but he was pleased for a more worthy reason as well. Bethe Danlo was far too fine a woman to be relegated to the position of a replacement, even for Commando-Colonel Islaen Connor. He knew now that this was not the case here, that she was loved for her own self and sake, as she deserved to be.

The Sergeant awoke slowly. She allowed the padding of the seat to continue taking her weight. She was tired from the activity and tension of the raid and from loss of blood. Bethe glanced at her shoulder. It still oozed somewhat, but the major flow had stopped.

The electric fire that still occasionally jolted through her weary body, albeit with much lessened force now, had induced a burning thirst that soon overshadowed the actual pain of the wound. Islaen picked up her need as it crystallized and told Varn to give her one of the canteens.

The woman drank eagerly, then hesitated, training functioning once more.

"Go ahead," he reassured her. "We are home."

So they were, she saw. Almost as the Arcturian finished speaking, the flier came to a stop amid the familiar trees near the clearing in which they had established their chief camp.

Jake dropped to the ground as lightly and noiselessly as a cat. He cautiously made his way to the edge of the trees and thoroughly scouted the camp and the area around it. When he discovered nothing amiss, he signaled the others to come ahead.

Bethe moved steadily when Sogan helped her from the machine. Another ordeal lay ahead of her, and she was resolved to meet it with at least a reasonable show of strength. She should be able to manage that much thanks to her spacer upbringing. Life was hard in the starlanes and had grown harder still during the long years of the War. Everyone was expected to carry his or her cargo out there with no whining over difficulty or weakness.

"The pellet's got to be removed."

She looked from Islaen to her shoulder. Most of her jacket on the left side was thick with drying blood. "I'm at your disposal, Colonel. It does look worse than it is, though."

After the remaining cloth had been cut away and the surrounding area cleaned, the wound did show itself to be light, as the war prince had initially stated. It had cost her a considerable amount of blood and was again becoming painful, but once the pellet was out, she anticipated no further trouble from it.

Karmikel took up the first-aid kit and resolutely opened it, but when he started to reach inside, the Colonel smiled and shook her head. "My job, Jake. I've always been the one to play surgeon. You man the renewer."

He nodded. Her small, able hands were better suited for this work than his.

Islaen prepared and administered a syringe of local anesthetic and waited a few seconds for it to fully numb the arm, then she unsealed a sterile scalpel and began probing for the pellet.

The narrow instrument followed the course of the wound. Bethe fixed her eyes on Karmikel. Islaen's hand was steady. She would do her best to keep the scalpel away from the ravaged flesh, and if she did slip, the anesthetic assured that her patient would feel no actual pain.

The blade touched the pellet. The Commando jerked slightly as an unexpected shock ran up the metal to her hand, but she did not withdraw the scalpel. She worked it under the ball, trying to lift it

out. This lever action would be the most difficult part of the
operation, for it must be done quickly, with as little damage to the
surrounding tissue as possible. A renewer repaired injury, but
there was still blood loss and simple aftershock to consider.

At last, it was out. She triumphantly held up the small,
blood-smeared metal ball. It seemed very tiny to be able to cause
so much trouble.

"Knock out now," Islaen ordered when she had finished.
"You've had quite enough for one tour."

So had they all. "Bandit, you had a good sleep on the way back.
You'll stand guard and warn us if anything or anyone approaches
the camp. The rest of us really won't be of much use until we get
a proper sleep."

Bandit will watch! The gurry responded in delight. This was
something concretely helpful that she could do to aid her human
comrades. She had always taken her turn at sentry duty, but this
was the first time she had been permitted to do it for the whole
period. She was keenly aware of the trust Islaen was putting in her
and would not disappoint her. Gurries looked after those they
adopted.

TWENTY-THREE

BETHE DANLO'S SLEEP was deep and dreamless, and it was many hours before it loosened its grip on her. She kept her eyes closed and lay still even after she awoke, lazily listening to the world around her. She felt no discomfort either from her arm or in herself, but she was reluctant just yet to return fully to reality and the activity it entailed.

When she heard voices being held purposely low, though, she sat up. "Good morning, comrades. Or is it evening?"

"Morning," Islaen Connor told her. "Late morning. We all slept very well. None of us have been up for long."

The demolitions expert saw that the others were clustered around the tape reader, and the last blissful wisps of sleep left her. "Did we get what we went for?"

"Aye," Jake responded jubilantly. "We'll have to wait until we get back to the *Maid* to see what's on the disks, but we've got enough just in the stuff we've read thus far to hang the entire Britynon high governmental staff and all the ranking officers of this fleet with them."

"A good haul!"

"Aye, and it means our job is done," Sogan said, not bothering to conceal his relief. He had little feeling one way or the other for Anath of Algola, and he had no desire whatsoever to have any further dealings with her people. The Anathi might arouse a sense of kinship in Islaen and the other two, but they were a source only of discomfort to him. "We are now free to lift. Islaen faxmitted what we have, more than sufficient material to permit the Navy to make its move. An assault force is already on its way, and the invaders should be quiet and nervously on guard after our recent activities until it arrives to finish them off."

"But the Anathi!" she began in alarm. "Even assuming our people can come in secretly and mop up that lot without undue damage to the planet, suppose the sons decide to make a move before they arrive? They'll have to believe the attacks came from the on-worlders."

The Arcturian shrugged. "An Fainne will be lost. We could not prevent its destruction if we did remain."

The Commando-Colonel frowned, and her eyes darkened. "If that's all they lose."

Her companions looked at her sharply.

"What do you mean?" Karmikel demanded. "What else could happen?"

"I wish I knew, friend," she said with a sigh. "I just wish I could be sure they do believe it's the Anathi breaking out at last."

"Why shouldn't they?" Bethe asked.

"Think! The physical description of Anath's race wasn't classified. They would have discovered that in the materials they studied before choosing the planet."

"We have been careful about not showing ourselves," her husband reminded her. "The only ones who might have gotten a good look at us would be those manning the command center, and they should all be dead. Nothing human should have survived that blast."

"So they should, but chance plays strange tricks. There have been all too many times when we should've been dead." She pressed her fingers to her eyes. "I just wish I knew for sure what they know and what they intend to do."

"Vanya's people haven't reported any scouting parties," Jake ventured. Xenon had turned the transceiver over to the Chieftainess, and Islaen had contacted her as soon as she awoke.

"Aye," she responded grimly. "That's one of the things that's worrying me."

"Just what do you fear?" Varn Tarl Sogan asked quietly as a deadly chill swept through him. The history of his race provided a long catalog of the horrors that could be inflicted on a planet and her creatures by invaders from the stars.

"I don't know, Varn, but if they so much as suspect the Federation has anything to do with their present troubles, they'll have no choice but to move and move hard. Primitive locals can be managed at their leisure; we're another matter entirely. It doesn't take much imagination to envision the consequences if

word of this attempt gets out—and with it the evidence to give the
courts the teeth to respond to it. What those measures would be,
I can't say, but there is nothing, absolutely nothing, that I would
put beyond a Britynon commander if he believed it to be necessary
for his own system's welfare."

Bandit can help!

The gurry hen made that declaration deep in her own mind,
behind shields as tight as she had ever raised. If Islaen knew what
she intended, she would not be allowed to go. As long as she
wanted to have a real part in her life, she knew she had to obey the
Colonel's orders. That was the way these humans functioned in
their hunting down of their kind's renegades. Disobey, and she
would find herself confined to their ship or even left behind on
Thorne, never seeing those she loved except during the brief times
when they were given needed rest from their deadly work. All the
same, a gurry did have her responsibilities, and she knew she
could make a contribution, an important one, here. If she just
slipped away and then succeeded, she could avoid their anger
entirely . . .

She gathered her resolution. It would not be easy flying so far
and so fast, and there might even be danger at the end, although
she did not think that was particularly likely. No matter. Gurries
guarded their charges against renegades, even as Islaen and Varn
did, and by bonding with them, their broader duties had become
hers. She needed to do this to carry her proper part on Anath.

Bandit flitted from the flier to one of the supply packs. After
waiting there a few seconds to make certain that none of her
deeply engrossed companions became aware of her, she moved
again, this time darting through the crack the humans had left at
the door to allow for ventilation. Once free, she sped into the
trees, flying due west.

None of the others saw the gurry go. The possibility of such a
move on her part never entered their minds, and the questions their
commander had raised held them all in an icy grip.

The former Admiral fixed his eyes on the screen of the tape
reader. His mouth twisted bitterly. As far as he was concerned, the
green-eyed barbarians infesting this place could have the joy of
their King and take their chances with the invaders. Of a certainty,
he had no wish to risk death or to die for them.

That was not his decision to make. He had known the sort of
service that would be demanded of him when he had given his
oath to the Federation Navy and joined forces with Islaen Connor.

There had been no question whatsoever as to why they had been sent to Anath of Algola.

"We cannot lift, then, not at this point. We would be free to try to escape a disaster we could not prevent, but until we are definitely faced with such a doom, we must do what we can to safeguard the planet and her life forms."

He turned to the others again. "We should probably return to the *Maid* and go over the rest of the material we seized. Once we faxmit whatever is pertinent, we shall have restored our expendability." His lips curved into a bleak smile. "I would suggest remaining with the ship afterward to give ourselves some chance of getting off-world if the worst should happen. I have no particular desire to lose my life needlessly."

"Nor do I," Islaen agreed. "We'll move out as soon as we can load the flier."

She immediately began to sweep up the captured tape cartridges, but her mind touched his. *Thanks, Varn.*

His eyes narrowed. *Did you think I would propose otherwise?*

No. You simply deserve thanks. I wanted to be the one to offer it.

The woman stopped suddenly. She frowned and looked sharply around. There was silence in place of the string of questions and comments that should be pouring into her mind. "Where's Bandit?"

"Over . . ." Bethe began. "She was there before."

The Colonel's mind ran swiftly through the clearing and its immediate environs. "She's not here now, not anywhere around." *—Varn?*

Together they ranged farther.

Bandit! Answer us! she demanded sharply.

There! Her touch was clear. *Bandit, what do you think you're doing?*

Bandit's fine! Back soon! With that, her mind snapped shut.

Bandit!

Sogan's hand brushed hers. *Let her alone, my Islaen. Perhaps there is something she must do.*

Heading west?

Even so.

His thoughts reached out again. They seemed to meet no response, but somehow he did not believe the gurry had closed them out completely, not yet. *Let us know if you get into trouble and when you are ready to return. —Not knowing hurts, small one. Remember how it was when Islaen was missing.*

Yes, Varn. Then her shields went up for a fact.

That little demon, the Noreenan sputtered in fury. She reined her temper in the next moment as she caught something of what Varn was trying to close behind his own guards. The war prince did not find it easy to trust, and it was more difficult still for him to love after all that had happened to him, but he had opened his heart to the little Jadite creature whose very nature they could not so much as define. Bandit's loss would be a wrenching sorrow for her. For Varn Tarl Sogan, it would be devastating.

Looking at the situation realistically, she had to admit that was not likely to happen on the hen's self-appointed mission, although its nature was not difficult to guess given their earlier conversation. Bandit, for all her eagerness and seeming innocence, had never shown herself to be stupid. Gurries were not minute, strangely formed infant children but an intelligent, highly successful species of their own world. Their comrade fully appreciated danger and could be expected to guard herself as well as circumstances permitted.

"Our adventurous friend seems to have turned spy," she told the others. "We might as well lug this stuff back to the *Maid* and keep ourselves busy until she reports in."

"Aye," Jake agreed, "and prepare ourselves to move real fast. With the kind of warning she could give, it might just be possible to block any plots those Britynon sons decide to hatch."

Bandit's pace never slackened all that day or during most of the night following it. In the end, though, she faltered as exhaustion began to weigh ever more heavily on her. At last she realized that, whatever the need to press on, she could go no farther without rest.

Her mind swept the world below. She was far out on the prairie, very far, and only a few of the larger plains dwellers lingered here; the shadow of Britynon hunters hung too heavily over that part of their range to encourage their presence. The junner population had suffered no similar reduction. They were not the goldbeasts of her native Jade, as capable of conversation as Islaen Connor or Varn Tarl Sogan, but she could make her needs known to them, and they were obliging little creatures. Even though they usually slept away the hours of darkness, she had no trouble rousing a series of individuals who, albeit grumpily, agreed to carry her in the direction she wished to go. They were small animals and could not bear her any great distance, but she was light enough that she

would not overtax her porters as long as she did not remain with
any one of them too long.

Morning found the gurry deep in the highlands, in full sight of
the major peaks, the great mountains separating her from her goal.
Her bright black eyes fixed on the topmost spire. She was still
weary, but she had rested sufficiently to complete her journey on
her own wings. Altitude itself was no source of dismay to any of
her kind, nor was a brief exposure to the chill and thin air that
were its outriders. Besides, the hen thought practically, there was
no reason to go right over the summit. There were plenty of lower
spots where a flying creature like herself could cross with no
inconvenience whatsoever and no loss of time such as a poor
surface-bound climber had to endure.

She thanked the junner on whose back she was snuggled and
took wing, shivering in the early-morning air, whose bite she had
scarcely noticed in her nest of living fur. A seemingly impossibly
short time later, Bandit was looking down on the Britynon fleet.

So many ships and so many humans, she thought. It could not
compare with Horus, of course, but otherwise she had not seen its
like before. These were all dangerous craft, too, and dangerous
people, renegades, not like those who carried the things that kept
colonies alive and thriving or those who protected them.

The gurry hen studied the big encampment carefully. She would
be taken for nothing more than a small bird if she were seen, and
no human not utterly depraved or completely in the grip of a
powerful, violent emotion would want to harm a gurry, but she
still could not simply sweep down there and sit open to all eyes.
Those people liked to kill, to hunt. Maybe it did not matter to them
that a creature was little if it were strange—and she knew they
could not have seen anything like her on Anath of Algola. Also,
their scientists could be bad, those who did not like studying live
things. According to Islaen, there were all too many of that kind.

Maybe someone had been to Jade and would know she was a
gurry . . .

No! She was making herself afraid. There was no point to that.
She must just be careful and make certain that she was not seen.
Surely there would be places in plenty amid all those buildings and
starships and machines to hide one gurry.

Gathering her courage, she began to descend, flying slowly and
keeping as much as she could within the mottled shadows created
by the irregular surface of the cliff. Perhaps nobody would try to

hurt her, but she still preferred to make her approach as unobtrusively as possible.

Once down, the hen darted under the short eaves of the nearest quan hut. She had managed that well, she thought smugly. The camp was awake and alive with early-morning activity, but no one had so much as glimpsed her. She knew that. She would readily have detected their surprise and curiosity if they had.

What now? She was safe where she was, but she would learn nothing here. Islaen would send her to listen to the commander or his chief staff, but where would this leader be? The invaders appeared to be living and working out of these buildings, but their officers might have stayed on the ships, on one of the big ones.

She watched the traffic around her. There was a pattern to it. The larger huts in the center were drawing the most of it, and those going in and coming out were moving very stiffly and formally, unlike the soldiers nearer to her. That must be the place, then. At least she should be able to pick up some information there.

It took a while to reach the building and longer still to move from window to window, but in the end her efforts were rewarded by the sight of five men, all with their uniform shirts comfortably open at the neck but bearing insignia on their shoulders and sleeves that she recognized as marks of rank, although they differed somewhat from those she had grown accustomed to seeing on Navy personnel. They were clustered around a camp table covered with maps and charts, some that she saw were star maps and other strange ones, all lines and irregular circles. Something to do with Anath?

Like most of the other windows in the camp, this one was open a little at the top. It was just a crack but more than sufficient for her purposes. A gurry possessed excellent hearing.

It was then that she was undone. Bandit could not understand what the Britynons were saying.

She had never had trouble with that before. She could comprehend perfectly any of the languages Islaen and Varn spoke although she could not converse with anyone but her own two humans. These were using something different. They had their own tongue, and Islaen did not speak it, or not really, not well enough to have transmitted the knowledge of it.

The hen was frantic. All this effort, and it was for nothing. She could not be of use after all!

She made herself control her panic. The men's emotions were as clear to her as those of any other members of their species. That should help her decipher the rest.

It might not be so impossible to do that either if she worked at it. Not everything that they were saying was totally unintelligible. By listening closely to the soldiers, she found that she recognized a lot of their words and could pick out a number of others that sounded enough like those she knew for her to make a reasonably good guess as to their meaning.

After a while, some of what they were saying began to make a little sense to her. They grumbled about clouds, and they spat out a comment about guerrillas so laced with hatred that she cringed to receive it into her mind. —They did have good reason to be angry, she conceded reluctantly even as her own anger rose in response. They might deserve punishment for the way they had forced themselves on Anath of Algola, but no human liked to be bested, and no one wanted to see friends die.

The little she could comprehend was not sufficient. She did not understand enough of what they were saying to make real sense out of it, and she did not think she would be able to recall all this jumble of strange words to carry back to her comrades verbatim. No, if there was anything to be learned, she would have to bring them here to listen to it themselves.

Bandit sent her mind out. It was not going to be easy to reach her friends, and she wondered if she would be able to do it at all. Islaen had very nearly failed, and she had been closer.

She had also been hurt, and the gurry was well aware that she had both a greater range with her gift and greater strength within that range than either of her humans. —Had she not been able to reach Jade's surface from space?

No. She had only helped. She had provided the link for Varn with the herd and its gurries. The effort had been his, and there had been a nearly countless number of receptive creatures below to receive his call. She had no one to bolster her attempt here and only two individuals to detect and receive her thoughts.

Even if she could reach so far, she was not at all sure she could sustain the effort long enough to transmit a coherent message, much less open up this meeting for them. Well nigh the full strain of long-distance mind talk fell on the one who initiated the contact. Would she be strong enough to endure it, to maintain the contact for the necessary length of time?

She would have to be! Bandit turned her thoughts from herself and concentrated the full force of her will on reaching her comrades and uniting with them mind-to-mind.

* * *

Varn Tarl Sogan quietly came onto the bridge. Islaen was seated in her flight chair, her hand still resting on the transceiver's switch. He said nothing for a moment until he was sure she had finished her transmission, then touched his mind to hers.

She turned and gave him a wan smile. He looked tired, she thought, but so, too, did she. Worry did that, and the pressure of almost constant mental searching. *The flier's ready?*

He nodded. *For anything we can anticipate. —You are finished here?*

Aye. The faxmitter paid for its passage this time out. Her mouth twisted in distaste. *They're a cold-blooded bunch for a fact. If I'd been a Britynophile before, I'd hate the lot of them now after seeing this stuff.*

It is enough? He could no more read Britynon than he could speak it.

More than enough, the Noreenan told him with satisfaction. *The Navy will be on its way to their system within an hour armed with warrants for the arrest of the better part of their government and with the power to back them up. Win or lose here, we'll have done that much.*

That is the main part of it, for the future at any rate, is it not?

It is. I would still prefer to make completely sure of this fleet. It has enormous potential for trouble.

Her eyes roved almost of their own accord to the observation panel. *Anything yet? I wasn't able to listen while I was on with Admiral Sithe.*

Sogan shook his head. *Nothing. —When that misbegotten daughter of Jade gets back, you had best make it clear to her that taking off without orders is as serious a matter as acting despite them.*

The scowl cleared from his face, and he took the hand she held up to him. He let her draw him to the arm of her chair. *If my former comrades heard me fretting like this over a seven-ounce ball of animated feathers, I should be in nearly as deep disgrace as I am now.*

Islaen smiled sympathetically. *I'd be a bit embarrassed myself. Pets may be acceptable to my kind, but a few of my associates that I could name'd still think my navputer was totally deprogrammed.*

Her eyes were soft when they raised to meet his. How did one tell a man like this that part of the reason she was so proud of him was precisely because he could and did worry about a missing gurry?

Both of them straightened as a faint touch brushed against their receptors. They united and reached out to embrace it. Immediately Bandit's thoughts rushed in to join with theirs.

For the first moment, there was a garbled flood of need and excitement, but the hen then gripped herself with a surprising speed and even more surprising maturity. She explained where she was and the difficulty she had encountered there.

You did right to call, Bandit, Islaen told her. *Now join your sight and hearing with Varn's. I'll stay linked with both of you and translate for all of us.*

Yes, Islaen.

The former Admiral barely had time to reach his own seat before the scene in the quan hut room opened up before him, as if it were his own eyes and ears that were feeding the information to him.

He had little trouble adjusting to the radical alteration in his perception. Bandit herself was stationary, sparing him the vertigo he usually had to endure as part of this sensory sharing.

The return proved equally easy when the long session at last ended, but he lay quiet for a couple of seconds to be sure of his balance before sitting up and swinging his feet onto the deck.

Islaen watched him. *You're all right?* she asked.

Aye. There was no movement to throw me off. He gave full play to his affection and admiration. *We owe you, Bandit. You did well today. You did well throughout all of this.*

You did indeed, love, the Commando-Colonel agreed, *but your work isn't over yet by a long shot. We'll need to know it when they decide to make their move. Don't let yourself get caught, though, or even seen if you can help it.*

Bandit won't, the gurry promised. She broke contact after that and returned to her watch of the invaders' camp and its Commandant.

Islaen Connor's small hand clenched. *They're just about everything I've ever believed and then some, aren't they?* she hissed.

She checked her fury. There was too much of too great importance to be considered to squander her energies on useless emotion. She activated the *Maid*'s intercom. "Bethe, Jake, come on up to the bridge. Bandit's reported in."

TWENTY-FOUR

JAKE KARMIKEL GLARED at his commander. "So that's the way it's to be, is it? Crisp the locals and their far-ranging assistants."

"More or less," the Colonel answered, showing no annoyance at his interruption of her report, "though it's us they really want to neutralize."

He frowned. "How, Islaen? Their biggest ship couldn't handle the equipment for even an extremely limited-area burn-off."

"Naturally not. They'd need a battleship, and a big one, for that. You should've let me finish." Her eyes smoldered as they turned momentarily to the west. "They don't have to go to those lengths to solve what they believe are their problems here."

Varn Tarl Sogan nodded. "The solution is simple, and they have more than sufficient power to implement it. As Islaen said, it is the presence of off-worlders, Federation Commandos or other agents, that they fear, not a surplanetary Resistance. Reason tells them that there cannot be many of us, and if they act quickly when they do decide to move, without giving us warning or a chance to flee, they stand an excellent chance of eliminating us."

"How?" the demolitions expert asked him, fascinated, as she often was, by his assurance. "We won't be easy to find."

"They need not do so, not precisely. They know from bitter experience where we are operating and must realize that we are basing out of the forest in this general region. The mountains would not offer nearly as good protection to off-worlders and would deny us access to the surplanetary forces they must believe we are utilizing. That means that we have to have mechanical transport. It is not difficult to calculate the approximate effective range of a flier or transport. Assuming we are not somehow

202

alerted well in advance, they would be able to obliterate our camp and transportation, including our starship, with their fleet's lasers discharged either from space or very high altitude. The inevitable secondary conflagration would almost certainly rage unchecked at least as far as the midcontinental river systems and would sweep up any chance survivors."

"What about their own ships and camp?" she asked. "The grasslands would burn as fast as the trees."

"They would make sure of the wind before they struck, of course, and have foam on hand to check any attempted backsweep by the fire. It would only become totally uncontrollable as it gained strength and sucked more and more fuel and oxygen into itself. By that time the seared land it left in its wake would make an impregnable firebreak for them."

Jake Karmikel's eyes were fixed on him. This was Admiral Varn Tarl Sogan of the Arcturian Empire talking, not the man he had come to know since their chance meeting on Visnu of Brahmin. "It'll be a bit hard on the Anathi," he drawled. "If you're right. You did miss out on the better part of that conference."

"We heard enough coupled with what we read in their records to let us make some damned good guesses," Islaen Connor replied. "The effect of such an assault on the local populace is one of the basic reasons why they haven't struck already, that and the fact that they don't like destroying so much valuable timber."

"That would be a moving factor right enough," the Noreenan man said dryly.

"We have to give them some credit for humanity. Their Commandant's not a totally bad sort. Emotions were running pretty high during the part of the discussion we caught, and I had no trouble reading them. He's honestly reluctant to order slaughter of that magnitude with nothing more than a possibility to drive him. There's still not much more than a strong suspicion of off-world involvement in the attacks on his forces."

"They were planning to wipe out the Anathi anyway," Bethe reminded her.

"Aye, but not directly. To the Britynon mind, dropping a missile or two on a barbarian populace's stronghold to render them incapable of effective resistance and then watching the beaten race slowly wither into oblivion once their identity as a people was destroyed isn't the same thing at all as genocide in one quick rush."

"He will follow the more direct course all the same," Sogan

stated flatly. "He has no other choice. The potential risk to his system is too great for him to do anything else."

"How can you be so sure?" the spacer protested. "Varn, you don't even know these people!"

"I know the situation. Too many of my own kind were caught up in very similar dilemmas." The war prince looked at her somberly. "Most of us are not the unfeeling butchers we are portrayed to be. Few of us liked some of the things our duty, or what we saw as duty, forced on us."

"You managed to grit your teeth and kill very efficiently all the same," Karmikel said.

"Aye—I was not boasting, just stating a fact. From what I observed in that conference and from what you have told me of them, these men will do precisely as we did."

"I'm sorry, Sogan. You didn't deserve that one."

He shrugged. "No offense. History supports you. I was simply fortunate to have been faced for the most part with lighter choices."

Yet when he had been ordered to destroy a world, he had spared her and thereby destroyed himself instead. "All the same, I am sorry. I was reacting against this whole mess and used you to vent my spleen."

"I know, Jake. Forget it. I want to tear something myself." The invaders preferably, although everything reasonable within him was praying they would be able to avoid a full confrontation with them. "Is there any chance your Navy will get here in time, Islaen?" he asked, turning the subject.

"Not likely. They had to hold too far back to avoid giving our suspicions away. Admiral Sithe's doing all he can to push them, but even the fastest ship can travel only so much of the starlanes in a day."

"What about those heading to Empress' system?" Bethe asked.

"No, worse luck. Our troubles, or the worst of them, will be over once they do strike. There'll be no way that word won't reach the invaders on Anath, and burning anyone or anything would be pointless then. Whatever their other faults, I don't see Britynons going in for vengeance killing on a large scale, at least not the men in charge here."

All of them were silent for several minutes.

"Any ideas what we're going to do, Colonel," the Commando-Captain asked at the end of that time. "There's no convenient ledge to drop into a waiting ocean this time, and we don't have the wherewithal to blow that cliff down on them."

"I wish I had a good answer, Jake. I've been trying to come up with a viable plot since I became afraid something like this might happen, which means since we were given the damn assignment. I haven't been able to think of much, nothing that wouldn't prove just about as costly to Anath even if we did make the sons pay full interest for the resulting damage. Even warning the Anathi won't do much good. They won't be able to get far enough away in time to have a hope of avoiding the conflagration."

The former Admiral had drawn a little away from his companions. His fingertips casually caressed the *Fairest Maid*'s weapons controls. "Those ships are pretty tightly packed, are they not?" he asked suddenly.

"Aye, almost dangerously close. To make guarding them easier I imagine," Islaen answered.

"A starship's lasers would do a lot of damage if they were to suddenly open up on them."

"Forget that one!" she told him sharply. "The *Maid* can't take on those odds. She'd be blown before she could accomplish anything of any use. They're monitoring near-space. Even our fleet will have a time when it gets here."

"I was not thinking of the *Fairest Maid*," the war prince said softly. "Of all the vessels in that camp, the flagship should be the least well guarded since she seems to be the safest there in the center of the whole lot. She is also the most powerful and is best placed to sweep all the rest."

"Varn!"

He smiled despite the gravity and probable outcome of the course he was proposing. "You Commandos excel in surplanetary warfare, battling in hell-hole wildernesses. My element is the bridge of a starship." His eyes bored into hers. "Let me reach her command dais undetected, Colonel Connor, and I guarantee you that few of her sisters will trouble Anath's denizens or anyone else again."

"And what in space do you think the other ships will be doing while you're blowing the fleet to bits?" Jake Karmikel demanded. The man's self-assurance was phenomenal, insane even, but the audacity of his idea was well-nigh irresistible if it could be made to work in reality.

"Burning." Sogan smiled again. "I have neither lost my mind nor turned suicidal," he assured them. "Actually this is not even an original idea. It very much resembles one of the first big assaults Federation Commandos made against the Empire. It might not succeed. It will not if luck goes against us, but there is good reason to hope that we can gain our ends and confine the battle to its rightful participants."

"Go on," Islaen Connor said wearily. She knew the raid to which he referred. Few had returned from it, none of those who had boarded the Arcturian battlecraft.

"The attack will be totally unexpected and will come from one of their own ships. They will have no screens up, no defenses whatsoever, for the first few crucial seconds, perhaps even for several minutes. Mine will be firmly in place long before they are ready to respond."

"But do you think you can take out enough of them?" the demolitions expert asked. "It won't mean anything if you don't."

"I believe so, aye. Remember, this is technically a fleet, but it cannot be classed with the one I once commanded or with that basing out of Horus. There is nothing like that number of craft involved, and nearly all of them are very small, quite vulnerable to the effects of even a single solid laser strike. If I can hit them before they become aware of their danger, I should be able to do them enough damage that they will not be able to retaliate for several days, more than long enough for our people to reach Anath.

"That is all we need do, create sufficiently severe havoc to delay their ability to respond. The Navy will handle the rest.

"The entire burden will not be on me either. That would be begging fate for a blow. You three will be stationed on the cliff above with some of the *Maid*'s lasers to see that no one makes space and to finish off some of those that I miss. It would be unrealistic to assume that I shall be able to get them all."

It was not necessary to say that the probable cause of that failure would be his death. None of them believed these Britynons were incompetents, and Varn Tarl Sogan had not proposed the plan on the premise that he was likely to return from it.

"Lasers designed for space use are difficult to fine aim in atmosphere, but a stationary or lifting starship, however small, is not an easy target to miss."

"Commandos know how to shoot, Admiral," Jake informed him. "Just let us worry about that part of it." He was quiet for a few minutes, as were the others. "I have to hand it to you, Sogan. It might possibly work. I'm mainly wondering if we won't wind up doing as much damage to Anath as we want to avert. There's going to be a lot of fire loose in that camp."

Varn looked to Islaen. "Colonel? You understand the dynamics of such places."

"Barring a disastrous gale, it should stay confined. The whole camp has been well cleared of vegetation."

The Noreenan woman frowned despite her assurance. It was a good plan, one that might well succeed. If only it were not Varn who would be carrying this through . . .

"How will you get aboard?" Bethe Danlo asked. "She'll be heavily guarded at night, and there'll probably be a good part of the crew on her then. Besides, you'll need light to shoot. You'll never be able to man the weapons controls and any of the instruments simultaneously on a ship that size. The panels'll be too far apart."

"I know." His eyes wavered for the first time. "That is the weakest part of my idea." The Arcturian felt embarrassed. His suggestion was too melodramatic, more like fictional heroics than a legitimate battle plan.

He had made the audacious work before and had seen a Commando-led Resistance make it work, and so he went on. "It is a given, I imagine, that we shall have to base on the mountain above the invaders. I will have to climb down after dark . . ."

"No go," the Commando-Colonel interjected. "You'd never make it without stumbling at least once. In a site that quiet and with an enemy already nervous after our previous attacks, a few loose pebbles rattling downslope'd be the same as announcing your arrival with an old-fashioned fanfare of trumpets."

"I must rappel down, then, or partway down. The flier is silent enough not to be heard, and it will not be seen against the cliff as long as it does not come too close to the ground. We have mountaineering gear since Hades, so I will not even have to jury-rig a rack."

"Once you reach bottom, assuming you don't wake the camp on your way?"

"I would find my target, hoist myself into one of her drive tubes, and hold on there with magnetic oversoles and gloves until morning. When she emptied out, or emptied as much as she would, then I could slip aboard and seize the bridge. Once secured there, I should be able to carry through my plan more or less as I have described, if luck and the Spirit of Space are with us."

The auburn-haired woman watched him somberly for a moment. "It should work," she agreed reluctantly, "especially since the Britynons will probably be expecting us to hit the vacant outposts next to prevent their being taken over. An attack of any real magnitude on the fleet itself should seem too farfetched anyway to represent a serious threat." Her expression tightened.

"Hopefully, it'll remain a threat. I don't want any shooting stars moving in unless we absolutely must."

Varn Tarl Sogan laughed. "No fear of that, Colonel! I would very much prefer the idea of sitting quietly on top of some mountain for a few days to slithering down a long rope in the pitch-dark."

TWENTY-FIVE

NEITHER ISLAEN NOR Varn said much to each other after the flier set out, moving rapidly west, or northwest rather. They planned to make a wide sweep around their target to come in from a nearly seaward direction even though the ruse would cost them almost a full day's additional travel. It would be well worth the lost time in terms of safety gained, and they knew from Bandit's reports that it was unlikely nearly to the point of impossibility that they should be needed there before they would reach the invading fleet.

At last the woman looked at her husband. His expression was grave and thoughtful, in keeping with the seriousness of their position, but despite that, she thought, he looked almost happy, relieved even.

Boarding that flagship should be my job, she said abruptly. *I am commander, and . . . I am the one who likes Anath and her people.*

But I am the one best qualified to carry it out, Colonel, he replied calmly.

You don't have to gloat about it, she muttered.

Only a menial would gloat in such circumstances, Colonel Connor, not an officer—former officer—of the Empire. I only stated a self-evident fact.

And gloated about it! Her eyes shadowed, and she dropped them. *You'll be facing several times the danger the rest of us will, however involved we get. I can't help being afraid for you.*

He smiled. *I am plaguy hard to kill, Islaen Connor, as I have proven on many occasions during and since the War.* His tone became thoughtful. *If it does come to the worst, it is better that I*

*bear the brunt of it. You will survive my loss better than I would
yours.*

Varn, don't . . .

*I do not love you the less or feel less loved myself for being
realistic, my Islaen,* he replied gently, but he saw how his remark
troubled her and did not press it further.

Time passed strangely, as was often the case before a major
raid, sometimes crawling interminably, with each second magni-
fied into a seeming hour, sometimes flying, shortening even more
the little that might be left of their lives.

Rapidly moving or slow, the four off-worlders strove to use it as
well as they could, refining their plans and developing alternates
to counter the many snags that might develop during the attack or
the period of waiting before it.

That held their full attention for the first part of their journey,
but once those details were settled as well as was possible, they
had only sleep, the mechanics of preparing and eating their
rations, and occasional quiet talk among themselves to block too
deep dwelling on what might be lying ahead for all of them.

There was too much time for that sort of reflection, Varn Tarl
Sogan thought regretfully. That was not good, certainly not good
for him. He was careful to appear confident, relaxed, as he guided
the flier over the prairie. To a degree, he was. He knew what he
had to accomplish and how to do it, and he had enough experience
behind him not to permit himself to worry about the vagaries of
chance at this stage. Still, he could not blind himself to the likely
outcome if he was forced to put his plan into action, and he did not
want to die. He did not want to die at all, much less for the
mutants Anath of Algola had spawned. He did not want to
sacrifice so much as half an hour's sleep for their menial-minded
ruler.

He sighed to himself and tested the tightness of the shields
covering his thoughts. He did not even blame the invaders the way
his companions did. His own race had done the same, aye, and far
more, for millennia in the building of the Empire and did not so
much as consider that history regrettable.

The war prince's eyes darkened. That was no longer true, he
realized. He did condemn these Britynons in his heart, and for
more than their violation of their ultrasystem's laws. He had been
too long with Islaen Connor and her comrades. The forces
motivating them had begun to move him as well, altering some of
his own concepts.

His opinions or beliefs did not matter anyway. The Anathi, all Anath's creatures and Anath herself, were his responsibility by reason of his oath. If he was required to surrender his life in their defense, so be it. His duty here was no different from that which he owed to peoples he found it easier to favor. All he could do was try to see to it that he was not cast away needlessly.

Sogan smiled then as his eyes flickered to his consort's delicate profile. He had other reasons too, for defending this world. Islaen Connor genuinely cared for Anath of Algola and her denizens. She had fought hard in the past to oust invaders from her surface and was as willing to do it once again. It was his as a man and a friend to stand beside her in her battle.

His eyes returned to the windshield. At least the bulk of the weight would be on him this time. It was far better that he carry it instead of her, instead of any of the others. The Spirit of Space knew, he would fight to live, but he was in every sense the most expendable of them all . . .

The woman beside him stirred and looked quizzically at him. He made himself smile and opened his shields after carefully banishing the thoughts he had been concealing. *Just thinking, my Islaen,* he said softly. He did not speak again after that but left his mind joined with hers in a wordless communion that was comfortable and tender as neither speech nor physical caress could be.

The highlands were plainly visible despite the deepening gloom when the Arcturian stirred in his seat, flexing shoulders that had grown stiff from the strain he had not really felt slowly building in him.

"No sign of trouble yet," he said, unnecessarily but to break the heavy silence that had gripped them all for the better part of an hour.

"We've been lucky," Karmikel agreed. "No patrols since noon, and the few we saw before were so far south that we had no trouble avoiding them." More thanks to the quick action they had been able to take in response to the forewarning given them by his comrades' unique talents than by any instrument on their vehicle, he thought rather grimly, but he did not say that. None of them wanted or needed a dose of gloom at this point. Besides, they had to expect an army already twice attacked to have some defenses out. "No word from Bandit?"

"None," said Islaen. "That's a good sign. She'd be calling if there were any changes, particularly for the worse."

"Shouldn't you two be contacting her soon to let her know we're almost there? It shouldn't be too much of a strain holding a conversation at this distance."

"No strain at all. We were going to wait a bit longer, but you're right. Now's as good a time as any."

Sogan joined with her to strengthen her search. He felt no compunction about retaining his place at the flier's controls as he did so, knowing there would be speech only and no linking of senses to confuse his perceptions.

It took them a few minutes to locate the gurry, but then a sleepy mind answered their call.

Bandit, are you all right, love? Islaen asked anxiously.

Yes, she replied, rousing rapidly. *Bandit was going to sleep. Awake now.*

Don't disturb yourself too much. We just wanted to let you know we should be camped on the mountain above you before midnight. We'll tell you our full plans then.

Good? You'll have dinner? Bandit's hungry!

Haven't you eaten anything? the woman asked in alarm.

Bandit takes care of herself! she replied indignantly. *The things I find don't taste good!*

Well, you'll just have to keep on eating them until this is over, or you'll wind up giving all of us away. You took the job on yourself, remember?

Yes, Islaen. —What's wrong with Varn?

The Arcturian was half bent over the control rod, his shoulders shaking with silent laughter.

Nothing's the matter with him, Islaen Connor told her severely. *Go to sleep now. We'll be wanting a proper report from you once we get settled.*

Yes, Islaen! the gurry said again, then she obediently withdrew from the conversation.

"She's absolutely hopeless!" Islaen told her comrades. "She could wind up dead at any moment, and all that's worrying her is the poor quality of her meals!"

Bethe laughed in delight. "She's probably the sanest and most sensible one of all of us."

"It proves that she is a professional in our business," Varn told them. "My command would have walked through a solar flare of laser fire without a murmur if ordered to do so, but let the chefs over- or undercook some side dish and they were martyrs."

"Arcturian warriors complained at a hardship?" Jake asked archly.

"Plenty when it came to food." Sogan smiled. "I have observed certain Federation Commandos respond to their survival rations, and it has rarely been with heroic silence."

"Quiet!" the Colonel hissed. "A flier!"

Even as she spoke, Sogan lowered their vehicle into the deep blackness of the oddly shaped shadows cast by the irregularities of the hilly landscape, heavy, miniature nights in an evening already far advanced. No sooner had it touched ground than he cut power and dove for cover in company with his comrades.

They heard the enemy machine almost in the same moment. It was moving fast and was slowly climbing to accommodate the heights ahead, very probably on its way back to camp after a tour of sweeping the region behind it for signs of intruders. They had not run across many such sentries in this direction, but the Britynons were not stupid and could hardly be expected to ignore it entirely.

The patrol would pass nearer than any of the others that they had encountered, but it was dark enough that they should not be sighted. If the invaders were using scanners on the other hand . . .

Islaen sought the minds of those aboard. She relaxed almost immediately. The soldiers were tired and bored, interested only in a hot meal and a chance to stretch their legs. There was none of the tension that would have accompanied vigilance and nothing of suspicion or fear.

Soon the vehicle vanished into the distance, and the Federation party was able to return to their own craft. When they took to the air again sometime later, it was even more cautiously than they had been traveling before. They were comparatively near the fleet now, and it was unrealistic to assume that, day or night, they would not meet traffic in the air above them.

Fortunately they did have a goal, a place to go. Before they had set out, the Colonel and Sogan had contacted Bandit again and, despite the difficulty of conversing over that distance, had told her to check out the mountain above the camp for potential watch posts and report back to them. The best of her discoveries was excellent, a very low but broad overhang large enough to shelter both their machine and themselves. It was open to the wind, and they would not be warm, but they would be secure.

TWENTY-SIX

ALMOST TWO DAYS passed without alarm or apparent change in the Britynon camp, and the guerrillas began to seriously hope that no action would be required of them. In another couple of days, their own fleet would sweep into Anath's space and down upon the invaders. If their enemies made no move before then, they were away with it.

No visible change did occur, but Islaen Connor began to detect an undercurrent of mingled excitement and regret among some of the host below, enough of them to make their emotions stand out above the jumbled feelings and thoughts of their fellows. Moments after it had begun, Bandit informed her that the fleet Commandant had just summoned his ranking officers, all of them, into conference.

Both her humans linked with the gurry when she settled herself in her by-then customary post at the invasion leaders' window, and they had soon learned what they needed to know. The meeting was not a long one. The Britynons had already made their preparations. They needed only to be given their orders and told when to carry them out. Anath's forests would begin to burn two hours before noon on the following day.

Varn Tarl Sogan checked out his equipment for a final time and then settled back to take what rest he could. He would make his move when the night had reached its darkest point.

He slept only a little but did not mind that. Islaen was sitting beside him, silent for the most part, her mind lightly brushing his. Even Bandit, who had returned to them now that her work was done, had little to say.

214

The Arcturian at last glanced from the luminous dial of his timer to the blackness beyond their lightless shelter. *It is almost time for me to start,* he said, not trying to conceal his regret; he was comfortable here with his consort and would not have wanted to leave even under happier circumstance.

Aye. He felt her eyes and mind fix on him. *How do you feel, Varn? Anything-unusual?*

Scared. He heard her breath catch and shook his head strongly enough for her to be aware of the motion. *Not like the other times, or I do not believe so. I know I am going into real danger, and I think I am merely responding to that. I should be meat for the psychomedics if I did not.* His fingers brushed her cheek. *Your Federation is worth defending, and I am willing to work for its sake, but I love you, my Islaen. I do not want to lose you or to be taken from all we have built together.*

Sogan came to his feet. *It need not end that way, not if I am careful where that is possible and have a reasonable share of good fortune.*

You are fighting for yourself, too, Varn. You're part of the Federation, very much a part of it.

In a sense, I suppose. —The flier is ready?

Aye.

Jake watched him pull on his harness. "Don't come down with too loud a bang when you hit bottom," he advised.

"Tell that to our commander. She is in charge of the flier. I shall merely be cargo dangling from it."

"Never mind that nonsense, you two," the woman told them, "or I'll give the pair of you an example of some real flying on the return from here that I guarantee neither of you will forget quickly."

The war prince chuckled and fastened his rappel rack to the rope itself.

It was a simple device, very old in design and effective. By feeding a line through a series of smooth, round bars, tightening and loosening them to create or ease tension and drag, a climber was able to control his speed of descent quite precisely. He had felt from the start, and the others had seconded his opinion, that this would be his best course. The rope was too long to be managed easily under any conditions, and in the deep black of Anath's night, a man dangling passively from the end of it was in considerable danger of being smashed against some pinnacle of stone, however careful Islaen tried to be. One capable of exerting even minimal command over his position stood a far better chance of reaching the ground unscathed.

He nodded to Islaen that he was ready.

She squared her shoulders. A show of emotion now would only weaken him. And herself. "Don't make yourself too comfortable down there," she warned aloud for the benefit of her comrades; they would have to carry through for her if she fell. "Finish up fast. I'll pick you up with the flier as soon as you're ready."

"Do not be a fool! I can try to slip out again in the confusion. The flier would be a painted target."

"Not if you do your job properly, Admiral," she told him archly. Her mind opened into his. *Varn, you have to do this, but we're not throwing you away. If it's possible at all, I'll come to get you, or one of the others will. Don't give up on survival when you board that cruiser.*

The flier lifted in absolute silence, without so much as its usual soft whisper. Sogan glanced up at it anxiously. It was moving even more sluggishly than he had anticipated. The sound baffle did its own job well but drastically cut back the machine's speed and the power on which it was able to draw.

He relaxed again after a moment. Everything was normal, as it should be.

Varn clung to the suddenly frighteningly thin line, his rack locked tightly to prevent any movement before he was ready to start his descent. His eyes closed, then opened again. It made no difference. He could see nothing. Although still only a few feet away, the cliff beside him was more a blackness he knew existed than a perceived menace. The ground far below might not be there at all.

He counted the seconds, trying to estimate how long he would have to remain suspended like this. It had seemed like a good idea to eliminate the delay and maneuvering that would be required if he jumped off from within the flier, but the actual doing was proving decidedly unpleasant.

Varn, now.

He had to make himself loosen the bars on the rack to begin his drop. Once before, he had gone down a similar distance by this method, deep below the surface of Hades of Persephone. He had not enjoyed it, and that had been a relatively safe maneuver, not this fall into a dark nearly as complete as that of a starless space. Now . . .

Varn gasped as the panic he had felt that other time gripped him with redoubled force, but after a moment, it ebbed, and he was able to take hold of himself again. The perils he faced here were real, and the fear they aroused was realistic. A man could understand and acknowledge it and then use his will to counter it.

It was well founded, he thought. There was potential for disaster in every stage of the descent, and it would only increase the nearer he came to its end. Islaen dared not move too far from the cliff for fear of making herself a target or of setting him down too close to the quan huts, maybe quite literally on top of one of them, instead of on this side of the rubble ridge separating the camp from the mountain itself. There should be good room, but she had only limited control over the motion of a line this long. There was no significant wind, praise the Spirit ruling space, but he could still swing too far in and strike some stone projection with more force than his muscles would be able to counter.

That possibility was not the only threat the war prince had to consider. He was far more concerned about his rate of descent—and what would happen to him when he came to a stop. If he went too slow, he would hold them needlessly in the air, subject to detection and destruction by their foes. If he dropped too fast . . . His eyes closed. The Commando-Colonel was flying purely by instruments with no visible check on the state of the rugged ground beneath. She need be only a little too low and he could slam into it; a little too high and he might be left dangling dangerously far above it. In the latter event, if he were also going too fast, the rope could escape the rack altogether, pull out of it, leaving him with no support at all if he was not quick enough to grab its fast-flying end.

His mouth felt as dry as if it were filled with sand. He made himself breathe deeply for several seconds until the terror passed and then turned his mind from that gristly image. There were other hazards that were more likely candidates for putting an abrupt stop to his attempt. Even now, snipers might be waiting below, taking aim at him through night sights.

No. That, at least, would not happen, or not in the immediate future. Islaen Connor would know they were discovered the moment that it happened. The surprise and quickly following anger and excitement would be unmistakable, and the transmissions of one preparing to kill were more powerful still and were absolutely distinctive. He could be sure they were as yet undetected if nothing else was certain in this mad mission of his.

All this while, the former Admiral had been keeping as close a count as he could of the distance he had covered. He knew he was drawing very near the rope's end and slowed down accordingly to prepare himself either to stop short or to touch ground gently, whichever the situation demanded.

There was no rope between his ankles! Sogan's heart wrenched painfully, but he was in good control of himself and of his equipment, and he stopped himself with more than a foot of line to spare.

Cautiously, he stretched his legs down. Nothing. He could be inches from the ground or a hundred feet. It should be near.

His nerve failed him at the thought of just dropping off, chancing that the ground was close, nor was such folly necessary. *Islaen,* he called, *you are too high. I do not know by how much.*

You're nearly right according to the instruments. Hang on, and I'll bring you down a bit more.

Tense seconds passed as he was lowered inch by inch, then his boots touched solid stone. *Hold! I am on the ground!*

Immediately the man freed himself from his harness. He froze as it jingled but then went on. The sounds had been in reality very low and would not have carried even in the silence around him.

The quiet was indeed deep, but he realized after a few moments that it was not total. There were faint machine noises, the blurred murmur of low voices and movement that was part of a large military installation even during the hours of minimum activity.

He gathered his courage. Islaen Connor had fulfilled her part. The rest of it was his business.

Before he could even begin, he would have to cross the miniature ridge separating him from his target, no mean task in itself under these circumstances. This rubble was hardly an impressive barrier. It was neither high nor unbroken, and by day or in twilight, he could have passed over it almost without thought save for the care necessary to avoid setting any loose stuff rattling around him. Moving through it in Anath's full night was another matter.

Sogan had known from the start that he would not be able to do it at all without some light, and he reluctantly activated his raditorch. The beam was thin nearly to the point of nonexistence and tightly shielded, but it was sufficient to guide him through the blackness ahead.

It could also be sufficient to tell anyone happening to glance in this direction once he found the miniature pass he was seeking that humans were active in this place, he thought grimly, a danger he knew would drastically increase the closer he drew to the invaders' stronghold.

Slowly and carefully, the Arcturian worked his way over the pocket range, moving chiefly in a low crouch that left him equally ready to drop to the ground or to leap aside at the first hint that he had betrayed himself. On several occasions he was forced to go down on all fours when he encountered terrain more than usually steep or rugged or where small, loose debris made the footing treacherous and difficult to cross silently.

Varn stopped to rest after the third and longest such stretch. He switched off his torch and lay still, rubbing a bruised elbow and silently cursing the rock that had done him the damage more to relieve the tension building within him than out of reaction to the momentarily sharp but insignificant pain of the blow. The Britynon camp was before him, clearly visible through the breach in the ridge at whose mouth he was lying. He could even discern some detail despite the fact that he was still somewhat dazzled by the brightness of his own beam.

He pressed his forehead against his forearm to completely block out every ray of light, taking great care to put no pressure on the eyes themselves. He could not afford any distortion of his vision now.

He gave himself five minutes, then lifted his head. He smiled in satisfaction. Not much light was escaping the blacked-out camp, but there was more than enough to bring him into the place without the need to use his own again. After that he should have no trouble at all.

None from this cause, Varn Tarl Sogan corrected himself. Once inside, he could expect that any mistake on his part would be his last.

This was his first opportunity to study the installation at close range, and he took a few minutes to observe it before making his move.

Its Commandant had probably had no experience in the great War, but he was no fool. He had seen what his forces had already suffered and realized full well that those attacks could well be only the prelude to much worse. The conflict so recently ended had shown all too clearly how much well-armed partisans could accomplish, and he had to realize there was at least the potential for disaster on Anath of Algola.

It was patent that he was concerned about more than savages outfitted with leftover weapons and matériel taken from the raided arsenal. Those would have been met by a normally lighted camp enclosed within a glaring picket of deadly energy. The blackout was proof that the invaders were guarding against a sizable airborne attack.

That meant they were scanning as well. His party had been fortunate, that and smart, to have made their approach from the direction they had despite the time the detour had cost them.

His eyes glittered coldly. Their vehicle had worked for them as well. Like his own people before them, the Britynons were watching for something much larger coming in at a higher altitude. Conventional reason simply did not accept the idea of a handful of soldiers in a single flier attacking a company of this size. He himself had quickly learned not to underestimate his opponents in that manner and so had lost fewer ships and men than most in his position, but not many of his brother officers had been able to completely readjust their thinking in the same way. He was relieved now to see that large segments of the Federation's population also shared that failing.

Did it matter? He was here, but he still had to make his way through those orderly rows of quan huts and through the encircling lesser warcraft to reach the flagship. There was light in that camp, directed downward and so efficiently screened that little of it escaped out or up, but it was present all the same, not high quality illumination perhaps, but of sufficient intensity to permit the sentries to perform their duties. If he ran afoul of any of them or otherwise gave himself away, he was done, and so probably were his comrades.

Sogan wished heartily that Islaen Connor or Jake Karmikel were here instead of him. This was their kind of work. They could move easily over such threatened ground, smoothly, nearly by instinct alone, whereas he had to laboriously think out his every move. If he blew this through his ineptitude . . .

Keep your mind on what you have to do, not on your performance.

Damn you!

He felt her smile. *That's better! —Go on, Varn. You're plenty good.*

We shall soon see if I am good enough.

You are, or I wouldn't have let you try it.

Any change in the readings? He did not want to link with her at this stage. With the enemy this near, he preferred not to confuse his perceptions even momentarily.

None. No one expects trouble. The sentries' minds're sleepy, and they're not likely to jump at shadows.

I can expect no better than that, he said, then severed contact and began inching his way forward before his nerve gave out on him.

At least he was able to move with complete certainty with respect to his route. The long hours he had spent on the mountain above with distance lenses pressed to his eyes were repaying him a thousandfold. He knew where to go, the shortest and safest way to reach his goal. There would be no time wasted groping for the right road through the Britynon living quarters or ships.

The quan huts provided better cover than he had anticipated. The strange partial lighting created large, fairly deep pools of shadow welcoming to one engaged in dark work. The Arcturian clung gratefully to these patches. Fortune and the care he and his comrades had taken in their preparations might have made his work easier than it could have been, but it remained a daunting business. If he were discovered now . . .

There was too strong a possibility that he would be. Sentries patrolled the camp in pairs or in larger companies, each group crossing others at frequent intervals, providing an effective check on one another. The individual Yeomen might not be expecting trouble, but their officers were not taking any chances that they would be unprepared if it did come. One man would not find it easy to avoid them all; it would have been almost impossible for several to do so.

Sogan froze as a pair drew near him. Too near. Had they altered their patrol pattern or actually seen him?

He shrank against the wall behind him. Would they never stop? All they had to do was turn their heads and peer a bit closely in his direction and they had him. —Space! He could knife either one of them without extending his arm to its full length.

Killing them would be pointless. They would soon be missed and their bodies discovered, announcing his presence to the entire fleet.

The two men passed him by. He felt shaken by the narrowness of his escape but moved on without so much as pausing to draw a breath of relief. He might not be so lucky when they made their return swing.

There were no other misses that close, although he froze again on four separate occasions when he heard Britynon guards active in his vicinity. Time seemed to be suspended, as if he were trapped in the same nerve-wrenching instant, but in the end he came to the starships themselves.

The former Admiral paused a brief moment to look at them and sighed in his heart. Needle-noses every one. They were rather too squat, too heavy in the middle, to be considered classic examples of their type, but they were still tall, fair vessels. Fighting ships, he thought in disgust at the thing he was about to do. It would have been one matter to meet them in battle in space and destroy them there, facing equal danger from them. Cutting them down as they stood docked here on-world was an obscenity.

No one had assigned him the task. He had proposed the plan, and he had to carry it through if he was to fulfill his responsibility to Anath of Algola. What these Britynons had in store for her was even more obscene.

Varn stepped away from the wall of the final hut. He clung to the shadows as much as possible, but he must not appear in any way furtive. The cover was not so certain amid the less regularly placed and differently sized battlecraft, and sentries were considerably more numerous. They were also, he realized almost at once, somewhat more alert than their counterparts patrolling the quan huts. It did not take much intelligence to realize that these rather than their living quarters would be the targets of any attack that might be made against the camp. If he were spotted, he had to appear at ease, as if he belonged here, that and keep the Britynons at a distance. Too close observation would quickly betray the fact that he was not wearing their uniform, however poor the light.

He did not let himself dwell on his danger or on the consequences of failure, not now. Only the task of flitting from ship to ship, from the patch of night beneath each one to that under the next, could be given any place in his mind.

He gained the flagship's shadow. No sense of triumph accompanied that success, and he merely made haste to draw on the magnetic gloves and oversoles he had carried with him. The worst of the mission still lay ahead.

Sogan stretched to his full height in an effort to reach the great exhaust tube gaping above him. For several fractions of a second, it seemed he was just a little too short, that he would not be able to grasp it and would be forced to make his entry at once, taking his chances with the sizable night crew quartered and working aboard her. Desperately, he made a last try. The tips of his fingers touched metal and clung as the powerful magnets did their work.

He was not home yet. The strain was excruciating, and he did not know if he would be able to hold out under it until he could get a more secure and comfortable grip.

That could not even be considered. He fought his way up until he got first one and then the other hand on the solar steel wall.

Seconds later, he was able to bring his feet up as well. After that his task became almost easy. The gloves and oversoles were standard spacer tools, designed to operate in zero or low gravity but also allowing a crew member to work in difficult-to-reach locations under normal weight conditions, for a brief span of time at least. Islaen had used similar gear on Omrai of Umbar, and countless Commandos before her had used them. He had known they would work for him here.

How long they would continue to support him, or, more precisely, how long the muscles behind them could stand this kind of pressure, was another matter. Islaen had suffered considerably in her assault on his renegade kinsman's ship, but she had used gloves only so that her arms had been forced to bear the whole of her weight, and she had been actively climbing the entire time. He had his legs to help hold him, and he need go no higher. It was dark enough at this point that he need not fear any casual upward glance even should some sentry think to check for intruders up the fins of his fleet's most important battlecraft. Had his position been comfortable enough, he might have safely slept what remained of the night away.

Varn Tarl Sogan smiled. He wished he could manage to sleep! If anything could top his two Commando comrades, that would have done it.

It was out of the question, of course. The discomfort of his position might be endurable, but it was ever-present. Already every muscle in his body was demanding relief, and they would be screaming a hell of a lot more insistently before the time came for him to make his next move.

TWENTY-SEVEN

LONG, SLOW HOURS crawled by before a perceptible dawn at last brightened Anath's sky. Varn stretched as best he might, but he did not move, not yet. It should not be too much longer before those who had spent the night on the cruiser disembarked, leaving her nearly deserted for a while. It was then that he would try to board her.

Voices. He straightened. They were coming out, not only from the flagship but from the others as well.

The war prince waited until all was nearly quiet again, as quiet as he judged the port section of a military installation of this size was likely to get, then he deactivated the magnets holding him in place and cautiously dropped to the ground.

Ignoring the almost exquisite agony in his limbs and back, he looked quickly around to assure himself that he had not been seen. He tested himself to be certain that he would be able to move smoothly and darted for the seemingly abandoned hatch.

He knew that it was not so in fact. It had to be guarded, most probably by a single sentry. Islaen had not been able to confirm that, to fix on one or two unknown, unruffled patterns amid so many, but reason argued for only one man.

Logic could more or less pinpoint his station as well. He should be just inside the air lock where he could sit or stand—very likely the former—out of the wind and still keep watch on all who approached his charge.

Almost all. Sogan was not about to let himself be seen at this stage. He passed under the ship, then hugged her skin, resisting the temptation to crane forward in an effort to peer up and within. When he reached the ladder giving access to the flagship, he went up it fast, scaling its side rather than its center in as much a spacer's as a guerrilla's maneuver.

This was the moment that would make or finish him. If he had erred in judging the placement of the guard or if there was more than one man, if he moved clumsily or too slowly, if his blow did not fall true at the first stroke, then he was not likely to succeed in his aim, not completely and not without a great deal of trouble.

Varn Tarl Sogan gathered himself and leaped inside. A lone sentry was sitting there, not half a foot from the spot where the Arcturian's reasoning had placed him. The Yeoman's lips parted in sheer astonishment, but before he could speak or move, Varn's hand shot out, striking him a brutal blow in the throat that shattered larynx and windpipe. A nearly simultaneous thrust of his knife completed the ending of the man's life.

Sogan wasted no time in closing and sealing the air lock, wedging it tightly so that it could not be readily breached should the fact that it was shut be noted prematurely.

A vessel this size was amply supplied with interior locks to protect the whole against fire or leaks in any one compartment. Each of these he treated as he had the entrance. There were other Britynons, a few of them, still aboard, and he wanted to prevent or delay interference from them, at least until he was well into his deadly work.

At last he reached the bridge. This, too, the former Admiral sealed, then he looked around him approvingly. A well-designed ship. She was not the equal of her counterparts in either ultrasystem's Navy, but her master could rightly be proud to walk this deck.

He had no more time to waste on observation. It was time to see how well she could fight. He went first to the panel controlling her screens. Activating her defenses would cost him precious seconds and would alert his enemies that something was radically amiss with their flagship, but he would not last long without protection.

There was no certainty that he would have any. Devices meant for use in space were notoriously unpredictable in their performance under gravity and in an atmosphere.

He relaxed. Even as his doubts formed, he could see the shimmer of the forming force screens through the cruiser's generous observation panels. How well they would function he did not know, but at least they were in place. It was a good sign that they had responded so quickly and that they were clear. Corrupt screens nearly always blurred vision, sometimes severely so.

It might be the lasers themselves that would fail to operate, Varn thought wryly, but then shook his head. Those always functioned, although they were difficult to direct effectively against any sort of small target.

His proposed victims were hardly that. His head raised in determination as he reached for and switched on the weapons control panel nearest him. This was a fairly big vessel with five bays operated from her bridge. The panels managing each one were well spaced throughout the cabin, and he would have to keep moving to utilize them all, but that was still to his good. He would be able to sweep the entire camp even if one or a couple of them were taken out, assuming that he could manage to remain enough unscathed to continue operating them.

His eyes fixed on the smaller cruiser to the flagship's right. With all but her maintenance systems inactive, there would be no burst of stellar-bright light and rapidly expanding cloud of glowing particles, but a well-placed hit from an artillery-class laser would finish her as a threat to Anath of Algola.

She, like the rest of her sisters out there, presented him with a brace of targets, the nose that was her nerve center and the fuel coils encircling her tubes. The war prince went for the former. His fingers stroked rather than depressed the firing button, sending a single, wide beam of blue light searing into the unsuspecting starship. Sogan whipped the laser back and forward again so that it swept his entire bridge, then swung his weapon away from the blazing wreck to cut down those behind her.

The smaller craft in the outer rings were more difficult targets. They were shielded to a great extent by the nearer vessels and were rendered even harder to see despite his advantage of height by the flames and smoke rising all around him from his earlier hits.

What matter? They were stationary targets, and they were fairly densely packed. He did not have to see them well to strike them, or to strike a good many of them.

Varn widened his beam to maximum and dropped his aim. Those ships were not large, and they were far enough away that the exploding fuel should not . . .

He cried out, and his eyes screwed shut as the coils of three fighters went up nearly simultaneously.

He whirled around, away from the panel and the madness rending the world beyond the observation panel. Light and sky-tearing flame colored the bridge the orange of the Arcturians' deepest hell, and the roar of a seemingly endless series of explosions reverberated through even the well-shielded bridge. What in all space must it be like outside?

The detonations continued. He had never set off so many, not directly, but the untouched ships were being swallowed up in the awesome violence ripping their neighbors apart, and some of these took out those nearest them in their turn.

The former Admiral did not delay to monitor the chain reaction. He sprang across the cabin and seized the laser stationed there. The time in which he would be able to act this freely was now very short, and he hastened to avail himself of whatever was left of it.

The remaining fifty-class cruiser was his primary target, and he seized the laser facing her. Varn shook his head and rubbed his eyes. They were still tearing so badly that he could scarcely make out the ship, close as she was. He was able to sight on her at last, and before his vision blurred again he loosed a long burst to ravage her bridge as he had her sister's. Without taking his finger from the button, he swept the laser back and forth in a wide arc to net the brigs standing immediately behind her and serve them in the same fashion.

More fire joined his in battering the camp, other lasers, streaks of shimmering light so intensely blue that they were nearly intolerable to the human eye, paling those he was wielding into visual insignificance. Navy weapons. His comrades had entered the fight.

They were none too soon. Several of the battlecraft that had been his next targets suddenly seemed to expand in size as a ghostly mist enveloped them. Their crews, or part of their crews, were aboard at last, and their own screens were in place.

His expression was grim. The Britynons had wasted no time, and more of them were reaching their surviving ships with every passing moment despite his efforts and those of his comrades to keep them back.

He had not done enough, not yet. He had taken out a lot of their fleet, all or nearly all their bigger craft, but those that did remain were still of sufficient number to recover fighting ability before the Navy arrived. They could be expected to wreak havoc on Anath in revenge for what had happened to them this day.

Several were still vulnerable. He went after them with cold purpose, trying to cripple as many of them as he could while they were open to attack. Once their guards were up, he would have no more easy targets, just a brutal slugging match whose end was inevitable given the numbers against him.

He sighed to himself at the irony of the situation. This cruiser

could probably have blown away the screens of any of those
fighters had she been able to bring her firepower to bear against
them, but he was only one individual, capable of manning only
one laser at a time. He could do less against them in the long run
than they could do against him.

Force screens were a powerful defense, the best ever developed
against any form of energy attack, but they all had one inherent
defect. They had to open to permit a ship to discharge her own
lasers. An opponent's gunners watched to locate her laser ports,
then either concentrated full power on that relatively vulnerable
spot until the energy plates sprung open, or else they tried to fire
simultaneously with her to send their beam through the port before
it closed. A very large ship could survive several such strikes if
she were lucky, possibly losing only one firing bay or a single
section with each hit. A smaller craft inevitably died. The fact that
they were not fighting this battle in space and most of the
contestants' highly active systems were idle would help reduce the
potential damage they could take from an individual blow, but the
flagship's fate was fairly assured. He could not permit himself to
blunt his awareness of that by underestimating those he faced, and
even if they were scramble-circuited utter tyros, there were
enough of them that luck alone would eventually send one or more
of their beams home to finish him. He could only hope he would
be able to do enough damage to fulfill his mission before they did
get him.

Islaen Connor's hands whitened on the grip of her laser. They
had entered the battle almost as soon as Varn had struck his first
blow, hitting the side of the fleet opposite that which he had
chosen, but they still had not moved quite fast enough. All too
many of the ships below had their screens up in spite of the
explosions ripping the docking area and the streams of laser fire
sweeping the rough bays to discourage any approach to the
surviving ships.

The tip of her tongue ran over her lips. What else had she
expected? Did she imagine those Britynons lacked guts or that
they were incompetents because their fleet was poorly guarded
against a guerrilla attack of this scope? She had encountered that
among some of the best troops of the Arcturian Empire.

Soon now, they would start trying Varn's defenses and would
sweep the mountainside to take out her party. She would have to
order a withdrawal before that happened, leaving the war prince to
his own devices. They had been able to dismount some of the

Maid's lasers but not her screens, and their only chance against those beams was to be gone when they struck.

A deep sickness filled her. Varn Tarl Sogan could not retreat, nor could she bring the flier in for him yet. It would only be blown out of the air.

Her eyes closed. The Spirit of Space knew, she did not want to leave him to die. She did not want to send out her mind at the end of all this and find only a void in place of his soul!

The Noreenan drove that thought from her mind and compelled herself to be calm. She was a seasoned soldier, a Commando officer, and the work before her did not allow for panicked reactions or hysterical judgments.

Two more starships went up, then she reluctantly brought her communicator to her lips and ordered her team to retreat. They would be of no use to Sogan or to anyone else if they allowed themselves and their weapons to be crisped where they lay.

The Colonel scrambled up the rope she had dropped at the start of her night's vigil and drew the heavy laser up after her. Only when she had pulled it over the crest and put a sound thickness of solid rock between it and the invaders' gunners did she return to the ridge herself and once more train her distance lenses on the embattled camp.

It was a spectacular sight, terrible in the manner of most of the works of war. Everywhere, starships and the shards of starships were blazing. Vicious streaks of pale blue light sizzled through the duller red of the flames to lick at the tall needle-nose standing high in the midst of the chaos she had wrought or darting out from her to bring more and still more disaster upon those who had been her fellows.

A fierce sense of triumph surged through Islaen's heart and mind and with it a delight in destruction she had not known when she had dealt a similar fate to Arcturian and to pirate craft. That men were dying down there in large numbers as well gave her no pleasure—for that she was infinitely grateful when she recognized her feelings for what they were—but to see that fleet go down, to watch Britynon strength and power brought to nothing, was glory itself to her.

Another fighter was gone. Varn was not firing as often now that there were no unprotected vessels left, but when he did, it was rarely without effect.

She battled the urge to reach out to him. No. It was better thus. Distract him at the wrong moment, and he could die.

He made another hit. His aim had not been so precise this time, and his victim's screens re-formed briefly only to be torn asunder an instant later when his second strike battered through their overstressed seams to finish her.

The woman gasped. A Britynon laser discharged in almost the same moment that Sogan's did. The beam seared through the flagship's open screen into the port itself.

The war prince knew the chance he was taking in firing again so quickly—and predictably—from the same port, but if he did not take that fighter out now, he would lose the opportunity. He loosed a strong burst, then switched the laser off and leaped back and to the side.

Scarcely had he taken himself out of line with the weapon than the panel shattered in a blast of metal pieces and sparks that were half fire and half pure angry energy.

Sogan fell flat, allowing the fury to pass over him. Had that laser still been in operation . . .

Although shaken, he was unhurt, not so much as singed, but he had no time to revel in his narrow escape. The bridge was ablaze.

Not bothering to rise, he rolled to the nearest foam canister, whose position he had noted during his initial inspection of the cabin, seized and discharged it. He gave one sigh of relief as the specially formulated chemical first contained and then smothered the fire. A few seconds longer, and it would have been beyond such quick control.

More fire! Another laser, but this beam came from below! —The Britynon crew! He had forgotten those sealed on board with him.

The Arcturian's body coiled into a crouch. It was easy enough to figure out what had occurred. The Britynons had managed to free one of the lower lasers from its bay—no easy task since, unlike the *Fairest Maid*'s, most starship artillery was not meant to be removable—and then had burned their way through each succeeding hatch until they reached the cabin beneath this one. Battle in an atmosphere was a far sight from the eerie, silent business it was in space, and they had probably judged his position by the simple expedient of listening to the havoc he was creating and their own side's response to it and had then decided to try to take him this way instead of alerting him to their intentions by a direct assault on the door. It was not a bad plan. He had not heard them at all in the general confusion. Had it not been for his own quick reaction to the hit on the flagship, he would now be a dead man.

The former Admiral let them at it for another long three seconds, although the bridge was now rather seriously aflame. When he judged they had opened up enough of a hole in the deck for his purposes, he crawled toward the eldritch blue fountain. The heat forced him to stand. His feet were burning even through his boots, but he should be able to keep most of the rest of his flesh intact for a while longer. He had to do so if he was to continue to act effectively.

The laser light vanished, and he heard noise below. The invaders would be turning their weapon on another site, perhaps the hatch since he had not yet responded to their fire and they could well believe him dead. He had to move fast. He would have but one chance, and surprise must be with him. A blaster against a laser was not an equitable fight.

Sogan squatted down, balancing on his toes to keep himself as much as possible away from the glowing metal, and peered through the narrow hole the beam had drilled. Two men were below, a Sergeant and a Yeoman. Only two to manhandle and use that dismounted laser? —Whatever the failings of their government and culture in general, he would have been proud to have had that pair serve under him at the height of his power.

His face hardened. They had earned a better fate than he would give them.

It would be a soldier's end, at least, preferable to the alternative, to years or a lifetime in a Federation penitentiary for their part in their system's crime and intended greater crime against Anath of Algola.

Hating himself, he fired, dropping both men with one broad bolt.

As he fell, the Sergeant's hand closed on the firing button in a convulsion so powerful that it jammed. The laser jerked away from his hold, discharging wildly, spinning and twisting under the whip of its own fierce energy. Within seconds, it had holed the hull in several places, and it would be only seconds more before it whirled upward to cut through the deck and into the bridge again, this time lashing the upper cabin without reason or pattern.

The weapon's erratic movements made it a poor target, big as it was. The Arcturian fired once and then again. His second bolt struck its controls, fusing them so that it lay still at last, as dead as the now-charred corpses of those who had tried to wield it against him.

The cabin was an inferno. Sogan first took care of the lesser blaze on the bridge, then threw open the hatch and poured canister after canister of foam into it, all he had available to him. It was enough, just enough, and once again he succeeded in extinguishing laser-started fire.

He had been lucky that last blaze had not been on the bridge with its welter of delicate and often highly flammable equipment, not to mention its four remaining lasers, he thought as he slammed the door shut once more to block the fumes already rising from below. There would not have been a hope of putting out a fire of that violence up here.

Sogan coughed violently. The air was bad, better here than in the cabin beneath but still foul.

Starship controls were fairly standardized, and he was not long in locating those directing air circulation and purification.

His mouth tightened when he saw them. It was pointless to try for a response from that mess, although the will to survive made him do so. The shrapnel from the exploding laser had spared him, but it had not shown any similar consideration for the instruments on the opposite side of the cabin.

So. He had only succeeded in trading one form of death for another, then, but he had come here expecting to die, had he not? He could not expect his luck to hold forever, and he had no right to curse it for failing him now. It had sustained him longer than he had started out with any reason to anticipate.

His shoulders squared. He had some time left, and the fight was not yet over.

Varn Tarl Sogan went to the observation panel. Only a few ships remained, amazingly few out of all those that had stood here before his attack had begun, but then, he of all men should hardly be surprised at the power of a well-coordinated Commando assault. He had fought to prevent a disaster like this for six long years.

None of the Britynon battlecraft had escaped into space. He could thank his comrades for that. Their lasers had picked off the few who had tried to lift, striking them through their vulnerable tubes even as they rose into Anath's air. After their destruction, no others had made the attempt.

The Arcturian doubled over in a spasm of coughing as his lungs tried to clear themselves of smoke and fumes. With the controls shattered, he could not close the vents giving that stuff access to the bridge, nor did he have any materials to manually seal them. His clothing would not suffice.

He was already weakening badly and judged that he would not be able to finish off more than another couple of his foes.

No, he thought dully. Not even that. As a fighting force, he was finished. The Britynons were keeping up a constant barrage against him, each ship centering her fire on the port nearest her. Either the cruiser's screens would eventually buckle, or his port would be invaded when he tried to fire one of his own weapons. He was beaten.

His comrades were not. They still had power in plenty and they would have retreated to safer positions by this time. They must realize that his screens were severely threatened and were only withholding their fire for fear of inadvertently striking the flagship.

There was one more thing that he could do. It went against their battle custom, but that made no difference now. His mind went out, seeking contact with his consort.

TWENTY-EIGHT

THE COMMANDO-COLONEL stiffened at her husband's call and
threw her mind open to receive him. *Varn?* she demanded half in
relief at hearing from him after the cruiser's long silence, half in
dread of what she knew in her heart he would say.

Do not spare the flagship any longer, he told her briskly. *I am
finished.*

Because his strength was failing in truth, he merely let his mind
picture for her all that had occurred since the laser had exploded,
then he withdrew from her, not even allowing himself to bid her
good-bye lest he weaken her. She had tried to conceal her anguish
at his fall, but he had been all too aware of it . . .

Islaen Connor lay as one frozen. It had come at last, then, after
all they had encountered and bested. They had all known from the
beginning that there had been only an outside chance of pulling
him free, but recognizing that fact did not help now, with her
man's death imminent. There had been hope before . . .

She gripped herself and raised her communicator. "Pour it on.
Try to avoid the cruiser, but Varn's about done."

She grasped her laser and glared at the burning camp with a
hatred intense enough in itself to consume it, it and her. The fact
that the invaders were proving themselves to be disciplined and
brave soldiers did not lessen what she felt and willed against them.

Neither should compassion, but the sight of the flaming quan
huts told her how many men must have died and be dying down
there. Her unit had made a slaughterhouse out of the Britynon
installation, and almost despite herself, against her conscious will,

she sought a way to bring it to a stop without betraying the need
that had pushed them to this in the first place.

It might be possible, she thought after a moment, possible even
to save Varn, although in her heart she believed it was already too
late to help him.

It was not something she could try on her own authority.
However slim the possibility, she could not risk blowing the
assault on Brityne herself, turning it into active, bloody battle, or
allowing the chief perpetrators of the atrocity to make good their
escape.

"Take over, Jake," she said into her communicator. "I've got to
contact Ram Sithe."

The Noreenan woman was not long in reaching their flier,
which she had removed to this side of the mountain and carefully
camouflaged as soon as she had finished lowering Sogan.

Bandit was huddled there, miserable and terrified, but she
rallied as soon as she saw the Colonel. *Islaen, Varn's in trouble!*

"I know, love," she whispered. "There's nothing we can do to
help him yet."

But, Islaen . . .

"Not now, Bandit!"

Islaen turned on the interstellar transceiver. She did not think
she would have any difficulty getting through, however busy the
Admiral might be. Sithe had always treated communications from
her as high priority, and he should be even more willing to receive
her call under these circumstances.

She was not disappointed. There was a wait of no more than
five minutes while he was called out of a meeting, but in very
short order after that she had both the news she had been waiting
to hear and permission to act as she judged best, that and his
promise of rapid backup.

The Federation Admiral had given Islaen the Britynon fre-
quency, and she used that to contact their enemies rather than
interstellar ship-to-ship. She also opened the communicator so
that her comrades would know what she was doing.

"Britynons," she said, speaking slowly and clearly, although
she knew that every one of them was as fluent in Basic as she was
herself. She wanted no one to be able to say that he had
misunderstood her. "This is Commando-Colonel Islaen Connor,
Federation representative on Anath of Algola. Your mission here
is known to both the Senate and the Navy, and because it is

known, it has failed. Utterly. Your homeworlds are under Navy control, and your Prime is under arrest along with most of his government and also those members of your military and private sectors who helped mastermind this outrage. Even as I speak, the fast fighters of another fleet are entering Algola's space and will be planeting here within the hour.

"Lay down your arms now. You may have a little time, a very little time, to contact your superiors and confirm the truth of what I have told you, but remember that any action you choose to take either against us or against this planet will be considered rebellion against the ultrasystem and will be treated accordingly. Such folly will stiffen not only your punishment but also that of your home system that sent you."

The woman ended the transmission as abruptly as she had begun it.

"Stay here, Bandit. There's nothing for you down there."

Varn?

"I'll try, little Bandit. Sure as space is black, I'll try."

She took the flier back to the crest, bringing it to a stop just below Jake Karmikel's position.

"Any move yet?" she asked as she crawled up beside him.

"No. They've stopped battering the cruiser, but that's all." He glanced at her. "It could be that they've just guessed Sogan's down."

"Aye."

She had promised the invaders time, and time she had to give them. They still had the power to fight and to avenge themselves, and they were not likely to surrender without confirming that the Britynon planets were indeed in government hands.

Twenty minutes went by, and the Colonel was about to demand a response when the screens suddenly vanished from around the fighters below. A great white banner, Terra's ancient symbol of surrender, rose over the camp. The remnant of the invading host was formally acknowledging its defeat.

Islaen Connor gave no thought to her victory. The flagship still retained her defenses. If those screens did not come down, they would never be able to reach the war prince. If their help could still profit him.

Varn? her mind called in desperation. She sought him on the bridge, and for a moment relief flooded her, washing out every other emotion and thought. Sogan was there, barely conscious now but still living.

Reason quickly reasserted itself. *Varn! Varn, can you hear me? We've won. The sons have just surrendered.*

I know. My communicator . . . Well done, my Islaen.

You'll have to turn off your screens.

I . . . cannot. It-is over for me.

None of that!—Get those screens down, Admiral. If you don't, and damn soon, they're bound to suspect treachery and will probably wipe the lot of us out when we show ourselves.

Sogan tried to rise. Summoning all his will, he struggled to his knees. The air was hotter, more poisonous, even that little distance from the floor, but he tried to ignore it. The difference was academic anyway, or soon would be.

Luckily the panel he wanted was close. He dragged himself to it, raised himself, supporting himself against it, then moved an arm that felt weighted with lead across it. Painfully thinking through every movement, he released the controls.

In so doing, the last shreds of his strength were spent. He fell, striking the floor heavily, and lay still, unaware and unmoving except for the heaving of lungs seeking for the remnants of oxygen left in the reek filling the starship's topmost cabin.

Islaen's eyes closed when the cruiser's screens went down. "Praise the Spirit of Space," she whispered. "Jake, take care of that lot down there. I'll get Varn out."

"How?" the Captain asked her calmly. "Even if he's conscious when you get to him, I doubt he'll be much help. What're you going to do with him? Sling him over your shoulder?—No, Colonel, I fear this is my job. Yours is to handle the surrender. You are our commander."

She nodded numbly, unable to refute either of his arguments, however much she might wish or need to do so.

His hand closed over her arm. "Try to be easy, lass. I owe that demon up there on more than one count. If he's alive when I get to him and oxygen can still do him any good, I'll bring him down to you."

"I know, Jake. It's just . . ." She steadied herself. It was time for the two of them to go. Bethe would remain where she was, to avenge them at least if the capitulation proved to be not all that it seemed.

The off-worlders looked around the ruined camp in silence. The destruction they had wrought was both awesome and awful.

Men were waiting for them near their remaining quan huts, as far as possible from the burning battlecraft with their ever-present danger of further explosions. All were drawn up at grim attention with one standing out before the rest whose bloodied uniform proclaimed him to be the fleet's Commandant.

He, like the rest of his troops, stared at the single flier and its two occupants.

The woman returned his gaze coolly. "We are Commandos," she said haughtily, "and you will have to pardon us if we don't choose to reveal our full strength at this stage."

There was work to be done, lives to be saved now that the battle was over. "Collect your wounded," Islaen told the Commandant. "Do what you can for them until our fleet gets here with renewers and regrowth equipment. Set men to containing these fires as well. The rest of the cleanup can wait."

"Our dead?" he asked stiffly.

"Leave them where they are for the time being. They'll be honorably interred later. That much grace I do promise, but right now, it's the living who need attention."

"Very well."

"Stack your small and personal arms. I don't want anyone slipping a circuit and imagining he can redeem Brityne's lost fortunes single-handedly."

She eyed him coldly. "I'm not keen on suicide, either, but if some of you choose that route, I won't bother stopping you."

Jake's surprise and sharp look brought the woman back to herself. The invaders had fought well enough, some of them heroically, even if they were not the equal of a similar Arcturian force. They had not deserved that last remark or the personal cut she had given by purposely thickening her Noreenan accent.

She did not feel compelled to apologize or to retract her suggestion of self-destruction. Suicide was totally repugnant to Britynon thought save in instances where such sacrifice was essential to general welfare. Any of them despondent enough to consider it would be carefully monitored by their own comrades.

The Commando-Captain had delayed only long enough to pick up oxygen packs and masks for himself and Sogan once Islaen drove him to the cruiser. He went up the boarding ladder with a spacer's speed and threw himself against the entrance, but it totally defied him. The former Admiral had apparently not trusted completely to his screens, or trusted that he would get them up in time.

He felt the Colonel's eyes on him and shook his head. He came back down the ladder. "Leave it to an Arcturian to barricade himself in so a rescuer can't get to him," he muttered as he shoved onto the seat beside her.

Jake Karmikel knew a lot of ways of gaining access to a sealed starship, but rarely had he possessed such a key as was currently at his disposal. They had fixed both his laser and the Colonel's on the machine on the chance that they might have to fight their way out of the camp. Unscreened solar steel would not withstand that pressure for long.

It did not. Seconds later, he was up the ladder again and diving into the ominously silent cruiser.

The Noreenan gagged as he passed into her and hastened to pull on his mask. He glanced once, grimly, back in the direction of his commander and then began ascending the core ladder. The taint from the fires was strong even down here, and he had not at all liked some of the odors he thought he had identified. That boded very ill for what he might expect to find on the bridge.

He shook his head when he reached the cabin beneath it. The whole place was blackened and ravaged by fire, stained and glistening with foam residue. The air was dark and heavy with a filthy smoke. His lips tightened. It would be thicker still except that so much of it had risen through those open vents.

The metal was still hot but not dangerously so as long as he kept away from the places the laser had actually cut.

Jake finished his climb. He had to use his strength against the door, but fortunately it was only shut, not sealed and wedged the way the entrance hatch had been. The time lost in blowing it might too easily have cost Sogan his life.

He saw the war prince as soon as he got inside. He reached him in a few strides and turned him over.

Varn's face had a deadly blue cast, and he was scarcely breathing. But then, the Commando thought, there was not a whole lot here to breathe. He got the mask on the other and opened the feed nozzle wide so that the inrushing gas would force his lungs to expand, then he set the pack for automatic respiration.

After several tense minutes, the unconscious man's color started to look a little more lifelike, and he appeared to be breathing more strongly on his own, but he was still too far under even to cough the remaining poison out of his lungs.

"Come on, my friend," he said as he caught hold of Sogan's arms and hoisted him onto his back. "You should be fine once I get you out of here and under our good Colonel's care."

TWENTY-NINE

VARN STRETCHED OUT on his flight chair with a sigh of contentment. His chest still felt sore and he tired far too easily, but for the
moment it was not weariness that had moved him to lie here, only
the desire to enjoy fully the spectacle beyond the *Fairest Maid*'s
observation panels.

It was so beautiful, that vast, star-filled void, peaceful and
clean. His head lowered. The contrast between this and the
burning, destruction, and death he had left was painful . . .

Varn?

On the bridge. He carefully slipped his shields into place. Islaen
would be troubled if she detected regret or gloom on him. *Come
on up. Bandit, too,* he added, feeling the gurry's eager touch.

The pair soon joined him. His consort sat on the arm of the
pilot's seat. He reached up and took her hand in his. *I cannot seem
to have you both close enough,* he told her softly. He paused, his
eyes fixing briefly on space once more. *I owe Jake for this one.*

*If we start trying to keep score on that, we'll addle ourselves for
a fact,* she told him dryly.

The woman studied him closely. *Are you sure you're well
enough to be up?* she asked.

*Aye.—You cannot keep me confined to my bed forever, Colonel
Connor.*

No. Her eyes darkened. *You took in space only knows what
bastard gases on that ship. You'll have to have your lungs
scrubbed out thoroughly once we reach Horus.* She saw his
frown, although he masked it even as it formed. *Thorne, then.
Our doctors there don't really trust Navy physicians anyway. They
much prefer keeping full charge of us.*

Thorne's better, Bandit agreed enthusiastically. *Everyone's happier there.*

Islaen thought that Varn would bridle at that, but he only nodded. He was as comfortable, as content, on Thorne of Brandine as he could be anywhere on-world.

We will have to go back for the wedding, she reminded him.

He smiled. *That is one event I would not willingly miss,* he assured her with genuine enthusiasm.

The Arcturian fell silent, and his attention drifted to the distance viewer. Algola had retreated until she was now no more than another point of light indistinguishable from the countless others of her size and color spotted throughout the void. *What will happen to her now?* he mused half in question, half to himself.

To Anath? Hopefully she'll be left in peace to develop and change and eventually take her place in the starlanes, if she doesn't tear herself apart in the process.

A number of promising planets have been destroyed by those they bore, he reminded her.

Too many of them, but she does have a good chance, better than most, with that homogeneous, tightly centralized population.

A population carrying the seeds of fratricide.

The breach can still be healed, but that'll be up to Xenon. He'll have to initiate all the first moves in An Fainne, and he'll jolly well have to forget his reluctance to overstep Coronus to do it.

So you do believe that one will remain King?

Her eyes shadowed. *I don't know. He probably will, but he's damaged himself badly. One more mistake, and he will be out.*

He shook his head sharply. *According to you, his people have the power to get rid of him. I shall never understand why they do not. He is no credit to them.*

The Noreenan sighed. *Because he's Magdela's son, because his line is old and royal and proven strong, because he is good, Varn. When it comes to an Anathi King's real work, he's very good, better than Herald would ever be. It's only when he starts pushing into other areas that he gets into trouble. He'll have to check himself with respect to that from now on, or Xenon'll have to check him.*

Her head bowed. *That's none of our business. They'll have to work it out for themselves.*

I am sorry, my Islaen, Sogan said softly. *You care about those people. It is not easy for you to leave them to their fate, even though it is basically promising and of their own making.*

She smiled faintly. *You cared enough yourself when caring was important, Varn Tarl Sogan.*

Bandit cared, too! the gurry interrupted.

"Aye, you did, love, and you proved it very concretely."

No more Anath? she asked.

"No. We're not to go back there unless she has more trouble from the stars, and we'll have to hope that nothing like this happens to her again."

Yes! Invaders are bad! Renegades!—No more nectar?

Both humans laughed.

"I'm afraid not, small one," Varn told her, "not once the supply we shipped with us is gone."

That may not be quite accurate, Islaen Connor announced, her eyes sparkling. *I brought a few seeds with me. They'll have to be tested for adaptability and safety on Thorne, naturally, and it'll take time, but we could eventually be harvesting quite a crop for ourselves.*

Islaen saw her husband's quizzical look, and the tone of her thoughts became graver. *The Thornens have been very good to us. I've wanted for some time to make them some return for their hospitality apart from the fighting we've done for them. A couple of products like nectar and power nectar would do very nicely.*

For us as well, he observed shrewdly.

Naturally. I'm hardly oblivious to that fact.—The Doge considers me his daughter, and I have no objection at all to becoming a merchant princess in fact, in my own right.

Bandit whistled in delight. *Then we can live on Thorne and not have to fight anymore!*

"I didn't say that," the woman warned hastily. "This'll be a long time in coming, if it does at all, but you're right in a sense. The time may arrive when . . . we'll want some other kind of life. I'm not about to neglect that possibility merely because our current profession isn't very conducive to an extended future."

The former Admiral was frowning. *What are you saying, Islaen?*

What I did say. Despite that assurance, she was quick to raise her shields. The sacrifice she had dreaded was before her. It was going to be as difficult as she had imagined, but she knew she was fully prepared to make it, and make it without whimpering later on over what she had surrendered.

The Commando-Colonel let a silence develop, as if it came naturally. She walked over to the observation panel. *What were you thinking about just before we joined you?* she asked after a moment.

Sogan looked sharply at her, then shrugged. *That I seem to blow up a lot of good starships in this new life of mine.*

Rather than commanding them? she pressed him quickly.

Most of this latest batch were too small to be of much interest, he countered carefully.

It might not be impossible, Varn, the Noreenan told him quietly.

Varn Tarl Sogan eyed her coldly. "I am realistic in my expectations," he told her, reverting to verbal speech, as he usually did when uncomfortable or afraid of revealing too much of himself. "Give me credit for that at least. Your Admiral Sithe has done all he can for me in getting me my commission and in placing me with you. There is no possibility that he will ever be able to turn over a fleet or any part of one to a renegade Arcturian officer, however skilled or well qualified he knows me to be."

"I wasn't thinking of a Navy command," she replied evenly, accepting his wish and using normal speech as well.

Varn stared at her. "What, then?"

"I met with the Doge just before we left Thorne. Harlran wants to push Thornen trade and at the same time both increase profits and cut down on the number of off-worlders planeting there by transporting her goods in her own ships, Thornen merchantmen handled by Thornen crews, as soon as he can get enough of his people trained to manage them."

"That will take time."

"Aye, he recognizes that. He'll use off-worlders as long as necessary. He also recognizes that for the whole of this generation and probably for all of the next at the very least, Thorne's starships will have to be fighters, even as all the freighters currently operating on the rim are effective battlecraft."

Islaen Connor took a deep breath. "It won't be an easy job putting that fleet together.—He would like you to take it on, Varn. To build and then command it." Her eyes met his. "It's a real offer, and a good one even though it's a civilian rather than a military post."

"Why have you said nothing about this until now?" he asked evenly.

"How could I, with a mission on us? I wasn't about to create any more distractions than we were already facing.—What else would you have had me do?"

"Sorry. You acted as I would have done." The war prince was

silent for several minutes after that. "It is indeed a good offer. As an honor and a trust, it is well nigh overpowering."

He came to his feet, and slowly walked over to stand beside her, although he did not look at her. His head lowered. "I wish I could accept it. I will do all I can to help establish Thorne's fleet, but I cannot command it. My place is in the Federation Navy, at your side."

"Varn!"

He faced her. "I will not be severed from you, Islaen, to grow a stranger to your life, to see you only when you are between assignments and free to be on Thorne for a brief time, to wonder whenever we are apart whether you are alive or dead or in peril at any given moment."

"There would be none of that," she told him very quietly.

"No." His voice was low and calm, but there was that in it that told that his will was irrevocably set. "The Navy is your life. Can you seriously imagine that I would permit you to throw it over?"

"I would still maintain contact, keep myself available for special duty.—It's no more than I was considering doing before meeting with you on Visnu, and it's not like I'd be burying myself somewhere. I'd be transferring into other pretty significant work."

"Not significant enough. Not for you or for me." For once he allowed her to see the pain, the longing, on him. "I do want a real command again, aye. Every time I see a major starship that wanting increases, but I am a war prince, Islaen Connor. My needs go beyond personal desire."

His head lowered and raised again, proudly, as befitted one of his rank and heritage. "Your ultrasystem is at war as surely as it was when it fought the armadas of my Empire, a war no less vicious and deadly because so many do not even recognize that it is being waged or realize the stakes at hazard. If the Navy and Stellar Patrol cannot contain those subbiotics eager to conquer and rape to their profit and lust for power, then that vermin will most assuredly tear this ultrasystem apart in very short order. It is mine to do all in my power to prevent that from happening. That duty is as much laid on me by what I am as by the word I have given."

"No one could do or ask you to do more than you already have.—You have a right to your own life, Varn. That's part of the Federation, too."

"I have given my oath, Islaen."

His eyes fixed for a moment on the distant spark that was Algola, then returned to his companion. "Maybe in a few years' time, conditions will change, stabilize to the point that I can think of moving into some other path if I so desire, but for now, there is no question in my mind as to where I belong."

"The Thornen position will no longer be open then."

"No. That I must accept. It is not the greatest of the losses I have endured, my Islaen."

"I know," she said bitterly, accepting her defeat. "I just wish you might start having some gains again."

Islaen turned away from him in disgust at herself. She was unworthy of this man. He had given up the only hope he would ever now have of even partially regaining the sort of command he had been trained to hold, for the sake of his duty and his love for her, and she felt only relief because she would not have to surrender her own commission. "I want you to be happy," she whispered, "complete . . ."

Varn Tarl Sogan smiled and gently touched her arm. "I have had some of those gains, Islaen Connor. Do not underestimate either yourself or the life you have opened for me." His dark eyes sparkled momentarily. "Perhaps it is just that you are overly proud, Colonel, not satisfied to be united to a mere Navy Captain."

The Noreenan tossed her head. "That doesn't merit an answer, especially since I'm not married to any such man."

She laughed at his puzzled expression. "I've been on the transceiver with Ram Sithe, and it seems my husband happens to be a Commando-Captain."

"Commando?"

There was a strange note in his voice, and Islaen did not know whether he was gratified or angry. His mind was sealed tight.

"Aye." If this had backfired . . .

Bethe, too! the gurry informed him. *Jake's telling her!*

"Since you're doing the work, both Admiral Sithe and I thought you should be collecting full pay for it, and getting your proper share of the glory," the woman explained. "It took a while to push the paperwork through, but the transfers have cleared at last."

"You knew this was in the works, Bandit?"

Yes! she replied proudly.

"For some time?"

Yes, Varn! Islaen said not to tell you.

"So it seems you are not congenitally incapable of keeping a secret. Maybe you will remember that the next time you pick something out of my mind that I would prefer not to have broadcast to the ultrasystem at large."

But, Varn . . . She realized that he was teasing her and purred happily and with great energy.

Islaen took courage from his good humor. *I wasn't sure it would come through just yet, but I did take the liberty of having uniforms made for you,* she said tentatively, using mind speech since he no longer seemed to be setting himself against receiving it, although his shields still prevented any delving of his inner thoughts.

His eyes were laughing, but he kept both his tone and his expression grave. *It would not do to appear on Thorne improperly dressed,* he agreed solemnly.

Varn, you are pleased about this? she asked, unable to stand her uncertainty any longer.

Sogan opened himself to her, allowing her to experience the full extent of his satisfaction. *Aye, Islaen Connor, I am pleased. Arcturians are fame-oriented, and the Commandos were the most elite company in either Navy. Had they been ours, the competition to gain a place among them would have been even fiercer than it was throughout Federation ranks. I am deeply honored to have been granted this privilege.*

You've earned your place with us! she snapped. Her great eyes looked hurt. *You've wanted it all along, haven't you?*

Aye, of course. How should I not, being who I am? I would gladly have surrendered my Navy rank for a Yeoman's place with you.

Then why in the name of space didn't you say something? she demanded hotly.

Because you would then have worn yourself out trying to secure a commission for me when my history might have made that a dream as hopeless as gaining control of a full armada, he replied simply.

Oh, Varn . . .

Islaen, no man can win everything. I have you, and through you I once again have purpose in my existence.

He rested his hand on her shoulder, physically establishing contact with her even as his mind brushed and remained with hers.

That was sufficient. It had to be. He would not stop desiring what he had lost. He accepted that fact even as he accepted the reality of the loss itself. Rather, the longing would probably only increase the more comfortable and securer he grew in his present life. That, too, he would have to accept and expect, but he would have to control it. The Federation's gods and the Empire's had granted him a second chance, a life that was again honorable, significant to others besides himself, and . . . happy. It was his to seize it and make of it all that he could.

Varn looked down at his consort, and he shuddered deep within himself at the memory of how close he had come to losing her, not once but several times over since their association had begun. He remembered all too vividly what he had felt and thought in those black moments.

No, he vowed as he poured a fierce love into her that caused her to stare at him in surprise and then answer it fully in kind. No. He would not waste, not squander, all that he had gained by looking only to the past. Islaen Connor was his, and his work was his. He would not fail either.

He would not fail himself. He was still a war prince of the Arcturian Empire. Being stripped of privilege did not alter that. His kind did not wail over fortune's blows. It was only right that he should walk well on the path fate and the gods had set for him.

Once more his eyes and his love fell on the auburn-haired woman beside him, and his head raised in pride and in hope of a future promising light and life and real purpose. That was his to claim, and he did not have to seek or to live it alone.